"Three charming authors invite you to the Hartwell House holiday ball, where just about anything can happen—and does!—to the delight of readers who enjoy short, light, delicious love stories that encourage them to feel the pleasure of the season."

—*RT Book Reviews*

"I thoroughly enjoyed each of these wonderful Regency romance stories. Each author has penned a tale that you will find yourself wishing were longer . . . each of these fine authors have more than done their job in this fantastic anthology."

—*Night Owl Romance*

McALISTAIR'S FORTUNE

"Johnson delights while touching hearts as she puts an unlikely pair of engaging characters into a witty plot and a lively adventure."

—*RT Book Reviews*

"Ms. Johnson brings together a spirited and original heroine determined to pave her own path and a hero who provides the adventure of a lifetime while contending with their differences in social station and his past. It's an engaging romance that will send readers to Ms. Johnson's backlist for other exciting reads."

—*Fresh Fiction*

CURIOUSER AND CURIOUSER . . .

"Curiosity is a powerful motivator. It's how we learn," Mr. Hunter said.

Kate traced the wood grain of the piano case with her fingers. "It's also how we end up"—*kissing handsome pirates in sitting rooms*—"with dead grasshoppers."

"Beg your pardon?"

"Nothing." She glanced up at him. He was standing very close. She could smell his soap, and she wondered if he would once again taste like spearmint. Her eyes shot back down to the wood. "Curiosity isn't always beneficial."

"Shall we put that to the test?"

She found it impossible to meet his gaze. "And how might we do that?"

He didn't answer. He simply stepped forward and pulled her into his arms.

Alissa Johnson

Destined to Last

LEISURE BOOKS NEW YORK CITY

For Emmanuelle Alspaugh and Leah Hultenschmidt.
Thank you.

A LEISURE BOOK®

April 2010

Published by

Dorchester Publishing Co., Inc.
200 Madison Avenue
New York, NY 10016

ISBN 10: 0-8439-6252-6
ISBN 13: 978-0-8439-6252-9
E-ISBN: 978-1-4285-0839-2

Visit us online at www.dorchesterpub.com.

Destined to Last

❋ Prologue ❋

The Countess of Thurston was perfectly aware that it was most unseemly for a lady to run in public. Which was why she chose to step briskly—*very* briskly—across Benton's small snow-covered town square.

"Lady Katherine Anne Beatrice Cole!"

The countess was also quite aware that it was unseemly for a lady to raise her voice in public, but every mother had her limits, and her five-year-old daughter, Kate, had an astonishing talent for pushing her past those limits. Lady Thurston had turned her back for only a moment in the shop to greet Mrs. Newman, and when she had turned round again, Kate had vanished.

What had followed was a frantic search of the shop, the two neighboring shops, and then the town square, where she had finally spotted Kate's little blonde head peeking out from over a row of decorative evergreen hedges.

Lady Thurston had managed to control her pace, but restraining her voice had been quite beyond her. Fortunately, by the time she arrived on the other side of those hedges and found Kate seated next to another child on a bench, her fear, and the accompanying temper, had eased enough for her to speak in the moderate tones far more suitable for both a woman of her rank, and for reasoning with an impetuous and impossibly stubborn child.

"Katherine Cole, how many times have you been told you are not to run off without permission?"

Kate cocked her head, her light blue eyes squinting in thought.

Oh, good heavens, five-year-olds were so literal. "I am not in search of an exact number, Kate. The point I am making is that you know better. You shall not be allowed to play the pianoforte tonight."

Kate's mouth fell open. It was, for her, the most grievous of punishments. "But, *Mama*—"

"No pianoforte," she repeated. "If it happens again—"

"But I *had* to go," Kate insisted, and pointed at the other child on the bench. "I saw Lizzy. She might be five."

Lady Thurston took a deep, calming breath and then, for the first time, took a very good look at the small child next to Kate. The girl did appear as if she might be near to five years of age. She had sweet brown eyes, hair that was in desperate need of a wash, and the sallow complexion of one who had recently suffered an illness. She was bundled in an old but warm-looking coat two sizes too big. And the remainder of her was covered in rags—even her feet, the poor dear.

Not a local child, Lady Thurston decided. She knew all the children in Benton, and she made certain all of them had decent clothes on their backs and shoes on their feet . . . All but her own, it would seem. Kate's feet were bare except for stockings. Lizzy was holding her boots.

"Why are you holding Kate's boots, dear?"

"I weren't stealing 'em," Lizzy proclaimed with a slight lisp. She tossed down the boots. "I weren't."

"She weren't," Kate echoed.

"She was not," Lady Thurston corrected before stooping to pick up the discarded shoes. "Here now, they are Kate's to do with as she pleases. Do you want her to have them, Kate?"

Kate nodded. Which did not surprise Lady Thurston in the least. The child adored giving presents and would have jumped at the chance to replace Lizzy's ragged footwear.

She held the boots out to Lizzy. "Where are your parents?"

"In heaven," Lizzy replied, snatching the shoes back without further argument.

"I am very sorry to hear it." She watched a moment as the girl fingered the soft leather. "How did you get here?"

"Puck brought me. I'm to wait for him here. Well, *there*," she amended, pointing to an alley between the modiste's and the booksellers. "But I like it better here."

Of course she did. The bench, unlike the alley, was warmed in the sun. "I beg your pardon? Who did you say brought you?"

"Puck. My friend."

"I see." Puck? That couldn't possibly be a real person. Lady Thurston turned to scan the square and surrounding shops. No one appeared to be looking for the child. A pang of anger and sadness clutched at her chest. The poor darling had been abandoned, like as not. It was an all too common occurrence.

She crouched down in front of the girl and spoke gently. "I think, Lizzy, that it would be best if you were to come to Haldon with us for a time. I shall ask one of my footmen to wait here and bring . . . er . . . Puck along when he arrives, and then we shall see what is to be done."

"Haldon," Lizzy repeated. "The big house what everyone here talks about?"

"The very one. Would you like that?"

Kate tugged on her sleeve. "Mama?"

"Is it warm?" Lizzy asked.

"Quite."

"Is there food?"

"Oh, plenty," Lady Thurston assured her.

"Mama?"

Lizzy bit her lip, clearly tempted. "And Puck can come too?"

"Certainly."

"Mama, who is that?"

"Hmm?" Lady Thurston looked away from Lizzy briefly. "What is it?"

Kate turned to point across the square. "Who is . . ." She trailed off and dropped her hand. "He's gone."

"Who, darling?"

"A boy."

"There are many boys in Benton, Kate."

"Yes, but . . . this one was different."

"Every child is different," she said distractedly and rose to offer Lizzy her hand. "Shall we go?"

The little girl hesitated, then reached out and placed a small, cold hand in hers.

❊ *One* ❊

$\mathcal{L}$ady Kate Cole was, by most accounts, a young woman of exceptional beauty, extraordinary talent, and notable charm. She was also, by *all* accounts, a woman so remarkably prone to accidents that it was generally considered wise to back away if she happened to be standing next to a steep hill, a large body of water, an open window, or any sort of material that might cut, discolor, burn, spill, break . . . It was probably best if one simply kept a bit of distance from the girl whenever possible.

There were times Kate rather wished she could do the same. Now, for example, would have been an ideal moment to back away from herself—while she was standing on the grassy lawn of Haldon Hall with her pale rose gown conspicuously splattered from hem to neck with mud. *Again.* And while her blonde hair was damp at the ends, coming out of its pins, and likely sporting a number of leaves in various stages of decomposition. *Again.* And while one Mr. Hunter was striding toward her from the house to witness her in all her

rumpled, mud-covered, frightful-haired embarrassment. Ag—
Well, no, that was a first.

"Oh, blast."

Why, *why* had she not taken care where she walked along
the pond instead of humming the new waltz she'd composed
whilst daydreaming about what it might be like to dance that
very waltz with the gentleman of her dreams? She'd imagined
what he might look like and sound like and talk about
and . . . and then suddenly it *hadn't* been a waltz she was
hearing in her head, it had been a sonatina. And she'd no
longer been walking gracefully along the muddy shore, she'd
been lying on it.

Grimacing, she watched as Mr. Hunter drew closer, and
wondered if it would be unforgivably rude if she turned away
and walked—or quite possibly ran—around to the side of the
house. Then she wondered if she cared overmuch whether it
was unforgivably rude. She decided yes on both accounts,
which was something of a disappointment, because of all the
people currently attending her mother's house party, there
were few she would rather see less.

There was something about Mr. Hunter that put her on
edge. To begin with, the man was impossibly well groomed.
In Kate's opinion, it simply wasn't natural that one should
never have a spot on one's clothes or have a button go missing or a hair fly out of place. Mr. Hunter's attention to the
details of his attire seemed more in tune with the fussy habits of a delicate London dandy than it did with a gentleman
of his size. Which was another thing about the man that put
her on edge—he was, aside from the local blacksmith, quite
the most imposing person of her acquaintance. He was even
taller than her brother, Whit, and notably broader across
the chest and shoulders. Perhaps the broadness was the reason that, while she found Whit's size and strength to be
reassuring, Mr. Hunter's large frame made her feel a mite
overwhelmed.

The rest of his appearance only enhanced that feeling. His eyes and hair were dark as night, his jaw hard, his cheekbones sharp, and his full mouth often curved into a small, but wicked smile, so that she rather fancied he looked a well-dressed pirate caught in a private joke.

What troubled her most of all, however, was that he sometimes used his size, dark gaze, and impossibly polished appearance to stand over her and make her feel ill at ease.

The man *loomed*, there was nothing else for it. Even when they were separated by an entire ballroom—and she generally took pains to see that they were—he still managed to loom. It was most disconcerting.

Resigned to an inescapable spot of looming that morning, Kate indulged in a brief but heartfelt sigh, and a futile but equally heartfelt wish that she had not forgotten to bring her bonnet. It would have gone a long way toward covering up the damage done to her hair.

She waited until he'd drawn close enough for her to see that he was impeccably turned out in fashionable tan breeches, dark coat, and intricately knotted cravat; then she pasted on an extremely bright smile, having long ago come to the conclusion that the next best thing to avoiding embarrassment altogether was pretending it didn't exist. She'd become depressingly adept at that pretense over the years.

"Good morning, Mr. Hunter," she chimed in her cheeriest voice. "Have you come out for a stroll? It's a lovely day for it."

Had Mr. Hunter been a typical gentleman of the *ton*, he likely would have floundered a little at her appearance—not to mention her apparent ignorance of said appearance—and then very courteously played along as if nothing was amiss while he assisted her back to the house.

Unfortunately, Mr. Hunter was a man of great wealth but inauspicious origin, which made his connection to the *ton* rather loose and his position as a gentleman decidedly suspect. Kate didn't hold with the notion that a man's status as a gentleman should be awarded solely by right of birth. She felt strongly that it was a man's character and behavior that marked him as a gentleman . . . or not, as she rather thought to be the case with Mr. Hunter.

He stopped in front of her, raised one dark brow, and took a long, thorough look at her bedraggled form before running his tongue along his teeth. "Am I to pretend I don't see the mud? Is that how it's done?"

Kate gave up the smile to roll her eyes and step around him to begin a hurried walk toward the house. "If you were truly interested in how it was done, you would not have asked."

He fell into step beside her. "How is one supposed to learn if one doesn't ask?"

"The fact that I did not wish to acknowledge the mud should have been obvious to anyone with even the most basic powers of perception." She pursed her lips. "Perhaps you did need to ask."

He chuckled at that, a low and soft sound she was irritated to discover she found pleasant.

"Let us assume for a moment," he replied after a pause, "that I do possess some very basic skills of perception. Why then, do you suppose I did ask?"

She glanced and saw that his lips were curved up with humor. "Because you wished to amuse yourself by discomforting me."

"Patently untrue," he returned. "You looked sufficiently uncomfortable already. I had hoped to make you smile."

"I . . ." That was another thing about Mr. Hunter that set her on edge. He was charming to the point of being glib. "Well . . . thank you."

"It would have been my pleasure," he responded smoothly, "had I succeeded."

"I believe I was smiling when you arrived," she pointed out.

"Because of me? How gratifying."

She felt a bubble of laughter form in her throat and ruthlessly swallowed it down. Nothing good could come from encouraging the man. Then again, *not* encouraging him had done very little good as well. Perhaps a more direct approach was required.

"Your arrogance is astounding," she informed him.

"No point doing things in half measures."

She wanted to laugh at that too. Instead, she increased her pace. "Just because something *can* be done, doesn't mean that it *should* be done."

"Just because something *shouldn't* be done, doesn't mean it can't be done *well*." He waited a beat before adding, "I imagine you fell into the pond spectacularly."

"I . . ." The laugh escaped, and she blamed what happened next solely on the distraction of that laugh.

He sidestepped a large root from a nearby oak tree.

She did not, and likely would have added grass stains to her poor dress had he not reached out and gently caught her arm as she toppled forward.

"Easy." He stood very still, his large hand keeping a firm grip on her arm as she righted herself. "May I assume by your energetic pace that you were unharmed by your accident this morning?"

Ignoring the amusement in his voice, as well as the sudden fluttering of her heart, she carefully extracted herself from his grip. "Yes, you may. Thank you."

"I am relieved to hear it."

She gave him a wry smile. "Relieved enough to go about your business and leave me in peace?"

"Disturbing your peace was the business I had in mind when I came outside."

"Ah." She titled her head up at him. "Is that why you've come to Haldon, simply to vex me?"

"Not entirely, or I'd have made the effort to arrive sooner."

There was no arguing with that bit of logic. It was the last full day of her mother's house party and Mr. Hunter had made the trip from London only that morning. Just in time, it would seem, to find her returning from her walk.

"You've come for tonight's ball," she guessed.

Rather than answer, he took a step closer and bent his head to catch her eye. "Tell me Lady Kate—and to be clear, I ask not to make you uncomfortable, but because I am genuinely curious—what is it about me that ruffles your feathers so?"

You're too large. You're too charming. You make my heart race. I'd wager a year's allowance you were, at some point, a pirate.

She couldn't tell him any of those things. Particularly the last, which she knew to be the influence of a long-standing weakness for torrid novels.

So she said instead, "You loom, Mr. Hunter."

"I loom."

"Yes." She searched desperately for something to add to that. "It's very ill-mannered of you."

"I see." His lips twitched. "You're an honest creature, aren't you?"

"I try to be." She waited for him to step back, or look away, or give some indication that her honest, if not exactly complete, confession had made an impact on him. He remained utterly still. "Are you going to *cease* looming?"

"No." He moved, *finally*, but to her shock, it was only to lift his hand and lightly brush a strand of hair away from her cheek. "I rather like ruffling your feathers."

His hands were ungloved, and the warmth of his fingers was answered by a shiver along her skin. It was Kate who took a step back. "Your behavior is presumptuous."

"Is it?" His lips curved up in a wicked smile. "I'd have asked first, but anyone with even the most basic powers of perception could see you're curious—"

"Good day, Mr. Hunter."

Hunter made no move to follow Lady Kate as she stormed toward the house, and not because he knew she wouldn't welcome his company, nor because he felt ashamed for having been, in fact, very presumptuous. No, he stayed where he was because following Lady Kate now didn't suit his purpose.

And everything Hunter did suited a purpose. In his opinion, anything less was a useless expenditure of time and energy.

Fortunately for his purposes, he didn't consider it a waste of time to watch Lady Kate make her way toward the house. He didn't consider it a waste of time to watch Lady Kate doing most anything. The woman was a vision.

A diamond of the first water, that's what the *ton* called her. The very picture of fashionable beauty—pale blonde hair, ivory skin, wide blue eyes, thin blade of a nose and a perfect rosebud mouth. She was elegantly tall and slender, and yet possessed enough curves to catch, and hold, a man's attention. She was exquisite, a testament to grace and beauty . . . provided she was standing utterly still. When she wasn't, well . . . He thought her occasional missteps only added to her charm.

There were those who believed her lack of coordination was the reason she remained unmarried at three-and-twenty, but Hunter knew that to be a misconception. He'd heard members of her family grumble over Kate's unwed state on more than one occasion, but a lack of suitors wasn't the problem. She'd received well more than a handful of offers. The problem was that she'd turned down every one. It seemed the gentlemen weren't offering anything she cared to accept.

In Hunter's opinion, they were merely offering it too easily.

Confident that her lack of interest in other gentlemen afforded him the opportunity, he'd spent a bit of time studying Lady Kate. He'd approached her at balls and dinners from time to time, or simply caught her eye from across the room, but for the most part, he let her be in favor of watching, listening, and learning what he could about the woman.

And what he'd discovered was that Lady Kate Cole was a dreamer. She might appreciate the attention she received from her suitors, but she would never be captivated by their overt fawning. Because, like all dreamers, what she wanted most was that which was just out of reach.

Hunter had made a point of being just out of her reach. He'd made a point of being impossible for her to ignore as well, but anyone could manage that. It was the element of elusiveness, the piquing of curiosity that could capture Kate. And make no mistake, he *would* capture her.

No other woman would do for his wife. True, there were a few who were higher in rank, one or two with more generous dowries, and it was possible, though he rather doubted it, that there was a more attractive young woman somewhere in society he'd yet to meet. But only Lady Kate Cole had it all— rank, fortune, *and* beauty.

She was, in essence, the very finest young lady the *ton* had to offer. What was the phrase—the *crème de la crème*? For a man raised on bread and water, a woman like Kate was nothing less than the promise of ambrosia. She was the definitive luxury, the most extravagant acquisition, and perhaps most important, the perfect symbol of his rise from pauper to prince.

All of which, he could admit, he would have learned to do without, were Kate not also a woman whose company he could enjoy. Granted, he'd sampled that company in limited quantities, but it had been enough for him to decide that he genuinely liked the girl—her wit, her humor, her loyalty to those she loved, even her clumsiness and distracted nature was something he found appealing. And to top it all off, he desired her more than he could remember ever desiring a woman.

What man could ask for more?

Feeling every inch as arrogant as Kate had charged him of being only minutes ago, he stood where she'd left him on the lawn, and patiently waited for her to reach the door, hesitate, then turn back to sneak a peek at him.

"There we are," he murmured.

He considered giving her a wave, but thought that might be overdoing things a bit. Instead, he simply waited until she whirled around again and went into the house, before he casually strolled away.

Contrary to what Kate had guessed—or accused, depending on how one wished to take her tone at the time—he hadn't come to the Thurston estate simply to attend the ball. Nor had he stepped outside with the hope of catching Kate trudging back from the pond covered in mud, although that had been a pleasant surprise, indeed. He'd come on business, and having a spot of time before that business was scheduled, he'd chosen a walk about the Haldon grounds over conversation in the parlor.

He was inordinately fond of Haldon Hall—the massive house with its generations of rambling additions, the extensive gardens, the open fields, and deep woods. But it wasn't just the sheer size of the estate that he found appealing—although that did, in fact, greatly appeal to him—it was what the place represented that captured his imagination. Generations of Coles had resided there, each one of them sure of, and comfortable with, his place in the world. Even when the Thurston fortune had been at its lowest, the residents of Haldon Hall had remained insulated in a thick cocoon of status and rank. No member of the Cole family had ever known what it meant to be truly impoverished, nor was any member ever likely to.

They were a charmed lot—particularly the current generation. Not only had the present earl, Whittaker Cole, seen to it that the Thurston coffers were well stocked, the family also had the good fortune of being a remarkably tight-knit clan. He'd yet to meet a group of people more secure in their love for one another and in their belief that love always endured.

Perhaps it did, he mused, for people like the Coles.

In his experience, nothing lasted forever.

"He is not . . . ideal." Kate's mother, now the dowager Lady Thurston, stood at the library window and watched as Mr. Hunter disappeared around the side of the house. "His behavior is most presumptuous."

Next to her, William Fletcher, head of England's War Department, scratched at his bulbous nose. It was a thoughtful habit he was only vaguely aware he possessed. "Hunter is a good man. I rather thought you liked him."

"I do. Very much." His friendship with Whit, and his loyalty to the Coles in times of trouble, had made Mr. Hunter an honorary member of the family in her eyes. A sort of nephew, she mused. She didn't know him well enough to think of him as a son. But she knew her daughter well enough to be skeptical with William's notion of making Mr. Hunter into a son-in-law. "And I am not above admiring a well-delivered spot of presumption from an attractive gentleman. However—"

"He stepped in front of a bullet for Whit, you know," William cut in casually as he continued to look out the window.

She drew in a hard breath. "Someone shot at my son?"

"Your son was a soldier for a time," he reminded her. "I imagine any number of people have shot at him."

Her eyes narrowed. The months Whit had spent on the

continent were not something she cared to remember. "And the circumstances surrounding *this* particular shooting?"

"Nasty bit of business in London a few years back. A Mrs. Georgiana Clemens attempted to dissuade Whit and Hunter from arresting her traitor of a husband."

"A woman?"

William bobbed his head and watched a squirrel dart across the lawn. "That's the trouble with new agents pulled from the nobility. They never suspect the women."

"Mr. Hunter is not of the nobility."

"Indeed. He saw the pistol, pushed Whit away and took the bullet in his side. Well, *across* his side," he amended. "He insists it was only a scratch."

"I see," she murmured, and ruthlessly shoved away the image of her son having guns aimed at him. It didn't do to dwell on such things. Nor was it advisable to act on the swell of gratitude she felt, and the accompanying impulse to seek out Mr. Hunter and offer him anything his heart might desire, including the hand of her only daughter.

William turned from the window, his expression a bit smug. "And there is no denying the effect he has on Kate."

"Kate appears to be denying it with very little effort," she pointed out, mostly because she felt it wouldn't do for the man to become overconfident.

"Bah." William waved that away, his confidence clearly unscathed. "She merely gives herself ample opportunity to ignore it by avoiding him."

Lady Thurston thought about that as she crossed the room to take a seat on a settee. "Kate has never before shied away from matters of the heart. Rather she has been quite diligent in seeking them out."

"It seems this time they shall have to be brought to her."

She smoothed the skirts of her bronze gown and thought of her soft, romantic daughter, and the cunning and ambitious Mr. Hunter. "No."

"No? What the blazes do you mean, no?"

"Do watch your language, William. And I mean, no. Regardless of my gratitude toward, and personal affection for, Mr. Hunter, I do not believe him the best match for Kate."

"He is."

"He is not."

"He . . ." William straightened his shoulders. "Mrs. Summers is in agreement with me."

"Mrs. Summers is in the unenviable position of having to choose between me, her friend, and the man with whom she has formed an attachment. Naturally, she would agree with you."

He ran a hand through what remained of his hair. "That is not—"

"And Mirabelle agrees with me."

William took a seat across from her, sitting down with a huff. "Your daughter-in-law is nearly always in agreement with you. You've raised an outspoken group of young women."

She smiled at what she considered a compliment. "Indeed, I have."

"Two for Mr. Hunter, and two against. We are at an impasse."

"I am Kate's mother," she said and gave a small sniff. "My choice takes precedence."

He gave her a bland look. "I am the man with a deathbed promise to the late Duke of Rockeforte to fulfill."

"Matches for five children," she remarked with an amused shake of her head.

"*Love* matches for five children," William corrected with just enough derision in his voice to make perfectly clear his opinion of the endeavor. "Which is why it must be Mr. Hunter."

"Mr. Laury is a far more suitable candidate. He is a charming but earnest young man, and his romantic nature will appeal to Kate. They even share the common interest of music."

"It's Mr. Laury you want, is it?" William fell silent for a moment, and tapped his finger on the arm of the chair. "I suggest a compromise," he eventually announced. "We try them both. See which of the two fits."

Lady Thurston rather thought that plan made the gentlemen sound like bonnets, but she couldn't argue with its practicality. "How?"

"I believe your Mr. Laury has made mention of attending Lord Brentworth's house party next week?"

"He has, yes."

"I'd planned to send Hunter on a mission to Cornwall, but upon further reflection, I've decided his services would be put to better use at Brentworth's."

Lady Thurston nodded in understanding. "I shall see to it Kate attends."

"Well, then." William's smug smile returned. "May the best match prevail."

❋ *Two* ❋

*K*ate closed the door to her room with a heavy sigh of relief. By virtue of sneaking up a back staircase and quietly ducking into an empty room or two, she'd made it all the way through Haldon Hall without being spotted by a guest. Even better, she'd managed to avoid her closest friends and family, who were more apt to see she was troubled by something other than the sorry state of her gown, hair, and the nearly unrecognizable pair of half boots in her hand.

"I am not troubled," she muttered to herself. "I'm annoyed."

And, in truth, she *was* bothered by the mess she'd made of her gown. The damage could be repaired, but it would require a great deal of effort on the part of her lady's maid, Lizzy. Kate would just as soon see to the chore herself, as she'd been the one who created the mess, but she knew full well Lizzy wouldn't hear of it.

Feeling guilty, she decided the least she could do was change on her own, instead of interrupting whatever Lizzy was doing at present to help her undress. It took several long minutes of contorting into a series of uncomfortable positions, but eventually she succeeded in struggling out of her gown. After noting with considerable relief that her chemise was still clean and dry, she carefully folded the wet and dirty material and searched for a spot in the room where she could set it down for a moment without damaging anything else while she removed her damp stockings.

The deep windowsill seemed her safest option, though it required she move a small pile of novels stacked there. She set the dress down with one hand, and with the other, picked up the book she was currently reading. It was a fairy tale in essence, the adventures of a beautiful maiden and her valiant prince. It was tremendously far-fetched, undeniably melodramatic, and not the least bit educational. She thought it quite delightful.

Already, the prince had plucked his true love from the back of a runaway horse, rescued her from a band of highwaymen, *and* fought a duel to defend her honor. And the book wasn't yet halfway over.

Kate fiddled with the binding. Is that what she wanted, she wondered, a prince to ride to her rescue? That didn't seem quite right. She longed for adventure and romance, without question, but she didn't feel an overpowering desire to be rescued. She snorted a little at the idea of any of her well-intentioned suitors ever having the chance to play knight-errant. As the only daughter and youngest member of the Cole family, she was, to put it lightly, *exceptionally* well looked after. Particularly by her brother, Whit.

There were worse things than being well looked after, she reminded herself, and turned the book over in her hand. Perhaps it was the sentiment of what was to be found between the pages that she wished for—the certainty that her suitor loved her with such ardor that he would be *willing* to ride to her rescue.

And if that suitor happened to look anything like the handsome, fair-haired prince from her book, well—

"Was there a mishap, Lady Kate?"

Kate looked up at the sound of Lizzy's voice at the connecting door to their rooms. "Beg your pardon?"

Lizzy gestured at her. "You're standing in your undergarments."

"I . . ." She glanced down at herself, then lifted her head to give Lizzy a sheepish smile. "I'm terribly sorry. I fell in the pond."

"Off the dock?"

"Not this time." She sighed heavily. "I was on the shore."

Lizzy wrinkled her nose and stuck out her tongue. "Muddier on the shore."

"I know," Kate replied, laughing a little at Lizzy's comical expression. "I am sorry. I'll brush out the gown if—"

"You'll not." Lizzy crossed the room to Kate's armoire. "I only mentioned the mud because it'd be an unpleasant bit of nastiness to fall in."

"It was, rather."

While Kate removed her stockings, Lizzy rummaged about for a clean dress. She was a young woman of average height and build, with dark blonde hair, soft brown eyes, and a round face. A nose that was just a little too long, a mouth that was just a hair too wide, and a chin that was notably pointed kept Lizzy from being a true beauty. But her extraordinary use of those somewhat ordinary features had made her a favorite among staff and family alike at Haldon Hall. Kate had never met a woman with such a remarkable assortment of facial expressions.

"I can't fathom why you wouldn't let your mother talk you out of this green gown," Lizzy commented from somewhere inside the armoire. "The color makes you look as if you escaped from the undertaker."

Kate rolled her eyes. Lizzy also had a remarkable amount of cheek—not a distinction most ladies of the *ton* would countenance from their abigail, but Kate wouldn't have it any other way.

Lizzy stepped back from the armoire. "This should do, I think."

Kate took one look at the peach gown her friend held out for her, and sighed yet again. "It's a shame dark colors aren't fashionable for young ladies. We'd have a much easier time of it."

"But fewer excuses to go shopping," Lizzy replied with a grin as she took the stockings from Kate's hand and stuffed them in a pocket of her apron.

"That's true." She accepted the gown and pulled it over her head. Lizzy worked the buttons up the back.

"Was there anyone else about?" Lizzy inquired after a moment.

"At the pond, you mean? Yes, unfortunately." Kate winced. "I came across Mr. Hunter on my return."

"Mr. Hunter," Lizzy repeated thoughtfully. "I do wish I could put my finger on why he seems so familiar."

"As do I, but like as not, he simply resembles someone we've both met in passing—a shopkeeper in London, perhaps."

"Perhaps. I suspect it'll come to you first." Lizzy fastened the last button to step around and give Kate a decidedly cheeky smile. "You spend more time looking at him than I do."

"I do nothing of the—"

"And he spends considerable time looking at you."

"I . . ." Well, yes, there was no arguing that.

"You may as well admit you're curious," Lizzy commented with a shrug. "There's no harm in it."

Without thought, Kate lifted a hand to her cheek. She swore she could still feel the lingering warmth where Mr. Hunter's fingers had brushed along her skin. Perhaps she *was* a little curious about him. And Lizzy was right, what harm was there in that? Then again, if memory served, she'd been curious at the age of six as to what would happen if she tried to keep a grasshopper as a pet.

She dropped her hand. "Curiosity killed the cat."

It had certainly killed the poor grasshopper.

"Satisfaction brought it back," Lizzy countered. "But they do have nine lives."

A soft knock on the door kept Kate from responding. A young maid entered, carrying a letter in her hands. "A missive for you, Lady Kate."

Kate crossed the room in several quick strides, excitement and nerves fighting for control of her system. She'd been expecting a letter from a London publisher for some time. "Thank you, Alice."

Alice handed her the letter, bobbed a curtsy, and left.

"Which one was this?" Lizzy asked, stepping up to peer over Kate's shoulder.

Kate stared at the sealed paper, biting her lip. "The waltz I composed last summer."

Lizzy bounced on her toes. "Well, go on, then. Open it."

"Right." Marshalling her courage, Kate broke the seal and unfolded the letter. She read the first line and the excitement and nerves quickly turned into the familiar weight of disappointment. "I don't know why I let myself become hopeful," she grumbled, refolding the letter. "It's always no."

"They've no sense," Lizzy said loyally. "They'll never make a go of their business with poor judgment such as that."

They'd been making a go of their business for nearly a half century, but Kate couldn't see the good in pointing that out. "Thank you, Lizzy."

"You'd not have such trouble, if you led them to believe you're a man," Lizzy commented. "Or if you let Lord Thurston put a word in for you. Or you could pay them—"

"I could do all those things," Kate agreed and crossed the room to place the letter in a drawer of her desk, on top of a stack of similarly worded rejections. "But I won't. I want my work to be accepted on its own merit. And I want credit for that success." She scowled at the stack of letters for a moment before turning to Lizzy. "Does that make me dreadfully vain?"

"Not *dreadfully*," Lizzy hedged. "A mite stubborn, though."

Kate reached back to close the desk drawer. "If being a mite stubborn is what it takes, so be it. I'll send out another inquiry tomorrow."

And she would send another inquiry after that, and another after that, and however many it took after *that* until she received a satisfactory answer. Seeing her music published and hearing it played in a public venue wasn't her only dream, but it was the only one hard work and perseverance would make come true.

As the sun set, Hunter settled on a stone bench in a secluded section of Haldon Hall's vast garden. He gave the man sitting on the bench across from him a hard look. "Was it really necessary for me to come here on the last day of a house party?"

He didn't mind visiting Haldon Hall, of course. He just preferred those visits occur in the time and manner of his choosing.

"It was necessary," William Fletcher informed him. "I've a mission for you."

"Why couldn't you give me my orders in London?"

William smiled at him pleasantly. "Because that would have required I go to London when I'd rather stay here."

Hunter snorted and leaned back against the bench. "What's the mission, then?"

"Right." William nodded once. "Lord Brentworth is holding his own house party next week at Pallton House on the coast. I want you to attend."

"To what end?"

"To keep an eye on Lady Kate."

Hunter straightened up. He couldn't have heard that correctly. "I beg your pardon?"

"Interested now, are we?" William chuckled, then wisely continued on in a businesslike manner before Hunter could respond. "It has come to my attention that Brentworth's son, Lord Martin, has decided to try his hand at smuggling. I'm afraid the information my source was able to acquire is rather vague, but there exists the possibility of young Lord Martin using his father's estate as a base of operations. And it is well known that young Lord Martin has a *tendre* for Lady Kate."

"You can't possibly be serious. Lady Kate embroiled in a smuggling operation?" The idea of Kate being connected to a criminal operation was absurd under any circumstances, but that she would be involved with the foppish Lord Martin was nearly laughable.

"She's not embroiled at present," William explained. "Your job is to make certain she stays that way."

"Wouldn't it make more sense to have Whit or Alex see to her safety?"

William raised a brow. "And have them keep her locked away at Haldon?"

"Does seem the safest course of action." Not necessarily the course he would choose, but certainly the safest.

"In this case, the safest course of action is not the wisest course." William twisted his lips. "If Lady Kate fails to attend the house party so, likely, will her admirer."

"What sort of smuggler ignores his operation in favor of chasing after a woman?" Hunter scoffed.

"The sort that fancies himself in love."

"Idiot." Hunter sat back once more, a sneer firmly set on his face. "We'll have him in under a fortnight."

"Not necessarily," William countered, scratching at his nose. "He's either the venturer or the sole investor or both, but he's hardly the type to dirty his hands unloading cargo on the beach. I highly doubt he would make the trip to the coast at all if there was nothing else there for him. He'd arrange for the goods to be brought to him."

Hunter's lips pressed into an annoyed line. "We won't catch him in the act, then."

"It is unlikely, but with any luck, he'll use his father's house to store the goods, or meet with his cohorts . . . that sort of thing."

"Lord Brentworth is a suspect as well?"

William shook his head. "I know Brentworth well. The man's not got a thing to do with it." He tapped a knee with his finger. "His leg has been giving him trouble since he took a fall from his horse last year. By his own admission, he hasn't been in the basement of Pallton House in over a year."

Hunter found it difficult to imagine anyone would be bold enough to store smuggled goods right under his father's nose, but then, one never knew with the nobility. They had a tremendous capacity for conceit. "What sort of goods are we in search of?"

William didn't trouble himself over the transport of everyday items. He was, he often remarked, head of the War Department, not an excise man. Hunter had noticed William was more likely to point this out when near a fine bottle of French brandy.

"There will be the usual sort of smuggled items brought over, no doubt, but it's a bit of paperwork we're after," William responded. "I can't provide you with further detail."

Hunter gave him a humorless smile. "Afraid I'll slip back into old habits?"

"If I were worried over you slipping back into old habits, I'd not have you slipping in and out of locked doors, would I? You were a thief longer than you were a smuggler."

He'd been better at it too. "You've no proof of that."

"Don't need it, do I?" William asked with a smile before waving his hand dismissively. "I can't provide you with further details because I haven't any. As I said, the information I've acquired is vague. It's possible we'll not find anything beyond a bit of brandy." William shrugged. "Acquiring paperwork isn't your objective at any rate. I've decided to task another agent with that matter. There's a London connection for him to explore, and he'll take primary control of the investigation at Pallton House after that."

"While I play nursemaid." In truth, Hunter had no intention of limiting his role to nursemaid, but he saw no reason to advertise as much to William with an easy capitulation.

William raised his eyebrows. "Would you prefer the alternative?"

The alternative, unfortunately, was to stand trial for his own ill-fated foray into smuggling almost seven years ago. Apparently, that time round, William's source hadn't been at all vague on what sort of paperwork was to be found among the harmless crates and barrels. "I prefer my neck the length it is, thank you."

William gave him a disgustingly patronizing smile. "Cheer

up, Hunter. Another six months and your obligations will be met. Out before you're thirty, eh? And perhaps the prince will see fit to grant you something extra for your service. Wouldn't you like to be a baron?"

A corner of his mouth hooked up. "Prinny can keep his titles."

"I rather thought you aspired to be a member of the elite."

"I aspire to wealth," he corrected, "and what it can acquire."

"It can't acquire happiness," William pointed out.

"True, but insufficient amounts of it will certainly afford a man a great deal of misery." Cold, hunger, and loneliness came to mind.

William brushed his hands along his thighs and rose from his seat. "Well, then, if having coin and what it *can* acquire is what you seek. I would venture to say you are a success."

He would be, Hunter mused. There was just one more acquisition to make.

❊ *Three* ❊

$\mathcal{I}$t came as a surprise to no one that the dowager Lady Thurston's ball turned out to be an unqualified success. Particularly not to Kate, who'd been privy to the extensive preparations and attention to detail—or minutiae, to hear her brother tell it—the event had received. According to her mother, there were but three things a lady need worry herself over: the children she loved, the charities she supported, and the parties she threw. Kate had been tempted to ask where husbands fit in, but knew better. Her parents' union had not been a love match. It had been civil and grounded in some level of affection, but not a love match. In the end, that had probably been best, as her father had died some years ago in a duel over a woman who was *not* his wife.

Her mother's ball, however, was not the time or place to dwell on unhappy memories. It was *supposed* to be the time and place a young unmarried lady paid attention to the young unmarried gentlemen in attendance. Particularly if they happened to be gathered about her chair in the corner of the ballroom.

"What say you, Lady Kate? Red or Green?"

She hadn't been paying attention. "Er, green."

Two of the young gentlemen said something akin to "ah-ha!" Another groaned in defeat, and the last gentleman, who really wasn't all that young, chuckled and slapped the back of one of the victors.

"Um . . ." She rose from her chair. "Do excuse me. I . . . I need some refreshment."

She walked away swiftly, wondering if she would ever learn what sort of opinion she'd just expressed by saying "green," and made her way across the room. From the corner of her eye, she saw another gentleman start toward her, hesitate when he saw the direction she was headed, and then quickly back away when she reached her destination.

She bit the inside of her cheek to keep from smiling and quietly hummed along to the tune the musicians were playing. Her little ruse never failed. Whenever she wished for a little peace from her suitors all she needed to do was stand next to the refreshment table.

She was not, it would seem, to be trusted with food.

Kate stifled a snort and reached for a glass of lemonade. No wonder she'd not fallen in love with any of the men who courted her. They would never risk their lives to save her from a runaway mount. They wouldn't even risk their cravats to speak with her.

She might have thought on that a bit longer, but she was

distracted by the rare sight of her cousin, Mrs. Evie McAlistair, engaged in a dance with her husband. Now *there*, Kate thought with a sigh, was a love match. The sort she dreamed of finding with her own handsome prince.

"Lady Kate, will you do me the honor of dancing with me?"

Kate jumped at the deep male voice, sloshing the lemonade in her glass onto the skirts of her blue silk gown. "Oh, bother."

Mr. Hunter stepped around from behind her and produced a handkerchief from his pocket. She nearly told him she didn't need it—she had enough sense to bring her own—but she bit back the sharp retort. Being rude to the man only seemed to encourage him. And reason dictated that if he pursued her merely for the fun of ruffling her feathers, she need only *stop* allowing her feathers to be ruffled and he would lose interest and let her alone.

She daintily accepted the square of linen. "Thank you."

"The least I could do, after startling you."

She rather thought it was. "It was my error. I was woolgathering."

"We can debate the matter over our dance. You will dance?"

She'd rather not. "Yes, of course."

"A waltz."

A waltz? After he'd been so forward that morning? And when he'd never before asked her for so much as a reel? Suddenly the man expected nothing less than a waltz? Oh, she *desperately* wanted to make another comment on his arrogance.

"A waltz would be lovely." She sincerely hoped the words didn't sound quite as ground out as they felt. "How very kind of you to ask."

"Not at all."

The best she could manage in response was a tight smile.

She assumed he would leave after that—she was more than a little surprised he'd braved her company at the refreshment table at all—and return for her when it was time for their waltz.

He didn't. He just stood there, watching her in silence, his lips curved up in a half smile as if he knew full well what she was about.

Let him look, she thought, he'll see no ruffled feathers. She turned away to watch the dancers, sip at the lemonade remaining in her glass, and even tap her foot in time to the music. She glanced at him, once . . . twice . . .

She couldn't stand it. She had to talk. She had to make him stop looming over her.

"Will you return to London on the morrow, Mr. Hunter?"

His lips curved up just a hair more. "Briefly. And your plans?"

"We've a house party to attend in Sussex next week. Lord Brentworth's affair. Mother forgot to inform me of it until today. This afternoon, actually." She licked lips gone dry. Did the man never blink? "I realize it's not the most fashionable of parties, but . . ." She gave up and leaned forward to hiss at him. "Would you kindly refrain from staring at me that way?"

Rather than appear abashed, he merely raised a brow. "Nearly every man in the room is staring at you."

"I rather doubt it, but if so, they have the courtesy to pretend otherwise," she chastised. "Or, at the very least, blink now and again."

He had the unmitigated gall to actually wink at her. "Will that do?"

"*No.*" The absurdity of it, however, did create a tickle of laughter in her throat.

"Are you certain it wasn't effective?" Mr. Hunter inquired with a grin. "Because you look as if you might like to laugh."

Either she wasn't nearly as accomplished at hiding her feelings as she thought, or the man was too perceptive by half. Better if it was the latter, she decided. She didn't care for the idea that everyone could read her so easily.

"Are you not familiar with the phrase 'looks can be deceiving'?" she asked pertly.

His smile grew and there was a pause before he answered. "I've a passing familiarity with the saying."

Kate thought it sounded as if he might have more than a passing familiarity, but the sound of the musicians beginning the first bars of the waltz kept her from responding.

Mr. Hunter offered her his arm. "I believe this is our dance, Lady Kate."

She laid her hand lightly on his forearm and was surprised by the swell of muscle beneath her fingers. She looked down at where the ivory of her glove rested against the black of his coat sleeve. How strong did a man have to be, she wondered, to have noticeable muscle in his forearms?

She'd not felt it with any of the other gentlemen she'd danced with in the past, and that accounted for a respectable number of gentlemen. Did it have something to do with his mysterious past? She recalled Whit mentioning that Hunter's father had been a merchant of some sort, but a father's profession needn't always dictate the son's. Had he been a blacksmith? Were pirates known for their strength? She rather thought it was just agility, but perhaps—

"Is there something the matter with your glove?"

She jerked her gaze up, a little bewildered to find they'd already reached the dance floor. "Beg your pardon?"

"You've been staring at your glove for the last thirty seconds. Is there something the matter with it?"

She hadn't been staring at her glove, she'd been staring at him, but she had no intention of correcting his mistake. "No, I . . . No, nothing the matter."

"Shall we dance, then?"

"Certainly." She cleared her throat and carefully placed one of her hands in his and the other on his shoulder. A shoulder, she couldn't help but note, that was also considerably muscled.

Mr. Hunter slid his free hand around her waist to rest at her back. She had only a moment to wonder why such a light touch should feel so significant before he swept her onto the dance floor.

Kate immediately applied herself to not thinking about her waltzing partner's physique, an effort that might have met with more success had she been doing most anything *besides* waltzing. Waltzing required touching, an obvious impediment to her goal. Furthermore, dancing was one of the very few activities where she was able to exhibit a respectable amount of grace with very little effort. As long as the music maintained a consistent tempo, it was simple, almost instinctual, for her body to move in time. In short, the task provided no distraction whatsoever from thoughts of Mr. Hunter's unusually muscled form.

Thoughts she was going to stop having, immediately.

"A penny for your thoughts, Lady Kate."

Had dancing *not* come so naturally to her, she very likely would have tripped upon hearing that question. Not for all the pennies in the world would she tell him where her mind had been.

"I, er, I was thinking you're a very fine dancer." It was entirely possible that thought had flitted through her head at some point. It was even true—for a large man, he displayed a surprising amount of grace.

She waited, expecting him to deliver a compliment of his own. Gentlemen usually commented on her dancing skills. She suspected they did so in part to be polite, but mostly because they were stunned to find she wasn't trodding on their toes.

In retrospect, she should have known Mr. Hunter would not do what she expected. Instead of returning the compliment, or thanking her for the one he'd received—as she rather felt he ought—he subtly bent his head, lowering it just enough for her to see the taunt in his dark eyes, and the humor.

"Liar," he whispered.

The tickle of laughter returned. "If you don't keep the proper distance, there will be more lies circulating about this ballroom than you find amusing. People are watching, you know."

"You're the sister of a wealthy earl and the daughter of an influential countess. People are always watching you," he returned, lifting his head and neatly sweeping her into another turn. "Tell me, do you find it disconcerting to have so many following your every move?"

It wasn't so very many, in her opinion. And she was quite certain her "every move" was a considerable exaggeration— he was the only person she felt looked at her too often and with too great an intensity—but since she was determined not to display any ruffled feathers, she let both matters go.

"I do sometimes wonder what people are thinking while they watch others dance," she told him.

He tipped his chin toward two austere-looking matrons whispering behind their hands at the edge of the dance floor. "Just now, I imagine the majority of them are wondering why you're dancing with an upstart and known rake."

"*Are* you a rake?" she asked before she could think better of it. She might have asked even if she *had* thought better of it. She'd heard rumors that Mr. Hunter had seduced legions of widows and opera singers, but what was fact and what was . . . well, rumor, it was impossible to say. It was equally impossible to say why she cared, except perhaps that she was a bit more curious about the man than she realized.

He carefully led her around an elderly couple exiting the dance early. "Would my being a rake make me more appealing in your eyes?"

"No, it would simply make you a rake." She studied him

for a moment as he laughed. "Do you know, I don't believe you are."

"Oh?"

She shrugged. "I've never once heard a rumor of you seducing an innocent young lady."

"That merely suggests I'm not a debaucher of innocents."

She frowned thoughtfully. "Is there a distinction made between being a rake and being a debaucher?"

"There is by men of sense," he informed her. "Only the latter is liable to end with dueling pistols at dawn."

"Oh." She considered that. "The distinction is purely self-serving, then? Morality isn't factored in at all?"

"We *are* discussing rakes and debauchers."

That was true. And how very strange that they should be. And how exhilarating. No other man of her acquaintance would ever think to have such an unconventional conversation with her. A gentleman simply did not discuss rakes and debauchers with young ladies. And young ladies were not to discuss them at all.

She looked about at the other dancers. If anyone was listening—

"You're safe, Lady Kate," Mr. Hunter assured her. "No one can hear."

He was right, of course, they were speaking too softly to be heard over the music. Still . . . "It really isn't a discussion we ought to be having."

"Should we change the subject?"

They should. They really should. And she would, in another minute. After one more quick scan about her, she lowered her voice and asked, "What of men who seduce other men's wives? Are *they* rakes?"

"Cuckolders."

"I see." She bit her bottom lip a moment and nodded. "But equally likely to find themselves on the field of honor, I imagine."

"Depends on how the husband feels toward the wife, and his honor."

"So a rake pursues only certain kinds of women, such as actresses and opera singers?" She thought about that. "Doesn't that make every man a rake?"

"Not every man. England doesn't have that many theaters."

She laughed as he swept her into another turn. "Tell me this, if a man pursuing a married woman is a cuckolder, what is a woman who pursues a married man?"

"Welcomed, generally."

"Certainly not by the gentleman's wife."

"Oh, you'd be surprised." He nodded toward a middle-aged man standing near the doors to the veranda. "Lord Renort's wife encourages him to visit his mistress as often as possible."

"Really?" Kate glanced at Lord Renort and thought about what she knew of his union to Lady Renort. It was a second marriage for both and had been heralded among members of high society as a most sensible match. The gentleman had obtained a fortune, which would certainly be of use to a man with two sons and three daughters, while the lady had acquired a title—the accompanying benefits of which would no doubt be of value to herself and her two children. In truth, the vast majority of marriages within the *ton* were arranged purely for financial and social gain, but that fact didn't make Lady Renort's plight any less regretful in Kate's eyes.

"It's very sad," she remarked with a sigh.

Hunter's dark brows winged up in mild surprise. "Do you think?"

Kate's brows lowered in confusion. "Do you not?"

"I might," he admitted after a moment's thought, "if Lady Renort had desired, or expected fidelity from her husband. But in this instance, the union was strictly a business transaction, and by all accounts, the terms of that transaction were readily agreed upon in advance by both parties."

"I . . ." In advance? She couldn't decide if that sort of heartless union was more, or less sad. "It's still very sad."

He glanced over to where Lady Renort was smiling and giggling with a small group of friends. "She appears a happy woman to me."

"I suppose she does," Kate conceded, though in her opinion, it was *still* very sad. The woman had traded the chance to love for a title. "Would you care for that sort of match?"

"Would I be comfortable in Lady Renort's slippers, do you mean?"

The picture was enough to make her laugh. "Or Lord Renort's boots."

"Absolutely not," he replied. "I'd not abide infidelity in my marriage."

"And what of the terribly businesslike quality?"

Hunter shrugged. "I'd no more want an impractical union than I would a faithless one."

"Why assume a marriage based on . . ." She trailed off as a more pressing question occurred to her. "How could you possibly know the details of Lord and Lady Renort's marriage?"

His lips curved up once again. "Any rake worth his salt keeps apprised of which women of his acquaintance might be open to a spot of debauchery. Lonely wives are generally a fair bet."

"I . . ." Her eyes widened in shock a split second before they narrowed in suspicion. "You're making the lot of this up as you go along, aren't you?"

"Not the *whole* lot," he assured her and grinned as she laughed.

In truth, she really didn't care if it *was* the whole lot. It was still a most intriguing conversation. She'd have liked to continue it, but the musicians were playing the final notes of the waltz, and before she knew it, Mr. Hunter was leading her off the dance floor.

"Shall I escort you to your mother?" he inquired.

Kate glanced to where her mother stood in a small gathering of her friends. Several gentlemen were standing nearby, quite obviously waiting for Mr. Hunter to deliver Lady Kate into her mother's care.

"I think perhaps I could use another glass of lemonade," she declared.

"You must be exceedingly uncomfortable by the end of these events."

She glanced up at him. "I beg your pardon?"

"How much food do you have to consume in your little ruse to keep the gentlemen at bay?"

She opened her mouth, closed it again. Was there nothing the man missed?

Mr. Hunter steered her around a small grouping of chairs. "Are you going to tell me I've mistaken the situation?"

She thought about it, and decided there wasn't any point. They'd both know she was lying. "It isn't necessary that I consume it," she replied with a shrug. "I need only be near it."

"That's it?" he asked with a quick look at the men standing near her mother. "They're as easily frightened as that?"

For some reason, she felt the need to come to the defense of her suitors. "Occasionally, I have to actually hold something." She smiled as they reached the refreshment table, remembering a ball in her second season. "I chased off Sir Patrick Arten with a cream pastry once."

He laughed softly and lowered his arm. "As much as I would like to hear the details of that spectacle, I'm afraid I've engaged another young lady for the next dance." He bowed low. "Lady Kate, it was a pleasure."

He turned and walked away, and it took an enormous act of will for Kate not to gape at his back. Good heavens, had she just been dismissed?

Yes, she realized as he crossed the room without a single backward glance, yes, she had been. Kate frowned after him.

She'd never before experienced dismissal from a gentleman, and wasn't quite sure how she felt about it. After a moment's consideration, she came to the conclusion that her pride and confidence were still perfectly intact, but she was rather disappointed.

They'd shared a lovely waltz and one of the most entertaining conversations she'd ever had with a man, and then he'd simply walked away . . . to dance with someone else. How disheartening.

Mr. Hunter was allowed to dance with whomever he chose, of course. She certainly didn't expect him to stand about speaking to her the entire night. But would it have killed him to give some indication he'd enjoyed the dance as much as she? True, he'd said it had been a pleasure, but *everyone* said that. She'd even said it to Mr. Marshall, and he had a tendency to spit when he spoke.

Confused by his sudden lack of interest, and her sudden increase in interest, she continued to watch as he made his way to a small group of young women standing at the edge of the ballroom. Recognizing the women, Kate clenched her jaw in annoyance.

If he had given up an opportunity to discuss rakes and debauchers with her in order to dance with Miss Mary Jane Willory, she was going to . . . Well, she couldn't think of anything she *could* do, actually, except staunchly refuse to ever dance with him again. Miss Willory was a malicious creature. A nasty, selfish, snobbish, cruel and—

She broke off her mental diatribe when she recognized the young woman Mr. Hunter led to the floor not as Miss Willory, but Miss Rebecca Heins. That changed things entirely.

Kate didn't mind being dismissed for the likes of Miss Heins. She was a tremendously sweet young woman with an unfortunate propensity for underestimating her own worth. That propensity and its accompanying shyness had consigned Miss Heins to the position of wallflower since her first season.

As Mr. Hunter and Miss Heins began the first steps of their reel, Kate remembered something her brother's wife, Mirabelle, often said. The very best gentlemen were those who made a point to dance with at least one wallflower at every ball.

Did Mr. Hunter dance with a wallflower at every ball? Having taken pains not to pay attention to the man, she couldn't say. But he was dancing with one now, which counted for something—

"He'll notice if you keep staring."

Kate snapped her eyes away from the dance floor to find her cousin, Evie, standing next to her. Petite but curvaceous with light brown hair and dark eyes, Evie was a lovely woman despite a thin scar than ran from her temple to her jaw, and a barely perceptible limp, both acquired in a childhood carriage accident.

Evie was also an extraordinarily clever young woman with a well-honed talent for ferreting out other people's secrets. Ordinarily, Kate admired and benefited from that skill. At the moment, however, she rather wished her cousin had taken up watercolors instead.

Kate reached for more lemonade. "I'm sure I don't know what you mean."

Evie merely raised her brows and waited.

Kate winced. "I *loathe* when you do that."

"Yes, I know. Wouldn't be nearly as effective otherwise."

She gave up the pretense. "I was only looking at him," she grumbled.

"Nothing at all wrong with that," Evie replied. "He's very nice to look at."

"He is handsome," Kate admitted.

"And quite charming."

"He's *exceedingly* charming."

Evie titled her head at her. "If you've an interest in him, why do you avoid him?"

"Because . . ." Frustrated, she turned back to look at Mr. Hunter yet again. "I'm not certain what sort of interest it is. There's something about the man . . ."

"That niggles at your memory," Evie finished for her. "Yes, you and Lizzy have mentioned it before."

"It's not just that," she replied with a shake of her head. "He's . . . I don't know. He's *too* charming, when he's not being impossible. I don't trust him."

"You hardly know him."

She looked at her cousin again. "You've spent some time with him."

A little over a year ago, Evie had spent a considerable amount of time with Mr. Hunter and three others—including her future husband—at a coastal cottage some distance from Haldon. She'd been secluded away in an effort to protect her from a man who'd threatened her life.

"Yes," Evie replied with a nod before turning to study Mr. Hunter. "I think . . . I think he's a good man, at the core."

"At the core?" Kate frowned thoughtfully. "What of the rest of him?"

"He has some darker spots, I'll admit."

"You make him sound like a piece of fruit on the verge of going bad," Kate said on a laugh.

"No, just one with a few bruises."

"Pity they can't be carved out like the soft spots on an apple."

"Pity apples can't mend," Evie countered, reaching for a sandwich. "Then we wouldn't have to carve them up."

Did Mr. Hunter need mending? Kate looked back at him, considering, and then, because she was doing entirely too much looking at Mr. Hunter, turned her eyes and her attention away.

"Where is Mirabelle?" she asked Evie.

"As attempts to change the subject go, that lacked subtlety," Evie commented, then shrugged. "She's is in the library having a discussion with Whit."

Kate glanced in the direction of the library. "A discussion or a debate?"

"Well, I didn't hear any glass breaking when I walked past, so I assume the former."

Kate smiled at that. Her brother and sister-in-law displayed a passion for arguing that was only exceeded by their passion for each other.

"They're terribly in love," she sighed.

It seemed as if nearly all her friends and family were terribly in love. Alex, the Duke of Rockeforte, was happily married to her friend Sophie. Mirabelle was a perfect match for her brother, Whit, and Evie was clearly blissful in her union to James McAlistair. Even Mrs. Summers, her mother's friend and Sophie's one-time governess, appeared to have developed an attachment to Mr. William Fletcher.

It bothered her to be the only one who had yet to find a love match, and it bothered her that she should be bothered. It made her feel small and selfish to be anything but delighted by the happiness of those she loved. And it was ungrateful of her not to be content with the blessings she could all ready claim—a loving family, financial security, a passion and talent for music and the engaging goal of one day being recognized for both. It should be enough. It was enough, she told herself firmly.

But where was the harm in indulging, just now and then, in a dream of something more?

❊ *Four* ❊

$\mathcal{L}$ord Brentworth's house parties were not fashionable events. Unbeknownst to the host, they were not merely dull, but *famously* dull. Most notably for the ladies in attendance. A widower of many years, Lord Brentworth apparently had no notion of how to go about entertaining a houseful of women, and clearly had, at some point, decided that the best solution was to leave them to their own devices while the gentlemen did . . . something else. Most young ladies who had attended in the past would admit to never having been interested enough to inquire what that something else might be. Because taking into consideration the sort of gentlemen who found the exceptionally boring Lord Brentworth to be good company, they all felt it could be safely assumed that whatever the gentlemen were doing, it was dull.

Kate couldn't have disagreed more. In her estimation, Lord Brentworth's house parties weren't dull. They were simply . . . sedate. She rather liked the sleepy feel of the gathering. It allowed a change of scenery and company without the pressure often experienced at a gathering of the highly fashionable. She could sit in her room and work on her music, or read a book on the veranda, or spend the afternoon with Lizzy, all without being chastised for not being adequately sociable. In addition, Pallton House had a library of enviable size and admirable variety, a lovely pianoforte to play, and a French chef of some renown in residence.

But to Kate's mind, the finest quality Lord Brentworth's house party had to offer was its proximity to the English Channel.

She adored visits to the sea—the way it smelled, the way it sounded, the way it engendered a sense of serenity even as its enormity and power made her feel small and insignificant. What drew her most, however, was something she had discovered on her first visit as a child—the sea was the one thing on earth that could completely silence the music in her head.

Kate didn't mind the string of notes and tunes that so often clamored for her attention. She imagined they were no different than the melodies she heard others go about humming, except that what she heard was detailed, persistent, and *hers*. They were her melodies, her notes and tunes, and they'd brought her a lifetime of pride and pleasure. But sometimes, just every now and then, she wished for a way to silence the music at will.

In a way, the sea afforded her that ability. Whenever she walked close enough, any music she might be hearing stopped. She supposed it was because it had a music of its own—the crescendo as a wave grew near, the crash as it toppled onto the shore, and the soft decrescendo as the water slid back out to sea. It held a power and rhythm as distinct as any well-constructed symphony. And yet it wasn't something one could hope to put to paper.

Kate very much hoped a spot of quiet would be just what she needed to move past whatever it was that was keeping her from completing her own symphony. It was her first attempt at such a challenging endeavor, and she felt no small amount of pride at having nearly completed the work. And no small amount of aggravation at having *nearly* completed it for several months now. No matter what she did, no matter how hard she tried, a small section in the third movement remained stubbornly, relentlessly silent.

With any luck, the sea, and the peace and control it offered, would change that.

Eventually, she would have to go inside Pallton House

where the sounds of the waves would be too muted to be effective, but for now, she simply stood on the sandy beach and listened, quite content to be at a sleepy house party and equally content to hear nothing but the movement of water.

Until a deep, familiar voice said, "Good afternoon, Lady Kate."

With her heart firmly lodged in her throat, she whirled about to discover Mr. Hunter standing not six feet behind her. From his relaxed stance and the tousled state of his dark hair, she gathered he'd been standing there for some time . . . watching her.

"How long have you been standing there?" she demanded.

"I am delighted to see you as well," he replied, gripping his hands behind his back. "And my journey was quite pleasant, thank you for inquiring."

"I . . ." She didn't bother to hide a wince. "I beg your pardon, that was very rude of me. It's only . . . you surprised me. I hadn't realized you were there . . . or here, I should say. That is, I hadn't realized you'd accepted an invitation from Lord Brentworth. My mother and I only just arrived yesterday afternoon and—" And she was rambling, an irritating habit often set off by nerves. "You surprised me," she concluded lamely.

He angled his head to the side. "A welcome surprise, I hope?"

She considered that and decided there was no point in answering dishonestly. "I'm not certain."

"An improvement over the outright no I would have received a week ago." He straightened again, his dark eyes twinkling with humor. "Was it my waltzing abilities that softened you, or my charm?"

"Apparently, it was your absence," she drawled. "It allowed the memory of your arrogance to dim."

"Ah."

"Quite sharp in my mind now, though," she informed him. Even sharper was that she found the slight disarray of his black hair distinctly appealing. The small flaw softened his otherwise impeccably polished appearance and made him seem more approachable. She supposed that meant it wasn't a flaw at all, but rather an improvement. Or maybe it was just a simple matter of—

"Delighted to know I'm in your thoughts."

She blinked at him. Good heavens, had she voiced her opinion of his hair aloud without realizing it? She didn't think she had, but it wouldn't be the first time she'd made such an embarrassing error. Surely he'd been referring to her earlier comment. The one about his arrogance and—

"Lady Kate?"

She winced for the second time in as many minutes and wished she had spent the morning catching up on the rest an unfamiliar bed had kept from her the night before. She was much easier to distract when she was tired. "I beg your pardon. I was . . . distracted."

"By thoughts of me?"

Yes. "Certainly not. I was thinking . . ." She lifted a hand to fiddle with the blue ribbons of her bonnet. "I was thinking . . . about the scenery. I like the sea best this time of day."

His lips curved up, and he took a small step toward her. "Your back is to the sea."

"I needn't look at something to ponder it," she replied, dropping her hand, and involuntarily taking a small step back. "*Some* of us are capable of abstract thought."

His smile turned just a little wicked, and his next step was just a little bigger. "That would explain how you managed to think of me in my absence."

She adamantly refused to back away again. Admittedly, that decision was bolstered by the knowledge she could only back up so far before stepping into the sea. Still, she felt it should count for something that, despite the way her heart raced and her mouth had gone dry, she managed to stay in place, tip her chin up, and say, "Did you come all the way to Pallton House just to ruffle my feathers, Mr. Hunter?"

He laughed softly, and to what she was certain was her relief and not disappointment, he made no further move toward her. "No. As it happens, I've come on business."

"Oh? What sort of business?"

"The financial kind, among others. Have you an interest in business?"

None whatsoever, she just wanted to change the subject. But she *was* intrigued by the idea that he would ask if she was interested. Like rakes and debauchers, business—particularly that of a financial nature—was not something a gentleman offered to discuss with a woman.

"Would you tell me of it if I said I was interested?" she inquired.

His mouth turned down at the corners, as if he wasn't quite certain why she'd asked. "Naturally, I would."

"Oh." Her mouth turned *up* at the corners because she was surprised at his answer. "Well. Thank you."

"*Do* you want to hear of it?"

"No," she replied with a shrug. "But the offer is appreciated."

She studied him as he laughed, and wondered what it was about him that seemed so familiar to her. Was it his eyes? The shape of his face? She was certain it wasn't the sound of his voice. She'd gotten the sense they'd met before the first time she'd seen him, and that had been prior to hearing him speak. Perhaps it was the way he smiled, or . . . Oh, she had no idea.

"Have we met in the past?" she asked abruptly. Much too abruptly. She hadn't meant to just blurt the question out, but there it was. And since it was too late to take it back, and because he was looking more than a little perplexed, she thought it might be best if she at least tried to clarify the question. "In the distant past, I mean. The first time we met, I felt as if we'd met before."

He shook his head. "The first time we met was at Haldon."

"You're sure of it?"

"Quite sure." He leaned forward to speak in a tone that was both teasing and sly. "I'd have remembered meeting the likes of you, Lady Kate. Believe me."

"Oh, well . . ." She cleared her throat. "I'm sure it's just my imagination, then."

"You've been imagining—?"

"Oh, look, there's Lizzy," she cut in, her voice sounding unnaturally high even to her own ears. She pointed to where Lizzy was waving at her from the back lawn. "It would seem I'm needed for something. Do excuse me."

She moved to walk around him, only to have him fall into step beside her. "No need. I was headed in that direction, at any rate."

She glanced at him, wondering if he had come outside just for her. Pure vanity, she told herself. Just because the man enjoyed vexing her didn't mean he sought her out for the opportunity to do so. Probably he'd been taking a walk along the beach for his own pleasure and happened to come across her. *Then* he'd enjoyed vexing her.

Kate set the thought aside as Lizzy reached them and bobbed a curtsy at Mr. Hunter.

"Lizzy." He inclined his head politely, and Kate couldn't help but notice that the teasing tone and wicked smile he so often employed in her presence was absent as he spoke to Lizzy. "I find you in good health, I trust?"

Lizzy smiled at him, and in such a way that made Kate realize it wasn't the first time Mr. Hunter had shown her such regard. "I'm perfectly hale. And you?"

"Quite well, thank you."

Good heavens, were they friends? How could she not

know they were friends? Lizzy had mentioned in the past that Mr. Hunter was always well behaved in her company, but she'd never given any indication that the two of them had developed any sort of bond. Surely if Lizzy had formed a friendship with Mr. Hunter, she'd not have kept it to herself. Lizzy was incapable of keeping *anything* to herself. They weren't friends, they were simply friendly. Weren't they?

Lizzy turned her attention from Mr. Hunter. "Your mother sent me to inform you it's time for tea."

"Right. Thank you." Kate took a step toward the house, realized the error in manners and turned round again. "Will you be joining us, Mr. Hunter?"

"I will after a time. I promised Mr. Abbot I'd have a look at his new mare first." He tipped his head toward the side of the house where the stables were located. "But save me a seat, won't you, Lady Kate?"

Before she had a chance to respond to that, he bowed again and turned away.

Kate watched him saunter off in the direction of the stables. "I don't understand that man at all."

"Mr. Hunter?" Lizzy took her arm and led her toward the house. "What's not to understand?"

"Who he is. What he wants. Why he . . ." She trailed off and glanced at Lizzy. "Does he always show you such regard?"

Lizzy stopped walking, her eyes widening considerably. "Beg your pardon?"

"Oh, I don't mean to imply anything untoward. I . . ." A horrible thought occurred to her. "I *needn't* be implying anything untoward . . . need I?"

Somehow, Lizzy managed to widen her eyes further, and even gape a little. "With Mr. Hunter? How could you think—?"

"I'm sorry. I truly am." The idea had come entirely unbidden, and she was equal parts ashamed and confused by it now. "It's only . . . well, he was most polite to you just now."

Lizzy tipped her chin up a hair. "What's wrong with that, then?"

"Not a thing." Oh dear, she wasn't improving matters. "It's only . . . he's *not* polite in my company. I assumed he was equally forward with everyone."

Lizzy relaxed her stance. "Ah. He's unpleasant toward you?"

"No, not unpleasant. Not entirely. Just not quite so respectful. Are you . . . friends?"

Lizzy's expression changed to one of inquisitive amusement. "That would bother you some, wouldn't it?"

Kate felt her own chin tip up. "It would not."

Lizzy studied her a moment before nodding once in a supremely knowing sort of manner. "It would. And it'd not have a thing to do with my being a maid."

"I would *not* be bothered," Kate insisted, and resumed their walk toward the house at something less than a ladylike pace.

Lizzy fell into step beside her. "You *would* and—" She broke off with a laugh. "I feel as if we're eight again."

Kate leapt at the chance to change the subject. "Shall I pull your hair until you admit I'm right?"

"You never pulled my hair," Lizzy replied with a snort.

"No, but I recall you pulling mine once. Revenge is long overdue."

"I can't believe your brother didn't take a strap to me for that," Lizzy commented with a dramatic wince.

"Whit isn't the sort to take a strap to anyone, least of all a child. And you were sent to bed without dinner, if I recall."

Lizzy smiled. "You tried to sneak me a bit of roast."

"I did, didn't I?" Kate murmured, remembering. She'd put the meat in a napkin, and the napkin up her sleeve. "Dreadful idea."

"The gravy did create something of a mess. Evie fared better with her buttered roll."

"Evie's better at being sneaky. Where did she hide that, do you suppose?"

"I didn't ask."

"For the best, no doubt," Kate commented as they pushed their way through a back door of the stone manor. It was also for the best that the topic of Lizzy's relationship with Mr. Hunter had been dropped.

Kate didn't want to dwell on the knowledge she *had* experienced a moment of irrational discontent at the idea of Mr. Hunter being friends with Lizzy. And that the discontent had nothing to do with the notion that a gentleman was not supposed to count a member of staff amongst his friends.

A silly rule, to Kate's mind, but that unusual opinion stemmed from having been reared in the company of several outspoken and unusually democratic women. Had Mr. Hunter been also? Was that why he was so polite to Lizzy? He needn't have been raised by women, of course. Men were just as capable of being democratic as women.

Lost in her thoughts, and absently tapping her finger against her skirts to the beat of a lovely violin concerto that had begun in her mind once they were inside, she followed Lizzy toward the front of the house.

Whatever Mr. Hunter's political and social leanings, she still didn't trust him. Because respectful to Lizzy or not, tousled hair or not, he was still a man of too much polish and charm who took pleasure in discomforting her. And if she didn't trust him, then she shouldn't trust her curiosity with him, nor her reaction to his dark gaze and . . .

The concerto faltered, slowing in tempo. Something hard nudged her hip, and she looked down just in time to see a vase go toppling from a side table she'd just bumped into. She reached for it with both hands, but it was Lizzy who caught it.

"Oh, dear," Kate whispered as Lizzy calmly replaced the vase. "Oh, thank you, Lizzy."

"Nothing to it."

"There would have been a great deal to it if it had broken and Mother caught wind." After a year of extensive deportment lessons had failed to curb the worst of Kate's clumsiness, Lady Thurston had given up any hope that her only daughter might display the grace the only daughter of a countess really ought. But that wouldn't stop her from lecturing over a host's broken vase.

"I do wish Lord Brentworth would keep his windows open," Kate sighed.

"So you can hear the waves?" Lizzy guessed. She was one of the few people who knew of the music that sometimes danced about in Kate's head, and the only other person who knew of the sea's ability to silence it. Given Lizzy's loose tongue, it was something of a mystery as to how she'd managed to keep the secret for more than ten years.

Kate nodded and sighed as they resumed their walk down the hall.

Lizzy brushed at a bit of dust on her apron. "Well, we can keep the windows ajar in your room, anyway. And mine, as it's connected. That should help—"

"You needn't keep yours open unless you want them open, Lizzy."

"I don't mind."

"It isn't a matter of minding. It's a matter of what you would prefer."

"I'd prefer you not knock anything over in either of our rooms," Lizzy said dryly.

Kate liked to think she would have come up with a very clever retort to that comment, but before she was given the opportunity to try, they reached the end of the hall leading to the foyer. The front door was open, and though a maid was blocking Kate's view of whoever was on the other side, she caught the sound of a familiar and very unwelcome high-pitched titter.

Oh, no.

She and Lizzy stopped in their tracks. The maid shifted and Kate saw a flash of elaborately coiffed blonde hair.

Oh, *no.*

The maid stepped aside and admitted one Miss Mary Jane Willory.

Kate felt her jaw fall open at the sight. *"Oh, no."*

Next to her, Lizzy made a small noise in the back of her throat. If Kate hadn't known better, she would have sworn it was a growl.

Though she would feel a little ashamed for it later, instinct made her grab Lizzy's arm and drag her back into the hall, out of sight of the front door.

Mouth pressed into a grim line, she stared around the corner at the petite young woman turned out in an insufferably tidy gown of white. Kate scowled at the woman and the gown. *Her* lavender traveling gown had been wrinkled from hem to neck and sporting several large stains by the time she'd arrived at Pallton House. Not exactly the most pressing issue at present, but annoying nonetheless.

Miss Willory moved aside to allow an elderly woman through the door behind her. Her chaperone, Kate imagined. A widowed aunt or distant spinster cousin or some other poor soul marked for punishment. Which was, again, not the most pressing issue.

She shook her head in bafflement. "What on earth is Miss Willory doing here?"

And why on earth did Miss Willory look so delighted about it? The woman was still tittering. Miss Willory was not the sort of young lady who tittered with delight to be attending Lord Brentworth's house party, unless . . . Unless there was someone in attendance she very much wished to see.

Oh, Kate *dearly* hoped that someone wished to see her back. And that the someone was Baron Comrie from Edinburough. How much more pleasant would life be were Miss

Willory to become Lady Comrie and spend the remainder of her days comfortably tucked away in Scotland. Kate had a difficult time imagining Miss Willory *wanting* to be tucked away in Scotland, but the woman did want wealth and a title, and after six seasons searching for them, and with people beginning to smirk a bit at her advancing age, she might just be—if Kate was very lucky—desperate enough to seize them from an unsuspecting Scotsman. Or maybe not, Kate mused, maybe she'd come with the hopes of luring the handsome young Mr. Potsbottom into her web and . . . No, no, Mr. Potsbottom had pockets to let, and if the rumors were true, the Willory family's extravagant tastes had put them in their own financial straits. Miss Willory was in search of a fortune. It must be the baron.

Lizzy plucked at her sleeve. "Lady Kate?"

Kate craned her neck to watch as Miss Willory imperiously ordered the staff to take special care with her trunks. "What is it?"

"We can't stand here all day."

Kate turned her head. "Do *you* want to go out there?"

"I'd rather eat slugs. A bucketful. But your mother is expecting you for tea." With her head poking over Kate's left shoulder, Lizzy pointed at a door on the other side of Miss Willory. "In that parlor."

Kate swallowed a groan. "Is there another way in, do you suppose?"

"Through the window."

"I'd like to retain some pride, thank you."

"Bit late, if you ask me."

Kate grimaced. "I suppose we can't dally here forever."

"Dallying," Lizzy repeated. "Is that what we're doing?"

No, they were hiding, but Kate didn't feel like admitting to that out loud. It wasn't that she was afraid of Miss Willory, not in the least. But spending time in the woman's company was, in fact, very much like eating slugs. Unlikely to cause harm, but unpleasant enough to justify taking extensive measures to avoid the experience.

Kate watched as Miss Willory and her chaperone were ushered into the parlor. *Blast*, there went any hope that the woman would retire to her room after her long journey. And stay there for the duration of the party.

To her complete shock, Mr. Hunter's dark head quite suddenly peered over her right shoulder. "What are we looking at?"

❈ *Five* ❈

$\mathcal{K}$ate jumped and spun around at the sound of Mr. Hunter's voice. In retrospect, it might have been a better choice to stay as she'd been, peering around the corner of the hall, because jumping and spinning only resulted in her catching Lizzy in the side with her elbow, and then coming to a stop with the hard wall at her back and Mr. Hunter's hard form not three inches from her nose. She *knew* his form was hard, because she'd caught him in the belly with her *other* elbow in the spinning process, and he hadn't emitted so much as a grunt.

Her heart leapt up to lodge in her throat. The air backed up in her lungs. And both reactions, she assured herself, were from the surprise—they hadn't a thing to do with his nearness. She blinked at his cravat for a second before slowly lifting her eyes to meet his.

The blighter had the nerve to grin down at her. "Startled you again, did I?"

Finding her breath once more, she wedged her arm between them, placed the flat of her hand against his chest—his decidedly hard chest—and pushed him back a step.

"How long have you been standing here?" she demanded for the second time in less than a half hour.

He continued to grin. "Just long enough to wonder how long the two of you have been standing *there*."

"We've not . . ."

"Three minutes, at least," Lizzy supplied, rubbing at her ribs where Kate had elbowed her.

Kate swallowed a groan, along with the apology she'd been about to offer. "You really *are* incapable of keeping anything to yourself."

Lizzy shrugged, clearly unrepentant. "I can if it's asked of me."

"What were you watching for the last three minutes?" Mr. Hunter inquired.

"Nothing." Kate threw a hard look at Lizzy before continuing. "It really isn't anything you need concern yourself over. I thought you were inspecting Mr. Abott's mare."

"Never said I'd inspect the mare, only said I'd look at it, which I have," Hunter replied easily. "And I'm not quite so concerned by what you and Lizzy have been watching as I am intrigued." He leaned a little to glance around the corner. "Was there a spot of mischief happening before I came along? A lover's spat? An assignation?"

"An assignation?" she repeated, a bubble of laughter forming in her throat. "In the foyer?"

"It would certainly merit three minutes of staring."

"We were not staring for three minutes." At least two of them had been reserved for contemplation.

"It was closer to four, really," Lizzy said with a sly smile for Kate. "You've still not asked me."

"Lizzy," Kate ground out, "would you please be so kind as to keep our business to yourself?"

"Certainly, though I don't see why it need be secret."

"Neither do I," Mr. Hunter remarked.

"It's not a secret, it's . . . Oh, never mind." She pushed at a lock of hair that had come loose when Mr. Hunter had startled her. "Lizzy, Mother's waiting."

Lizzy pulled a face. "Must I go?"

Kate hesitated, torn between desiring Lizzy's reassuring presence in the parlor, and wanting Lizzy's comfort. The latter won out fairly quickly, but she let the silence drag out a few extra seconds in retribution for Lizzy's loose tongue. "If you'd rather not, I'm sure I can manage it on my own. Although—"

"Excellent. I'll just be in my room, then."

Kate sighed as Lizzy made a rapid escape down the hall. "So much for loyalty in the face of adversity."

"You could have insisted she come," Hunter pointed out.

"No reason for the both of us to be miserable," she grumbled.

He bent his head to catch her eye. "What's changed since I left you on the lawn?"

"What do you mean?" she asked, noticing for the first time that he'd smoothed the flyaway locks of his hair. She wondered if the man was vain, or just very neat.

"You were happy enough to go in for tea when I saw you last," he explained. "What's changed?"

She shook her head. "Nothing that warrants the waste of three perfectly good minutes." She positively refused to admit it might have been closer to four.

He offered his arm and a reassuring smile. "Whatever it is, we'll brave it together."

She looked at his arm, then him. She couldn't find a trace of arrogance in his dark eyes, nor teasing in his tone. "Are you offering to be my friend, Mr. Hunter?"

His expression didn't change, but unless she was much mistaken, his voice softened a little. "Would you like me to be?"

Yes.

Kate bit back the instinctual reply. The man was too arrogant by half all ready. No reason to go adding to his vanity with instantaneous agreement simply because she was curious. And given the fractious nature of their encounters thus far, it might serve her well to think the offer through a bit before accepting. It might serve her *very* well if he knew she was thinking the offer through before accepting.

"Lady Kate?"

She held up a single finger and bit the inside of her cheek to keep from smiling. "A moment."

He *was* clever and witty, both points in his favor. Whit seemed to think highly of him, which helped. Furthermore, he'd been willing to speak with her of rakes and debauchers and matters of business. He'd danced with Miss Heins, and he treated Lizzy with respect.

"Right." She nodded once. "Yes. I would, I think."

He dropped the arm she'd been rather surprised to see he was still holding up. "You needed that long to decide?"

She decided, in the interest of friendship, to hide her amusement at his disgruntled tone. "It really isn't a decision one should make in haste."

"It generally isn't one that requires extensive deliberation either," he said dryly.

"I found this to be an exceptional case."

A spark of humor entered his dark eyes and he offered up his arm once more. "A man can do worse than be exceptional. If you've made up your mind, then?"

Kate didn't square her shoulders before entering the parlor, but only because there was a chance Mr. Hunter would notice and comment. She did, however, immediately scan the room for a chair that would put the greatest possible distance between herself and Miss Willory. With that accomplished, she none too subtly attempted to steer Mr. Hunter in that direction. A futile effort, as it turned out. Miss Willory was out of her seat and coming toward them, false smile in place, before Kate had taken more than two steps into the room.

"Lady Kate! Mr. Hunter! How marvelous to see you both."

Even with her mother, that relentless champion of etiquette, looking on, Kate couldn't manage a more polite greeting than a tight smile and a simple, "Miss Willory."

Next to her, Hunter made a noise that sounded suspiciously like, "Ah."

Miss Willory made a show of taking Kate's free arm and pulling her away from Mr. Hunter. "Lady Kate, I'm so relieved to finally see you arrive for tea. Your mother was just saying that you'd been expected for some time. I was growing worried you'd met with a mishap."

"I'm quite well, Miss Willory, thank you. I trust your journey was uneventful?"

There, that should please her mother. Or maybe not, Kate thought after a moment's reflection. The dowager Lady Thurston wasn't fond of Miss Willory either.

"Exceedingly," Miss Willory replied with a dramatic sigh. "I vow, I nearly perished from boredom."

"I am sorry to hear it." She carefully pulled her arm free as they passed a small settee and she bent to place a kiss on her mother's upturned cheek. "Afternoon, Mother. I'm sorry I'm late."

Lady Thurston returned the gesture. She was a small woman with soft gray hair, cheerful rosy cheeks, gentle blue eyes, and a backbone constructed entirely of iron. "Quite all right, dear. Did you enjoy your stroll on the beach?"

"I did, very much. I—"

"You went to the beach?" Miss Willory cried. Her voice came out shy of hysterical, but not shy enough. Every head in the room turned in their direction. "You went *alone?*"

And so it begins, Kate thought, with a sigh. "Yes. I—"

"But what if you had fallen in?"

"I imagine I would have climbed back out again." She'd been strolling on the beach, for pity's sake, not sailing deep waters.

"But you might have drowned—"

"In a few inches of water?"

"Certainly the beach is safe enough for *most*, but *you* might have hit your head as you tumbled in, or tangled yourself in your skirts, or—"

"Miss Willory," Lady Thurston cut in coolly. "Your concern is *noted*." She let that word hang between them, countess to ambitious commoner, for a heartbeat before daintily reaching for her cup. "But it might be better served by allowing Kate to take her seat and drink her tea."

"Of course," Miss Willory fairly cooed. "How thoughtless of me. You *must* sit down and rest, dear. You can tell us all about your little adventure, and—"

"I'm afraid I promised to take my tea with Mr. Hunter," Kate cut in. He'd told her to save him a seat, anyway, and that very nearly qualified as the same thing. She turned and gestured to where he was standing on the far side of the room, his hands clasped behind his back and a smile playing on his lips as he watched the exchange.

Miss Willory sniffed and smoothed her skirts. "You may suit yourself, of course."

Kate felt a moment's guilt at leaving her mother to deal with Miss Willory alone, but the excuse to leave had been made almost involuntarily. And there was nothing to be done about it now. Everyone in the room expected her to sit with Mr. Hunter. Conscious of being watched, Kate very carefully made her way across the room. If she stumbled, she would never forgive herself.

Mr. Hunter was still smiling when she arrived. "Should I be flattered you thought of me first," he asked quietly as he led her to a seating arrangement by the window, "or worried how easily that lie tripped off your tongue?"

"Flattered," she told him. "And it wasn't a lie. It was an assumption. You asked me to save you a seat. Naturally, I assumed you wished to sit next to me."

"Mostly I was afraid I'd be the only one left without a place to sit. Awkward for a man to stand about in a parlor, dainty little cup in his hand."

"Oh, look," one of the ladies suddenly exclaimed, pointing out the window to where a rider was coming up the drive. "It's Lord Martin, isn't it?"

"Come to see his father, the dear boy," someone else commented.

"Come to see a certain lady is more likely the case," someone else said softly.

Kate pretended not to hear, just as she pretended not to see several heads once again turn in her direction, and just as she pretended not to feel a small pang of disappointment as the rider drew close enough for her to be certain that it was indeed Lord Martin. It was silly of her to be disappointed. She'd known he might come, and he hadn't done anything to make her uncomfortable in his presence . . . not lately.

Kate glanced at Miss Willory. Had *she* known Lord Martin would attend? It would certainly go a long way toward explaining her visit. An earl's only son was a far better catch than a Scottish baron, provided the earl was wealthy and not too stingy in his allowance, or too sturdy in health, or unlikely to allow the match, or . . . perhaps it wasn't Lord Martin.

She took one more look at the newcomer as he climbed down from his horse. He certainly was handsome—tall and fair-haired with soulful blue eyes, an aquiline nose, and the narrow waist and wide shoulders all the dandies strove for. She'd been disappointed to discover on the occasion of their first waltz that he obtained that appearance by the use of padding. The result of which was that his shoulders felt—as Mirabelle had once put it—rather squishy.

With a small smile at the memory, she turned away from the window to find Mr. Hunter watching her, his expression unreadable.

"Particular friend of yours?" he asked.

"I've known him most of my life." She glanced back at Lord Martin as he carefully smoothed his blonde hair. "But no, he's not a particular friend."

"Kate, dear, look who arrived not two hours ago. You remember Mr. Laury, do you not?"

Kate turned her head at the sound of her mother's voice. Lady Thurston stood before them with a tall, thin, and rather nervous looking young man at her side. He had light brown hair and intense, dark green eyes hidden behind spectacles.

"Yes, of course." She'd spoken with Mr. Laury only a handful of times and just briefly on each occasion. But those short exchanges had been more than enough for her to discover Mr. Laury, although a very polite gentleman, had markedly little talent for conversation. He fidgeted, blushed, appeared to have difficulty forming whole sentences, and always cut the conversation short.

Kate wondered what her mother meant bringing him over in such an obvious fashion. Lady Thurston made no secret of her desire to see her only daughter wed, but she was generally much more subtle in her efforts. And the maneuver had clearly made poor Mr. Laury uncomfortable. The man was sweating a bit about the hairline.

As introductions and greetings were made, and Mr. Laury took a seat next to Mr. Hunter, Kate couldn't help noting the difference between the two men. In contrast to Mr. Hunter's large frame and confident bearing, Mr. Laury looked rather like a frightened schoolboy.

Lady Thurston took her own seat and gave Kate a pointed look. "Mr. Laury has just returned from an extended stay in Stockholm. He was fortunate enough to attend one of Baroness Cederström's salons."

"Oh." Kate scooted forward in her chair. That put her mother's maneuverings in a whole new light. Christina Cederström was an artist and composer who had managed to obtain considerable recognition for her work. "I'm a great admirer of hers. I should dearly love to attend one of her salons. What was it like?"

Mr. Laury cleared his throat, twice. "Quite nice. Quite nice."

"I imagine it was." She imagined "nice" was a pitiful understatement. The woman was an honorary member of the Royal Swedish Academy of Arts and the Académie des Beaux-Arts in France. While such success was not entirely unheard of, neither was it commonplace. Certainly not for a woman. In Kate's opinion, meeting the baroness would be the experience of a lifetime. "Were any of her musical pieces played?"

"Yes." He adjusted his spectacles and wiped away a bead of sweat on his forehead. "Yes, indeed. Tal-talented woman. Mite warm in here, isn't it?"

She gave him an encouraging smile. "A bit. Which of her pieces, Mr. Laury?"

His face took on a bright red hue. "'Välkommen, o måne, min åldrige vän', I believe."

"The most well known of her works." Kate wondered if disappointment had something to do with Mr. Laury's obvious discomfort with the topic. She tried for a tone of understanding. "I suppose you were hoping for something new from her?"

"Er, indeed . . . indeed."

Lady Thurston blinked at Mr. Laury, as if surprised by his reticence. "Well, no doubt the others in attendance—"

"Ah, Martin's arrived," he cut in, suddenly jumping to his feet. "Must say hello. Do excuse."

Lady Thurston smiled in a strained manner as the

young man made a dash for the door. "Such a nice young gentleman."

"I'm sure he's delightful," Kate returned, simply because it was expected of her. Just as it was expected of her not to comment on either the private wink Mr. Hunter gave her over the rim of his cup, nor the suspicious eye he turned on Mr. Laury as the young man left the room.

Hunter hadn't been suspicious of Mr. Laury. He'd been curious, mildly amused, and a little perplexed. Arms folded, he leaned back against the wall in Mr. Laury's bedchamber, and watched as the young man scribbled something at his writing desk. "Do you intend to spend the whole of the house party hiding in your chambers? Because you won't be of much use to us, this way."

Mr. Laury glanced up from his papers and Hunter imagined, with some amusement, what Kate's reaction might have been had she been present to see that the nervous young man present in the parlor only an hour ago had vanished. In his place sat a confident young agent from the War Department. One who gave a wry smile and wink. "The young ladies do tie my tongue in knots something dreadful."

Hunter chuckled at that. He'd never worked with Mr. Laury directly, but he knew the man to be perfectly capable of charming a young lady, if it was to his benefit. "I thought you had a mission to see to in London before taking over the investigation here."

"I'm not taking over this investigation. There's another man tasked with that responsibility. He's expected shortly."

Hunter straightened from the wall. "A third agent wasn't mentioned."

"My involvement wasn't decided upon until the last minute." Mr. Laury set his pen aside. "This surprises you?"

"No." Missions weren't static, they required constant reevaluation of strategy and dispersal of resources. Still, it would have been nice to have been informed of Mr. Laury's possible involvement. "I'm just irritated. If you're not here to help with the investigation, why have you come?"

Mr. Laury sat back in his chair. "I am to fill the role of 'transitional agent,' as William put it. If the investigation moves beyond the house party, it becomes my responsibility."

"Why?"

"I imagine William has other plans for you and whoever William has put in charge—who, by the way, is not to know of my connection to this mission, under any circumstances." Mr. Laury shrugged a shoulder at Hunter's raised brows. "William said you'd understand once the agent arrived."

"You've never met this other agent?"

"Apparently not in connection to the War Department. It falls to you to keep me informed of any major developments that might warrant my involvement." He reached for his pen again, and tapped the end of it against the desk. "Also, it would help, *considerably*, if you could keep Lady Kate from seeking my company."

Hunter grinned. "She's quite eager to speak to you of the baroness's salons."

"Bloody hell." He stopped tapping the pen. "I should never have accepted that mission to Stockholm."

❋ *Six* ❋

As the clock in the hall struck eleven, Kate snuggled into the cushions of an overstuffed chair, sighed happily, and opened her book. Probably, she should feel a touch guilty for leaving Lizzy up in her room while the guests laughed in the parlor and she hid in the small, out-of-the-way sitting room, but as much as she loved Lizzy, there were times when a person wanted a spot of solitude to sit and think . . . or read a silly novel without suffering through eye rolls from her lady's maid.

She wasn't to have that solitude. Within a few minutes of sitting down, the door swung open, and Mr. Hunter stepped inside.

"Good evening, Lady Kate."

"Mr. Hunter."

Kate's pulse sped up in pleasurable anticipation as Mr. Hunter crossed the room. She'd not had a chance to speak with him in private since her mother had joined them in the parlor, which had preceded Lord Martin joining them, and that had preceded nearly every young unmarried lady in the room joining them. After tea, she'd gone to her room to work on her music until dinner. At dinner, they'd been seated at opposite ends of the table, and *after* dinner, he'd gone to the study for brandy while she'd made polite conversation in the parlor. She'd managed to sit through nearly an hour of the last before she'd made her excuses and gone to her room for her book.

She'd thought not to see Mr. Hunter again until breakfast, but with their new friendship established, she was happy to be mistaken.

He took a seat across from her and tilted his head to read the spine of her book. "*The Adventures of Lady Amelia and the Valiant Prince Edward.*" He straightened and smiled at her. "Not a particularly creative title is it?"

She felt the color rise to her cheeks and berated herself for not hiding the book in the cushions when he'd come in. Clasping the book in tight hands, she waited for him to say more.

When he didn't immediately, she frowned at him in confusion. "Aren't you going to poke fun?"

"Didn't I just?"

"I meant at me, for reading it."

He leaned back in his chair. "If I wanted to mock you for your choice of reading material, I would have done so long before now. Whit's mentioned your penchant for such novels in the past."

"Oh." She would have to have a discussion with Whit about what he should, and should not, tell his friends. "He shouldn't have."

Hunter considered her. "Why read them if they embarrass you?"

"I'm not embarrassed to read them," she argued. She was embarrassed to have been *caught* reading one by *him*, which was an entirely different matter.

"If you insist," he returned generously. "But that doesn't answer my question. Why do you read them?"

She shrugged and fiddled with the binding of the book. "I find them diverting. I like the adventure." And the romantic aspects, but she wasn't about to admit that.

"You wish for adventure," he guessed.

"Doesn't everyone?" she asked, looking up.

He gave a slight shake of his head. "Most prefer the security found in a life of monotony."

"I don't think that's true. Human beings are naturally drawn to drama."

"As long as it's someone else's."

"Yes, you may be right." She tapped at her book thoughtfully. "Perhaps I'm no different."

A weighted pause followed that statement, and she looked up to find him watching her closely, his dark gaze unreadable.

"You're different," he said softly.

She wanted to look away, or at least shift in her seat a bit. The room seemed too still all of a sudden, the air between them loaded with tension. Through a considerable act of will, she sat perfectly still, looked him in the eye, and berated herself for being foolish. Air was physically incapable of becoming tense.

"Are you attempting to compliment me?" she asked, and if her voice came out a little breathless, it couldn't be helped.

His lips curved up, and he let the silence draw out a heartbeat longer before responding. "Compliments aren't attempted. They're given, or they're not."

"Well, which was yours?"

"Do you feel complimented?"

She blinked a few times, thought about it, then said, "I honestly don't know."

"Then you have your answer."

She opened her mouth, closed it again.

"You needn't look so crestfallen," he told her on a soft laugh. "It wasn't an insult, merely an observation."

"I'm not crestfallen," she countered. She was, however, inexplicably disappointed, and hoping it didn't show.

Rather than respond, he considered her for a second, and then very smoothly, and quite unexpectedly, rose from his chair. Kate had a moment to wish she could move about with such elegance, and to wonder why she felt let down that he should abruptly decide to leave, and one last moment to wonder why he wasn't headed in the direction of the door. And then, quite suddenly it seemed, he was standing over her. Or, to be more precise, *looming* over her.

There was so very much of him. His broad form blocked out the light of the fireplace and cast a shadow over her figure. He wasn't touching her, there was plenty of space between every part of her and every part of him, and yet she felt completely overwhelmed. Not for the life of her could she manage a single syllable of speech or even a flicker of movement. She could barely string two coherent thoughts together.

She felt trapped, utterly enthralled. And too confused to know if she cared for the sensation or not.

He reached down and she watched, a bit dumbfounded, as he slipped her book from hands gone lax. "Tell me, Lady Kate, is this the sort of adventure you long for? A dashing prince who will shower you with compliments?"

It came as some surprise to her that she was able to find her voice. "What . . . what sort of adventure would that be? One doesn't do anything when complimented. Except say thank you."

"There are an infinite number of ways to say thank you." He set the book aside and took her hand to draw her to her feet as easily as he had drawn the book. "Some of them very, very adventurous."

He slipped his free arm around her waist and ever so slowly pulled her to him. A small voice in the back of her head told her to resist, to pull away. She ignored it. She didn't want to resist. She wanted to see where the excitement dancing under her skin would lead.

She wanted to be adventurous.

He drew her near until his hard chest was pressed against her breasts, and he brought his other hand to curve firmly around the back of her neck. Everything inside of her thrilled at the feeling of being held so close. He seemed to be all around her at once. His body, his scent, his voice.

Had she really thought him overwhelming before? How could she have, when that sensation had been nothing, *nothing*, compared to this.

He bent his head toward hers. "I've never in my life met a more beautiful woman. Now . . ." His breath brushed her parted lips. "Say thank you."

Enthralled, enchanted, and wildly curious, Kate let herself be led by instinct. She placed a hand on his chest, closed her eyes, and pressed her lips to his.

If Hunter was surprised by her acquiescence, he gave no indication of it. His mouth moved over hers in a soft and skillful rhythm, and she felt the excitement inside her build. Dimly, she noticed his breath tasted like spearmint tea and he smelled of clean soap and the sea air. Wanting to savor both impressions and discover more, she lifted her arms and wrapped them around his neck.

The hand at her neck slid down to her shoulder, then lower to brush along her breast on its way to her hip. She gasped at the sensation, then gasped again when his mouth left hers to trail warm kisses along her jaw and down her neck. Each kiss left a delicious prick of heat in its wake.

His mouth found hers again, and his hands caressed her back in a long, slow stroke to the top of her gown. She felt the warmth of his fingers brush her skin and then they were working on the buttons of her gown.

She pulled away, just enough to find her breath and her voice. "Wait. Stop."

His hands stilled but he continued to brush his lips softly, teasingly against hers. "Are you sure, Kate?"

"Yes. No. *Yes*."

He slowly straightened and let her go, but lifted a finger to trail along her cheek.

"I wonder," he said softly. "You spend your days dreaming of a man who will offer you adventure, but do you have the courage to reach for what you want when it's handed to you on a platter?"

The burn of anger and shame instantly replaced the heat of passion—most of it, anyway. Did he think her a common doxy, then? Did he expect her to throw herself at the first gentleman who offered her a bit of *adventure*?

"Do not presume to know how I spend my days, nor what it is I dream of, Mr. Hunter. Furthermore, while *you* may fancy yourself a storybook hero"—she coolly pushed his hand away—"I see only a man with a grossly inflated opinion of himself."

His face took on a darker cast. "Is that so?"

"That is so," she replied with a succinct nod and a very subtle step backward.

She should have made it a little less subtle, because he was on her before she could take her next breath.

If the first kiss had been a dance of gentle seduction, the second was a war of wills. There was nothing soft in the way Mr. Hunter held her against him. Nothing coaxing about the way he moved his mouth over hers. It was hard and insistent—a dare and a demand at once. She wasn't sure she could answer either. What she did know was that she desperately wanted to wrap her arms around his neck again. She wanted to give in to the excitement that was building once more, not in the slow and steady progression of before, but in a climb so rapid it left her light-headed.

She felt herself shifting to try to get closer. Perhaps she'd give in for just a moment.

Without warning, he let her go and stepped back to leave her cold, gasping, and to her mortification, leaning just a little.

"What do you think of my opinion now, Lady Kate?"

She wanted to gape at him, nearly as much as she wanted to throw something at his head. He looked smug. She felt dizzy, hot, and muddled, and he looked smug. The rotter.

"You, Mr. Hunter," she managed through gritted teeth, "are no prince."

His lips curved up in a humorless smile. "You have me there."

She searched for something to say to that, but found her options were limited as he was, essentially, agreeing with her. She gave him a cold, hard look instead, then spun on her heel and left.

Minutes later, she let herself into her room with the careful stealth of a thief, or tried to anyway. She did stub her toe on the doorframe and tripped a bit on the rug as she crossed the room in semidarkness, but the resulting noise wasn't enough to alert Lizzy of her presence, which was the entire reason she was trying to be stealthy.

She didn't want to see anyone right now, let alone an inquisitive friend. She wanted to be left alone to think, and to fume.

What do you think of my opinion now, Lady Kate?

She didn't need to think on it at all to know Mr. Hunter was absolutely not the romantic prince of her dreams. He wasn't even a gentleman. Perhaps he *was* a rake, after all. Perhaps he was the dangerous pirate she'd thought him earlier. The fact that she'd read a number of novels featuring pirates—and that she'd had her fair share of dreams involving those pirates—wasn't something Mr. Hunter needed to be made aware of, ever.

She set the candle she'd pilfered from the library on the fireplace mantel and stared at the flame without seeing it.

What was she to do with the man, now? A friendship clearly wasn't going to be feasible. Friends didn't go about kissing their friends senseless in out-of-the-way sitting rooms. She didn't at all care for the idea of being enemies, or even adversaries. Being openly at odds with someone made her distinctly uncomfortable. She preferred avoidance to active confrontation, even with the very few horrid individuals of her acquaintance. And despite her displeasure with him at the moment, she wouldn't go so far as to describe Mr. Hunter as anything approaching horrid.

Perhaps it would be best if she returned to her original plan of pretending his actions didn't concern her in the least, which meant she would also need to pretend the kisses hadn't bothered her, which was really only another way of saying she would need to pretend the kisses hadn't happened at all.

She could do that, she decided with a decisive nod. She could most certainly do that.

In her first season, she had allowed Lord Martin to briefly

press his lips to hers in her mother's garden. Not long after, she'd decided it would be best if she behaved as if that event had never taken place. She'd managed that well enough, and Lord Martin could be a deuced persistent young man.

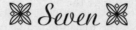

❦ *Seven* ❦

*B*y five o'clock the next day, Kate had come to the conclusion than in comparison to Mr. Hunter's skills of persistence, Lord Martin was a mere novice. And a clumsy one at that, because while Lord Martin had a tendency to trail her about like a child stepping on her heels, Mr. Hunter kept a respectable distance even as he followed her from room to room.

It was the oddest thing, to see him appearing everywhere she went. Even now, as she sat outside on the back veranda, a book of poetry in her hands, she just *knew* he was watching her from the windows behind her. What could the man be thinking? In the past, he seemed to loom whenever they happened to be in the same room, but he'd never before stalked her.

Perhaps he was working up the nerve to form an apology, she mused. Perhaps she would accept it.

She swallowed a laugh at her false conceit. *Of course* she would accept it, provided it was sincere. She detested being at odds with someone and always took advantage of the first reasonable opportunity to smooth things over.

Besides, now that she'd had the night for her temper and embarrassment to cool she had to admit that he hadn't done anything worse than kiss her . . . and then act monstrously arrogant about it.

Perhaps she'd make him squirm a bit before she accepted his apology.

He would not be apologizing.

Hunter didn't mind apologizing as a rule. A well-crafted appearance of contrition was capable of smoothing many a rough path. For the time being, however, his purposes were better suited by keeping the path between him and Kate a little uneven.

From his position at the window, Hunter rolled his shoulders and thought through his next move. It was going to be a challenge, both keeping close to Kate and maintaining the appearance of being just out of reach. After careful consideration, he decided that the most expedient way of doing both was to inform her of the smuggling operation and offer her an opportunity to participate in the investigation. The benefits were twofold. First and foremost, there was no possible way for him to continue following her about without arousing her suspicions. Which brought him to his second reason—he bloody well wasn't going to be following the chit about.

She could come to him, and appealing to her sense of adventure would assure she did.

He'd always meant for her to come to him, he'd just forgotten that pertinent bit of information for a moment in the sitting room last night. His jaw clenched at the memory. It hadn't been his intention to let things get quite so out of hand. He'd intended to kiss her, certainly, but that kiss was meant to be no more than a test. He'd wanted to know how susceptible Lady Kate was to seduction, and as he had expected, she was open to it, but not easily blinded by it.

What he hadn't expected, was what an unholy temptation kissing Lady Kate would be for him.

He'd never intended to take her innocence in the sitting room. Reaching for the buttons of her gown had only been part of the experiment. And yet a small, irrational part of his mind had hoped she wouldn't demand he stop. Some part of him had wanted to forget the purpose of the kiss, and see if she could be persuaded to ask for more.

And that was nothing, *nothing* compared to the temptation he'd felt the second time they'd kissed. She'd fallen into the heat of it within moments, and it would have been an easy thing for him to press his advantage. He'd come close to doing just that, so close to letting all his careful planning go to waste for a few minutes of pleasure . . . Well, an hour of pleasure at least, but that wasn't the point. He didn't want Kate for a few minutes, or an hour, or even the duration of a house party. He wanted her for a lifetime. And a spontaneous tumble was not the best way to go about acquiring that lifetime—an expedient way, certainly, but not the best. He'd be damned if his marriage would be founded on something as flimsy as a compromising.

Confident he could, and would, do a better job of remembering what he wanted from Kate in the future, he smoothed his cravat, brushed a bit of lint from his coat and stepped outside onto the veranda.

"Good afternoon, Lady Kate."

She spared him a brief glance over the top of her book as he walked around to take a seat beside her. "Is there a particular reason you've been following me about all day, Mr. Hunter?"

"Several, in fact. Would you care to hear them?"

"Not really," she replied and turned the page. "I'd rather you just stop."

"Can't, I'm afraid. I've orders."

"Orders?" She laughed a little at that and looked up. "From whom?"

He hid a smile when her eyes darted to his mouth. He'd known she would try to pretend the kisses hadn't happened, just as he'd known she would not be able to pull it off.

"William Fletcher," he told her.

"You don't take orders from Mr. Fletcher," she said with a roll of her eyes. Her gaze dipped to his mouth once more before she blushed and stuck her nose back in her book. "He works for the War Department."

"That's not common knowledge," he commented, although he wasn't particularly surprised she knew of it. Only to be expected, really, since a number of her friends and family members—including her brother Whit—worked for the War Department.

She twisted her lips but didn't look up. "It's not entirely uncommon knowledge."

"Whit let something slip, or was it the duke?" He sincerely doubted it was the ever reticent James McAlistair.

"I'm sure I don't know what you mean," she demurred.

"I'm sure you do, and while I can appreciate your circumspection on the matter, I'll remind you that when Evie's life was in danger, I was one of the men Whit and William chose to guard her." That had been a remarkably shortsighted and precarious choice, in his opinion. He'd suggested they draw out their adversary by using Evie as bait.

"That's true." Kate seemed to think about that for a moment before inclining her head in acknowledgment. "Very well, I do know what you mean, but I don't believe for a moment that you work for the War Department in any official capacity. Also, nothing was 'slipped,' as you put it. I am not so sheltered that I am unaware of what goes on in my own home. "

He'd wager she knew only what had been gleaned in bits and pieces. And he had no intention of filling in the blanks.

"As it happens, I do work for Mr. Fletcher in an official capacity." He stretched his legs out before him. "And he has ordered me to keep an eye on you."

She seemed to consider that, and him, then lowered her

head a little, just as he had not long ago at her mother's ball, and whispered, "Liar."

"Liar, is it?" he asked on a laugh.

"Yes." She straightened again. "To begin with, you're not the sort to work for the War Department."

"And what sort might that be?"

She frowned a little in thought. "Oh, patriotic, selfless, brave, perhaps a little reckless."

"I'm an unpatriotic and selfish coward with a cautious streak?"

"I didn't say that. I simply don't believe you possess those qualities to the degree necessary to risk life and limb in the name of crown and country."

The patriotic bit, he'd give her. The lack of selflessness as well. But damn if he'd have her thinking him a coward. It would better serve his purposes, however, to have that argument another time.

"Second," Kate continued, "Mr. Fletcher would not employ one of his men as a chaperone for a young lady at a house party."

"He would if he thought that young lady in danger."

"What a lively imagination you have," she said, and with enough amusement in her voice to tell him she didn't think the less of him for it. "In danger of what?"

"From whom, actually. Your admirer is heavily invested in a smuggling operation."

"Which one?"

"Which . . ." He nearly gaped at her. Holy hell, could he have been that mistaken about the girl's innocence? "How many smuggling operations are you aware of?"

"Oh, all of them," she drawled with a roll of her eyes. "Which admirer?"

"Ah. Lord Martin."

"Really?" She stared at him, her blue eyes going round. "You're in earnest?"

"Never more so."

"Lord Martin a smuggler?" She blew out a long breath, glanced back toward the house as if she expected to see the gentleman in question coming out the door, then turned back again. "Goodness, I shouldn't have thought he'd have the spine."

"You say that as if he's risen in your estimation."

"I suppose he has, in a way. I've always thought him something of a milksop. Well, not always. There was a period of time, a significant period of time to be honest, when I was quite attached to him. Or at least the idea of him. He seemed terribly dramatic and romantic, and . . ." She trailed off. "I beg your pardon. I have a tendency to ramble."

"Yes, I know."

She shot him an annoyed look. "What I am trying to say is, I don't think more of him for smuggling. I simply think more of him for being *capable* of smuggling. One can admire a talent without approving of how it's put to use."

He wondered how she would judge the use of his talents. Not well, he imagined. "Did you miss the part where I said his talents place you in danger?"

"No."

"You don't appear concerned."

She shrugged. "I'm not particularly. Lord Martin shares a closer bond to others in residence than he does with me. You'd be better off following them about."

"Which others?"

"Oh, Mr. Kepford and Mr. Woodruff come to mind. I believe the three of them attended school together."

"I rather doubt he fancies them."

"I rather doubt his fancying me puts me in any sort of jeopardy," she returned. "Particularly in light of the fact that I do not fancy him. What do you expect him to do, exactly? Recruit me into his merry band of outlaws?"

"Robin Hood wasn't a smuggler."

"And Lord Martin isn't especially merry. Neither of which is the salient point."

It was fascinating the way her mind worked. "What is the salient point, as you see it?"

"That I am not interested in Lord Martin, smuggling, or any other outlawed activity—particularly the sort that runs to high treason, which I assume is suspected if the War Department has become involved—and therefore I am not in any real danger."

"Regardless of where your interests and fancy are directed, his interest lies with you. The danger to you may be limited, but it still exists." He smiled at her pleasantly. "And that makes you, Lady Kate, my newest mission."

She frowned down at her book. "Is this the sort of mission Alex and Whit have been sent on in the past? I always imagined them engaged in something a tad more active. Bit disappointing, really."

"You'd prefer they risk life and limb?" he asked, surprised by her comment.

"No, I would prefer they have nothing at all to do with the War Department. But that's not likely to happen, is it? That being the case, I see no reason not to appreciate the work. Or I didn't, until now . . . I suppose I'll have to take back what I said about it requiring bravery."

"Absolutely fascinating."

"I beg your pardon?"

"Nothing."

Kate looked at the man before her—or more accurately, at his very tidy cravat as she was having some difficulty lifting her eyes to his face without her gaze becoming stuck on his mouth—and marveled at what he'd just told her. After first wondering what he meant by "absolutely fascinating," anyway.

Mr. Hunter, an agent for the War Department. She could

scarce believe it. Oh, she'd known that Mr. Fletcher trusted him, but she never would have guessed Mr. Hunter was actively engaged as an agent.

Nor would she have guessed that after a mere two days at the *ton*'s most sedate house party she would already have been kissed, twice, and embroiled in a smuggling operation. Which reminded her . . .

"Your mission is to keep me from becoming involved in a smuggling operation?"

Mr. Hunter inclined his head in acknowledgment. "Correct."

"I should think telling me of it is rather like involving me in it." She smiled at him pleasantly. "Do you fail all your missions this quickly?"

He chuckled at that. "My orders were to see you weren't involved in Lord Martin's endeavors. William didn't say a word against your participation in the investigation of those endeavors."

Kate knew full well William Fletcher wouldn't have said a word *for* her participation either, but she had absolutely no intention of arguing that point. She snapped her book shut and scooted forward in her chair. "Do you mean it? You'll let me help?"

"That depends. Can you resign yourself to my giving you orders?"

"I am the daughter of the dowager Lady Thurston and sister to the earl," she informed him in a dry tone. "I assure you, I long ago resigned myself to being ordered about."

Following those orders was another subject altogether, and one she very much hoped he did not broach.

"Will you resign yourself to being ordered about by *me*?" he pressed.

She gave him a decisive nod. "As those orders relate to this mission, yes."

"Excellent, then—"

"And provided they are sensible."

He lifted one dark brow.

"I only mean I'll not endanger myself simply because you ordered it," she explained.

"I see. You needn't worry on that score." He gave her a hard look. "Your involvement will be limited."

She didn't care for the sound of that. "How limited?"

"That remains to be seen."

Kate wrinkled her nose. She well and truly hated that phrase. Her mother employed it whenever she wished to avoid answering one of Kate's more sensitive questions, which meant her mother employed it with depressing regularity.

"If it wasn't remaining to be seen," Kate grumbled. "I wouldn't have had to ask. I'd have seen it."

"Beg your pardon?"

She shook her head. As that argument had never worked on her mother, it was a safe bet it would be equally unsuccessful with Mr. Hunter. "Never mind. What am I to do?"

"For now, keep your distance from Lord Martin."

"I already do that. I declined an offer to go riding with him just this morning," she informed him. "Couldn't I do something else? Perhaps charm a bit of information from him? I could express an interest in acquiring smuggled goods of a harmless variety, like brandy. Surely, he means to bring at least some over."

"No doubt, but that is too much involvement."

"What if—?"

"Another time, Kate."

She blinked at him, first at his sudden refusal to continue the conversation, then at the realization he had called her "Kate," and finally because he was clearly looking at something behind her. She twisted in her chair to see Mrs. Keenes and Mrs. Lubeck enter the terrace.

Kate stifled a sigh at the interruption as Mr. Hunter rose

and bowed to the women. They inclined their heads in turn, but there was little to no respect evident in the greeting. From the quick jerk of their heads, to their ramrod-stiff backs, they made it perfectly clear that they tolerated his presence, but it was not to be forgotten that he was not really one of them.

Kate felt her hackles rise. The very nerve of them, she fumed silently. It was one thing for *her* to have been dismissive of Mr. Hunter—or attempt to be dismissive, if one wished to be exacting—he'd given her cause with his looming and ruffling of feathers. But it was another thing altogether to dismiss a man, *this* man, out of hand.

Kate stood and gave a haughty nod of acknowledgment of her own. She may have been the only unmarried lady present, but she was also the only one related to a wealthy and influential peer of the realm.

"Mrs. Keenes, Mrs. Lubeck. I believe you made Mr. Hunter's acquaintance last night at dinner?"

Mrs. Keenes sniffed through her overlarge nose. "Indeed."

"Your husbands, I am sure, have made his acquaintance in the past." In truth, she wasn't entirely sure of that, but it seemed a fair bet their husbands had had *some* financial dealings with Mr. Hunter. According to Whit, Mr. Hunter saw to the investments of half the *ton*, and held the vowels of the other half.

By the way Mrs. Lubeck blanched and stammered, Kate concluded she belonged to the second half. "I, er . . . yes, of course." She pasted on a sickly smile. "Good afternoon to you, Mr. Hunter."

"Good afternoon," Mrs. Keenes mumbled halfheartedly before turning to Kate. "Mrs. Lubeck and I were just headed for a stroll about the grounds. Won't you join us?"

"We'd hoped for our dear Miss Willory's company as well," Mrs. Lubeck informed her, "but she declined." She leaned forward to whisper dramatically. "I daresay she worried she would damage what is left of her wardrobe. Did you see her traveling gown, Lady Kate? Mended in several places."

"*And* a full season out of date," Mrs. Keenes's added with a gleeful tone.

Kate couldn't help but feel some sympathy for Miss Willory in the face of such pettiness.

"How charitable of you to take such *interest* in your friend's circumstances," she bit out. "I believe I shall forgo the stroll, thank you."

Mrs. Keenes looked momentarily stunned, but after a spot of rapid blinking, managed to regain her composure. "Yes . . . well, if you'll excuse us?"

"With pleasure," Kate said sweetly.

Mrs. Keenes's lips briefly thinned into a white line before she hooked her arm through Mrs. Lubeck's and hurried them both away.

"Officious old biddies," Kate muttered at their retreating backs.

Resisting the urge to stick her tongue out at them, she turned away to find Mr. Hunter watching her. At first glance, his expression seemed to be one of mild amusement, but upon closer inspection, she saw a hint of darkness as well—the taint of anger and wounded pride.

He smoothed the front of his coat. "Did you just defend me, Lady Kate? *And* Miss Willory?"

"No," she said quickly, unsure whether she was trying to further spare his pride, or save her own. "I-I was defending a principle."

"And what principle was that?"

"Um, the principle of, er, good manners," she finally managed. To her relief, the sound of voices coming from around the side of the house meant she wouldn't be required to defend or explain that less than ideal response.

Mr. Hunter glanced at the noise. "It looks as if we'll have to continue this conversation another time."

"Yes, how unfortunate. I . . ." Kate trailed off and cleared her throat as her mother and Mr. Laury came into view.

Her mother smiled as she drew near. "Ah, Kate, there you are. Mr. Laury and I are for a stroll on the beach. Do join us."

Kate watched the blood drain from Mr. Laury's thin face. Oh, dear. It was thoughtful of her mother to press Mr. Laury into her company so that she might hear of Baroness Ceder-ström, but not at the expense of the man's health. He looked near to fainting. "I'm not certain—"

"Excellent." Her mother reached for her, neatly drawing her next to Mr. Laury, whose Adam's apple began to work up and down with disconcerting speed.

"Mother, I—"

"And will you be joining us, Mr. Hunter?" Lady Thurston inquired in a very, *very* polite tone.

Kate felt her eyes widen. She knew that tone. It was one reserved for individuals Lady Thurston was quite fond of, but would rather be rid of in the given moment. She'd been known to use it on her own children. And the only conceiv-able reason she'd want to be rid of Mr. Hunter was for the purpose of matchmaking between her daughter and Mr. Laury.

"Yes, do say you'll come, Mr. Hunter," Kate said quickly and in a voice that sounded a touch desperate even to her own ears.

"I've other business to attend to, I'm afraid," he replied, a smile playing on his lips. "I'll leave you in the capable hands of your mother."

Oh, blast.

"Such a pity," her mother chimed, linking their arms to-gether. "Come along, Kate."

"Lady Kate," Mr. Hunter called out as her mother ushered

her away. He waited for the group to turn around. "I understand you're an unforgiving opponent at chess. Could I interest you in a match after dinner?"

"I could see my way to having a match sooner—"

"After dinner," Lady Thurston broke in, turning Kate about again. "Good day, Mr. Hunter."

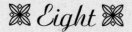

❈ *Eight* ❈

Never had dinner taken such an inordinate amount of time to begin, progress, and end. Kate was not a patient woman under the best of circumstances, and there were moments as she waited for her chess match with Mr. Hunter that she could have *sworn* the clock turned backward.

Her stroll with Mr. Laury and her mother had been painfully awkward for five very long minutes, which was the approximate amount of time the gentleman had remained in their company before making a hasty excuse and an even hastier retreat to the house. Then it had been a solid hour of listening to her mother list all of Mr. Laury's very fine attributes. Kate did not argue. Her mother was certain to push at least one gentleman at her daughter during the house party and Kate thought it rather convenient that the gentleman of choice was in the habit of fleeing. She saw no reason to urge her mother toward choosing someone else.

But the event that had taken the most amount of time had been dinner itself. A normally pleasant event was made disagreeable by having Mr. Woodruff seated on her right, Mr. Kepford on her left, and the both of them alternating between leaning away from her in fear of mishap, and toward her to sneak furtive glances at the neckline of her gown.

She'd been tempted to have a mishap involving her wine and both gentlemen, but chose instead to distract herself from thoughts of vengeance by imagining what role she might play in the investigation.

It wouldn't be anything dangerous, of course, she mused now. Mr. Hunter had more sense than to give her—and she had more sense than to accept—a task she wasn't qualified to perform. But she did hope it would at least be challenging.

It was a shame he wouldn't allow her to charm a bit of information from Lord Martin. She looked across the table to where Lord Martin sat drinking too much, laughing too loudly, and spending entirely too much time gazing at her and talking about himself.

Nothing at all unusual about that. Apparently, he wasn't nervous about his little operation. It would stand to reason, then, that a few carefully worded questions could be handed to him without arousing his suspicions. In truth, a few haphazardly worded questions could probably be *tossed* at him without arousing his suspicions. He wasn't the cleverest of men.

It was a trifle embarrassing, really, that she'd mooned over him for so long.

"Kate, dear."

Kate looked up from her untouched bread pudding to discover the other ladies rising from their chairs and her mother nudging her arm. "Oh, right."

Only a little time left now, she thought. As soon as the gentlemen were done sipping their brandy, they would join the ladies in the parlor. She hoped they sipped quickly.

To Kate's irritation, they sipped slowly. It was another hour before the gentlemen arrived and Mr. Hunter set the chess game up in a quiet corner of the room.

She managed, just barely, to keep her peace until they were seated and she opened the game by pushing forward a pawn. She'd not have been able to manage even that show of patience if her mother hadn't been watching the pair of them from across the room with a sharp and faintly disapproving eye.

"What are we to do next?" she whispered.

"What's that?"

"About Lord Martin." She glanced to where Miss Willory had trapped the gentleman in question on the other side of the room. Or perhaps Lord Martin had trapped the lady. It was impossible to say as both looked a mite disgruntled. "What are we to do?"

Hunter pushed one of his own pawns forward. "You draw less attention to yourself by speaking softly than you do by whispering."

"Oh." She supposed that made sense. Nothing said "secret" quite so loudly as a whisper.

"I'll speak softly," she assured him. "Tell me what we do next."

The wait was killing her.

"We wait," Mr. Hunter informed her. "And watch."

She felt her shoulders, her back, her *everything* slump in the chair. "You *must* be joking."

"I'm not," he assured her with a small laugh. "And it's your turn."

She'd waited all day to hear her role in the mission, only to discover it was to wait? She glanced at the board and brought out a bishop. "That's *all*? I'm to do nothing more than wait and watch?"

"Did you expect everything to happen all at once?" he asked, moving his knight.

"No, but I'd rather hoped to be doing *something*."

"You will be." He smiled at her. "You'll be watching."

She sighed and pushed a pawn forward. "What will I be watching for?"

"Unusual behavior from the staff."

She perked up a little. This was a bit more interesting. "Why? Do you suspect—?"

"If this house is used as a base of operations, then at least some of them are apt to know of it."

"Oh, of course." She couldn't help but glance at the maid who came in carrying a glass of milk for Mrs. Ifill. The girl looked to be no more than fifteen years of age, and harmless as a kitten. "How am I to distinguish between harmless unusual behavior and *truly* unusual behavior."

"I'm afraid that question requires some clarification on your part."

"Well, every staff has their own way of running a house and keeping their employer happy. Some ways might seem a little odd to you and me, but really aren't—"

"Try an example."

She gave him one she'd never been able to puzzle through. "The staff at Mr. Reiter's estate always move to the far side of a hallway when he passes. Always."

"Ah." He took her pawn with his knight. "He pinches."

"He . . . ?" She shook her head. "He's not the sort to hurt a servant."

His waggled his eyebrows at her, his smile turning devious. "It's not the sort of pinch meant to hurt."

"Oh . . . Oh." She never would have guessed it of sweet old Mr. Reiter. No wonder both her mother and her brother had avoided answering that question. "I can ask you near to anything, can't I?"

"I don't see why not."

That answer, Kate decided, was *infinitely* better than, "that remains to be seen." The possibilities it opened up were endless. Well, nearly endless. She couldn't expect him to have an answer for everything, or even be willing to answer everything. But he was willing to listen to her questions, just as he'd been willing to speak with her of rakes and—

"It's your turn again, Kate."

"Right." She pushed her rook forward two spaces without really looking at it. He'd called her Kate again. Did he mean to, she wondered, or even realize he had? She didn't mind if he did, not in the least. With the exception of Lizzy, none of her friends—and she rather thought she and Mr. Hunter were back to being friends—referred to her as Lady Kate. But if he did realize, why had he not yet asked her to call him by his first name as well? She decided there was really only one way to find out.

"Are you going to invite me to call you by your first name?" she inquired, grateful her mother wasn't close enough to overhear that terrible breach of etiquette.

He frowned absently as he studied the board. "Do you need an invitation?"

"Well, yes. That *is* generally how it works."

"I don't recall waiting for your invitation."

He *had* known, then, and not asked her in return. She twisted her lips in annoyance. "I can't . . . I'm not . . ."

"Not what?"

"Not you," she replied with a frustrated huff. "I can't go about ignoring the rules of propriety simply because it suits me." Push at their boundaries a little, certainly, but not ignore them entirely.

He angled a bishop out and looked up from the board. "Why not?"

"Because . . ." She moved a pawn. "Because it *doesn't* suit me. I like the rules of propriety. Some of them," she clarified. "*This* one. Are you going to invite me or not?"

Chuckling, he brought his queen into the game and leaned back in his chair. "Lady Kate Cole, would you do me the honor of using my Christian name?"

"Yes, thank you. I believe I shall." She maneuvered her knight so that he couldn't take her rook without sacrificing his queen, then straightened in her chair. "What is it?"

* * *

"What is . . . ?" Hunter gaped at her a moment, then threw his head back and laughed. The woman was a gem.

"Do you mean to tell me you don't know?" he asked when he could speak again.

"Of course not," she replied, apparently unfazed by his reaction. "How could I? I've only ever heard you called Mr. Hunter, or just Hunter by Whit and McAlistair. Do *they* know your Christian name?"

"Yes."

She frowned a little, then shrugged. "Hardly signifies as I couldn't have asked them."

"Why not?"

"Because they'd have wondered why I was asking."

"There is that." Still chuckling, he moved his bishop to threaten her knight.

"Well, what is it?" she demanded. "Your name, I mean."

"It's Andrew."

"Andrew," she repeated, a line forming in her brow. "Andrew."

"Does it not meet with your approval?"

"I don't think it's a matter of approving," she mumbled absently and just as absently sacrificed a pawn to his bishop. Her mouth formed his name again, as if she were tasting it, and hadn't decided yet if she cared for the flavor. "It's a matter of becoming accustomed to it."

"I see." He took her pawn and watched her quietly say his name again. "And how long might that take, do you think?"

"I'm not sure," she said before silently repeating his name.

He hoped it would take a few moments more at least, because watching Kate mouth his name was nothing short of an erotic delight. Particularly the way she drew out the "rew" so that her perfect rosebud mouth remained puckered even after she was done sounding the word. He imagined covering that mouth with his own. He imagined her lips forming his name on a whisper as he lowered her to the floor. He imagined her whispering it again and again as he stripped away the layers of clothes to stroke the heated skin beneath. He imagined taking his time, all the time he wanted, all the time he needed. He imagined tasting, and touching, and teasing until the whisper became a moan. Until the moan became a plea. Only then, when she was begging, when she was writhing beneath him in tortured ecstasy would he give her what she wanted—

"No, I don't think I like it."

It actually took him a moment to realize she was referring to his name, and not his sexual prowess.

"What do you mean you don't like it?" he demanded, shifting a little in his seat. Bloody hell, how long had it been since he'd had such a powerfully erotic daydream, in public no less? Ten years? More? Not since he'd been a green boy, surely. He couldn't decide if he was more amused or embarrassed. He shifted again and decided he was mostly just uncomfortable.

"It doesn't fit you," Kate explained, clearly unaware of his current line of thought. "Not as well as Mr. Hunter does, at any rate."

"Call me Hunter, then." It made very little difference to him, as long as he could get her to moan it.

"Hunter," she murmured, then gave a decisive nod. "Yes, I believe that will do."

Pity she didn't want to try it out a little longer. "Certain you wouldn't care to practice—?"

"Kate, dear, it is growing late."

The sound of the dowager Lady Thurston's voice as she rose from her seat across the room had them both looking up.

Kate glanced at the clock. "It's not yet midnight."

"Quite late enough." Lady Thurston replied as she arrived

at their side. She gave him a pleasant smile. "You understand, Mr. Hunter."

"Of course." He understood the lady didn't care to have her only daughter too long in his company. He wondered how much of that was a result of her preferring someone else as a possible son-in-law, and how much of it was her preference for *anyone* else as a possible son-in-law. More the former, he guessed. She had, after all, agreed to his looking out for her niece, Evie.

Kate rose from her chair with a sigh. "I trust I'll see you at breakfast?"

He'd be seeing her all day. "You will."

Lady Thurston ran her eyes over the chessboard. "You might as well finish the game, dear."

Kate glanced at the board. "Oh, yes."

Finish the game? "I thought you were—"

He broke off as she leaned over to push her queen halfway across the board.

"Checkmate. Good night, Hunter."

It had been a very long time since Hunter had gaped at a woman as she left a room. About as long as it had been since he'd lost himself in an erotic daydream in public, and just as long since he'd been put into checkmate within eight moves. Or had it been nine? He hoped it had been nine.

Whatever the number, it left him gaping at her as she left, then smiling as their footsteps echoed down the hall.

And then he was grinning. Oh, yes, Lady Kate Cole was, indeed, the finest life had to offer.

Nine

By two o'clock on her first full day as an agent of the crown, Kate was forced to admit that it was probably best she wasn't asked to fill the role with any regularity. She was, as it turned out, demonstrably bad at waiting and watching.

She'd tried her hardest, she truly had. It was just that her task turned out to be rather unengaging and the presence of Hunter much too distracting. She had assumed that after breakfast he would spend the day fishing with Lord Martin and the other gentlemen. Instead, he had spent the day in the house, making it all too tempting for her to go seek him out. It was absurd that she should do so, but she couldn't seem to stem her curiosity. Was he searching the house? Questioning the staff? Counting the floorboards?

Desperate to know what he was about, she had *ever* so casually tracked him to the veranda after breakfast, where they had sat speaking to other people. And then she had trailed him at a *very* respectable distance to the library where he had read a book and she had pretended to. And finally she had followed him, after a *perfectly* suitable amount of time had passed, to the parlor where he was now looking over a paper in a chair some distance from where she sat writing an imaginary letter to the Duchess of Rockeforte.

She snuck a quick glance at him. His clothes, she noted, were as tidy now as they had been first thing that morning. Her white muslin gown, on the other hand, was a mite wrinkled, had a brown smudge of unknown origin on the hem, and a small black ink stain near her waist. She scowled at the spot, then scowled at the pen in her hand. How ridiculous did one have to be to acquire a very real ink stain as a result of writing an imaginary letter? She set her pen down, brushed at a wayward lock of blonde hair, and once again glanced at Hunter.

How fastidious did one have to be, she wondered, to always look a veritable fashion plate?

Well, no, that wasn't quite right. Hunter's clothes were stylish, yes, but they were too subdued in color and cut to be considered the fashion *du jour*. There were no brightly colored or outrageously patterned waistcoats for him. She knew for a fact he didn't pad his shoulders, and he seemed to avoid the impossibly high and stiff collars favored by some other gentlemen. There was nothing about Hunter that marked him as a dandy or a fop. He was simply . . . polished.

She recalled that her brother, Whit, had once remarked in passing that Hunter was a man who possessed an inordinate amount of self-control. Perhaps that was what drove him to keep his appearance so well ordered—a desire to be, and look to be, in absolute control.

A simple enough appearance for one to obtain—provided it was someone other than herself—when one did nothing more than go from breakfast room, to library, to parlor. Clearly, the man was not about searching the house or questioning the staff. He didn't look to be about anything at all, not even counting the floorboards. Her curiosity got the better of her. She pushed away from the desk and rose from her chair.

"Good afternoon, Mr. Hunter," she chimed loudly for the benefit of several ladies gathered at the far side of the room. "Can I interest you in another game of chess before tea?"

He waited for her to reach him before giving her a wan smile and a simple, "No, thank you."

She opened her mouth to respond to that, then changed her mind when she noted he was still sitting. She gave him an inquisitive look. "Are you aware that it's rude of you to still be seated while I'm standing?"

"It won't be when you sit down."

Apparently, he was aware. As the question had been mostly an academic one, she shrugged, unoffended, and took her seat. "Why won't you play chess?"

"I don't think my pride could take it."

She fought back a smile. "Yes. That's understandable."

A corner of his mouth hooked up. "Evie told me that the two of you are the most evenly matched players at Haldon."

"We are."

He closed his book. "You bested me in nine moves."

"Eight," she corrected. "You shouldn't have brought your queen out so early."

"Eight," he conceded. "My point is, she wasn't able to do the same."

"Yes, well, the *most* evenly matched, and evenly matched *in truth*, aren't the same thing, are they?"

"Clearly not." He set his book aside. "Did you come all the way over here to discuss chess?"

"It was less than twenty feet. But no, I did not." She glanced warily at the other guests before lowering her voice even further. "Isn't there something you should be doing?"

"I'm speaking with you."

She rolled her eyes. "I meant in regards to the investigation."

"Perhaps I'm doing both, as you are. You're watching the staff and talking to me at the same time, aren't you?"

She could barely walk and breathe at the same time. She gave him a sheepish smile. "No, to be honest, I'm not. With very few exceptions, I'm rarely at my best when trying to perform simultaneous tasks."

"You played chess and spoke last night."

"As I said, there are a few exceptions." She looked down to the ink stain on her gown. "You may count yourself fortunate that I didn't upend the table midway through the game."

"Wouldn't have bothered me in the least. I find your lack

of coordination to be one of the most charming things about you."

She looked up and laughed. "Oh, you do not."

"I do, in fact."

"I . . ." Good heavens, he was serious. She couldn't fathom why he should be. Gentlemen often liked her *despite* her clumsiness, not because of it. She shook her head at him, baffled. "Why?"

"Because you've been gifted with extraordinary beauty, wealth, position, and talent. If it weren't for your ungainliness, you'd be insufferable." He smiled at her. "Everyone should have at least one flaw."

"I . . ." She had difficulty responding to that, which really ought to have kept her from responding at all. "I have *loads* of flaws."

The inability to recognize when I ought to keep my mouth firmly shut, for instance.

"Is that so?" He tilted his head at her a little. "Care to share what they might be?"

"Um . . ."

"Oh, Mr. Hunter!"

For the first, and what Kate was certain would prove to be the only, time in her life, she was happy to see Miss Willory enter a room. Even if Miss Willory was wearing a peach gown with a neckline cut almost, but not quite, low enough to be considered vulgar. Kate strongly felt it to be a case of revealing more than the view warranted.

Miss Willory reached them and sighed heavily. "I vow, I have been looking for you everywhere. That is . . ." She tittered, then blushed. The latter was something Kate knew the woman could do entirely at will. Which was, in her estimation, a perfectly stupid talent. "Well not *everywhere*. That would be silly of me, wouldn't it? I would never . . . Goodness, I'm making a terrible ninny of myself."

Hunter waited for the wave of tittering to pass before asking, "Is there something I can assist you with, Miss Willory?"

"Oh, yes, please." She blushed again. "There is a book I should like in the library, but I'm afraid I simply cannot reach it. I thought, perhaps, as the tallest gentleman in residence, I might trouble you to reach it for me."

Kate blinked at her. "Isn't there a stepladder?"

Miss Willory barely spared her a glance. "It's broken. Mr. Hunter—"

"Odd," Kate remarked. "It was intact when I used it."

"*You* used it recently? Well then, that would explain . . ." She cleared her throat delicately. "I'm sure I've no idea how it might have come to be broken."

Kate swallowed down a retort. Arguing that she'd had nothing to do with whatever had happened to the stepladder would likely only give her a headache. When it came to Miss Willory, the best course of action was to get rid of the girl as quickly as possible, not drag the conversation out. "Would you like me to ask one of the footmen to assist—?"

"Oh, no, Lady Kate. I'm sure it would be best for all if you kept your seat."

Inevitable headache or not, Kate would have responded to that if Hunter hadn't spoken first.

"Show me the book, Miss Willory," he said coolly, rising from his seat.

"Oh, you are too kind," Miss Willory simpered.

"You really are," Kate muttered, but neither seemed to hear.

Kate didn't glower at Miss Willory's back as she left the room with Hunter, but only because there were others in the parlor who might see. Perhaps, *that* was why Miss Willory had come to Pallton House, she thought. Not for Mr. Potsbottom or Lord Comrie, or even Lord Martin, but for Hunter. Unable to hold back any longer, Kate looked down at her ink stain once more and glowered at it. She should have guessed earlier, she fumed. She should have realized it might be Hunter Miss Willory was after. True, he hadn't a title—it was possible he hadn't even a traceable lineage—but he did have the fortune to buy half of England. And wouldn't Miss Mary Jane Willory just *adore* owning half of England?

Irritated, and unaccountably nervous, she stood to pull a small nearby table between their chairs, and fetch the chessboard.

Ten minutes later—which was five minutes longer than Kate felt was necessary—Hunter returned from his task and eyed the table dubiously. "Didn't I mention I'd rather not play chess?"

"I can't sit here talking to you while you read a book," she informed him. And she had every intention of talking to him, just not on the topic she'd originally planned. "But if your vanity is so easily bruised that you tremble in fear at the mere *thought* of—"

"I'll play."

"Excellent." She pushed a pawn forward and strove for a casual tone. "Did you retrieve Miss Willory's book?"

"That is why I went," he reminded her, taking his seat.

"You were gone an awfully long time for just one book," she commented as he studied the board. "Did you run into difficulty?"

"Miss Willory had a spot of trouble remembering where the book was located."

"It's a library," she drawled. "They're arranged by author and subject according to—"

"She had a spot of trouble remembering who wrote it as well."

Kate rolled her eyes. "Of course she did."

He looked up at her with brows raised. "Beg your pardon?"

"You *are* aware she's attempting to flirt with you?" She flatly refused to give Miss Willory the accolade of having accomplished the deed.

"I've eyes in my head," he replied by way of answer.

She waited for him to expand on that. He didn't. "Do you *like* her attempting to flirt with you?"

He leaned back in the chair and crossed his arms, his expression one of smug amusement. "Are you jealous, Kate?"

Rather, was her initial and entirely unwelcome thought. "Curious," is what she told him.

Hunter idly shrugged one shoulder. "I might like it, were she a different sort of woman. It's no compliment to receive the attentions of someone like Miss Willory."

"Oh." She stifled a sigh of relief. "Good."

He grinned at her. "You *were* jealous."

"I certainly wasn't," she countered, smoothing one of the many wrinkles in her gown. "I was merely worried you couldn't see past her charms."

"And that you'd lose me to them?"

Do I have you to lose? That unbidden thought was even more unwelcome than the last. Uncomfortable with both, she strove to steer the conversation in another direction. "You'll twist any comment to suit your purposes."

"*I'll* twist any comment?" He threw his head back and laughed. "Lady Kate, I have never met another human being so adept at modifying a comment for her own benefit than you."

"I—"

"Yes," he cut in with a patronizing smile and nod, "that was a compliment."

"It wasn't," she countered. "And I was going to say that you obviously haven't spent enough time in the company of those who are so *clearly* in the right."

"I've spent considerable time in my own company."

"I do so hate to repeat myself," she said smartly, "but you obviously haven't spent enough time in—"

"Oh, Mr. Hunter!" Miss Willory once more sailed into the room blushing and giggling. "I'm *dreadfully* sorry to trouble you again, but I'm afraid I must ask on behalf of Mrs. Ifill if you would be so kind as to assist in the library one more time."

Having been an unwilling witness to Miss Willory's brand of flirting on numerous occasions, Kate knew, without a doubt, that it would not be merely one more time.

"Perhaps it would be wise to fetch a footman instead," she suggested, "and have him repair the ladder."

"What a clever idea," Miss Willory said sweetly. "And how generous of you to offer."

"I'll fetch the footman," Hunter said quickly, rising from his chair. He headed for the door once more. Miss Willory followed, but not before throwing a disgustingly self-satisfied smile at Kate.

She'd stall him for the next twenty minutes at least, Kate fumed. With a sigh, she left to search out one of her own books with the idea that by the time she found something appropriate for reading in the parlor, Hunter would have returned. Considering that the only other appropriate book in her possession, besides the volume of poetry she'd had on the veranda, was a book on musical theory Lizzy may, or may not, have unpacked and placed on the vanity, it was possible she would return to the parlor to find him waiting for her.

She made a point of not finding her book until twenty minutes later, even though Lizzy had, as it turned out, placed it on the vanity. With the volume tucked under her arm, she made the return trip whilst pondering Miss Willory's sudden campaign for Hunter's hand.

How desperately did she want that hand? Kate wondered. And how far would she go to obtain it? Would she attempt to maneuver him into a trap? Feign being compromised? It was a dangerous game to play with someone like Hunter, but Miss Willory was conceited, conniving, and possibly just desperate enough to try.

It seemed the staff at Pallton House were not the only

people she would need to keep an eye on. Resolved to keep a close eye on Hunter as well, lest he not recognize a marital trap when he saw it, she reached the bottom of the stairs just as a maid opened the front door to admit, of all people, her brother.

Her mouth fell open. "Whit?"

Her brother looked up, his blue eyes crinkling at the corners as he grinned at her. "Good afternoon, Kate."

"What in the world are you doing here?"

"Such a flatterer, you are," he laughed, handing his gloves to a waiting maid. "I was invited."

"You're the Earl of Thurston. You're invited to everything," she pointed out as she crossed the foyer. "Why would you want to come here?"

As soon as the question left her lips, she hit on a possible answer. He may have come to help Hunter watch over her. Whit was inordinately fond of watching over her. It was strange that he'd allowed her to come to Pallton House at all if he'd known of the smuggling operation, but she wasn't in a position to demand an explanation.

Whit bent down to place a kiss on her forehead. "Delighted to see you as well. And to see that you *are* well."

"I've been gone less than a week. What else would I be?" Putting aside for now the question of what Whit did and did not know, she looked behind him at the open door and asked, "Where is Mirabelle. Did she—?"

"Still on the other side of the carriage, I imagine. Mrs. Warrings snagged her before she could make it to the front—" He broke off when she shoved her book at him and headed for the door. "Where are you going?"

"To greet Mirabelle."

"You've barely greeted me."

She tossed a teasing smile over her shoulder. "Well, you're not Mirabelle, are you?"

Kate found Mirabelle just where Whit had indicated, on

the other side of the carriage being held captive by the exceptionally friendly Mrs. Warrings. To her further surprise, she was also in the company of her mother's friend, Mrs. Mary Summers.

Mrs. Warrings fluttered her hands dramatically as Kate arrived. "Lady Kate, had you any idea? Your brother, Lady Thurston, and our dear Mrs. Summers here? What a delightful surprise."

"It is that," Kate agreed and stepped up to give both ladies a kiss on the cheek.

Mrs. Warrings glanced at the house. "I simply must make my hellos to the earl. He managed to sneak straight into the house without my seeing him."

"He did, indeed," Mirabelle commented dryly. Of average height and build, with dark eyes and hair an unremarkable shade of brown, some considered the current Lady Thurston a somewhat plain woman. It was Kate's opinion that those people were idiots. When Mirabelle smiled, a person would be hard pressed to find a more beautiful lady in all of England. It lit up her whole face and made it impossible for one not to smile in return. But Mirabelle wasn't smiling at present. She was scowling at the house, and though Kate couldn't be certain, she thought perhaps Mirabelle muttered something under her breath. Something along the lines of "traitorous blighter."

Mrs. Warrens didn't appear to hear. "Do excuse me."

"I shall join you," Mrs. Summers said in an uncharacteristically quiet voice. "I am quite done in."

Tall, rail thin, and with sharp, hawkish features, Mrs. Summers looked every inch the imposing governess she had been for the last two decades. But her eyes, which usually betrayed the warm and kind heart hidden behind the disapproving air, now showed only exhaustion.

"Are you well, Mrs. Summers?" Kate asked.

"Quite, dear." Mrs. Summers patted Kate's arm. "Just a

trifle tired from the journey. A brief lie down will serve to restore me."

Kate didn't believe that for a moment, but she waited until Mrs. Warrens and Mrs. Summers had moved out of earshot before turning to her friend.

"Whatever is the matter with her? Is she ill?"

"Not at all," Mirabelle assured her. "She's melancholy. That's why we've come."

"Melancholy?"

Mirabelle nodded and took Kate's hand to lead her around the side of the house at a clipped pace. "We need a spot of privacy for this." She stopped and scanned the side lawn impatiently. "Isn't there a gazebo or the like about?"

"There's a bench just on the other side of that half wall." She pointed at a decorative stone divider. "We could just as easily speak inside, you know."

"Yes, but first I'd have to go through all the greetings, and I don't want to wait to tell you—Oh, yes, this will do nicely." Clearly impatient, she tugged Kate down on the bench. "You'll never guess what has happened."

"Whatever it is, it must be very exciting. This is most unlike—"

"Mr. William Fletcher offered for Mrs. Summers."

Kate sighed with delight. "Oh, that's *wonderful.*" Not quite as shocking as she'd expected given Mirabelle's uncharacteristic enthusiasm. It had become fairly clear the two were attached after all, but still it was very nice and—

"Mrs. Summers refused him."

Kate gasped. That *was* shocking. "What? But she's violently in love with him."

That statement garnered a raised brow and a smirk from Mirabelle.

"*Madly* in love with him anyway," Kate amended. "Mrs. Summers doesn't do anything violently, except perhaps disapprove, although I suppose she's really more quietly severe in that regard than she is violent. I don't think one can be quiet *and* violent at—"

"Kate."

"Yes. Right. Why did she refuse him?"

Mirabelle nodded and bent her head forward conspiratorially. "She wouldn't say at first, so I wrote Sophie with the idea that she would know her former governess well enough to guess."

"What did she write in return?" Kate asked, wondering how the Duchess of Rockeforte felt about her lifelong companion remarrying.

"She didn't. And this is where things become very exciting." Mirabelle leaned in a little more. "Sophie came to Haldon the very next day. She dragged Mr. Fletcher and Mrs. Summers into the library, closed the doors, and demanded to know what was the matter with them."

Kate opened her mouth, closed it. "How do you know what she said if she closed the doors?"

"She demanded violently. At any rate, Sophie exited the library a few minutes later leaving Mr. Fletcher and Mrs. Summers inside. They were arguing—something about how her first husband died, and—"

"A moment," Kate cut in, holding up a finger. "Mrs. Summers was shouting?"

"Of course not."

"Then how do you know what *she* was saying? Were you eavesdropping?"

"No, Evie was."

Kate bobbed her head. "Of course."

"The argument grew quieter after a few moments, and then Mrs. Summers began to cry—"

Kate winced. "Oh, dear."

"That's what Evie and I said, but then she stopped, and Mr. Fletcher said he would consider the matter, and Mrs. Summers said something too quietly to be heard, and then they came out of the library appearing quite ill at ease with each other. Mr. Fletcher left for London immediately, and Mrs. Summers expressed a desire for a change of scenery. We brought her here."

Kate shook her head as if to settle all the pieces of information into place. It didn't help. "They're not to be married, then?"

"I don't know," Mirabelle replied, straightening up. "Mrs. Summers refuses to speak of it except to say that Mr. Fletcher would need to see it through, or she will not accept."

"See what through?"

"We've no idea. And you know how Evie is about ferreting things out, but attempting to pry information out of Mrs. Summers is rather like trying to keep information *in* Lizzy, it's a fool's pursuit. At any rate," she continued as Kate laughed, "we're bound to find out eventually, and it's still intriguing news. Plus, it was a very convenient excuse for me to come. Do you know, I've never been to a house party not held by your mother or my uncle? I'm rather embarrassed by how delighted I am to be here."

"You'll not be delighted for long," Kate warned her. "Miss Willory is in attendance."

Mirabelle's face fell almost comically. "You're not serious."

"It's hardly a jesting matter, is it?" Kate glanced at the house. "I know she's been very unkind to you in the past—"

"And you and Lizzy and Evie and Miss Heins and—"

"Yes, I know. But her family has fallen onto hard times. And she hasn't any real friends to speak of. I find myself torn as to how to treat her."

"You'd give the devil a powder if he claimed a headache." Mirabelle held up a hand to forestall an argument. "We'll have to agree to disagree on that matter. Is there any other news, unsavory or otherwise, I should be made aware of?"

Out of habit, Kate opened her mouth to inform Mirabelle of each and every event that had occurred since they'd seen each other last. *I'm involved in the investigation of Lord Martin's smuggling operation. I kissed Mr. Hunter in a sitting room, twice. I'm hoping to do so again at the earliest opportunity.*

She shut her mouth. In part because she was stunned by the last thought, in part because informing Mirabelle of the investigation would *guarantee* Whit knowing of the investigation, and in part because she suddenly realized she wanted to keep how she felt about Hunter private, for now. Which was very odd, indeed. When she'd fancied herself in love with Lord Martin, she'd wanted to do nothing *but* speak of him. She'd nearly driven her friends and family to distraction with her incessant babbling. But then, she wasn't in love with Hunter, she was simply . . . growing more curious about the man.

She cleared her throat. "No, no, nothing that would be of interest to you."

❋ *Ten* ❋

*H*unter looked through the window of the Thurston guest room and smiled at the idyllic picture Mirabelle and Kate made sitting on the bench, the late afternoon light gilding their hair and the sea breeze tugging gently at their skirts. He made a note to regularly invite the Thurstons to visit once he and Kate were married. Mirabelle would like that, he mused. She hadn't often had the opportunity to travel. And he would like seeing his beautiful wife sharing tete-a-tetes with the pretty countess of Thurston on *his* coastal estate. On all five of them, actually.

He indulged in the daydream a moment longer before turning away to watch as Whit issued orders to the staff. In

Hunter's estimation, Whit was the quintessential peer of the realm—proud, arrogant, and exacting. Each of those traits Hunter could identify with and appreciate. Whit's unrelenting drive to be the most honorable earl in England, however, was something Hunter was sure he would never fully understand. Honor and nobility were all well and good but sometimes, for some men, the cost for both was too dear.

Hunter imagined Whit would argue that the price of *not* being honorable was the only thing a gentleman couldn't afford, but then, Whit had never had to choose between thieving or starving.

It was amazing what a man would do for a loaf of bread and a little dignity.

Despite their difference of opinion on that particular matter, Hunter genuinely liked and respected Whit. For a proud, arrogant, honorable and exacting peer of the realm, Whit displayed a remarkable amount of good humor. Which was why, after the last servant left, Hunter had no qualms about beginning the conversation with a smirk and an accusation.

"You brought your wife."

Whit glanced at him and tossed a small bag on the four-poster bed. "Not bringing her would have appeared suspicious."

"Does she know why you're here?"

"No, though I wouldn't be surprised if she suspected there was more to this trip than an outing to the coast."

The smirk grew. "She brought herself, didn't she?"

"It's my carriage, isn't it?" Whit asked by way of deflecting the question.

Hunter leaned against the wall and folded his arms. "I'm surprised at you. Allowing your wife to come, allowing your sister to stay. William assumed you'd lock Kate away at Haldon if you thought she might be in any danger. I'm amazed he told you of this mission, let alone put you in charge of it."

He was pleased as well. Whit wasn't going to insist Hunter remain completely removed from the investigation.

Whit twisted his lips in disgust. "He wasn't going to, the bastard. But he received word while he was at Haldon that the agent he had picked for the job came down with the ague. My being chosen as a replacement was a matter of expediency."

"Doesn't explain why you've not locked up your sister."

"If I thought Kate was in danger, I *would* lock her up." Whit shrugged. "Lord Martin poses no real threat. To begin with, William tells me we're not entirely certain he's bringing over anything more nefarious than brandy. In addition, a man doesn't seek to impress the object of his affections by dragging her into a smuggling plot, does he? Your presence here—and in all probability, mine as well—is merely precautionary."

Hunter rubbed the back of his hand across his jaw. No wonder William had ordered Mr. Laury's role as an agent be kept secret. Added manpower would not suggest to Whit a mission of limited danger. "You think so?"

"There's no telling how many gentlemen in the *ton* have their fingers dipped into a smuggling operation here or there. Am I to keep Kate away from all of them?"

A finger dipped in, was not the same as being the sole financier, Hunter thought, and most smuggling operations did not include the possibility of treason, but he wisely let Whit keep his illusions. He didn't want Kate to leave, after all. He was confident he could keep her safe, and he wasn't yet ready for the mission to be over. "It'll be enough for me if you were to simply keep an eye on her from time to time while we're here. I'd like a chance to spend some time with Lord Martin."

Whit's eyebrows winged up. "You're willing to trade missions for a day? Kate's company for Lord Martin's?"

"A morning here and there," Hunter replied with a shrug.

"A few hours in the afternoon. I can't spend every waking moment with your sister. People will talk." He didn't mind the usual amount of gossip that happened with any courtship taking place at a house party, but he'd just as soon avoid an outright scandal.

Whit nodded in acknowledgment of the point. "I'll watch her tomorrow. Have you spent much time with Martin in the past?"

"A little at dinners and balls, why?"

"Never a full day?"

"Never had the opportunity, or the desire. He's a little irritating. Again, why?"

"No reason," Whit was quick to assure him. "Let me tell you what I learned in London."

Whit hadn't learned a damn thing in London, a bit of news Hunter was still mulling over in the library a half hour later while Whit and Mirabelle finished settling themselves in their room.

It was unfortunate—though hardly unusual—that a fellow agent had wasted his time chasing down a false lead. But it was a relief to know they wouldn't be capturing Lord Martin the next day, putting an end to one of the finest excuses he'd ever come across to spend a protracted amount of time with a lady.

It also would have come as a disappointment to Kate. She was expecting an adventure, and he meant to give her one. He'd start, he decided, by instructing her to search certain portions of the house—now that he'd searched the whole of it and determined there was no danger. And he thought she might like to help organize the plan of capture—once they figured out where Lord Martin was planning to bring in and hide his smuggled goods. Probably, she would enjoy—

The sound of someone playing the piano floated in on the air. No, not just someone, he corrected, as he headed for the door. It was Kate. No one else could play like that. No one else could even come close. Others played well, or very well, or even splendidly. Kate's talent transcended those descriptions. It was nothing short of sublime.

He followed the sound to the music room and quietly stood in the doorway to listen.

Here was the final reason he would marry Lady Kate Cole—her unparalleled talent for music. If Kate's physical beauty offered a man secular delight, her art offered a glimpse of paradise. And what man wouldn't wish to spend the rest of his life watching and listening to the beautiful Lady Kate Cole coax the divine from a piano?

Lady Kate *Hunter*, he corrected and, not for the first time, made a mental note to have the instrument of her choice installed in every estate, manor, cottage and town house he owned.

Kate let her fingers rush along the keys as the sound and feel of the sonata rushed about the room.

Here, just as when she danced, she was graceful—her mind and body in accord. The music in her mind blended seamlessly with the music she created with her fingers. She never missed a note, a beat, a rest. There was no accent too nuanced, no emotion too elusive that she couldn't tease it from the keys. For her, playing the piano was as simple as speaking, as natural as laughter, and as necessary as air.

She slowed her fingers and let the deceptively light melody trip along while she built an underlying current of something stronger in the harmony. It simmered and gathered and then released as the two halves were joined for a dramatic finale.

She sighed happily as the final notes died away. What should she play next? Something darker? Something more complicated? Something—

A tickle crept along her spine and she spun on the bench to find Hunter leaning against the doorframe, watching her.

His stance was relaxed, but there was such an intensity to his gaze as he studied her that the tickle turned into a warm shiver, and she found it impossible to turn away.

Hunter broke the spell, stepping into the room, and pushing the door partially closed behind him. "That was exquisite, Kate."

She felt herself blush, both from the compliment and from the look that had passed between them. "Thank you."

"Your own work?" he asked easily.

She nodded and willed herself to match his light tone. "Evie's seventeenth birthday present."

"That would have made you what," he inquired, reaching her, "thirteen years of age?"

"I suppose, yes."

"Incredible," he murmured. "She must have been thrilled."

"Oh, yes, until she learned I had to write it after spending all my pin money on sweets and hair ribbons."

Hunter laughed and leaned a hip against the piano. "Whit tells me you play other instruments as well."

"A few, but my preference is for string instruments." She tapped a key idly. "This one in particular."

"The piano is a string instrument?"

"Yes, didn't you know?" When he shook his head, she rose and stepped around him to point inside the piano's case. "You see? The keys move the hammers, which strike the strings, hence a string instrument."

He peeked inside. "So it is."

"You didn't have a piano about as a child, I presume?" When he merely raised his brows, she shrugged and lowered the prop holding the lid open. "Children are inexorably drawn to anything with a lid. You can't keep them from trying to look inside."

"Curiosity is a powerful motivator. It's how we learn."

She traced the wood grain of the piano case with her fingers. "It's also how we end up"—*kissing handsome pirates in sitting rooms*—"with dead grasshoppers."

"Beg your pardon?"

"Nothing." She glanced up at him. He was standing very close. She could smell his soap, and she wondered if he would once again taste like spearmint. Her eyes shot back down to the wood. "Curiosity isn't always beneficial."

"Shall we put that to the test?"

She found it impossible to meet his gaze. "And how might we do that?"

He didn't answer. He simply stepped forward and pulled her into his arms.

Hunter was careful with the kiss. It wasn't a test, as it had been in the sitting room, nor was it an attempt to seduce. He wanted to tempt and entice. He wanted to reassure her that it was safe to give in to curiosity . . . as long as she was with him.

He teased his lips over hers in a playful game of attack and retreat. Curiosity and security. Adventure and protection. It was a fine line to walk with greed chasing so closely behind, demanding he take more, but it was more easily done than he might have envisioned before it began. Easier because the kiss wasn't for him. It was for her.

It just happened that kissing Kate *for* Kate suited both his pleasure and his purpose.

Lure her closer, closer still. That was the plan.

To that end, he wrapped his arms tighter and pressed the length of her body against his. Not too tight, he reminded himself, not too close. It was important to let her think she could get away. It was equally important to make certain she didn't want to.

To *that* end, he took the kiss deeper, letting his mouth settle over hers and gently teasing her lips apart so he could fully taste her, and she him. She gasped when his tongue slid inside the warmth of her mouth, then moaned and leaned forward seeking out more.

He wanted to give her more. Suddenly, he ached to take everything. Each sigh of breath, every brush of her lips and small movement of her hands stole away bits and pieces of his control, making it increasingly difficult to remember who and what the kiss was about.

It was tempting to forget while the sight and smell and feel of her all but drowned his senses. It would be an easy thing to let his purpose and plans slide away just long enough for lust to gain the upper hand. He could have her undressed in minutes, panting and moaning his name in seconds, and bent over the piano bench—

Bloody hell. His control, he realized, was nearly at an end.

He softened the kiss in stages, until he was once again holding her loosely and teasing his lips across hers. He kept them that way for several long minutes in an effort to ease her out of the kiss, and not, he assured himself, because he was finding it difficult to let her go.

Finally, when her breath evened and his heart didn't feel as if it might pound its way out of his chest, he pulled away.

"Do you see?" he whispered, taking her face in his hands. "Nothing to be afraid of."

"I'm not at all certain of that." She licked her lips and eyed him warily, which he didn't mind, and a little suspiciously, which wouldn't do.

"Well, if you require more convincing . . ." He bent his head toward her slowly, and grinned as she danced out of his reach on a laugh.

"I believe I've had enough convincing for one day, thank you."

He took a step toward her. "Oh, I don't know . . ."

She skipped out of reach again, moving around to the back of the piano. They eyed each other over the wood. He grinned wolfishly. Her light blue eyes sparkled with laughter.

Better, he thought, much better than the suspicion. He would do well to remember she was skilled at games of strategy.

As if to illustrate the point, she feinted left, then dodged right, leading him around the piano until their positions had switched. Then she spun around and bolted for the exit behind her, knowing full well he'd not have time to come around the piano before she reached the door.

She stopped at the threshold to turn about and give him one very smug smile as she stepped backward out the door. "Good day, Mr. Hunter."

And then she was gone.

Hunter stood alone in the room, his own self-satisfied smile firmly in place. He hadn't intended to catch her. Not this time. This was one game of strategy he was going to win.

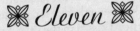

❈ *Eleven* ❈

It was with some disappointment that Kate discovered the following morning that Hunter had gone into town with Lord Martin and several other gentlemen. It was so disappointing, in fact, that she spent the first hour after breakfast sitting on the veranda moping a little.

If she had known Hunter was to leave that morning, she wouldn't have taken dinner in her room the previous night. Probably, she shouldn't have taken dinner in her room last night no matter Mr. Hunter's whereabouts today. But the seating arrangements in the dining room would have put Lord Martin on her right, Miss Willory on her left, and Mrs. Keenes directly across the table. One of them she could have handled, two she would have suffered through for the chance to eat the very fine food and speak with Hunter after the meal, but all three at once was more than anyone should have to bear. And because she had *expected* to see him at breakfast the next day, and because it wouldn't do to appear *too* curious, she'd chosen to spend the evening in her room where she'd spent the majority of her time dwelling on the kiss she and Hunter had shared in the music room. Strangely, the longer she dwelled on it, the more she suspected something had been a bit . . . off. Which was another reason she felt a little mopey.

Oh, it had been a lovely kiss, without question. She'd experienced the same building excitement she'd felt the first time he'd kissed her in the sitting room, the same dizzying loss of breath, the same restless heat. But the memory of that wasn't enough to keep at bay the misgiving that something had been amiss with, or perhaps missing from, both kisses.

If she hadn't known better, she would have said that something was Hunter. But that didn't make any sense at all. Obviously, the man had been there. He'd just seemed *more* there the second time they'd kissed in the sitting room—when he'd seized her and held on.

It was very confusing. And she wasn't going to be able to figure through the mystery without spending more time in Hunter's company. Probably it would help if he kissed her again as well.

She huffed out an irritated breath, turned her face into the soft breeze, and then, because she wasn't fond of moping, made an effort to turn her thoughts toward something other than Hunter and his kisses. She looked over the pages of notes she'd brought out with her. They were a detailed description of what she was attempting to accomplish by composing a symphony, written in an effort to inspire completion of the work. That had been weeks ago, and they'd yet to inspire a single note. She set the pages aside.

Perhaps she should go for a ride. Maybe she should explore

the house and grounds. *Maybe* she could convince Mirabelle to explore the house and grounds with her.

"Good morning, Kate."

Kate turned at the sound of Mirabelle's voice.

Perfect.

Mirabelle took a seat next to her on the bench, brushed at her apple green skirts and sighed happily. "What shall we be doing today?"

Again, *perfect.* "What would you like to do?"

"Whatever Lord Brentworth has planned for the ladies."

"You might want to reconsider that," Kate told her, "unless you wish to spend the day doing absolutely nothing."

"What do you mean?"

"Lord Brentworth isn't in the habit of arranging diversions for the ladies in residence."

Mirabelle blinked. "None at all?"

"At all," Kate confirmed, before continuing on in what she hoped was an offhanded manner. "Though I did hear Mrs. Hatcher suggest needlework in the parlor this morning."

"Needlework," Mirabelle repeated, making a face. "Why would anyone want to do needlework at a house party? One can do it just as well at home."

"Or just as poorly, as we do." Kate shifted to face her friend. "We can entertain ourselves well enough. Why don't we take a tour of the house and grounds?"

"I've already had a tour," Mirabelle told her. "Whit and I were given one after we arrived."

"Yes, Mother and I were as well." Kate gave an impatient wave of her hand. "But that was a guest's tour. Much too abbreviated."

Mirabelle narrowed her eyes. "You want to go snooping."

"I want to go exploring," Kate corrected. "We needn't rummage through anyone's bureau."

"I don't know that Lord Brentworth would appreciate the distinction."

"If Lord Brentworth doesn't care for how we entertain ourselves, he can give us something else to do."

"Lack of distraction is not a justification for objectionable behavior." Mirabelle threw a glance at the house. "If your mother caught wind . . ."

Kate grinned impishly. "If mother caught wind, she'd tsk at us, and then demand to know if we found anything of interest."

"That's true." Mirabelle turned back to look at her. "I'm surprised you've not explored already."

"Traversing unfamiliar terrain really isn't something I ought to do alone."

"It's a house, not a mountain," Mirabelle drawled.

"There are the grounds as well."

Mirabelle winced. "I see your point. Why haven't you taken Lizzy?"

"Because should anyone happen upon you and I while we're exploring—"

"You mean if we're caught snooping."

"Oh, very well," Kate conceded with a roll of her eyes. "If we're caught, very little is likely to be made of our—"

"Snooping."

"Exploring," Kate corrected. "Because we're guests. Lizzy—"

"Would be open to a censure we are not, because she's a lady's maid," Mirabelle finished for her with a nod of understanding.

"*Exactly*. Mother and Whit wouldn't be so unfair, of course, but the rest of the guests could be most unkind."

Mirabelle continued to bob her head for a moment before she turned to look at the house again, her teeth worrying her bottom lip. "I cannot *believe* I'm quite seriously considering snooping about Lord Brentworth's house."

"And grounds." It was paramount they check the grounds.

"And grounds," Mirabelle agreed, still staring at the house.

Kate lifted a shoulder and looked out over the lawn. "There's always needlework with Miss Willory in the parlor."

"Grab your papers."

"Oh, excellent." With barely concealed glee, Kate grabbed her notes and practically leapt from her seat. "You'll not regret this, Mirabelle."

"I sincerely hope not," Mirabelle sighed and rose as well. "What do you expect to find, exactly?"

"Nothing in particular," Kate answered truthfully. Nothing dangerous, at any rate, or she wouldn't have suggested the idea. She certainly wouldn't have asked Mirabelle to come along.

It was highly unlikely Lord Martin would leave proof of his treason lying about where any lost guest—and she had every intention of claiming to be lost should they be discovered—could stumble across it. What she *hoped* to find, however, was a locked door or two—something innocuous but suspicious. Something that might lead to something useful. She'd just leave picking the lock to someone with a little more experience.

Two hours later, Kate came to the conclusion that whoever would be responsible for picking the locks at Pallton House would need more than just experience. He'd need time, lots and lots of time. And patience, *vast* amounts of patience. Because nearly every room in the house was locked.

"Why would anyone have this many doors locked in their own home?" she demanded as they discovered yet another door that refused to open on the third level of the house.

"I don't know." Mirabelle stared at the door handle, a line forming across her brow. "It must be awfully inconvenient for the staff."

Or perhaps, Kate mused, it simply confirmed Hunter's suspicion that the staff was involved. Perhaps every smuggler kept half his house sealed up like a giant vault. She scowled absently at her feet. That didn't make sense. Lord Martin was the smuggler, but it wasn't his house. The doors wouldn't be kept locked without Lord Brentworth's approval, and Hunter hadn't mentioned Lord Brentworth being involved with the smuggling.

"Perhaps, he's just odd," she said, mostly to herself.

"Lord Brentworth?" Mirabelle asked. "He must be."

Kate blew out a short breath and fisted her hands on her hips. "I suppose there isn't much point in our checking the rest of this hall."

"I can't imagine why there would be."

Kate looked at the line of rooms before them. "Then again, if even one of those doors opened . . ."

Mirabelle rolled her eyes and leaned against the wall. "Go jiggle the handles, then. I'll wait here."

When the jiggling resulted in nothing more than . . . well, jiggling, Kate dragged Mirabelle outside for their exploration of the grounds. Unfortunately, that turned out to be an equally forgettable experience. Lord Brentworth's estate contained only the usual assortment of outbuildings, which in turn contained only the usual sort of supplies needed to run an estate.

"Goodness, one would think there'd be *something*," Kate mumbled as she and Mirabelle stood on the beach, looking out over the water.

"Beg your pardon?"

"Nothing. Shall we walk along the shore a ways?"

"If you like." Mirabelle pointed east. "See how the land rises and the shore curves out of sight? Whit says there are bluffs two or three miles farther down the beach."

"Bluffs?" Kate repeated. "Rocky ones do you suppose?"

Mirabelle blinked at her. "Does it make a difference?"

Probably not, except that it would increase the likelihood of caves, and caves were excellent places to hide smuggled goods.

"Merely curious," she told Mirabelle.

And simply delighted when they made their way around the curve of the shore and she spotted large rock outcroppings in the distance.

"Shall we continue along here for now?" Mirabelle asked. "Then follow the hill and look out over the top?"

Kate nodded and eyed the rocks in the distance with both excitement and wariness. If there were any smugglers' caves hidden amongst the bluffs, she'd just as soon not get too close. She couldn't imagine there being any actual smugglers about in broad daylight, but it really wasn't the sort of thing one should chance.

An hour later, Kate decided that the view from the top more than made up for any lingering discontent she felt at not being able to explore the rocks below. The English Channel spread out endlessly before them in a display of ever changing blues and greens and even gold where the sunlight cut through the clouds to sparkle on the water.

"Oh, it's beautiful," Mirabelle breathed as the waves crashed violently against the rocks below and seagulls soared overhead.

"It is, isn't it?" Kate agreed. "You can see forever."

But being able to see forever and being able to look forever were two entirely different matters. Knowing their time was limited, Kate took several minutes more to enjoy the dramatic view before dragging Mirabelle away. They walked another quarter mile along the bluffs until they discovered a small section of the rocky cliff that gentled into a slightly less rugged hillside. A narrow path, just wide enough for a single horse, cut back and forth along the face, working its way down to a small sandy beach far below. A *very* small beach,

Kate noted. And with so many large beaches available nearby, it didn't make any sense for someone to go through the trouble of cutting out a path to a very small one . . . unless they had a good reason.

Mirabelle pinned her with a hard look. "You are *not* going down that path."

Kate couldn't help shuddering a little at just the thought. Most people could probably manage the hike to the bottom without any great trouble. *She* would probably fall before she was a quarter way down.

She took an unconscious step back from the edge. "You'll have no argument from me."

Mirabelle nodded and looked up the coastline. "It's tempting to go a bit farther, but I suppose we should return before Whit comes looking for us. We've been snooping for the better part of the day."

"Exploring," Kate countered automatically and glanced back in the general direction of the house. "I'm rather surprised he hasn't come looking for us all ready."

Mirabelle shrugged and took Kate's arm to lead her away from the bluff. "He had business to attend to with Lord Brentworth. It must have taken longer than expected, or he would have come by now."

Kate glanced at her friend. "Are you going to tell him how we spent the day?"

Whether or not Whit was aware of the investigation, he'd be less than pleased with the news that she and Mirabelle had spent part of the day trying to open locked doors.

Mirabelle shrugged. "Only if he asks."

"Of course he'll ask." Hadn't they just been discussing how long they'd been gone?

"Allow me to rephrase that. Only if it becomes necessary that I answer him."

"Why wouldn't it be necessary—?"

Mirabelle smiled coyly. "He's easily distracted."

"How . . ." Kate made a face. "Never mind, I don't wish to know."

She might have—in fact, she would have demanded to know, in explicit detail, how one went about distracting a man—but not when that man was her brother. "I'll tell Mother you'll not be joining us for tea."

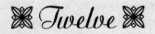

❊ *Twelve* ❊

*H*unter considered himself a patient man—a very patient man, in fact, taking into account the very determined, very methodical way he'd built his fortune over the years—but twelve hours in the company of Lord Martin and his two obnoxious friends, Mr. Woodruff and Mr. Kepford, was enough to try even the patience of a saint. And he was no more saint than prince.

He took the side steps to Pallton House two at a time, eager to put some distance between himself and the drunken lot of idiots trailing behind him from the stables.

No wonder Whit had found the idea of trading missions for the day so damn amusing. Lord Martin wasn't merely irritating, he was an *endurance*, a trial, a plague among men. Very well, that last may have been overstating things a bit, but after *twelve bloody hours* of following the man about as he shopped for fripperies, drank to excess, and talked incessantly without saying anything of value, Hunter felt he was entitled to a little exaggeration.

To make the day even more aggravating, he'd learned nothing more substantial than that Lord Martin knew how to get his hands on some very fine brandy. Even after he'd made certain to get the man well and truly foxed, Lord Martin hadn't let anything else slip. How the hell did a man that stupid, that enamored with talking about himself, and that drunk, find the fortitude to keep a secret?

"Hunder!" One of Lord Martin's friends called out from behind him. "Hunder, good man! Where are you—?"

"To the library for more drink!" he shouted over his shoulder.

He entered the house, closed the door behind him, and turned his steps away from the library. No doubt Lord Martin and his friends would reach that room, wonder a moment where he'd gone off to, and then promptly forget him as they poured another round of drinks.

Hunter wanted to forget them just as quickly. It wasn't yet ten o'clock, but he was officially declaring the day over. Lord Martin and his pack of giggling friends were once again Whit's responsibility, and he meant to inform Whit of that just as soon as he washed off the dust from the road. Probably, he should change his coat as well, as Whit was likely in the parlor with the rest of the guests. No doubt there wasn't one among those guests who would think twice about a man looking a little disheveled after riding in from town . . . if that man happened to be one of their own. In *his* case, at least half of them would consider it evidence of his inherent inferiority and—

"Mr. Potsbottom, you will cease at once!"

The sound of Kate's angry and slightly muffled voice coming from around a turn in the hall had him starting in surprise, then sprinting forward.

"*Honestly*, Mr. Potsbottom . . . what do you think . . . Enough!"

He turned the corner in time to see young Mr. Potsbottom attempting to wrap his arms around a struggling Kate, who was caught against the wall.

Hunter lunged forward, but before he could take more

than two steps, Kate took care of matters by lifting her skirts with one hand and bringing up her knee to deliver a sharp blow where it would do the bastard the most amount of pain.

Mr. Potsbottom squealed and dropped to the floor.

Hunter reached them in three more long strides, and he wasn't sure, but he thought he heard her say something along the lines of, "Goodness, it really does work."

"Kate, are you all right?"

"What?" She blinked up at him, her eyes wide, her cheeks pale, and her breath coming in pants. "Oh. Yes. Yes, I am." She stared down at the writhing Mr. Potsbottom. "I kicked him. I can't believe I kicked him."

"Kate, look at me." He tipped her chin up with his finger. "Are you hurt? Did he hurt you?"

"No." She gave a minute shake of her head. "No, I'm quite well. Honestly."

She *was* well, he realized, and not only physically unharmed, but apparently more stunned than frightened.

"I kicked him." She blinked once more. "Well, I didn't actually kick. I used my knee—"

"Yes, I know. I saw."

And he felt just a trifle deflated. As a rule, he wasn't inclined to play knight-errant to distressed maidens, but in this particular instance, it was not only his job, but the maiden in question was going to be his wife. Now he was itching to plant the pup a facer and he couldn't very well do it while the pup was rolling about on the ground whimpering. Well, he could actually, but it wouldn't be the same.

And he didn't have the time. Footsteps and female laughter heralded the approach of Miss Willory and at least two other women.

"Bloody hell." He threw open the nearby door to the music room, grabbed Mr. Potsbottom under the arms, hauled him up, and tossed him into the room where the young man landed in a whimpering heap. He shut the door and turned around just as Miss Willory, Mrs. Keenes, and Mrs. Lubeck rounded the corner.

Miss Willory's shrewd eyes darted from him to Kate before she pasted a bright and entirely insincere smile on her face. "Mr. Hunter, I'd not realized you'd returned."

"Only just," he returned smoothly. "I met Lady Kate on my way to the parlor."

Mrs. Keenes gestured toward the music room. "I thought you'd left our company to play the piano, Lady Kate."

"I . . ." Kate swallowed audibly. "I've developed a sudden headache."

"You do look *dreadfully* wan," Miss Willory commented. "Why—"

"And where might you ladies be headed?" Hunter cut in.

"To view a painting in the east wing," Mrs. Keenes said. "Miss Willory insists it—"

"Do you hear that?" Mrs. Lubeck inquired suddenly. "It sounds rather like whimp—"

"Is it one of the family portraits you're off to study?" Hunter asked quickly, and just a trifle loudly. Damn that Potsbottom.

"It *is* one of the portraits," Miss Willory chimed. "How wonderfully clever of you to guess."

It wasn't really. As far as he'd been able to tell, at least 80 percent of the artwork at every grand estate was comprised of family portraits. "Well, I'll not keep you from your quest any longer." He bowed low. "Ladies."

Clearly reluctant to leave, Miss Willory hesitated a moment before finally curtsying and departing with her companions.

Kate let out a long, shaky breath as the three women disappeared around the next corner. "Oh, dear. That could have ended very badly."

He took her arm in a light grasp and led her off in the opposite direction of Miss Willory's party. Whit would have to wait for his news.

Kate tugged a little on her arm. "What of Mr. Pots-bottom?"

"I'll send a footman for him later." When he was through taking care of Kate. "Where did you learn to defend yourself in that manner?"

"Evie taught me. She told me it might come in handy one day, but I never imagined . . ." She glanced behind them at the door to the music room. "Will he be all right?"

"You're *worried* about the bast—?"

"I'm not worried, not exactly. It's only that I didn't expect my, er, defense to be quite so effective. Did I do him a lasting injury?"

"That's worried, Kate, and no, unfortunately, Mr. Potsbottom will be whole and hale by morning." Except for the headache Hunter hoped turned out to be positively brutal.

"Oh, good. That's good." She shrugged hesitantly when he gave her an incredulous look. "He's harmless, really. Just a bit too enthusiastic in his attentions."

"He was pawing at you," he growled.

"Yes, I know, but he's young and he's had too much to drink."

"I can't believe you're defending him. The two of you are of an age, and drink is not an excuse." An explanation, perhaps, for why the idiot might have tried to kiss her, but not an excuse for why he'd not given up the effort once Kate had made her disinterest clear.

"Of course it's not," Kate agreed, softly. "I only meant that he's generally a good-natured sort and that I don't think he intended to hurt me."

"Intentional or not, he *was* hurting you."

"Well, yes, that's why I applied my knee," she explained reasonably.

Not feeling particularly reasonable himself, he led her

into the small, out-of-the-way sitting room, placed her in a chair, and went to a sideboard to pour her a glass of brandy.

She sat quietly as he brought it over and handed it to her. She sniffed it, took a tiny sip and immediately handed it back. "Ugh. I'll not drink it."

"It will settle your nerves."

"My nerves perhaps, but the rest of my system will likely revolt. I don't need . . ." She trailed off at his hard stare. "I'll take a glass of wine, or sherry, if you insist, but I'll not drink brandy. It's revolting."

"Fair enough."

He poured her a glass of sherry, which she sipped at gingerly.

"The whole thing, Kate."

Clearly lost to her own thoughts, she took another sip. "I can't believe Mr. Potsbottom did that," she said softly. "It isn't at all like him."

"You know him well?" he asked, pleased to see some of the color returning to her cheeks.

"I do, rather." She looked down at her drink, her long lashes shielding her eyes. "Or thought I did. We're of an age, as you said."

"What sort of man did you think he was?"

She gave a small shrug and looked up again. "He's not particularly clever, I'm afraid, but I always thought him to be rather sweet. He dances with wallflowers sometimes, and he's always polite to staff. I know he's exceedingly devoted to his grandmother and his young sisters. How could a man with sisters do something like that?" She shook her head as if to clear away the thought. "What could he possibly have been thinking? If Miss Willory and the others had come earlier—"

"You would have been compromised," he stated grimly. And he and Whit would be arguing over which of them got to shoot Potsbottom.

"I would have been ruined," she corrected. "I'd not marry a man who would press his suit on a woman, even if I'd not thought him capable of such boorishness before."

Hunter nodded in understanding. Now that the worst of his temper had settled and the threat to Kate minimized, he was beginning to understand something else as well. She was right—from what little he knew about young Mr. Potsbottom, the boy really didn't seem the sort to press his suit on a woman.

"If he's not the sort to do it," he mumbled, mostly to himself as he took a seat. "That begs the question as to why he did."

Kate seemed to think about that. *Seemed* being the key word, because what she said after a moment was, "Actually, begging the question indicates that a person has made an argument for their position on a matter by offering a point that is wholly dependent on their position having been correct to begin with. It's an assumptive, even circular sort of—"

"Kate," he cut in gently. It truly was fascinating the way her mind worked.

"What? Oh." She set the sherry aside. "I don't think I need any more of that."

He felt his lips twitch. "Tell me what you were doing when Mr. Potsbottom arrived."

Her brow furrowed in thought. "I was going to the music room from the parlor, just as Mrs. Keenes said. I ran into him in the hall. Or he into me. I'm not certain which."

"Was he in the parlor when you left?"

She shook her head slowly. "I don't recall, to be honest. He may have come in for a time with the other gentlemen."

"Did you speak with him earlier in the day?"

"No, Mirabelle and I were out for most of the day, and Mr. Potsbottom wasn't present when we returned to the house, nor at tea." She blew out a hard breath. "I simply have no idea what possessed him."

"We'll figure it out." But as he meant to see Mr. Potsbottom permanently removed from the house, his erratic behavior suddenly became a less pressing matter than the phrase, *Mirabelle and I were out for most of the day.*

"Where did you and Mirabelle go?"

"Oh, we went exploring." She sat up a little straighter in her chair, and pushed a lock of blonde hair behind her ear, excitement suddenly lighting her eyes. "Did you know there are bluffs to the east of here? Great rocky ones that jut out into the water and—"

"Who told you that?"

"No one. Mirabelle and I discovered it. We went for a stroll."

"A stroll," he repeated, drawing out the last word.

"Yes."

"Down more than two miles of beach?"

"Oh." She slumped a little in her chair. "So you did know."

"Yes. What I *don't* know is what you were doing there." And why the devil Whit had allowed it.

"I told you, Mirabelle and I were—"

"Going for a stroll, yes."

"More of a hike at that point, really. After a time, we followed the bluff rather than the beach." She smiled at him and shrugged. "Seemed safer, under the circumstances. But we did discover a small beach between two rocky outcroppings and a trail cut out of—"

"Tell me you had more sense than to go down that trail."

She blinked at his hard tone. "I had more sense than to go down that trail."

He opened his mouth, closed it. "Are you just repeating what I said because I told you to, or did you actually have—"

"I had more sense than to go down that trail," she said again, and with just enough emphasis to betray her irritation.

Good. Irritation didn't begin to cover what he was feeling. There was a sick knot of fear in his stomach, and another, tighter knot of it weighing on his chest. Something might have happened to her. She could have been accosted, abducted, fallen from the bluffs. The possibilities were endless, really. And horrifying. Unaccustomed, and uncomfortable, with being afraid for another, he retreated to the safety of cold anger. "But not, apparently, a sufficient amount of sense to keep from going down the coastline to begin with."

She tipped her chin up. "There was absolutely nothing wrong with me going—"

"What if someone had seen you?"

"Then someone would have seen two ladies taking a stroll along the beach," she retorted. "Hardly an uncommon sight."

"Had it been an actual stroll, yes. But two miles up to Smuggler's Beach while—"

"Is that really what it's called?" She gave a small snort. "One would think they'd come up with something a bit more discreet than that, or at least more creative."

"It's had the same name for . . ." He bit off an oath. It was nothing short of astounding how quickly she could steer a conversation off course. "Doesn't signify. It was reckless of you to go running about the coast looking for smugglers. For the remainder of the house party, you will stay in my sight every minute of the day that you are not in your room. Am I understood?"

Her mouth fell open. "That's *preposterous.*"

It was, probably, but he wasn't in a mood to argue with her, not while his stomach was in a knot. "*That* is an order."

Kate couldn't believe what she was hearing. Every minute of every day? Had the man come unhinged? The order wasn't just preposterous. It was impossible. What was she to do when it was time to leave her room, send a maid for him? What was she to do after dinner when the ladies went into the parlor and the gentlemen had their brandies? What was she to do if Lizzy or Mirabelle wanted a few private words with her when she was not in her room?

"You can't *order* me to stay in your sight every minute. What—?"

"I can, and I have."

"But it's ridiculous," she countered on a bewildered laugh. "It's beyond ridiculous. I can't—"

"You can, and you *shall*, or I'll inform your brother why I'm here."

"What?" Likely she would have come up with something more intelligent to say if her mind hadn't been swamped in utter disbelief. She couldn't have possibly heard him correctly. *Surely* he wasn't issuing a threat.

Hunter leaned back in his chair, his face set in hard lines. "I'm sure he'd be interested to know his only sister is attending a house party in the midst of a smuggling investigation."

Apparently, he *was* issuing a threat. She narrowed her eyes at him. "Neither I nor my brother is an idiot, Mr. Hunter. Whit knows of the smuggling operation." Probably, she amended silently. "And I know he knows of the smuggling operation." Again, probably. "Why else would he attend *this* house party—"

"He doesn't know you know, nor that I told you what you know." He pressed his lips together and grumbled something akin to, "I can't believe I just said that," before continuing. "He doesn't know of your involvement."

That was very certainly true. If Whit had any idea she was helping—even in the most limited sense of the word—with the investigation, he'd send her packing back to Haldon.

Her hands fisted in her lap. "You would compromise your own mission just to spite me?"

"I do nothing to spite you, Kate," he replied in a patronizing tone. "My primary mission is to protect you. And if that requires I inform your brother that you, and his wife, were traipsing about the beach looking for smugglers—"

"Leave Mirabelle out of this," she cut in. "She did nothing more than go for a walk because I asked it of her. Furthermore, I wasn't looking for smugglers. I was just . . . looking." She tossed up her hands in frustration. "It was the middle of the day, for pity's sake. Even I know smugglers don't bring their shipments ashore in broad daylight. And with Lord Brentworth's house full of guests two miles away? They'd have to be terrifically stupid to take such a risk. I can't imagine Lord Martin, for all that he is rather silly, investing his money in a ship full of fools. At the most, he'd—"

"You're rambling."

"What of it?" she snapped.

He merely lifted a brow at her sharp tone. Kate wondered how the movement of a single eyebrow could say so much, and then she wondered how what it said could be so *irritating.*

She didn't care to be looked at as if she were an excitable child. She wasn't in the habit of throwing fits of temper. On the other hand, she could probably manage a fairly respectable fit if he kept issuing asinine orders while he looked at her with that one irritating brow raised.

"I assume you felt the need to interrupt my rambling for a reason?" she ground out.

"Only way to get a word in edgewise," he returned.

"Then have your word."

"Thank you." He lowered his brow, but leaned forward to catch and hold her eye. "I am willing to compromise on the matter of you staying within sight at all times, but not on this—you will not, at any time, leave Pallton House grounds."

She considered that. It wasn't as asinine as his first order. And she had practically given her word that she would adhere to his orders. She had no intention of breaking her promise. But what if the ladies took it into their heads to go out for a picnic in the nearby countryside, or her mother asked her to go into town for a bit of shopping?

She pressed her lips into a line. Participating in the investigation was becoming more bother than it was worth. "What if I've need—?"

"No more arguments, Kate," he cut in for what she thought must be the hundredth time. The aggravating oaf. "You *will* remain on the grounds at all times, or I will inform your brother of your involvement in this mission and let him decide what's to be done with you."

"Decide what's . . . ?" She gaped at him yet again—just for a moment, just long enough for the waves of insult and indignation to solidify into the far more useful emotion of fury.

"You," she began coolly, rising from her chair, "*and* that ultimatum, may go straight to the devil. *I* shall inform Whit of my involvement, and *I* shall decide what is to be done with me after that." She sniffed once and looked down her nose at him. "I'll leave it to William Fletcher to decide what's to be done with *you*."

"Holy hell, you're stubborn." His voice was more awed than angry. "You're quite serious, aren't you? You'll tell Whit yourself."

"Yes."

"He's mentioned you can be mule-headed," he commented in an aren't-you-rather-interesting sort of way that turned the edges of her vision red, "but *this* I hardly expected."

"Apparently, you don't know me as well as you would like to think."

"Apparently," he agreed. He leaned forward in his chair and motioned toward the door. When he spoke again, his voice was soft and just a little taunting. "Go on and tell him, then. It should be interesting to see how he takes the news of your untrustworthy behavior."

"I beg your pardon?" Her tone was sharp enough to cut glass.

"You agreed to adhere to my orders." He sat back against the cushions of the chair once more. "You've broken your word."

Kate took a slow, deep breath through her nose in an effort to control the overwhelming wave of emotions that insult had provoked. Coles *never* broke their word, not since her father had passed. It was a matter of utmost pride for every member of the family. The accusation that she had failed to uphold that honor infuriated nearly as much as it wounded.

She didn't speak again until she was certain she could do so in a voice that was confident rather than thready. "Unlike you, my brother knows me too well to question my integrity. Had you let me explain myself rather than rushing to assume the very worst of me, you'd have known I was only looking for clarification of your order, not seeking to excuse myself from a promise."

His dark eyes searched her face. "You meant to keep your word?"

"I *always* keep my word." She spun on her heel, headed toward the door, and threw a parting shot over her shoulder. "And I give you my word that Whit won't cast aspersions on—"

"I'm ordering you not to inform your brother of your involvement."

She stopped in her tracks, but didn't turn around. She couldn't. She simply could not look at the man . . . not without risking doing him a physical injury.

"Not tonight, Kate." His voice had gentled, a fact that only added fuel to her fury. There was nothing more grating than being enraged and having the object of that rage remain calm and collected. "You're angry," he continued. "It would appear you've some right—"

She turned around for that, and found he'd risen from his chair, his hands clasped behind his back. "I've ample right," she bit off.

"Be that as it may, I am ordering you to wait twenty-four hours before making a decision you might regret."

She'd have given nearly anything in that moment to tell him she would speak to Whit at the time of her choosing, and the devil take his orders. But she couldn't, not without proving him right. Furious, she spun around again, reached the door, and spun back. "Don't forget to send a footman for Mr. Potsbottom."

Hunter didn't bother with the footman. His own temper still simmering, he followed Kate at a discreet distance to be certain she made it safely back to her room, then went directly to the music room where he found Potsbottom snoring in the very spot where they'd left him.

Hunter toed him with his boot. "Get up."

When that failed to illicit more than a loud gurgle, Hunter stalked over to a vase with cut flowers and stalked back to dump the contents over the boy's head.

Potsbottom lurched violently and flailed his arms as if warding off an attacker. "Wazzat? Wazzat?"

"Awake now, are we?"

Mr. Potsbottom stared at him, eyes wide and uncomprehending. "Wazzat?"

Awake, Hunter ascertained, but nowhere near sober. "Get on your feet. We're going to the stables."

Mr. Potsbottom required some assistance in fulfilling that command, which Hunter provided in the form of dragging him up and hauling him out the door. Under normal conditions the walk to the stable took under a minute, but with Mr. Potsbottom's stumbling, lurching, and tripping—all whilst babbling unintelligible nonsense—it was at least five before Hunter pushed through the doors, and then shoved Mr. Potsbottom against the wall of the nearest stall.

His instinct was to follow up that shove with a right jab to the nose, then a left jab to the jaw, and then a serious of blows to the gut, and then . . . Well, he just wanted to beat the man unconscious.

Pity a man couldn't answer questions when he was unconscious. While Hunter was debating his limited options, Mr. Potsbottom mumbled something about heaven, or possibly lemons, and his eyes began to roll back in his head.

Hunter shoved him again. "Stay awake, Potsbottom."

"What?"

That was an improvement, anyway. "You've questions to answer. Let's begin with why you thought Lady Kate would appreciate your attentions."

"Lady Kate?" Mr. Potsbottom squeezed his eyes shut on a groan. "Mistake . . . Terrible . . . Sorry . . ." His head began to loll to the side then snapped back up again when Hunter gave him a hard shake. "Didn't mean . . . frighten her . . . I'd never . . ."

"You did."

"Terrible . . . Said she wanted a kiss . . . She said . . ." He blinked owlishly and looked around a little. "We in the stables?"

"Lady Kate said she wanted a kiss?" He didn't believe that, not for a second.

"Huh?"

Hunter ground his teeth together. "Did Lady Kate ask you to kiss her?"

"No . . . No, don't think she wanted . . . Might have frightened her . . . Didn't mean . . . I'd never . . ." His face suddenly took on a green cast. "Gonna be sick . . ."

Hunter let him go and took a step back. Mr. Potsbottom staggered away a few feet and bent at the waist as if to toss up his wine. But rather than ridding his body of the poison, he kept bending forward slowly until he'd finally toppled to the ground headfirst.

Hunter curled his lip in disgust and wondered if it would be worth the effort to drag the sot up again. Probably not. From what he knew of Mr. Potsbottom, and what little— what *very* little—the drunken fool had been able to make clear, it was fairly obvious the young man had been drunk, clumsy, and stupid when he'd turned his attentions on Kate, but hadn't intended to harm.

He'd have another talk with him in London, a sober one, about limiting his drink. And to make certain he kept his tongue in his head.

Mr. Potsbottom snorted, gurgled, and began to snore.

"Waste of good air," Hunter grumbled.

A soft snicker sounded from overhead and he looked up to discover a large pair of brown eyes in a young face peeking out from over a bale of hay in the loft.

Hunter jerked his head in acknowledgment. "Evening, lad. You have a name?"

"Simon, sir."

"Well, Simon." He dug a few coins out and held one up for the stable boy to see. "Care to earn a bit of this?"

The boy crawled out from behind the hay to crouch on his heels at the edge of the loft. At least twelve, Hunter guessed. Old enough to hear a spot of rough language. He tossed him the coin. "Inform Mr. Potsbottom upon his rising that he is to get on his horse and go home. He can send for his things. If he takes one step inside Pallton House, I'll personally hack off the offending foot."

Simon nodded.

Hunter tossed him another coin. "Also inform him that if he speaks one word of what took place this night I'll personally hack off his head."

Simon nodded again.

"If he gives you any trouble, come for me. Understood?"

"Aye."

"Good lad."

"You hack off mine? If I talk?"

"Won't need to, will I? That's what this is for." He tossed him a wink to let him know the jest, and tossed him the final coin, a sovereign. "You're in no danger from me, Simon. But I expect you to earn that and be mindful of what you say."

"Aye," the boy breathed, he turned the coin over in his hand, his eyes wide. "That I will."

Though he would have preferred to go straight to his room for a drink, and the privacy in which to savor it and his foul mood, Hunter made himself stop by the library on his return from the stable. Cracking the door open, he looked inside to discover Lord Martin passed out on a settee, Mr. Kepford snoring loudly on the floor in front of the settee, and Mr. Woodruff slumped over in a high back chair, a thin line of drool seeping from his mouth.

He briefly considered picking each of their pockets for the keys to their chambers before deciding it would be easier and safer to simply pick the locks on their doors. He'd been a fine pickpocket in his youth, but he'd been a better thief.

He let himself into Lord Martin's room first, using the tools from a small leather satchel he rarely went anywhere without. He'd not had the benefit of those tools the first time he'd gone thieving. There'd been only one of his mother's hairpins, a small knife, and a very rudimentary understanding of how a lock worked.

He could still remember that night as if it had been only yesterday—the fear as he stood in the darkened hallway of the workhouse, the desperation for what was on the other side of the locked kitchen door, and the determination to acquire what was needed. But most vivid in his memory was what came after he'd found success and left the kitchen with his pockets stuffed with bread. He'd felt useful, confident, even powerful. There was something he could do to help, to make a difference. It was a heady experience for a boy—one he'd sought out time and again, even after the sense of power had proved to be false. He'd been able to keep what he'd stolen, but not who he'd stolen for.

Hunter shoved the memory aside. He was no longer a helpless young boy. And there was work to be done. He searched the room quickly but thoroughly, opening every drawer, turning over every scrap of paper, and delving his hand into every pocket. His search was met with success in the form of simple note in a desk drawer.

> My dearest Martin,
> As you are quite well aware, the shipment shall arrive within a fortnight. Please do attempt a show of patience.

Hunter turned the note over in his hand. It was neither signed nor dated. Clearly, it had been hand delivered, but whether that delivery had occurred at the house party or prior to Lord Martin's arrival was impossible to determine. What *was* clear, was that Lord Martin knew the sender well. The tone was chiding and that implied familiarity.

Hunter studied the note until he was confident he would recognize the handwriting if he saw it again, then tucked the note back into the drawer and made his way to Mr. Kepford's chambers. He searched that room and Mr. Woodruff's in under fifteen minutes and found nothing of interest. To his frustration, samples of both gentlemen's handwriting failed to match the note addressed to Lord Martin. The second party remained an unknown. He *hated* unknowns. A man couldn't strategize properly without knowing all the variables, all the players. As a thief, he'd studied his marks for weeks before making a move. As a businessman, he knew the personal and professional lives of each and every one of his competitors. As an agent, he was left studying cryptic, unsigned notes, penned by an unknown individual who may, or may not, be a threat to Kate.

He left Mr. Woodruff's room with a scowl, and headed for the parlor. It had been easier being a thief.

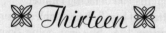

❊ *Thirteen* ❊

*D*espite her distaste for moping, Kate spent the next morning in her room doing mostly that. She would have much preferred to have spent her time doing something a little less disheartening, or at least a little more imaginative, like devising ways to make Hunter pay for his high-handedness, but she just couldn't drum up an interest in it.

Most of her anger had burned away the night before—*after* she'd stormed down the halls, painfully aware that Hunter was following her at a distance, and gone to her room to pace, fume, and kick at her bed a few times. When the latter had prompted Lizzy to hesitantly knock on the connecting door between their rooms, Kate had claimed clumsiness and pretended as if nothing was amiss. She'd allowed Lizzy to help her change her gown for a night rail, and then she'd gone to bed.

Though her sleep had been restless, what was left of her anger had melted away during the night, and now at midday she felt only weary, heartsick, and a strong desire to avoid Hunter for as long as possible. She also felt rather guilty for having told Lizzy and Mirabelle she wanted to spend the day composing. Guilty enough, in fact, that she'd been trying for the past three hours to put aside her foul mood and work on her symphony.

She hadn't managed to put two notes together. For some

reason, her mind kept going back to a silly little tune she'd made up as a child, and she couldn't open her windows and let the sound of the waves silence it because it was raining outside.

"I don't even like that song," she grumbled to herself. Nor did she like that she had misled her friends so she could mope about her room instead of facing Hunter.

"I'm not afraid of him," she grumbled again and rose from her small writing desk. She was going downstairs to find Mirabelle and Lizzy, and if she ran into Hunter, so be it. There was no reason for her to feel ashamed. *She* hadn't been the one to toss about asinine orders and heartless insults. Remembering, she felt a small revival of anger. She latched on to it greedily. It was so much better than despondency.

"See what's to be done with me," she muttered as she walked down the hall, her steps unconsciously matching the beat of the silly tune.

"Untrustworthy," she said under her breath as she made her way down a back staircase. That specific memory prompted the return of disappointment and hurt. Did he really think so little of her? Did he truly believe her so capricious as to give her word one day and break it the next? Or the day after the next . . . which was neither an improvement nor the point.

Had he *always* thought so little of her? Had she given him cause to? She could admit to being impulsive—*occasionally*—and she knew her distracted and romantic nature sometimes got the better of her common sense. But she wasn't an idiot, and she wasn't dishonorable. That Hunter should think her both—

The silly tune playing in her head rather suddenly became a lively minuet.

Her hip nudged something hard and she glanced down to see the vase Lizzy had rescued once before go toppling from its table. To her considerable shock, Kate actually managed to reach out and catch the thing. But she had only a heart-beat to revel in this unusual display of coordination, because in the next, her toe caught on the leg of the table and then *she* was toppling to the ground, vase in hand.

She landed on it—caught it right between her shoulder and the hard wooden floor. The sound of it breaking was like a gunshot in her ear.

Slowly, painfully, she sat up and surveyed the wreckage. The vase was in at least a dozen pieces. She looked at them numbly, the next twenty-four hours of her existence playing out before her.

She would try to pay for the replacement of the vase. Lord Brentworth would refuse. Her brother would press the money on him in private. Kate would press her money on Whit. Whit would refuse. She would give the money to her mother. Her mother would lecture. Everyone would feel terrible.

A stinging sensation on her shoulder provided an almost welcome distraction, until she looked down to discover a long slash in her gown and an accompanying blooming spot of red.

"Of course," she said wearily. *Of course* she would ruin yet another gown. Hadn't her brother worked so hard to restore the family coffers just so she could squander the money on one accident after another?

She rather felt like crying.

"Kate? What's all this?"

And *of course* Hunter would suddenly emerge around the corner to witness her disgrace.

To her mortification, she felt her eyes begin to water. Ruthlessly, she battled back the tears. She was not going to add to her pitiable circumstances by leaking like a sieve.

"I'm constructing a mosaic," she drawled in her most sar-castic tone, because honestly—*What's all this?* Was the man blind? He had to be, not to see she was sitting in the hallway surrounded by pieces of a broken vase. And to see her as an untrustworthy, dishonorable, and capricious idiot. The tears returned, and she fought them back again as Hunter crouched beside her.

"I deserved that, I suppose," he murmured. "Are you all right?"

Her shoulder hurt, her heart hurt, and humiliation sat like a heavy blanket on her shoulders. "Yes."

He bent his head, his dark eyes searching her face. Her misery must have been evident, because he reached out to take her hand in his. "It's only a vase, Kate."

"It's *Lord Brentworth's* vase," she countered. *That* was the point. It wasn't hers to break.

"I'll fix it for—"

"You can't fix it." She gestured angrily with her free hand. "It's ruined. I ruined it."

"Everything can be fixed." His eyes darted to the vase. "Or replaced."

"Oh, *please* go away."

"Not quite yet." He let go of her hand to brush an errant lock behind her ear. "Here now, stand up before someone comes along. You'll only feel worse if anyone sees you on the floor."

"I don't think it's possible to feel worse," she muttered.

"That someone could be Miss Willory."

She let him pull her to her feet. She was going back to her room and staying there, she decided. Coming downstairs had been a dreadful idea. It would have been much more sensible to have crawled back into bed and caught up on the sleep she'd lost last night. She was always more sensitive when she hadn't enough sleep, and when she broke someone's vase, and when the man she'd been growing steadily more attached to unfairly accused her—

"You're bleeding."

She blinked at Hunter's hard tone and followed his gaze to the injury on her shoulder.

"It's just a scratch," she said. It was *always* just a scratch, just a bruise, just someone else's vase. Why couldn't it ever be just a perfectly graceful walk from point A to point B?

"It's not just a scratch, and I haven't a handkerchief at the moment. We need—" Hunter broke off midsentence when she pulled three handkerchiefs from a pocket in her gown. "You carry three handkerchiefs about with you?"

"When I've somewhere to put them." Three was a minimum, and too often insufficient. She dabbed at her injury and hissed at the resulting sting.

Hunter scowled at her shoulder for a second, then retrieved a small leather satchel from a pocket, and within a minute, had a door across the hall swinging open.

Kate gawked at him, momentarily distracted from her wretchedness. "You just picked that lock, didn't you?"

Rather than answer, Hunter placed a hand on the small of her back and ushered her into a small parlor that looked to have gone unused for years. Most of the furniture was shrouded in dust covers, and the rest was covered in dust. He pulled the cloths off two chairs and led her to one. "Sit down. Let me see your shoulder."

"It's only a scratch," she insisted. "And I need to clean up the vase before someone trips over it." She moved to stand, only to have him nudge her back in the chair.

"Wait here."

It took him less than a minute to step out into the hall, pick up the pieces of the vase and return to dump them into an empty planter by the window.

"Now," he said pointedly, taking the seat across from her and pulling it forward until their knees brushed. "Let me have a look." He drew her hand away from her shoulder. "It's a nasty cut, Kate."

Frowning, she watched as Hunter carefully widened the tear in her gown, exposing the wound. It *was* a bit nastier than she'd realized. It was nearly two inches long and seeping more than she'd realized. She felt a trickle of warmth slide down her arm. "It's not very deep, is it?"

He refolded the linen to produce a clean square. "It should be all right."

"Should be?" That wasn't the most encouraging assessment of an injury that one could hope to hear.

He tenderly dabbed at the blood around the cut. "It's a clean slice, that helps."

"*Helps?*" She traded frowning at her shoulder for frowning at the top of his bent head. "You're not very good at this sort of thing, are you? Atrocious, really."

He glanced up at her. "Would you rather I lie?"

"Well, no, but couldn't you . . . I don't know, soften the truth a smidge?"

His lips twitched, but the humor didn't quite reach his eyes. "I think we can save your arm."

"Atrocious was too generous a description."

"You'll be fine, Kate." He took the hand of her uninjured arm and lifted it to place a kiss against her palm. "All right?"

The warmth of that kiss spread along her skin, bringing on a slight case of nerves. She found that rather annoying as she hadn't forgotten he'd called her honor into question. Carefully, she pulled her hand away. "Yes. All right."

Hunter nodded. "Good. Think you can sit still while I remove the shard?"

Warmth, nerves, and annoyance were immediately, and thoroughly, brushed aside by shock. "What?"

"The . . . you didn't notice, did you?" He winced sympathetically. "You've a shard of porcelain in the cut, sweetheart. It needs to come out."

"It doesn't. I don't." She twisted her neck in an effort to better see her wound. Oh, good heavens she *did*. She'd been distracted by the size of the cut and the blood coming from it and had not seen the small piece of ivory porcelain caught in the corner of the wound. How buried? she wondered uneasily. How small? It was difficult to tell from the angle of her perspective.

"Is it very large?"

"I'm sure it's not."

How could he be sure? For all either of them knew, the piece was buried an inch deep. But that would hurt more, wouldn't it? It hurt now, to be sure, but not terribly. "I'm surprised it doesn't hurt more."

"I'm afraid it's going to hurt a little more when I take it out."

"Oh." She grimaced. "Yes, I imagine it will." *Blast*.

"I'll be gentle," he promised and pulled out his leather satchel once more to retrieve something small and metal.

She turned away, quite certain the experience would not be enhanced by knowing precisely what the tool was, nor what he was going to do with it. Biting her lip, she concentrated instead on sitting perfectly still as he began to prod at the wound.

"You'll tell me first?" she asked wincing at a sharp sting. "Before you pull it out?"

Keeping the tool in place, he leaned over suddenly and brushed his lips softly across hers. "Of course I will."

The warmth spread quickly this time, before anger and annoyance had any say in the matter. "I . . ."

He pulled the shard out with a quick draw of his hand.

The pain of it was absolutely stunning. She jerked, cried out, and swatted at him. "Oh, *ow*! Oh, you *rotter*!"

"I'm sorry, sweetheart." He crooned to her as she rocked in her seat, gripping her shoulder above the wound and hissing through her teeth in pain. "I'm sorry. Shhh, it's done."

He tried to kiss her again. She swatted at him again. "You *lied*."

"I did. I'm sorry. I thought it might be easier if you didn't see it coming."

"Well we won't know *now*, will we?" she managed through gritted teeth.

"Not unless you care to break another vase?"

She stopped rocking to gape at him. "Are you making fun of me?"

"I am," he admitted and reached up to brush the back of his fingers against her cheek. "But only to distract you. Is it working?"

It was, rather. The pain had dulled to a throbbing ache. "It's possible."

"Poor Kate," he murmured and leaned in to press his lips to her forehead. "It's been a rough morning for you, hasn't it?"

It had been a rough night as well, but she didn't want to think of their argument in that moment, not while she was hurting, and he was being so kind. She'd think about their argument when she felt better and he was back to being a high-handed oaf.

She closed her eyes and sighed as the throb lessened. "I'm sorry I called you a rotter."

"Don't be. I did lie." He tapped her chin gently until she opened her eyes. "Better now?"

She nodded as he pulled away to retrieve her handkerchief. He used it to stem the fresh flow of blood.

"You'll need to take proper care of this," he told her, his voice taking on a serious tone. "Keep the wound clean, and keep it covered when you go to bed. I'll hunt up some bandages for you."

"Yes. Thank you." She glanced to where he'd set the shard he'd pulled out. It wasn't an inch, she was relieved to note, but she wouldn't have described it as small either. It was triangular in shape, with the base a good quarter inch wide.

"I can't believe this happened," she said, somewhat awed. "I never hurt myself. Not seriously . . . Well, I did give myself a black eye with a door once. And I think I may have broken a toe when I fell out of father's curricle, but—"

Hunter's head snapped up. "You fell out of a curricle?"

"There were no horses attached to it at the time." She gave him a sheepish smile. "A game of hide-and-seek with Evie when I was ten."

"Ah." He cleaned the cut a moment longer, then returned the handkerchief. "No one goes through life without acquiring an injury or two, Kate. Don't overthink the matter."

"I can't help it. Overthinking comes naturally to me."

"I see." He sat back in his chair and studied her. "And have you had second thoughts about speaking with Whit, yet?"

"No." It was a lie. She *had* reconsidered speaking with Whit, but she wasn't yet ready to hand Hunter that victory.

Hunter's lips twisted wryly. "And you accused me of being spiteful."

"I'm not being spiteful," she countered. "I'm being vengeful. It's entirely different."

"I can't believe I'm going to ask this," he muttered, "but how is it different?"

"Only the latter implies one is standing up for oneself," she explained.

"Vengeance isn't a virtue, Kate."

The smile she gave him was Machiavellian. "Oh, it can be."

He didn't smile back. "Would it make any difference if I were to apologize for last night?"

Apologies, when genuine, always made a difference. But she wasn't ready to hand him that either. "I suppose that would depend."

"On?" he prompted.

"Why you were apologizing, and what you were apologizing for. If you're going to offer a vague and sweeping sort of apology for 'last night' or 'the argument' just to make me more biddable, then I assure you it won't help. But if you're quite sincerely sorry about something specific—"

"I am," he broke in. He caught her gaze and held it. "I am genuinely sorry I called your honor into question. It was wrong of me."

"Oh, well, yes, that does make a difference." All the difference, or quite a bit at any rate, there was still the question of whether he believed it. She looked down and plucked at her skirts. "When you say wrong, do you mean wrong because you know it isn't true, or wrong because it isn't something you should say even when it is true?"

"Kate, look at me." He waited for her to stop plucking and look up. "I knew it wasn't true, but I was willing to ignore that because I was angry with you and wanted to twist the conversation to my benefit."

She nodded slowly. "Very well, apology accepted."

He nodded in return. "Excellent, now—"

"Are you sorry for initiating the threat to tell Whit as well?" she asked, not because she needed for him to be, but because she was curious.

"I might have been, had you not turned it back on me so quickly." His lips curved up. "I had no idea you were capable of such cold disdain."

"The benefits of being Lady Thurston's daughter are many."

He laughed at that. "I imagine they are. Is that where you acquired your stubbornness as well?"

"Oh, no, that I developed on my own."

"It's not a flaw I would have attributed to you without seeing it firsthand."

"I recall mentioning I have loads of flaws. Everyone does." She smiled at him sweetly. "Some more than others."

"I am aware of my flaws," he replied dryly, "thank you."

"Are you?"

"Certainly. Did I argue when you called me unpatriotic and selfish?"

He hadn't, nor did he look at the moment as if he was at

all unsettled by the idea of being considered both. "It's true that others would consider those flaws. Do you?"

There was a brief pause before he answered. "No."

She briefly wondered if he was in earnest, before deciding he couldn't possibly be. Everyone considered selfishness a flaw. Like as not, he was attempting to ruffle her feathers again. "What flaws are you aware of, then?"

He tapped a finger on the arm of his chair as he thought about it. "I'm overindulgent."

"Of yourself or others?"

"Myself, mostly."

She found that rather surprising. She'd thought him the disciplined sort. "You're wasteful?"

His finger stopped tapping. "No. Waste implies a resource has been discarded, not used to excess."

"Oh. Well, what do you overindulge in?"

"Whatever takes my fancy at the time. Land, art . . ." He gave her a wicked smile. "Sin."

She twisted her lips. "I don't believe that. Evie told me you're a good man at the core."

"Did she?" he asked, clearly intrigued.

"But that you're nicked a bit on the edges."

"Makes me sound like bruised fruit."

"Yes," she laughed, "that's what I said."

He didn't laugh in return. Instead, he sat very still in his chair, studying her. "And what do you believe, Kate?"

"That . . ." She shifted in her seat, uncomfortable with his intense gaze. "That I was wrong to call you selfish and unpatriotic."

"No," he said softly, "you weren't."

"Of course I—"

"Do you know why I work for William?"

He looked terribly somber all of a sudden. A storm had gathered in his eyes, but she couldn't tell if it was one of anger, or fear, or hurt. The man was impossible to read. "You . . ."

She shifted again. "Presumably for many of the same reasons Whit and Alex do."

He shook his head slowly, then caught her gaze to hold it without blinking. As if he was daring her to judge him for what he was about to say. Or perhaps asking her not to. She dearly wished she knew which.

"I take orders from William," he said carefully, "because my only other option is take a final set of orders from the hangman."

"I . . . *Beg your pardon?*" Given how significant her reaction seemed to be to him, it might have been better to come up with a more eloquent response, but that phrase was the best she could manage after hearing the word, "hangman."

Hunter nodded once. "My punishment for crimes committed against the crown was seven years in service to the War Department. Six months remaining." He leaned back in his chair and stretched his legs, as if suddenly deciding the whole business made very little difference to him. She might have believed him, if not for the lingering clouds in his eyes and the way his gaze was still fixed on her face. "Generous, really. William could have just as easily sent me to trial or confiscated all I had and impressed me into the navy."

"Seven years," she breathed. "What in heaven's name did you do?"

"I did nothing in the name of heaven. In the name of profit, there was very little I *didn't* do."

"But what was the crime that earned such a punishment? Did you . . . did you hurt someone?" Could he have actually been a pirate?

"No. Not the way you mean."

She let out a long breath she hadn't realized she'd been holding. If he hadn't murdered someone, or very nearly murdered someone, then she rather thought whatever he'd done could be forgiven. It had been nearly seven years ago, after all, and he'd paid for his transgression. More, it was clear he wasn't proud of what he'd done. Defiant, perhaps, but that seemed more a defense against her possible censure than—

"Decided if I'm a good man or not?"

She blinked herself out of her musings to find Hunter still watching her. "I've no idea who or what you were seven years ago," she answered honestly. "You've not told me what your crime was. Are you going to tell me?"

He shook his head.

"Pity," she replied on a sigh. "Because if I knew you'd stolen from a rich man to feed a starving child, then I'd venture to say you were a good man, but—"

"Robin Hood again."

"It's a lovely story," she informed him primly before continuing. "But if you stole food from a starving child and then sold that food for profit—"

"I didn't steal from children."

"Well then—"

"I didn't spend much time stealing from the rich to feed them either."

"I believe we can safely add persistent interrupter to your list of flaws," she drawled, delighted to see his lips twitch and the worst of the storm in his eyes subside.

He gestured in a prompting motion. "Please continue."

"Thank you. My point is, I don't know what sort of man you were seven years ago. I only know the man I see before me now, and yes, I believe that man is good." Because she wanted to see his eyes laughing rather than storming, she added, "At the core."

His eyes didn't clear, not entirely, but he did laugh and that was certainly an improvement. "Well, now that we've established that either I'm a good man or you and Evie are poor judges of character, it's time we left before someone discovers you're keeping company with me in a locked room."

She pulled a face. She wasn't ready yet to face Lord Brentworth, nor her mother. "I don't see why anyone should think twice about *this* locked room as *all* the rooms in this hall are locked."

There was a weighted pause before Hunter responded. "You took a stroll about the house as well?"

"Er . . ." She winced. "It's possible."

"It's all right, Kate. It was to be your next assignment, at any rate."

She straightened in her chair. "Was it really?"

He nodded, then seemed to hesitate. "I, ah, I'd already searched."

"Oh."

"But I wanted you to look again," he was quick to assure her. "It's always possible I'd missed something. And it's always best to use two sets of eyes rather than one."

"Oh," she said again, this time with a little more enthusiasm. "That makes sense, although I didn't find anything more interesting than the fact I couldn't get into most of the rooms."

"Ah, yes. You have the dowager Lady Brentworth to thank for that. She has a tendency to walk about in her sleep, and the staff keep doors locked to limit the danger."

"The dowager Lady Brentworth? But she's not in residence, is she?"

"Not at the moment, no. She's visiting her sister in Kent. The doors are locked by habit."

"Oh. That's something of a disappointment." She wondered if a great deal of what an agent did was follow false leads. Probably, an *authentic* agent would have been aware of Lady Brentworth's unusual nocturnal habits.

"Would it be less disappointing if I showed you how to pick a few of those locks?" Hunter asked.

Kate felt her eyes go round. She'd wanted to acquire that skill ever since she'd discovered Sophie, the Duchess of Rockeforte, possessed it. Unfortunately, Evie and Mirabelle had been more interested in receiving instructions in Sophie's other unusual talent, knife throwing, which was something Kate felt she had no business attempting. She'd considered asking Sophie to give her a separate lesson in lock picking, but the woman was a friend, not a governess.

She scooted forward in her chair. "Would you really teach me?"

"Certainly."

She beamed at him and rose from her chair. "Now?"

"Later," he replied gaining his feet. "The next time I'm at Haldon. Guests here might not appreciate a lady's interest in the art of lock picking, and we're taking enough risk with your reputation as it is."

She brushed at her skirts, caught between disappointment and embarrassment. Most of that risk had stemmed, not from the smuggling investigation, but from the time she spent with him behind closed doors. "Yes, perhaps you're right."

And perhaps it was time she stopped stalling and faced the consequences of the broken vase. With a sigh, she moved to walk with him toward the door, only to have the minuet shift back into the silly child's tune.

She caught her toe at the edge of a rug, and would have fallen yet again, if Hunter hadn't reached out to steady her.

Frustrated beyond measure, and dearly wishing she'd paid more attention to the curses Evie was so fond of collecting, she ground her teeth and gave the rug one futile—and admittedly rather foolish—stomp with her food.

"This wouldn't keep happening if Lord Brentworth had the decency to keep his windows open." She refused to acknowledge that it was still raining, and therefore none of the windows could be opened.

Next to her, Hunter cleared something from his throat. "Did I just hear you correctly? You tripped on the rug because Lord Brentworth keeps his windows shut?"

"Oh, never mind," she mumbled, embarrassed to have made the comment. "You wouldn't understand."

"I certainly don't at the moment."

"An explanation isn't likely to help."

"Why don't you try anyway?"

She found it impossible to meet his gaze. "Because I don't care to be looked at as if I've come unhinged." And she'd made enough of a fool of herself for one day.

"Have I ever looked at you that way?"

No, his gaze usually said he was thinking something entirely different. Something she wasn't going to dwell on. She had enough to occupy her mind at present. Like whether or not it was only fair that she share her secret after he'd shared one of his own, and whether doing so would help erase the vestiges of the clouds from his eyes. She wondered what it meant that those clouds should bother her so greatly, and—

"Kate?"

"I hear music," she blurted out before she could think better of it.

He looked in the general direction of the music room and cocked his head. "I don't hear anything."

"No, I mean . . . I mean in my head. I hear music in my head." She could scarce believe she'd said it. Those six words had felt like a cork stuck in her throat, bottling up everything she wanted to explain. And now that the cork was gone, the everything came out in one long rush. "Not all the time, but quite often. It's *my* music, the songs I compose. Sometimes it's a piece I'm working on, or something I've written in the past, but on occasion the arrangement is entirely new to me, and now and then, when the music changes abruptly, or some portion of it alters dramatically, and I've not been paying attention to what I'm doing—which is most always, isn't it?— then I have a tendency to do this sort of thing—trip on rugs and knock over vases. To be honest, I've a tendency to do so even when the music remains consistent, but a sudden change is more likely to—"

He held up a hand to cut her off, which she had to admit

was probably for the best. Her explanation, though extensive, was sadly lacking in coherency.

"You hear music in your head?" he asked, speaking each word distinctly.

The cork began to grow again. She nodded nervously.

"Music you've never heard anywhere before?"

Though that wasn't always what she heard, she thought it might be wise to nod again rather than attempt another explanation.

A line formed across Hunter's brow. "It just . . . comes to you?"

She nodded once more, hoping it would be the last time. Waiting for his reaction was excruciating.

His expression turned to one of amazement, and when he spoke he sounded more than a little awed. "What an extraordinary gift."

The cork disappeared and her nerves melted away. Nothing he could have said would have relieved or pleased her more.

It *was* a gift. Despite the toll it sometimes took, she had always recognized it as a priceless gift. She hadn't imagined, however, that Hunter would recognize it as well. She'd hoped for acceptance from him and had resigned herself to at least some level of sympathy. She hadn't even thought to hope for admiration and understanding.

Not that he looked all that understanding at the moment. He was peering over her shoulder with a decidedly confused expression on his face.

"What does it have to do with Lord Brentworth's windows?"

"Oh, right." She nodded. "It's the sea. When I can hear it clearly, the music stops."

"Does it?"

"It's the rhythm of the waves, I think. External music will replace my own. It's not as if I go to the opera and listen to two sets of musicians at once. And I'm less inclined to have—" She waved her hand at the rug. "This sort of problem when there's an external source of music. It's so much more consistent than what I hear. It's quite easy for me to follow the tempo and I needn't worry it will alter abruptly."

"Does yours often alter abruptly?"

"No, sometimes it will be the same for days or even weeks, sometimes the change is gradual, sometimes it's not the song or tempo that changes, it's the instruments. I'll hear a cello, and then the sound becomes higher and more hollow, and suddenly it's a piccolo." She scowled at nothing in particular. "That's jarring as well."

"I imagine so." He smiled at her suddenly. "Life must seem like one long theatrical production."

She laughed and shook her head. "The music is neither that consistent, nor that loud. It's not as if I've an entire orchestra playing in my ear." She shrugged. "Lizzy says everyone has music in their head from time to time. I don't think what I hear is all that different except I hear it more often, and it's a bit more detailed, I suppose. And I do have some control over it," she added, lest he think she was completely at the whim of her gift, or believed the music she put to paper came without hard work. "Usually, when I concentrate, I can hear whatever I like, change whatever I like. It's how I compose. But when I'm not concentrating, well . . ."

He nodded in understanding. "And what do you hear right now?"

"My mother lecturing me for breaking the vase," she said grimly, though it was actually still the child's tune. "I shouldn't put it off any longer."

He placed a hand on her back and gently urged her toward the door. "Your mother needn't hear of it."

"I won't lie to her, or to Lord Brentworth."

"Yes, you will." He unlocked the door. "I'm ordering you to."

"You can't do that."

"I believe I just did." He checked the hall to be certain it was free of guests before ushering her out of the room and closing the door behind them.

"I never promised to follow your every order," Kate laughed. "I only promised to follow orders as they pertained to the investigation."

"This does."

"How?"

She looked up to find his eyes dancing with merriment. "I'm ordering you not to ask."

Hunter left Kate laughing, and with the promise that he would handle the matter of the vase. The moment he turned the first corner in the hallway, he stopped, leaned against the wall and took two long, deep breaths.

You're a good man.

Bloody hell, what had he been thinking to tell her of his bargain with William? He snorted and dragged a hand down his face. *Clearly*, he hadn't been thinking of dazzling her with his charm. Nor had he been thinking of that last night, when he'd gone off issuing unreasonable orders. But *that*, at least, had come from somewhere, and led to something. He'd been furious with her for going anywhere near Smuggler's Beach and he wanted to be certain she never, *ever*, put herself in that sort of danger again. Granted, once his temper had settled he'd been able to admit the danger had been fairly limited . . . and his reaction fairly asinine. But asinine or not, there had been a *point*.

For the life of him, he couldn't figure out where the desire to suddenly share a piece of his sordid past had originated or what he had thought to gain from it. It had come from nowhere, this overpowering urge to give her some inkling of the kind of man he was, the kind of man she was getting involved with—which was perfectly stupid as he didn't intend to give her much of a choice in the matter, and then he'd been on the edge of his seat waiting to discover what she thought of that man—which was equally stupid as he had no intention of changing who he was for her or anyone else—and then, *finally*, she had called him a good man. Which had elated, baffled, and irritated him all at once.

He wasn't a good man. He was wicked. *Usually*, he was rather good at being wicked.

He'd been nothing short of ineffectual for the last eighteen hours.

That would stop, immediately. He knew how to be effective. He knew how to be damn near everything. He *had* been damn near everything over the course of his life—wily street urchin, elusive thief, cutthroat businessman, charming gentleman. He'd managed that last well enough *after* his bizarre little confession.

He certainly knew how best to go about getting what he wanted. And, *despite* his bizarre little confession, what he wanted bloody well wasn't for Kate to absolve him of his sins.

He *liked* being wicked, damn it, and he wasn't the least bit sorry for it.

He pushed away from the wall and resumed his walk to the billiards room where he knew both Lord Brentworth and Whit could be found. The former he intended to offer an unholy amount of money to keep quiet the matter of the vase. The latter he intended to have keep an eye—a *watchful* eye, this time—on Kate for a couple of hours.

He had a wicked and charming idea.

❈ Fourteen ❈

Kate returned to her room with the intention of changing her gown and hiding it in a trunk. With any luck, she could dispose of it once she was back at Haldon without anyone being the wiser.

Luck, it seemed, was in short supply. She opened her door to find Lizzy standing in the middle of the room, folding a blanket at the end of the bed. Lizzy dropped the blanket with a gasp and crossed the floor the second her gaze fell on Kate's bloody shoulder, which was exactly one second after Kate stepped inside.

"Lady Kate, what happened?"

Kate closed the door behind her. "It's nothing."

Lizzy stopped in her tracks and gestured at the blood-stained tear. "Nothing, is it? I've eyes, haven't I?"

"Yes. You also have ears and a mouth, which is why I'm not telling you what happened."

Lizzy sniffed, rather melodramatically in Kate's opinion. "I have been known to keep a secret or two."

"Only when it's my mother who's asked it of you."

"Well . . ." Lizzy eyes darted away and she began to tug at the ties of her apron. "Well, she asks me doesn't she? She . . ."

"She what, Lizzy?"

"She asks for my word."

Like a Cole, Kate realized, like family. How could she have failed to realize what that would mean to Lizzy? Rather than make an issue out of it, which would only make Lizzy more uncomfortable, she shrugged and spoke casually.

"Well, promise *me* you'll not breathe a word of it, and I'll tell you what's happened."

Lizzy gave one solemn nod. "I promise."

Relating a story to Lizzy was always something of a challenge. The woman asked an inordinate number of questions. But relating a story that involved a broken vase, an injury, a picked lock, and a substantial amount of time locked in a room with a handsome man—whilst simultaneously avoiding any mention of a smuggling operation, and changing her torn gown—was far more than a challenge. It was an *event*. And one that took the better part of two hours.

It would have taken even longer if a soft knock on the door hadn't interrupted Lizzy in midquestion.

"Come in," Kate called, fully expecting a maid to enter with news of tea in the parlor.

What she heard was Hunter's voice. "It is tempting."

"Good heavens," Kate bounded off the bed, flew across the room and threw open the door. After a quick glance down both ends of the hall to be certain no one was about, she grabbed a handful of his waistcoat and pulled him a foot into the room, then thought better of it and pushed him back into the hall. Ignoring his deep chuckle, she stepped out, closed the door behind her, and took his arm to drag him away from her room.

"What were you thinking, coming to my door?" she demanded. "If someone had been about—"

"If anyone had been about, I wouldn't have come to your door."

"That's—"

"The ladies are in the parlor and the gentlemen are in the billiards room, Kate, and I didn't feel like hunting up a maid to fetch you."

She rolled her eyes. "Have you never heard of a bellpull?"

"I'm not going to make a maid come all the way upstairs

just to deliver a message six doors down from my own. It would be a waste of time."

She stopped and turned to him when they reached the top of the back staircase. "It *is* ridiculous, I grant, but it is also the way things are done. And not doing things the way they are done can result in . . . in . . ." She trailed off, remembering what he'd said. "Six doors? You counted?"

He blinked once, then threw his head back and laughed. To her astonishment, he reached out to grip her face with his hands and placed a loud kiss on her forehead. "You never cease to surprise me."

She shoved him away, even as she battled the exceedingly odd combination of amusement and attraction. "*That* is not how things are done either."

"Come with me." Still chuckling, he took her arm and led her down the stairs. "I've a present for you."

"A present?" No doubt it was silly of her to be so easily sidetracked from her goal of educating the man on proper house party etiquette, but she couldn't find it in herself to care. She was far more interested in the fact that she was *excited* to be receiving a present from a man. Generally, whenever one of her admirers brought her a token, she felt awkward accepting it, guilty that she wasn't thrilled to be receiving it, and in the case of Lord Martin, a little annoyed that he kept bringing them.

Hunter pulled her down a hallway she knew went mostly unused by guests. "Where are we going?"

"The ballroom. I want a bit of space for this."

"There's quite a bit of space outside." Though why they should need it was a mystery. "It stopped raining, hasn't it?"

"It has, but we need to do this indoors. That reminds me, why is it your family has not taken up permanent residence on the coast?"

She couldn't imagine how the first part of that statement

could possibly remind him of the second. "I think perhaps you're spending too much time in my company."

"The music you hear," he began by way of explanation. "It stops when you listen to the sea, correct?"

"Yes."

"And sometimes you would prefer the music stop, also correct?"

"So why haven't we packed up and left Haldon for a place like this?" she guessed, and shook her head. "Haldon Hall is our home. It wouldn't be fair to my mother or Whit, or—"

"Is your family aware of the music you hear?"

"Mostly," she hedged.

"Most of your family, or mostly aware?"

"Mostly aware," she admitted. "They know I sometimes hear music and that it can be distracting."

"That's it? You've kept the details to yourself all these years?"

"You needn't say 'all these years' quite like that," she complained, only because it was a chance to change the subject. "I've had four seasons, not forty."

"Beg your pardon," he replied without sounding remotely apologetic. "Now answer the question."

"I've not kept the details entirely to myself. Lizzy knows." *And now you.*

She was relieved when he nodded and let the subject drop. It was an uncomfortable topic for her. She didn't like that she kept a part of who she was from those she loved, but she found the idea of her family rearranging their lives to accommodate her even less appealing. And goodness knew, if Whit or her mother thought it was something she truly needed, they would pack up their lives and leave Haldon for the coast. It was just the sort of overprotective nonsense Whit was fond of. And it would be dreadful. She adored Haldon. She'd met Hunter for the first time at the dinner table, Mirabelle for the first time on the grounds, and Lizzy not far away in the town of Benton.

"Here we are."

Kate looked at the large set of doors they stopped before. "Are you going to pick the lock again?" she asked hopefully.

He pushed open the door without trouble and smiled at her disappointed expression. "Sorry. I asked the housekeeper to unlock it earlier today. Seemed practical."

She pursed her lips and followed him inside. "Practical is rarely as much fun."

"Perhaps this will change your mind." He ushered her farther into the room and reached into a pocket.

Kate waited for him to pull out a book, or sweets, or . . . well it couldn't be flowers, not in his pocket, and that was really the only other thing a gentleman brought a lady.

He brought out a small hinged box and handed it to her. "Here you are."

She took it hesitantly. Oh, dear, what if he wasn't aware of what a gentleman could, and could not, give to a lady? What if he'd brought her something inappropriate, like jewelry?

Slowly, carefully, she opened the box just a crack, just enough to peek inside, as if a vastly inappropriate gift might become only slightly inappropriate if the look she took was very small.

"It's a pocket watch." She honestly couldn't think of anything else to say.

It was, indeed, a large gentleman's pocket watch fashioned of silver and heavily inlaid with gold in a complicated design of what looked to be leafy vines.

"It's . . ." Arguably, the oddest gift she had ever received. "It's, er, quite handsome."

"It's not," he laughed. "But you'll find it useful, I think."

"Yes, well, they are useful instruments," was the most diplomatic reply she could come up with.

"For you in particular, if we're lucky."

She hadn't the foggiest notion of how to respond to that.

He tipped his chin at her. "Have you any pockets on that gown?"

"Pockets? Er . . ." She ran her free hand along the sides of her dress and found a hidden pocket on the right. "Yes, this one does."

"Excellent. If this works, you should consider having them sewn into all of your gowns."

"If what works?"

He took the box, removed the watch to wind it up, and handed it to her. "Do you feel that?"

"Yes, of course." It was impossible not to feel the steady *tick, tick, tick* beneath her fingers.

Almost instantly, the silly child's tune shifted to follow the external rhythm.

She gaped at the instrument, suddenly seeing it in an entirely new light. "I . . . oh, my."

"I thought perhaps a larger movement would prove easier for you to hear and feel. Put it in your pocket."

Excited now, she did as he suggested. The steady rhythm of the watch wasn't strong enough for her to feel through the material of her gown and chemise, but when she put her hand in her pocket—"Oh, this is wonderful."

"Take a turn about the room," he suggested.

Kate was too enthralled with her new present to feel self-conscious about Hunter watching her as she made a circle around the ballroom. The steady ticking of the watch kept rhythm at a pace she could easily walk to, and it would be a simple enough thing to adjust the number of steps she took to each beat. Fewer steps per tick for meandering, additional steps per tick for a brisk walk.

Delighted and eager to discover all the possibilities a pocket watch had to offer, she turned to Hunter. "Stomp on the floor."

"Beg your pardon?"

"Stomp on the floor," she repeated with a grin and an impatient gesture of her hand. "I want to see if a louder rhythm from elsewhere has an effect."

He brought his heel down several times and she rolled her eyes. "Hard, Hunter. You're just tapping."

"I'm really not much for stomping."

"It is a bit unmasculine," she agreed. "Go kick something."

"I am not going to kick—"

"Too undignified?"

Laughing, he shook his head and went to retrieve one of the sturdy looking chairs lined against the walls. He picked it up by the back, brought it a few inches off the ground and then brought it back down again with a bang. "Will that do?"

"Yes, thank you."

He brought the chair down just hard and long enough for her to determine that the noise did not alter the watch's ability to keep tempo.

She took it out of her pocket and stared at it. "It's like . . . it's rather like a metronome, only better."

"A what?"

"A weighted pendulum used to keep rhythm," she replied with a dismissive shake of her head. "They're not at all practical. Much too long for slow tempos."

The watch, on the other hand, was perfect. As perfect as she could ask for, anyway. The songs themselves would still change, as would the instruments, but the tempo would remain constant for as long as she wished it.

"You can't walk about with your hand in a pocket all day," Hunter pointed out as she crossed the room to him. "But when no one else is about—"

"It's perfect. It's . . ." Unquestionably, the most thoughtful gift she had ever received. "It's brilliant. I don't know what to say."

She was so lost in the wonder of her present that she wasn't aware he'd stepped close to her until his warm hand cupped her chin and gently tipped it up.

"Say, thank you," he whispered, a heartbeat before his mouth covered hers.

It would have been easy for Kate to fall into the kiss. She wanted to. She could already feel herself slipping. It could have been only a matter of time before she was utterly seduced by Hunter's skilled mouth and clever hands. It would have been, had they been just a little less skilled, a little less clever.

He wasn't slipping with her. There was too much control in what he did, as if every slide of his lips, every warm trail of his fingers had been orchestrated in advance. Moves in a game, that's what it felt like. It was moves in a game she didn't fully understand and didn't want to play—not if she were playing alone.

Just like in the music room, she thought dimly. This was all just like the first kiss in the sitting room and the last kiss in the music room.

And it was quite enough. She didn't want a music room or sitting room kiss. She wanted a kiss just for the ballroom. She wanted him to slip and fall with her.

She wasn't entirely certain how to go about getting it, but she thought it might be a good start if she put her arms about him. She went on tiptoe, reaching around his neck with her uninjured arm, and resting the hand of the other against his chest. Her breasts brushed against him as she stretched up, and the sensation created a deep pull of longing she found thrilling. As it also made Hunter go very, very still, she decided to give in to curiosity and brush against him again . . . and again.

He made a wonderfully masculine sort of noise in the back of his throat, something between a growl and a moan, and his arms tightened, dragging her hard against him.

That was better.

Recalling the kiss in the music room, she hesitantly tasted his lips with her tongue. Hunter responded by spearing his fingers into her hair and slanting his mouth hungrily over hers.

Much better.

He broke away to trail a line of heat across her jaw and down her neck.

Worlds better.

His teeth scraped lightly over a sensitive spot at the juncture of her uninjured shoulder, and suddenly she lost the ability to think, lost the ability to do anything but feel.

There was only the weight of his mouth as it covered hers once again, the glorious slide of his tongue along hers, the heat of his arms banding her close.

He loosened his hold only to mold his hands to her hips and then drag them up over her waist, her torso, the sides of her breasts. Every inch he touched felt hot as his hands moved over her, and hungry for more when they'd passed.

Excitement built in a dizzying rush, until it grew into something else . . . into need. She needed to be closer. She needed more. She tasted the skin at his jaw, his ear, his neck. Her fingers pulled at his cravat, pushed at his waistcoat.

Suddenly, he broke away, leaving her reeling.

"Enough," he whispered hoarsely. "Kate, that's enough."

It was? Her blood was racing, her breath coming in pants, and every nerve in her body was screaming in protest at the rude interruption of the kiss. "Enough?"

"Yes, you need to go."

"Go?" She blinked at him slowly, willing her heart toward a normal rhythm. "Why?"

"Because it's not enough."

"I . . ." That incomprehensible bit of logic prompted her to concentrate a little harder on what he was saying and less on what she was feeling. Concentrating wasn't enough. It still didn't make sense. "I don't understand."

"I want more from you," he said gruffly. "I want everything. And nothing you should give on a ballroom floor."

"Oh." That perfectly comprehensible statement had her biting her lip. "I see."

"You should go now."

"I should, yes." She didn't want to. As imprudent as it was, she wanted to stay and offer what he wanted. Offer him everything, and take it for herself. Her eyes darted to his mouth. "I should go."

Oh, but she wanted to stay.

"*Now*, Kate." He fairly growled the command.

She pulled her eyes away from his mouth and took a look at all of him. And then she took a step back. Perhaps it would be best to attempt the everything when he was a little less . . . agitated. The man was practically vibrating. "Right . . ." She swallowed hard and began a cautious backward retreat. "Right. I'll just . . . I'll just see you at dinner then, shall I?"

He didn't answer. He just stared at her, his jaw locked tight, his hands curled into fists at his sides . . . his dark hair mussed where she'd run her fingers through the thick locks. She did so love when his hair was a little mussed. Maybe . . .

"Go."

"Right." She took two more steps backward, then turned around and walked through the door, certain she could feel his burning gaze on her back.

Instinctively, she headed toward her room, then turned back again and walked toward a side door to the house. The change in direction put her in the rather awkward position of having to pass by the open door to the ballroom, where a quick glance told her Hunter was still vibrating, but that couldn't be helped. She wanted a moment to herself before facing any other guests. She needed to right her appearance and settle her system. But most important, she needed time and space to reconcile what she'd suspected in her mind with what she now knew in her heart.

Somehow, somewhere, between the laughter, and the kisses, and the acceptance of her dreams, Mr. Andrew Hunter had turned into a prince.

Where had he gone wrong?

Hunter stalked across the ballroom to throw open a window. He needed air, and a drink, and possibly a hard punch to the head. What the *devil* had he been thinking?

He'd had it all planned. Everything, *everything* had been set to suit his purpose, and his purpose had been to remind himself, and Kate, of who was in control of this unconventional little courtship.

A small excursion to the ballroom, the judicial—albeit belated—application of charm, and the presentation of a carefully selected gift had all been delivered with the intention of wrapping Kate around his finger, and his arms around Kate.

The kiss had been carefully thought through as well. Absolute control on his part and the illusion of control on hers, just like in the music room. Things had gone swimmingly in the music room.

What the bloody hell had happened here?

She'd asked him about counting doors, that's what had happened. She'd started the whole business off by charming *him*. And then she'd been so genuinely delighted by the watch that he couldn't help but feel delight with her, instead of with himself for having thought to buy the thing.

And then she'd told him to go kick something.

And then he'd been kissing her.

And then she'd been kissing *him*. And that was where things had well and truly gone to hell.

He'd been a mere heartbeat away from dragging her to the floor. No, no that wasn't the trouble. The trouble was that he'd been a mere heartbeat from letting Kate drag *him* to the floor. If it had been *his* idea—if *he'd* had the upper hand—he'd not have broken the kiss.

But it hadn't been his idea—he hadn't planned to introduce his future wife to the pleasures of the marriage bed on a ballroom floor—and he hadn't had the upper hand, because he hadn't *just* lost control—he'd handed it to her as neatly as he'd handed her the watch.

Here you are. You'll find it useful, I think.

Giving Kate control had never been the plan.

He rubbed the heel of his hand against his chest in an effort to alleviate an uncomfortable tightness building there. A tightness he staunchly refused to acknowledge as worry.

Clearly, he needed a better plan. One that could handle the likes of Lady Kate Cole.

A competent strategist recognized when it was time to alter tactics. And any strategist who'd been a heartbeat away from letting a mere slip of a girl drag him to the floor would recognize that a little distance was in order. A day in town for himself, that's what he needed. A solid day alone to gain perspective and think through his next move. Whit could watch Kate. Mr. Laury as well, from a discreet distance.

By tomorrow night, the discomfort in his chest would be nothing but a bad memory.

❋ *Fifteen* ❋

$\mathcal{K}$ate tapped her pen against the small writing desk in her room.

A full bar of rest and then . . . Could she change keys? Would that be too jarring? Perhaps she should bring the oboes in first. No, the cellos—rich and low and hollow. No. No, that was much too maudlin. She wanted pensive, not despairing. Didn't she? Why couldn't she hear it?

Maybe it should be the oboes . . .

"Kate, are you coming?"

Kate looked up to find Mirabelle standing in her door. "Coming? Er . . ."

"You promised to take tea with Lizzy and me this afternoon."

"Oh, yes, of course. I'm sorry, Mirabelle, I lost track of time."

Mirabelle motioned at the mountains of paper on the desk. "It must be going well, then."

"It was. I thought it was." She sighed and set her pen down. "And now it isn't. It's the symphony. It's missing a section right in the middle of the third movement. I cannot seem to work it out."

"If you'd rather forgo tea and have something brought here, I understand."

Kate shook her head and stood to follow Mirabelle from the room. "No, I'd rather the tea than a headache. And a break might well do some good."

As long as that break did not include thinking of Hunter. The day before, she'd done nothing *but* think about the man, and her strong attachment to him. The phrase "strong attachment" to describe what she felt for him was, to her dismay, all that those hours of thinking had netted her. She hadn't the foggiest notion what to do about the strong attachment, or even if she should do anything at all— Well, yes, she was certain she should do something, but the what, how, and when—

"Hurry *up*, girl." Miss Willory's strident voice sounded from an open door at the end of the hall.

Mirabelle scowled. "Horrible woman. Abusing some poor maid, no doubt."

"I've not got all day to wait about for you," Miss Willory snapped.

"You're not waiting," a mumbled voice responded. "You're walking."

Kate and Mirabelle exchanged glances of alarm. *Surely* that couldn't be Lizzy.

Miss Willory stepped into the hall and tossed an angry look over her shoulder. "What did you say, girl?"

Lizzy stepped out behind her, a large pile of books in her arms. "Nothing."

"Nothing, *miss*." Miss Willory snapped, her voice holding none of the honeyed tones she reserved for individuals of her own rank. "Impertinent little monster. I can't fathom why Lady Kate keeps you about, stupid as you are."

What sympathy Kate had felt for Miss Willory in her current troubles was instantly, and thoroughly, obliterated. She opened her mouth to deliver a scathing rebuke, only to have Mirabelle beat her to it.

"Stop right there, Lizzy." Mirabelle went storming past Kate to snatch the pile of books from Lizzy's hands and shove them at Miss Willory. The latter had no choice but to grab hold or risk having them land on her feet.

"Miss Browning, what—?"

"It is Lady Thurston."

"Oh, yes, of course." Miss Willory scrambled to keep a book from dropping. "I don't know *why* I can't seem to remember."

"Because you are a selfish, spoiled, and monumentally spiteful individual, Mary Jane Willory, *that* is why." She ignored Miss Willory's gasp to continue on in a frigid tone. "And since you appear incapable of observing even the most basic forms of etiquette when in the company of myself and those in my husband's employ, you will no longer be welcome at Haldon Hall for any reason. Do I make myself clear?"

Miss Willory's eyes grew round. Banishment from Haldon meant exclusion from some of the most fashionable parties of the year. It wasn't a completely fatal wound to Miss Willory's social ambitions, but it was a grievous one.

"You can't do that. You . . . you're . . . you're . . ."

"Lady Kate, Miss Willory still seems to be having difficulty remembering who I am. Would you be so kind as to remind her?"

"Oh, it would be my pleasure." Kate gripped her hands behind her back and took a deep breath. "Mirabelle Cole, the Countess of Thurston and mistress of Haldon Hall, the Thurston town house, Holly Terrace, Hartright Castle, Fryerton—"

"You've a castle?" Mirabelle interrupted with a stunned look in Kate's direction. "Really?"

"*You* have a castle," Kate corrected.

"Oh. Right." She turned back to smile pleasantly at Miss Willory. "I have a castle."

Miss Willory blinked once. "I—"

"Fryerton Abbey," Kate cut in. "Dreibruken House—that's in Germany, I've never been—Poplar Cottage, Wain—"

"Enough," Miss Willory finally spat. Her fingers stood out white against the bindings of her books. "You're hateful. Both of you. This girl is nothing more than a servant. I had every right—"

"The London town house is now closed to you as well," Mirabelle informed her calmly. "Care to try for the castle?"

Kate bit the inside of her cheek. The castle was a moldering pile of ruins in Scotland.

"You'll regret this," Miss Willory hissed, and then wisely spun away to storm down the hall before she lost access to another Thurston holding.

Mirabelle watched her go. "Oh, I've wanted to do something like that for *years*." She sighed happily. "I do so like being Lady Thurston."

Lizzy worried her lip with her teeth, obviously caught between delight and worry. "I'm not certain you should have done that, my lady."

"Why ever not? She deserved it."

"She'll make a fuss."

"Yes, she will." Mirabelle grinned at Kate. "She'll make a fuss to your mother about being banned from Haldon and the town house."

Kate grinned back. "And then she'll appeal to Whit when mother refuses to gainsay you. Oh, I do wish I could hear those conversations."

Mirabelle turned to Lizzy. "Would you be so kind as to see if tea is ready, Lizzy dear? Kate and I will be along shortly."

"Eventually," Kate corrected. A successful bout of eavesdropping took time.

"As you wish, Lady Thurston." Laughing, Lizzy bobbed an exaggerated curtsy and headed for the back staircase.

Kate took Mirabelle's arm and led her toward the front stairs. Her mother was taking tea in the parlor. Miss Willory would not be so foolish as to air her grievances there, but she would take the opportunity to ask for a private audience, and that could take place anywhere.

"Kate?"

"Hmm?"

"Am I *really* mistress of all those places?"

"Of course." She frowned a little, remembering her list. "Well, not the abbey. That I made up."

"I see." Mirabelle swallowed hard. "Good heavens."

Kate's laughter died rather swiftly at the sight of Mr. Laury coming toward them down the hall. Mirabelle's countenance, on the other hand, brightened considerably.

"Mr. Laury, how very nice to see you."

Mr. Laury, whose gaze had been trained on the floor, snapped his head up. By the way his eyes widened and his face paled, Kate half expected him to turn about and flee. But to his credit, his step faltered only a little before he continued his walk toward them. "Good afternoon, Lady Thurston, er, Lady Kate."

Kate returned the greeting and would have ended the encounter at that, but Mirabelle reached out to subtly take her arm and bring her to a stop.

"We're to have tea in a half hour's time or so, Mr. Laury. Won't you join us?"

Mr. Laury started, blushed and stammered. "Kind of you. Most kind, but—"

"Not at all," Mirabelle assured him. "Your company would be welcome. Don't you agree, Kate?"

She had no other choice but to smile and agree. "Yes. Certainly."

"I-I . . ." Mr. Laury shifted his weight on his feet, clasped his hands behind his back, brought them forward again, and then went back to clasping. All the shifting and fidgeting put Kate to mind of a squirrel. Possibly an injured one. "Most kind of you. Most. I've another, I'm afraid. Engagement, that is. Another engagement. Do excuse."

"Oh, but . . ." Mirabelle trailed off as Mr. Laury made a dash down the hall. "How very odd."

"Odder that you should have invited him," Kate commented. "Why ever did you do that?"

"Why shouldn't I?"

"It's to be a ladies' tea."

"I was merely being polite." Mirabelle threw her a glance. "Don't you like Mr. Laury?"

"I hardly know him."

"Which is why I invited him to tea—so that you might better come to know him. He is a very nice man."

Kate watched as Mr. Laury threw a very uncomfortable glance over his shoulder before disappearing around the corner. "He is a very nervous man."

Mirabelle frowned thoughtfully. "A bit reserved in your company, that's all. I'm certain he would overcome his shyness upon better acquaintance."

Kate wondered how anyone could possibly be certain of such a thing, but decided not to ask lest Mirabelle take it as some sort of challenge. The last thing she wanted was both her mother *and* her sister-in-law seeking to regularly throw her into the company of Mr. Laury.

Hunter stood at the side of Pallton House and glowered at the door in front of him.

He wasn't in the habit of glowering at inanimate objects, but he felt the need to glower at something just then, and the damn door was there.

He'd missed Kate while he was in town.

Less than twenty-four hours away from the lady and he missed her.

He was appalled at himself. He didn't miss people. He'd had mistresses of great beauty, considerable wit, and *exceptional* dexterity in the bedchamber. Business had routinely taken him away for weeks at a time, but had he ever missed any of those women? No, he had not.

He'd damn well made sure of it, because missing implied one was significantly attached, and from significant attachment sprang inadvisable emotions like affection and need, and even love. All of which he'd spent his adult life avoiding like the plague.

A mild attachment was acceptable. The sort that had allowed for easy friendships and casual affairs. The sort one could lose, or have snatched away, without feeling as if one's beating heart had been ripped from one's chest.

That last was a trifle melodramatic, perhaps, but damned if it wasn't accurate. He could still feel the echoes of that pain when he remembered. He made a point not to remember.

He made a point not to become significantly attached.

And yet one hour after leaving the house, all he'd been able to think of was returning to Kate. He wanted to see her soft blue eyes, wanted to hear her airy laugh, wanted to see the way candlelight colored streaks of gold into her pale blonde hair.

He'd thought of her when he'd spent the day with Lord Martin as well, but only as a means of distracting himself from visions of ripping out Martin's incessantly flapping tongue. He'd pictured pulling the pins out of Kate's hair to watch the locks settle on her shoulders. He'd pictured running his fingers through the tresses. And he'd imagined taking a handful to pull her in for a kiss. It had been an idle fantasy, mildly erotic in nature, and one over which he'd had complete control.

Unlike today's embarrassingly tame daydreams of laughter, and candlelight and . . . heaven help him, he'd even thought of her nose. *Her nose.* No man daydreamed about a woman's nose. It wasn't natural.

It was just that Kate's nose had the smallest, most adorable dimple at the very tip. Just the faintest line one didn't notice until one was an inch away and, and being an inch away from Kate . . .

"Oh, bloody hell."

It *had* to stop. He would *make* it stop. And there were only two ways of seeing it done. The first, and most expedient, was to simply walk away. Surely, with adequate time and distance he would be able to regain perspective. Probably. He would never know for certain, because he had no intention of leaving. In part because there was still the mission to consider, but mostly because walking away was a retreat, and a retreat, even a strategic one, went against every instinct he had. He wanted to win the game, not give it up. He'd not dragged himself up from the gutters by crying defeat at every obstacle thrown in his path. He'd acquired his place in the world by removing, destroying, or simply ignoring those obstacles.

Which left him with the second, far more appealing, option. He could indulge himself a bit. In all likelihood, his preoccupation with Kate was due in large part to his not having done so. It had been a very long time since he'd denied himself something he wanted. A very long time since he'd had to.

And he'd been craving Kate as if she were a forbidden treat for what seemed like an eternity. So he'd indulge himself. Better yet, he'd *over*indulge. One satisfied an inconvenient craving by tasting. One eliminated it by gorging. He'd take all he wanted of laughter, candlelight, heady kisses, and damn it, even the dimple at the end of her nose. When he'd had his fill, he'd get back to the business of wrapping Kate around his finger.

Looking forward to both endeavors, and feeling considerably more cheerful than he had for most of the day, he pushed through the door and headed toward his room. He was going to wash off the dust of the road. Perhaps he'd have a drink. He didn't need to seek the woman out the very second he returned. He wasn't quite that preoccupied with her.

"Oh, Hunter. You've returned."

As if to prove him a liar and a fool, every nerve ending in his body sprang to attention at the sound of Kate's voice.

Bloody hell, he wasn't just preoccupied. He was obsessed.

Kate had the irrational and nearly irresistible urge to step right up to Hunter and throw her arms about his neck.

She'd missed him terribly.

While working on her music, she'd been able to push thoughts of him, if not completely away, at least far enough to the side that she was able to concentrate on the music. But without the distraction of her composition, she'd gone right back to thinking about him and her strong attachment to him and whether that attachment might be on its way to something more.

Even as she and Mirabelle had gone on their eavesdropping expedition, she'd been thinking of Hunter's dark eyes, and how they were so often guarded. And she'd thought of his deep laugh when she'd asked him what his Christian name was. And she'd thought of the strength in his arms when he'd wrapped them tightly around her in the ballroom.

Remembering now that she hadn't spoken to him since that encounter in the ballroom, she felt her cheeks heat and her heart begin to pound. Her gaze darted to his mouth. She'd thought of that as well—his firm, warm, wickedly seductive mouth. She dragged her eyes away.

"Did . . ." She had to clear her throat. "Did you learn anything of interest in town?"

"Not a thing," he replied, and she was delighted to see his gaze flick to her mouth. "Didn't expect to, really. The townsfolk are loyal to Lord Brentworth, and to his son by extension."

"Oh, well." She twisted her fingers behind her back. "Did you at least enjoy your visit?"

"Have you not been to Iberston?"

"Oh, yes." She laughed lightly and felt herself relax. "There's a tavern, a handful of shops, and very little else. Lord Brentworth is quite fond of it."

Hunter stepped back to lean against the wall. "He has been known to boast of its charms."

"It is rather charming, in its sleepy way. And in comparison to Pallton House, it is a marvel of entertainment. Particularly for the ladies."

"And how did you spend your day here?" he asked, folding his arms across his chest in a relaxed manner.

"Composing, mostly, and then tea with Lizzy and Mirabelle—a rather late tea due to an ugly spot of business with Miss Willory." And a brief and sadly fruitless attempt at eavesdropping. "And after tea, I ran into Lord Brentworth and Lord Martin. Lord Brentworth asked if I would play for the guests after dinner, and Lord Martin invited me to take a walk on the beach."

"Did he?" Hunter asked in a tone that somehow managed to be both casual and cool.

"Yes, and I had an excuse at the ready, you'll be pleased to know. But I never got the chance to use it, because Whit appeared, quite out of nowhere it seemed to me, and convinced Lord Martin to take up cards in the billiards room instead. Poor man looked fairly pained by the idea."

"Lord Martin?"

"Whit," she explained. "Lord Martin was delighted. He's even more easily distracted than I."

"Is that why you lost interest in him? His flightiness?"

"I . . ." The question startled her. Hunter hadn't broached that topic before, and she'd thought—hoped really—that he never would. She wasn't proud of the *tendre* she'd had for Lord Martin, nor happy with the way that *tendre* had ended, nor particularly eager to discuss either. But there was no getting out of answering a direct question.

"That would be rather hypocritical of me, wouldn't it?" she hedged, of the opinion that a direct question didn't necessarily require a direct answer. Hypocritical or not, Lord Martin's flightiness *had* irritated her a little.

"The two of you have different sorts of flightiness."

"There's more than one sort?"

"Aggravating and not aggravating. Yours falls into the second category," he said with smile. "If it wasn't his aggravating sort that cooled your ardor, what was it?"

She shrugged, unwilling to answer.

"Is it because your affection was returned?" he guessed.

She was willing to answer *that.* "I would *never* be so fickle."

She'd been thrilled when Lord Martin began to court her in her first season. She'd been infatuated with him from afar for years, and his immediate interest in her after her come out had felt like a dream come true. He was, she'd been certain, her prince come to life.

"Then what was it?" Hunter prompted.

"I . . ." She opened her mouth, closed it again.

She'd jested to Evie once that her *tendre* for Lord Martin had expired after she'd discovered he kissed like a fish struggling to breathe on land. But that hadn't been true. The one kiss she'd shared with Lord Martin had been rather nice. Not at all like the exhilarating kisses she'd shared with Hunter, but perfectly adequate for her at the time.

Her disillusionment had come the next day when, emboldened by that kiss, she'd shared with him her dream of one day writing a symphony, having it published, and hearing it performed in front of an audience, a *real* audience in a theater, not just a room full of house guests.

He'd laughed at her. Not with intentional cruelty, but with a distinctly patronizing air that told her he found her, and her dream, quite adorably silly.

She'd been crushed.

"Kate?"

Kate gave off twisting her fingers behind her back, for twisting them in her skirts. She wanted to tell Hunter. She did, but the words bottled up, just as they had when she'd wanted to tell him of the music in her head. "Martin . . . Lord Martin didn't care for my . . . for something I want."

"Would you care to try that again?" he asked in a gentle, but faintly amused tone. "With a bit more clarification, this time?"

She took a quick breath and blurted out, "I'm writing a symphony. I want to publish it and hear it played in a theater."

To keep from babbling incoherently as she had the last time she'd blurted out one of her secrets, she snapped her mouth shut, hard, and waited for his reaction. She braced for a laugh, or a sympathetic smile, or a patronizing pat on the head. She feared she'd receive all three. But what she got was a slight lift of his brows and the comment, "A challenging goal, but you've certainly the talent to obtain it. Is it coming along well?"

Acceptance of her dream, confidence in her abilities, and interest in her progress. All at once. If they hadn't been standing in the hall where anyone might come along and see them, she would have thrown her arms around him and kissed him soundly. She contented herself with just beaming at him.

"You mean that. All of it."

"Said it all, didn't I?" He tilted his head at her. "May I assume Lord Martin had a different reaction?"

Her smile faltered, then fell. "He thought it was silly. He laughed."

"The man is a fool."

"Yes, I know." But he'd been the fool she'd fancied a prince, and the disillusionment had been difficult to accept. She pushed the memory of it away. It had been a long time ago, and it no longer mattered to her what Lord Martin thought.

"I'm very near to being finished," she told Hunter, and how wonderful that she *could* tell him. "I've only a little left, a small section I'm working on now."

"It must be exciting, to be so close."

"And frustrating. It's not coming along as well as I'd like. It *will*," she was quick to inform him. No matter how frustrating the missing piece became, she'd not give up on it. "It's simply a trifle irksome at present. And it's a great deal of work for something I may never hear played as I'd like once it's complete."

"I imagine Whit would shoulder the expense of an orchestra for you."

"He would," she agreed. Whit had paid for orchestras to play at their mother's balls in the past. "But it wouldn't be the same, not really. It wouldn't be published. And it would feel as if . . ."

"As if what?" he prompted.

"As if I'd given up. As if I'd been bested."

"I hadn't realized it was a competition."

"It's more a duel of wills," she decided. "London publishers have been reluctant to recognize my other works for some time, and I've become rather persistent in my attempt to change their minds. They're forced to write out their regrets at least once a month."

"One word from Whit, or—"

"No." She shook her head resolutely. "That wouldn't be the same either. I'll succeed on the merit of my work."

He was quiet a moment before speaking. "If you were a man, you would have obtained that success by now."

"And if I were the daughter of a commoner, my requests for publication would likely be ignored entirely."

"It's a balance of injustices then?" he asked with a small laugh and pushed off the wall.

"I'm afraid so." She fell into step beside him as they began a leisurely walk down the hall. "Are you headed to the library? That's where the other gentlemen have gathered."

He shook his head. "I'm for my room. You?"

"I thought perhaps I'd practice the piece I'm to play tonight."

He glanced at her. "Is it necessary for you to practice?"

"In a general sense you mean?" she guessed, then continued when he nodded. "Of course. How could I improve otherwise?"

"I hadn't thought it possible for you to improve."

She felt her cheeks warm. "I thank you for the compliment, but one can always improve. And one should always strive to, in my opinion. I'd hate to think I was no more skilled today than I was five years ago. I'd hate to think I was the same *person* I was five years ago." She thought about that. "How disheartening it would be to know the person I am now is exactly the same as the person I was then, and exactly the same person I'll be twenty years from now."

"You want to be someone else?" Hunter asked.

"No, I just want to be better. I certainly want to be acknowledged as a skilled composer." She glanced at him. "Do you wish to be the same as you are now, twenty years hence?"

"No. I should like to be richer."

She laughed at that. "Is it *possible* for you to be richer?"

"I plan on spending the next twenty years finding out."

"And I suspect fifty years from now, you'll be willing to give up all your riches to be twenty years younger. So, who you are, and not just what you have, will have changed. In the end, it's only who we are that matters, isn't it?" They stopped outside the music room. "That's why I practice at the piano and, whenever possible, at being the person I want to be in twenty years."

There was a slight pause before he spoke. "Absolutely fascinating."

"Beg your pardon?"

"Nothing," he chuckled. "Enjoy your time in the music room."

Hunter walked away as Kate pushed through the door of the music room, but he didn't go far—just a few feet down the hall before he stopped, leaned against the wall, and listened as she began to play. As she began to *practice*, he corrected.

He folded his arms over his chest and scowled absently at the floor. Did he practice at anything? Was he a better man than he'd been five years ago? Certainly, in the eyes of the law he was *much* improved from the man he'd been seven years ago, but the law had never been the ruler by which he'd measured himself.

The accumulation of wealth was, and always had been, how he determined improvement. He was wealthier now than he had been five years ago, and he fully intended to be wealthier yet five years hence. It stood to reason then, that he *had* improved, and would continue to do so.

Fifty years from now, you'll be willing to give up all your riches to be twenty years younger.

He thought about that and came to the conclusion that it was absolute nonsense. If he gave up all his riches, he might very well starve to death within a fortnight. What bloody difference would it make if he was twenty years younger at the time? It was better to die old and rich than young and poor, wasn't it? In his estimation, it was also better to die young and rich than old and poor.

It was, he decided and pushed off from the wall, just all around better to practice at being rich.

Mirabelle accepted a biscuit from the dowager Lady Thurston. Having already partaken of tea and biscuits with Kate and Lizzy, Mirabelle couldn't claim hunger. She *could* have claimed an inability to refuse anything sweet, but she found it more appealing to simply claim manners. She was sitting in Lady Thurston's chambers, after all. It was only polite to accept what was offered.

She bit into the treat, and considered how best to bring their conversation around to a problem she'd been mulling over since before tea. She'd come with the excuse of wishing to discuss whatever had been said between Miss Willory and Lady Thurston—Kate and Mirabelle hadn't been able to make out but every third word—but Lady Thurston's response to that had been more or less what Mirabelle had expected. Miss Willory's plea to the dowager countess to overturn Mirabelle's decision had been denied. There was nothing else that needed to be said on the matter. In truth, what interested Mirabelle most at the moment was the subject of matchmaking. She swallowed her food and decided that a direct approach would suit best.

"I think perhaps we have been mistaken in regards to Mr. Laury."

Lady Thurston set down her plate of biscuits without taking one for herself. "What has led you to that conclusion?"

"I invited him to tea today." Mirabelle grimaced. "The offer produced some sort of nervous fit. I rather feared he might swallow his tongue."

"Yes. It was the same on our walk about the grounds. He is ill at ease in Kate's company." Lady Thurston pressed her lips together in annoyance. "I had not expected that."

"It is *most* odd. I don't recall him behaving oddly in the past."

"Nor I. Quite the opposite, in fact. I have always found him to be a charming young man."

Mirabelle blew out a short breath. "What do you suggest?"

"I suggest we not give up our efforts prematurely."

Mrs. Summers's voice sounded from the connecting door to Lady Thurston's room. "It would not be premature to cease in an effort you should never have begun. Mr. Laury is clearly not the gentleman for Kate."

"I should think I would be the best judge of that," Lady Thurston replied with a sniff.

Mrs. Summers crossed the room to take a seat. "I should think Kate the best judge of all, and she appears to prefer Mr. Hunter's company."

"Kate is simply as yet unaware of Mr. Laury's attributes," Lady Thurston insisted.

Mrs. Summers carefully selected a biscuit for herself. "And those attributes would be?"

"He *is* handsome," Mirabelle ventured. "In a soft, romantic sort of way. Rather like a poet. And he has a great fondness for all things musical."

"He has a quick mind, a kind heart, and a gentle disposition," Lady Thurston added.

Mrs. Summers raised her brows at that last in mild amusement. "You make him sound like a horse."

"One with an unfortunate propensity for shying, I'm afraid," Mirabelle admitted with a wince.

Lady Thurston waved that away. "He needs a firm hand, is all."

Mirabelle glanced at Mrs. Summers, who gave a barely perceptible shrug of her shoulders. "You shall do as you please, of course."

Hoping to avoid an argument between the two friends, Mirabelle changed the subject before Lady Thurston could comment. "You look well rested, Mrs. Summers. Much improved from yesterday."

"Thank you, dear. I feel much improved." A slight blush formed on Mrs. Summers's cheeks. "I received a letter from Mr. Fletcher not an hour ago."

Lady Thurston exchanged surprised glances with Mirabelle. "So soon?"

The blush grew. "It was delivered by special courier."

Mirabelle scooted forward in her chair. "And the contents of the letter?"

"Mr. Fletcher has expressed a desire to . . . to set things right between us."

"That sounds very promising." Mirabelle finished her biscuit and tried not to look at the full plate next to Lady Thurston. "Are you going to tell us what went wrong between you to start?"

"It was . . . it was his position with the War Department."

"I see," Mirabelle murmured, though she didn't really.

"I see," Lady Thurston echoed. And clearly, she did. "Your first husband?"

Mrs. Summers nodded and turned to Mirabelle. "He was an agent as well. He was in France, at court when the Terror began. An effort was made to retrieve him after the king fell, but it failed. He was lost to the guillotine."

"I'm very sorry," Mirabelle murmured.

"It would not have happened, had he been at home in England where he belonged." Mrs. Summers brushed her skirts with hands that were less than steady. "I will not have another husband in the War Department."

"That is understandable," Mirabelle ventured and made a pointed effort to keep her expression free of worry and doubt. According to Whit, William Fletcher had worked for the War Department since he'd been a boy. Would a man give up a life he loved to live his life with the woman he loved? Could he be happy with such a choice? For Mrs. Summers's sake, Mirabelle dearly hoped so.

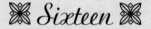

Sixteen

On the first few occasions Kate had played the piano in front of guests, she had been exceedingly nervous. It mattered a great deal to her what others thought and said about her music and, at the time, she'd been quite terrified someone would think and say it was dreadful. After a half dozen performances, however, she had come to the conclusion that it simply wasn't possible to please everyone. There would always be someone who said it was too complicated or too simple, too experimental or too common. The defining moment had been when one silly young man had declared it tolerable, but rather too high in pitch. She'd not ceased caring what others thought after that, but she ceased being terrified of a single person's opinion.

Perfectly aware that at least one person wouldn't care for what she'd chosen to play that night, Kate made her way to the piano in the music room as guests took their seats. She would have preferred a more casual atmosphere, with only a few chairs set out for the elderly guests, but Lord Brentworth obviously had something else in mind. He'd had the staff line up neat rows of seating in the room while the guests had been at dinner. Kate sincerely hoped that didn't mean he expected her to play for an extended period of time. She'd thought to play a song or two, not give an entire concert.

As the voices and movements of the guests settled, she took a seat on the bench. She frowned absently when it rocked a little beneath her. Odd, she didn't remember the bench being wobbly earlier in the day. Mentally shrugging the thought aside, she pushed back the lace cuffs of her pale gold gown, flexed her fingers once, laid them softly on the keys, and began to play.

She'd chosen a playful and energetic piece, one that rapidly dipped from high to low and back again. She rocked on the bench, stretching a bit to reach the keys, ignoring the twinge of pain it caused her injured shoulder, and enjoying the feel and sound of the notes as they swirled about the room.

And then the unthinkable happened. There was a loud crack. Her fingers slipped from the keys. The bench lurched back and sharply to the right, then collapsed with a bang.

Kate was no stranger to embarrassment, but bumping into furniture in the hall or spilling a spot of lemonade on her skirts or even coming across a guest when she was covered in mud was nothing compared to having a bench break under her weight while an entire roomful of guests had their eyes trained upon her. That sort of accident wasn't embarrassing. It was *mortifying*.

For what felt like an eternity—but was likely no more than a second or two—she could do nothing more than sit where she'd fallen, mouth open, hip aching, and mind reeling.

That couldn't have happened. That couldn't *possibly* have happened.

The sudden explosion of voices told her that yes, indeed, it had happened.

Her mother, Whit, and Mr. Hunter were the first to reach her.

"Kate, Kate, are you injured?" her mother murmured as she knelt down beside her. Later, Kate would marvel a little over the image of her extremely dignified mother kneeling on the floor, but for now all she could manage was a mute shake of her head.

Lady Thurston rubbed her arm and leaned forward to whisper encouragingly. "You'll want to get up then, dear."

"I . . . oh. Yes, yes of course." She took her mother's hand, and with the help of Mr. Hunter's supporting grasp under her arm, managed to gain and retain her feet without becoming entangled in the rubble of the bench. And it *was* rubble. One of the legs had broken off to go skittering across the floor, two others had snapped off at their joints, and the last remained loosely connected to the seat—the notably cracked seat—holding up one corner at a sickly angle.

"This wasn't me," she whispered to her mother before turning to Mirabelle and Mrs. Summers as they joined her. "This wasn't my fault."

"Clearly not." Her mother patted her arm again.

"It couldn't have been," Mirabelle agreed, exchanging a nod of agreement with Mrs. Summers.

Hunter bent to catch her eye. "Certain you're not harmed?"

"Yes, yes, I'm . . ." Mortified beyond words. "I'm fine."

"Lady Kate Cole," Lord Brentworth pushed through a small group of guests to stand before her, his wide gray eyes filled with concern. "My most sincere apologies. I had no notion the bench was defective. No one in the house plays, you see, and . . . and I am deeply sorry for—"

Kate shook head. "It's all right, Lord Brentworth."

"I humbly disagree. I should not have insisted—"

Miss Willory stepped forward to cut him off. "Please don't

trouble yourself too much, Lord Brentworth. Our dear Lady Kate *is* rather accident prone, after all."

"I had nothing to do with breaking that bench."

"*Of course* you didn't," Miss Willory cooed.

"Indeed, she did not," Lord Brentworth added, looking at Miss Willory askance. "The lady did nothing more than sit on it."

"Well, yes, but—"

"She can't weigh more than nine stone," someone interjected.

Oh, for pity's sake, Kate groaned silently. Were they going to begin a discussion of her weight? Hadn't she suffered enough?

"She does move around quite a bit when she plays," Miss Willory pointed out, clearly annoyed to have been gainsaid.

"Many a gifted musician do," Lord Brentworth argued. Had Kate not been so miserable, she would have beamed at him. Lord Brentworth was a lovely man, she decided, and he threw delightful parties . . . defective benches notwithstanding.

"Have you had the opportunity to see Herr Beethoven perform, my lord?" someone asked. "He's a sight more active in his performance than Lady Kate."

"I saw him play in Vienna," someone else offered. "Man weighs twelve stone, at least. Bench didn't so much as utter a creak, as far as I could tell."

"For pity's—"

"The legs were loose."

Every head in the room swiveled around at the sound of Hunter's voice. Crouched down with Whit next to the remnants of the bench, he held up one corner of the broken seat. "The nails worked free."

Lord Brentworth stepped forward to inspect the seat. "And so they did. Defective, just as I said."

To Kate's immense relief, the discussion in the room soon turned to craftsmen and how there was no longer a decent one to be found in the whole of England. She took the opportunity to whisper in her mother's ear. "Do you think you could encourage the other guests to return to the parlor?"

Her mother nodded and patted her arm one more time. "If you promise to come along after a time. You cannot hide away for the rest of the night, dear. You will only feel the worse for it."

"Yes, I know," Kate admitted reluctantly. "I'll be along shortly."

With the help of Lord Brentworth, Lady Thurston herded the guests out of the music room.

When the last had left, Kate rubbed both hands over her face and likely would have rubbed at her aching hip as well if Hunter's voice hadn't distracted her.

"Why don't you sit down, Kate?"

She spun around to find him standing in the doorway. "I'm quite through with sitting for now. I thought you'd left with the others."

He shook his head and crossed the room to stand before her. "I hung back, then slipped away." He reached up to lightly cup her face. "All right? Your shoulder?"

"Yes, yes, I'm fine." She closed her eyes and grimaced. "It was just terribly embarrassing, that's all."

"It was meant to be."

Her eyes flew back open. "What do you mean?"

His hand dropped away. "It wasn't an accident, Kate."

"Certainly it was," she argued, growing a little alarmed. "You said the legs were loose."

"There are hammer marks on the inside of the legs. Someone pounded them loose."

"But . . . why would anyone want to break Lord Brentworth's bench?"

"At best guess," he said in a gruff tone, "because they knew you were going to sit on it."

"I . . ." She stepped back to find a chair. She wasn't through with sitting after all. "Who would do such a thing?"

"Someone who wished to harm you, frighten you, or embarrass you." He pulled a chair in front of hers and leaned forward to rest his elbows on his knees. "Someone who would enjoy seeing you stripped of your status of most desirable young lady in the house."

Later, she would take great pleasure in being called the most desirable lady in the house, but at the moment, she couldn't get past the notion someone had humiliated her on purpose. "I can't envision anyone in residence going to such lengths to injure me. Not even those with whom I share little or no affection. Perhaps it was meant for someone else."

"Who?"

"I've no idea, but I'm not the only lady in residence who plays the piano. Maybe some of the younger gentlemen thought it would make a fine jest in general and hadn't a particular victim in mind. Young gentlemen are often forgiven for these sorts of antics. "

"It is possible," he conceded.

"I suppose the odds of someone coming forward with a confession are slim." She blew out a short breath. "Did Whit see the hammer marks?"

Hunter shook his head. "He was inspecting the seat, not the legs."

"Would it be too much to ask that you not mention the hammer marks to him? He has a tendency to . . . to . . ."

"Become overprotective?" he filled in.

"Words cannot describe."

He frowned a little, then shrugged as he sat up. "I see no reason he needs to know of it at present."

"'At present' leaves the option of telling him later."

"Does it, indeed?" he asked, his brows winging up in mock surprise.

She rolled her eyes. "Will you at least promise not to tell him without giving me warning first?"

"That I'll do."

"Thank you." She studied him for a moment. "You're not as protective as he. Just as high-handed, but not as protective."

"I'm not your brother."

"No." He certainly wasn't, and what she wanted from Hunter wasn't remotely sisterly. She wanted to nudge her chair closer until their knees touched and take his hand and . . . No, no that wasn't quite right. A brush of the knees and the feel of her hand in his wasn't nearly enough. What she *really* wanted was to crawl into his arms, lay her head on his shoulder and pretend the last half hour had been nothing more than a very bad dream. Once that was accomplished, she wanted to lift her face and brush her mouth against his. She wanted to kiss him until the excitement built as it had in the ballroom. Perhaps she could convince him to let her remove his cravat. She dearly wanted to know what the skin hidden behind—

"Not here, Kate."

She only half heard Hunter speak. She did, however, fully notice the movement of his lips. "Sorry?" she mumbled and watched a wicked smile spread across his mouth.

"Now isn't the time for what you're thinking."

That comment succeeded in pulling her from her daydream. She dragged her gaze up and found him watching her, a knowing glint in his eye.

Oh, dear, he'd known exactly what she'd been daydreaming of. She opened her mouth, intent on pretending ignorance, but changed her mind at the last second. They'd both know she was lying.

"I beg your pardon," she said softly instead, and felt the warmth of a blush touch her cheeks.

"Granting pardon would only make me a hypocrite."

"Oh." Certain she was blushing furiously now, she shifted a bit in her seat. "I see."

"Another time," he reiterated a little gruffly. "I believe we were discussing your brother."

"Right." She cleared her throat, shoved images of kissing Hunter as far away as possible—which, in truth wasn't all that far—and tried to remember the point she'd been trying to make. Something about how protective Whit was. "Right. You're not as protective as he. Well, you are, but not in the same manner. You . . ."

She wanted to say she felt as if he had more faith in her and what she was capable of, but that seemed both silly and rather unkind toward Whit. She knew Whit had faith in her, but unlike Hunter, he would never ask her to assist in the investigation of a smuggling ring, or speak with her of rakes or matters of business, and if it had been he who had discovered the hammer marks on the bench legs, he likely would have kept that information from her and sought out the culprit himself.

"Whit wants to wrap me in cotton batting," she continued. "He means well, and I don't fault him for it, except when he becomes unreasonably overbearing," she amended. "But it is nice to be treated as if I won't shatter under a little strain."

"I would tell you I'm happy to oblige, but I'm not. I don't particularly care to see you under strain."

"It's only a broken bench," she reminded him. She leaned a bit to eye the remnants sitting behind him. "Poor Lord Brentworth. First the vase, now this. At this rate, Pallton House will be in ruins by the time I leave. I'll never receive another invitation."

"He doesn't blame you for this."

"He must for the vase. Unless you—?"

"I distinctly recall ordering you not to ask."

"So you did," she agreed with a small smile. She took a deep breath and gained her feet. "I need to return to the parlor. I promised Mother I'd not hide away too long."

He offered his arm as if to lead her there, but she shook her head. "Better if we didn't arrive together. We've both been away from the group for some time. People will whisper."

Kate wondered as she left if there would soon come a time when they would no longer have to concern themselves over whispers. They were, after all, engaged in a sort of courtship . . . weren't they? He sought her out, brought her presents—*a* present, anyway—and stole kisses when no one was looking. That certainly indicated that it was a courtship. An unconventional one, certainly, but a courtship nonetheless.

Strange that she hadn't considered what they'd been doing in those terms before. A fortnight ago, she would have thought it stranger yet that she should be delighted to suddenly find herself courted by Mr. Andrew Hunter. Then again, a fortnight ago she hadn't known he was called Andrew Hunter.

"Andrew," she mouthed silently and shook her head. It really didn't fit him as well as Hunter. However, if a woman had a *possible* interest in one day becoming Mrs. Hunter, it might serve her well to learn to appreciate the name—

She tripped a little on the front hall rug and decided that a woman who had just picked herself off the floor in front of a room full of guests might also be well served by paying more attention to what she was about. The last thing she needed was to make another spectacle of herself.

Slipping a hand into her pocket, she felt the cool and reassuring weight of her new watch. She blew out a short breath, squared her shoulders, and headed into the parlor with the steady rhythm of the watch ticking against her fingertips.

* * *

Hunter turned the page of a book he had absolutely no interest in nor any intention of reading. He hadn't even intended to go into the library. After Kate's departure from the music room, he'd headed for his bedchamber thinking to have a drink while he waited for the appropriate time to return to the parlor. He'd made it halfway before he'd heard a door open quietly behind him, followed by soft steps trailing him down the hall. It hadn't been necessary for him to turn around to know it was Miss Willory. The girl had been watching him with a crafty gleam in her eye all night.

She'd been eyeing him craftily, obviously, or otherwise since she'd arrived at the house, but the gleam had never been as pronounced as it had become in the last few hours. He'd detected nerves and anticipation as well. And the premature glimmer of predicted victory.

He meant to douse that glimmer before the night was over. With that purpose in mind, he'd turned his steps away from his room and gone right to the library. He'd pushed through the doors, selected a book at random, took a comfortable seat by the fireplace, and waited for the show to begin.

He didn't have to wait long.

Miss Willory entered the library and closed the door behind her. She walked halfway into the room, then affected a startled little gasp and blush. "Oh, Mr. Hunter, I didn't see you sitting there."

"Didn't you?"

"No, I thought you'd retired for the night."

"And I thought you were still in the parlor." A lie for a lie, he thought.

Miss Willory gave a delicate shrug and moved farther into the room. "The conversation quickly grew tiresome. So much bother over one silly little bench and a clumsy . . . Well, at any rate, I thought a bit of light reading would be more enjoyable. We're of a mind, it would seem."

He ignored her last comment and waved a distracted hand at the shelves of books behind her. "I'm sure you'll find something."

She made a show of perusing the shelves for a few moments while he made a show of reading his book.

Under other circumstances, he might have found her pursuit of him amusing. It hadn't been a year since she'd last looked at him as Mrs. Keenes and Mrs. Lubeck had on the veranda—with lips pinched tight in disapproval. What a remarkable change a reversal of fortune could effect in a woman. Within weeks of her father losing a staggering amount of money in a poor business venture, Miss Willory had become all blushes and smiles in his presence.

Hunter couldn't blame her for it, despite her previous snubs. He understood desperation and the single-minded drive to create a secure place in the world for oneself and those one felt responsible for. He might have even dredged up some sympathy for Miss Willory now, in her bid to save her family from outright ruin. Might have, had he not suspected Miss Willory of having something to do with the broken piano bench.

"What is it you are reading, Mr. Hunter?" Miss Willory gave up her search for light reading to step forward and stand in front of him.

He didn't bother looking at her. "Too soon, Miss Willory."

"I beg your pardon?"

He nodded his head in the direction of a clock on the mantel. "You're making your move too soon. Your friends won't be arriving for a few moments more, at least. Given your vanity, I imagine you told them not to dally too long, but you have to give them some time to escape the parlor and find us. We could be in the billiards room, for all they know."

"I'm sure I have no idea what you mean."

"Don't you?" He shrugged and turned the page. "Suit yourself then. Far be it from me to dissuade a pretty woman from climbing into my lap at the time of her choosing."

"Climb into your . . . ?"

"No doubt you'd prefer to play the victim, but with me sitting in this chair, your options are limited. Unless you intend to drag me to the floor." He considered that. "Far be it from me to dissuade you of that notion as well."

"I . . . You . . ."

"Imagine your father will hold me responsible either way. But that *is* what dueling pistols are for." His mouth turned down at the corners, just for a moment. "Pity, rather liked him."

"Dueling pistols?" she fairly squeaked.

"Unless he prefers sabers?" he inquired, finally giving her his attention.

She gulped, her eyes darting to the clock, then the closed door.

"Having second thoughts, Miss Willory? Or perhaps you think the closed door will be sufficient to ruin you. Or perhaps you thought it would be a mere compromising." He gave her a long, cold, hard look. When he spoke, his voice was soft, but just as cold. "*Perhaps* you were laboring under the impression that I am a gentleman."

A woman could trap a gentleman into marriage with very little trouble. She needed only to close the right door or plan a kiss at the right time, and suddenly she had the gentleman neatly bound up, boxed in, and otherwise defeated by his own sense of honor. Bit like carrying your own rope to the gallows, in Hunter's opinion.

It was a sight more difficult to hang a man without that rope.

Too difficult for Miss Willory, it seemed. She glanced at the door one more time, then sniffed haughtily. "I've no idea how much you imbibed tonight, Mr. Hunter, but I suggest you severely limit the quantity in the future."

He went back to looking at his book. "I shall take that under advisement."

"Given that you are clearly deep in your cups, I shall endeavor to forget this unfortunate conversation by morning."

"I'd estimate two minutes left."

She spun for the door. "Good night, Mr. Hunter."

"Miss Willory."

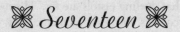

❈ *Seventeen* ❈

*A*s the bright light of the late morning sun streamed through the windows, Kate glanced at the parlor entrance for the tenth time in the past half hour. Ten, she assured herself, was a perfectly acceptable number of glances. At least insofar as it was unlikely to draw the notice of the other guests in the room. Guests who did not include Hunter, which was why she continued to glance at the door.

She'd not had the opportunity to speak with him privately again the night before, and he'd been missing from breakfast. Gone in to Iberston at sunrise, Whit had informed her. Determined not to obsess over his absence, she'd retired to her room to compose. Three hours later she'd emerged and headed to the music room to test the first quarter of a new sonatina.

She'd assumed she would have to stand while she played, but to her amazement and delight, there was a brand new piano bench sitting in front of the instrument. After questioning a maid and discovering Hunter was responsible for its purchase, she'd gone straight to the parlor where she had been awaiting his arrival ever since. Surely the man didn't plan on spending all day in his room.

"Would you care for a game of chess, Lady Kate?"

Kate glanced up from her sheets of music at Lord Brentworth's query. He'd been very solicitous toward her last night in the parlor and again that morning at breakfast, and now he'd elected to keep the gentlemen at the house rather than take them out for the day. He was clearly attempting to make amends for the unfortunate piano bench incident, and she hadn't the heart to tell him she wasn't especially interested in a game of chess at the moment, nor that she would have considered it a personal favor if he *had* taken the gentlemen out for the day. Particularly Lord Martin and Mr. Laury, both of whom were eyeing her from across the room. The first with more interest than appropriate given that he was currently engaged in a conversation with Miss Willory.

"A game of chess would be lovely," she replied politely.

"Excellent, my son was just expressing his desire to play." Lord Brentworth turned and gestured for Lord Martin. "Martin, Martin, my boy, come have a game of chess with Lady Kate."

Taken completely off guard, Kate wracked her brain for a way to excuse herself from the game. "Oh, er . . ." She looked about the room as if someone or something in it might offer inspiration, but nothing and no one did.

Oh, blast. She'd have to play. There was no possible way of getting out of it without insulting Lord Brentworth or Lord Martin or both.

She managed what she hoped passed for a smile but feared was really more of a grimace as father and son set the game up before her. She detested playing chess with Lord Martin. The man was a dreadful opponent. He tried to put himself in check at least once per game and seemed to be under the impression that being bested by a woman in under ten moves was quite acceptable if those ten moves were dragged out over the course of several hours. She'd never met anyone who took such an excessive amount of time at his turn.

She'd rather hoped the embarrassing spectacle in the music room would lessen his interest a little. But honestly, if the man wasn't to be dissuaded after more than three years of clear disinterest and two rejected offers, a broken piano bench wasn't going to see the job done.

"This is nice, isn't it?" Lord Martin remarked, taking his seat.

"Hmm," was the best she could manage.

"We've not spent much time together these last few days."

"I suppose we haven't." That had been *exceedingly* nice.

"You've been preoccupied."

She barely refrained from raising a brow at his peevish tone. He was jealous. *Very* jealous if the pouty set of his lips was any indication. She considered that as she moved a pawn forward to start the game. People were often rash and foolhardy while under the influence of jealousy. Lord Martin, already prone to silliness, was no doubt particularly susceptible to that pitfall.

She shouldn't, she told herself. She really shouldn't.

Oh, but it was such an ideal opportunity. And she wouldn't be breaking a promise to Hunter, not really. She *had* tried to keep her distance from Lord Martin, and she wasn't looking to charm information from the man. She was looking to goad him, which was entirely different. Under the current circumstances, it was also entirely irresistible.

"I *have* been rather anxious," she said with a small sigh. "My brother's birthday is only weeks away, and I've yet to find a suitable present." It wasn't an outright lie. Whit's birthday *was* fast approaching, and she hadn't yet settled on a gift for him. The fact that she wasn't at all anxious about the matter was a minor detail.

Lord Martin's lips relaxed into a pleasant smile. "Ah, well, I'm sure you'll think of something." He turned his attention to the chessboard. "Ask your mother to purchase a gift for him."

She wanted to ask him how that would make it a gift from

her, but knew that would not lead the conversation in the direction she sought. "I suppose I could, only I'd rather hoped to come up with something myself. A new cravat pin, do you think?"

"I'm sure that would be adequate. I just purchased—"

"Oh, adequate won't do. Not for Whit. It must be something special. What of new handkerchiefs? I could embroider them." She shook her head and continued before he could comment. "No, I gave him those two years ago. A fine brandy? Oh, he would adore that. Pity one can't find some sensibly priced . . ." She trailed off, as if embarrassed to have mentioned the subject of money. She began to fiddle with one of her pawns. "Never mind. Maybe I should ask Mr. Hunter to help me choose a new epee, instead."

Lord Martin's head snapped up. "I can help you."

"Hmm?" She looked up from her pawn and gave him a distracted and decidedly patronizing smile. "Oh, yes, of course. You're always so helpful, Lord Martin, thank you. Do you suppose Mr. Hunter knows anything about fencing? A new epee is not so ideal as a fine brandy, but he can't very well get me that. It will have to be the epee. After dinner, I'll—"

"*I* could get you the brandy."

She went back to fiddling with her pawn. "That's very nice of you."

He straightened his padded shoulders. "I could. Reasonably priced."

She reached over to pat his hand. "Certainly you could."

"Tomorrow morning. I'll have it then."

"I . . ." She drew her hand away, opened her eyes wide and blinked repeatedly. "You're quite serious, aren't you?"

"I am."

"Well, good heavens." She let her surprised expression grow into a delighted smile. "How wonderful. Oh, how fortunate for me. Lord Martin, this is *most* generous of you."

"It's nothing. Nothing at all." He waved off her compliment with false modestly. "You'll . . . you'll not ask Mr. Hunter to choose an epee for you?"

"I'll have no need now, will I?" In truth, she never had. She'd chosen one herself for Whit last year. Just because she had more sense than to try to use one didn't mean she was completely ignorant of them. Logic such as that would no doubt be lost on Lord Martin. "I can scarce wait to see Whit's reaction," she told him instead. "Won't he be surprised?"

"You mustn't tell him where you got it," Lord Martin said sternly. "You mustn't say a word of this to anyone."

"Of course not."

"Good." He nodded once and leaned over the board a little. "It's not my secret to tell, you see."

She didn't need to affect her shock this time, it was entirely genuine. "It isn't?"

He shook his head and changed the subject. "Tomorrow morning, meet me at the bench behind the half wall. Do you know the one?"

She nodded, still feeling a trifle bewildered by his secret comment. "Yes, I know it."

"Excellent. Shall we say five?"

"Five? In the morning?"

He nodded again. "That should give me just enough time. I'll bring a barrel of brandy, you bring—"

"A barrel? How are you going to bring an entire barrel of brandy?" And what on earth did he expect her to do with it once he had? Hide it in a reticule?

"Oh, right." A line worked into his brow.

Good heavens, the man was such a twit sometimes. She would have found it impossible to believe he was involved in a smuggling operation if he hadn't, in that very moment, been offering her smuggled goods.

"Right." Lord Martin continued. "Just bring the money, then. I'll—"

He broke off at the sound of Hunter's voice. "Good morning, Lady Kate, Lord Martin."

Kate turned away from Lord Martin as Hunter came to stand before them. She'd been so engaged in her small act of espionage, she'd not noticed his entrance. He didn't appear angry at discovering her in the midst of a chess game with Lord Martin. How lovely he'd not presumed she had orchestrated the game. Pity his good humor with her was sure to be short lived.

His eyes dipped down to the board, and Kate's lone pawn moved out of its starting position. "My apologies for interrupting what I'm sure is an engrossing match, but Lady Thurston would like a word with you, Lady Kate."

She searched for a way to indicate that she needed just a few more minutes—a wink or nod or gesture. Surely there was something. To her dismay, the best she could come up with was the question,

"Which one?"

He blinked once. "Which one?"

"Yes, which Lady Thurston? Mirabelle or my mother?" She happened to know that both Lady Thurstons were currently to be found in the dowager Lady Thurston's chambers with Mrs. Summers, but she'd bet a week's allowance neither of the gentlemen before her were aware of it.

"Both," Hunter replied, a coolness creeping into his tone. "They're in the dowager Lady Thurston's chambers."

"Oh." It was fortunate she wasn't given to making wagers. "Right. Er . . ."

"They're waiting, Lady Kate."

"Yes . . . yes, of course." She rose from her chair. "Do excuse me, Lord Martin."

Hunter ushered her out across the foyer, past the front staircase and down the hall—all in silence.

Kate bit her lip and glanced up at him. "Am I to assume neither Lady Thurston wishes to speak with me?"

When his only response was a cold look, she decided to choose discretion over valor and keep her mouth closed for the remainder of their walk down the hall. He brought her to the small private sitting room and led her inside. He closed the door, turned around slowly, and then stood there, staring at her—*looming* over her—for several painfully long moments. When he spoke, finally, his voice held both displeasure and a world of disbelief.

"*Which one?*"

"I . . ." Oh, dear. She cleared her throat. "I'd rather hoped for more time with Lord Martin."

"More time," he repeated.

"Yes." She took a deep breath and decided to get the conversation over and done with. Perhaps she'd be very lucky and he'd be pleased, even impressed with her resourcefulness. "Lord Martin has agreed to sell to me a barrel of brandy for an unspecified amount of money tomorrow morning. I'm to meet him at the bench behind the half wall at five."

By the muscle working in his jaw, it was fairly clear that he was neither pleased nor impressed by her resourcefulness.

"I'd have known the amount of money," she was quick to add in a rather frantic bid to delay his response. "But I hadn't the chance to ask. I hadn't a chance to convince him to meet me at a time and place less impractical either. He picked the details of our rendezvous with the notion he'd be hauling along an entire barrel of brandy. Are we quite certain he's in charge of this operation? Because—"

"Enough."

Hunter drew a deep breath through his nose and made an attempt to relax the tight knot of muscles between his shoulders and calm the sick rolling in his gut. He wasn't going to lose his temper. He was not going to begin issuing unreasonable orders just because Kate had *once again* put herself in danger. This time by questioning a known smuggler, whom she'd once had a *tendre* for, and who *still* had a *tendre* for her, and who now expected to meet her at dawn so that they might exchange money for illegal goods and—

"What the bloody hell were you thinking!"

Very well, he was going to lose his temper.

She shifted her weight and gave him a hopeful smile. "That the information might be of use?"

It was, but that wasn't the point. "I ordered you to avoid Lord Martin."

"And so I have, at every opportunity," she countered. "There was simply no way for me to do so in the parlor. Not without giving him the cut direct in front of a room full of people, and I thought it best to avoid that sort of attention. The rumors that would have resulted—"

"I also ordered you not to try your hand at charming information from him."

"Strictly speaking, you said it was too much involvement. You never explicitly forbade it."

The knot in his back grew tighter. "That is—"

"Also, what I did wasn't so much charm as goad." She shifted again. "Strictly speaking."

He bent his head to catch and hold her gaze. "I am ordering you, explicitly forbidding you, from doing anything, speaking to anyone, or going anywhere that has to do with the smuggling operation unless you do so under a direct order from me. Do I make myself clear?"

That, he assured himself, was a perfectly reasonable order.

Apparently, Kate did not agree. "You're being unreasonable."

"I'm not."

"You are."

"I'm . . ." He wasn't going to let the argument disintegrate into a childish string of accusations and denials. But bloody hell, if she had made herself a target . . .

"I am not. *And*," he was quick to interject, "if we continue on in this vein, we'll never get around to deciding what's to be done with the information Lord Martin gave you."

She pressed her lips together as if to physically restrain her tongue. Her eyes narrowed. She took a deep breath through her nose. And then, apparently, she caved.

"You are."

He wanted to laugh. Despite the anger and fear, and the considerable amount of energy it took to keep both under control, he wanted to laugh at that one monstrously stubborn comment.

"You are the single most bullheaded individual I have ever met," he informed her and watched her lips twitch. "Are you quite through?"

"That depends."

"On?"

"On whether you made that order simply because you're angry I managed to obtain in five minutes what you and Whit could not in days."

That hadn't occurred to him. Though now that she mentioned it, it was a trifle embarrassing. And he could certainly understand why she'd wonder. He could also see her bringing it up in an effort to shift the focus of blame from her to him. At a guess, he would say it was a little of both.

Taking her hand, he drew her to a chair, and then picked up another to set it close enough for their knees to almost, but not quite touch. He wanted to be near her, but not so near as to be distracted from his purpose.

"My purpose in issuing orders is not to spite or punish you, Kate," he told her as he took his seat. "My primary mission, you'll recall, is to keep you safe. My methods may be different, but I am no less determined than Whit to keep you from harm."

"Is . . . is that all this is to you? A mission?"

He couldn't help himself, he reached out to brush the

backs of his knuckles along the soft skin of her cheek. "You know better."

She gave a small nod, and he let his hand fall away.

Her hands plucked at a ribbon on her peach skirts. "It's only that . . . you've asked nothing of me in this investigation but to watch the staff."

"I'd have asked you to search the house as well," he reminded her.

"You'd have asked me to re-search the house," she corrected. "It's not quite the same."

"It's only been a matter of days."

"I know." She sat back in her chair with a small huff. "I hadn't intended on goading information from Lord Martin. But he was *there*. Right there and it was so easy. And to have to endure his company and *not* have him speak of the one thing that interests me about him was more than I could—"

"I know." He remembered well the long hours in town with Lord Martin.

"He's not at all suspicious, I assure you."

"You can't know that."

"I can," she retorted, frustration creeping into her voice. "I've known him longer than you. He's really not at all clever."

"I'm inclined to agree." He blew out a long breath. "An entire barrel of brandy at five in the morning?"

She nodded. "Oh, and he said something else. He said . . ." She scrunched her face up a little in thought. "That I couldn't breathe a word to anyone because it wasn't his secret to tell." She relaxed her features again. "That's odd, isn't it?"

"Very."

"What are we to do next?

He gave her a hard look. "I meant what I said, Kate. You do nothing else in this investigation unless I specifically—"

"May I at least offer suggestions?" she cut in with a roll of her eyes.

"I would welcome them."

"Then I suggest you and Whit investigate Smuggler's Beach tonight."

"Thank you," he drawled. "But there is a possibility these particular smugglers use a different beach. Unlikely, if Pallton House is the base of operations, but possible."

"But you will go to Smugglers Beach?"

"Yes."

"And I suppose it would be too dangerous for me to come along and—"

"Yes." Absolutely yes. The very idea made his gut began to roll again.

She sighed and nodded. "Pity."

He waited for another argument, or at least a spot of wheedling. When it wasn't immediately forthcoming, a sliver of unease ran up his spine.

"You're being very sensible about this."

She frowned at him. "What did you expect me to be?"

"Insensible."

"How flattering."

He eyed her suspiciously. "You're not agreeing so readily because you plan on following Whit and me, or sneaking down to the beach on your own in the dark?"

"That beach?" she said, taken aback. "Certainly not. Why ever would I do such a thing?"

"For the adventure."

"That wouldn't be an adventure. It would be an unmitigated disaster." She gave a delicate snort. "A midnight walk down a rocky slope to a smuggler's beach, when I can barely walk down a well-lit hall without tripping over my own skirts?" She pursed her lips thoughtfully. "Come to think of it, sometimes I *can't* walk down a well-lit hall without—"

"If you knew it was foolish, why ask to come?"

"I didn't," she countered, "not to the beach. I had hoped

you'd tell me it would be safe enough for me to take a lantern to the bluffs and watch from a safe distance."

"I see . . . It's not."

"Wouldn't have been able to see much at any rate," she commented absently, studying him. "You truly expected me to be foolish about this, didn't you?"

"I don't recall using the word foolish. But you are stubborn, and you are impetuous. The combination gives me some worry."

"When you cease being charming, you cease altogether," she grumbled. "Stubborn, I'll grant. But I'm not impetuous."

"Really?" he drawled. "I recall you arriving at Suffolk last year, having raced across the country on horseback to warn Evie of danger—"

"I didn't go *alone*," she cut in. "Whit, Alex, and Sophie made the trip as well."

"But you *would* have gone alone," he guessed, "because you're impetuous."

"I'd have gone alone," she corrected, "if I had no other choice. Evie was in danger. Would you *expect* me to ignore a loved one in danger?"

He expected she'd fight to the death for those she loved. But while he admired that about her, he had no intention of encouraging it. "You searched Pallton house and the grounds on your own."

"That wasn't impetuous. The amount of time it took to talk Mirabelle into it alone qualifies it as having been well planned."

"You arranged a rendezvous with a smuggler, and possible traitor, at night, not twenty minutes ago."

"At dawn," she corrected, for the sole purpose of irritating him, he was sure. "And it isn't impetuous to take advantage of an opportunity."

"It is when it's an opportunity to put yourself in danger."

"Of Lord Martin," she said with a humorless twist of her lips. "I think perhaps you *are* as overprotective as Whit."

The disappointment in her voice made him uneasy. The hint of anger made him defensive, which in turn made him uncomfortable. "You can't very well expect me, or anyone else who cares for you, to idly sit about while you blithely stroll into danger."

"Stroll?" She sat up in her chair slowly, her anger becoming quite evident. *"Blithely?"*

"There are limits," he tried to explain. "You have limits. You may not always be willing or able to recognize the full extent of them, but—"

"I am not an idiot," she snapped, her blue eyes sparking. "I am fully aware of my limitations. I know I'm clumsy. I accept that I am very easily distracted, and do occasionally speak or act before thinking things through quite as well as I ought. I am not so foolhardy as to dismiss those limitations on a whim, or even fail to take them into account when considering a venture such as searching the house or goading Lord Martin. I can, and do, distinguish between calculated risks taken for the right reasons and tossing myself into peril for no reason at all."

"Kate—"

"You wish for me to understand and accept your desire to protect, but you'll make no effort to understand and accept my desire to not be so . . . so . . ." She shook her head, and her lips thinned into a line as she searched, obviously frustrated, for the right word. "So bloody well protected."

He felt his brows rise. Kate didn't swear. He'd heard every one of her friends curse at some point, but never once had he heard so much as a "damn" from Kate.

"You don't swear." Not the most eloquent response he could have offered in that moment, but there it was.

"I just did." She rose from the chair and looked down at him with cool eyes, just as she had the first time they'd fought.

"I may not always make the right decisions, Hunter, but it shouldn't be assumed that I'll never make any but the wrong ones, nor be unable to weather the consequences should I do so."

With her speech concluded, she spun on her heel and left the room.

Hunter watched her go, equal parts baffled, frustrated and—and he'd suffer the tortures of the damned before he ever admitted it to Kate—just a little impressed. The woman was nobility, through and through.

She was also thoroughly aggravating. What the devil did she expect from him, an invitation to single-handedly apprehend the smugglers at her leisure?

Well she'd have to learn to live with disappointment. He was a man, damn it. His store of honor may have been limited, but even he understood that it was a man's duty to protect the woman he meant to make his wife.

She was being irrational. Unfair as well. She hadn't complained when he'd taken care of the business of the vase, had she?

That hadn't been done to protect her, a small voice in the back of his head reminded him, it had been done to charm her.

He ignored the voice and changed the subject.

He wasn't insisting he control every facet of her life, was he?

Not yet, the voice chimed in.

"She's too stubborn," he grumbled. *That* at least, he couldn't argue about with himself. The knowledge that he was, in fact, arguing with himself had him dragging a hand through his hair. Arguing with himself, daydreaming about her nose, nearly letting himself be ravished on a ballroom floor—the woman was well on her way to driving him stark raving mad.

He wanted a drink. It was barely noon and he wanted a

drink. He could add that to the growing list of unhealthy habits directly attributable to Lady Kate.

"Should've chosen a more biddable woman," he muttered.

Apparently, he could also add talking to himself to the list.

He was having the drink.

Kate, no doubt, had gone to her room to sulk. Women always took to their rooms when they were in a snit.

Brow furrowed, he rose from his chair and headed for the study.

❋ *Eighteen* ❋

$\mathcal{L}$ord Brentworth kept the best brandy in the house in a cabinet behind his desk. Hunter helped himself to a small drink and made a mental note to repay the man for the expense with a new bottle. Raising the glass, he took the first sip and let the heat of it burn away some of his anger.

A bit of time to think, and a spot of fine brandy to do it with, that was all he needed.

He imagined Kate had her own rituals for settling her temper. She'd not remained angry with him for long after their last argument—a night and part of a day until . . . well, until he'd apologized for doubting her word.

She wouldn't be receiving an apology this time round . . . probably. He'd see how he felt about it when he was through with his drink. The possibility of an apology, however, did not mean he was willing to change his position on any matter regarding her safety. There wasn't enough brandy in the world to see that accomplished.

But if he'd said something that had led her to believe he thought her an idiot—

"Ow! Let go of me!"

Hunter set the glass down. Bloody hell, he knew that screech. Miss Willory was in a scuffle with someone down the hall.

"Let go of me this *instant!*" Her voice reached a painful and very unattractive pitch. Clearly it wasn't an act. The woman was a dedicated actress, but she wasn't a particularly talented one.

Gritting his teeth, he abandoned his drink and headed for the door. How many ill-mannered sots could there be at one bloody house party?

To his complete shock, he found Miss Willory struggling not with an overenthusiastic admirer, but with, of all people, Lizzy. Even more astounding, was that Miss Willory appeared to have very good reason to struggle. Lizzy was forcibly dragging the woman along by—holy hell, he couldn't be seeing this correctly—her *ear.*

"What the devil is going on here?" he demanded.

"Oh, Mr. Hunter! Thank goodness you're here." That statement would have come as no shock at all, if it hadn't been uttered by both women simultaneously.

"Lizzy, let go of Miss Willory's ear."

"I'll not. She'll bolt." As if to discourage Miss Willory of the idea, Lizzy gave the woman's ear an extra twist.

"Ow!"

"*Now*, Lizzy."

Lizzy grumbled, but did as he ordered.

"Thank you. Now someone explain to me—"

They both began talking at once.

"I saw her—" Lizzy began excitedly.

"She accosted me," Miss Willory panted, rubbing at her ear.

"—giggling in a stall—"

"She's a *lunatic*."

"—she broke that piano bench—"

"Enough!" He turned cold eyes on Miss Willory. "Explain yourself."

"She lies," Miss Willory cried. "I cannot believe you would give credence to the word of a mere servant over my—"

She broke off with a yelp and jumped back when Lizzy reached for her again.

"You'll tell him the truth," Lizzy demanded, "or I swear I'll twist your ear clean off."

"I'll have you sacked!" Miss Willory shrieked, swatting wildly at Lizzy's hand. Lizzy merely reached up and grabbed hold with the other.

"Ow! Mr. Hunter!"

"I believe Lizzy means what she says."

"You can't be—ow! All right, all right! Let go!"

Lizzy looked to him. He nodded.

"It was just a spot of fun," Miss Willory whined, rubbing her ear when Lizzy once again let go. "I thought it would wiggle under her a little, that's all. It wasn't supposed to break."

Hunter held back his growing—or regrowing to be precise—anger. "And what was supposed to happen with Mr. Potsbottom?"

It was only a guess that Miss Willory had been involved in what had transpired outside the music room, but the coincidence of her showing up with two friends just moments after a typically good-natured man had been pawing at Kate made it an educated guess. A good one, by the way Miss Willory's eyes briefly widened before she pasted on an innocent expression.

"I'm sure I haven't the slightest idea what you're referring to." Her tone turned wheedling. "Did something unsavory occur between Mr. Potsbottom and Kate? I'd not be surprised. Everyone knows she's been hoping for a kiss."

"A notion you fed him along with drink, no doubt. And you brought the ladies around in the hopes of finding the two of them in a compromising position, is that it?"

"I've no idea what you mean—"

"Tell him what else you've done," Lizzy demanded. "She's done something else," she informed him before Miss Willory could answer. "She was giggling in the stables as Kate left and I know she's done something nasty."

Kate had gone for a ride instead of her room? Fear, cold and painful, seeped into his bones. "What did you do, Mary Jane?"

Miss Willory gasped at him. "You haven't permission to call me by my Christian name. I—"

"*What did you do?*" he barked.

She took a step back, but tipped her chin up and pressed her lips together in a thin, mutinous, and very guilty line.

"Bloody hell." He could argue with her all day and not receive an answer. He spun and took off down the hall at a dead run.

"I've not done anything!" Miss Willory shouted after him. "I was only in the stable for a—*ow!*"

Aside from dancing and playing the piano, riding was one of the few physical activities Kate was able to perform with some grace. The sound of hoofs hitting the ground and the feel of the horse moving beneath her had a similar effect as the sea, except that it didn't silence the music in her head, it simply gave it a rhythm to follow. Knowing an abrupt change in that rhythm sometimes caused her problems, Kate had learned to take extreme care in how she handled her mount. After all, a fall from a horse could be so much more than just embarrassing. It could be deadly.

Not that she *hadn't* ever embarrassed herself by falling from her horse. She had, but those few occasions had occurred when she'd let her mind wander while her mount meandered around at a leisurely walk and admittedly, once while her horse had been standing perfectly still.

But Kate was not in the mood to walk her mount for long. She wanted to race. She wanted to feel the wind blow past her face and see the earth fly by beneath her feet. She wanted . . .

She groaned. What she *wanted* was to march right back into the house, find the nearest liftable—and if at all possible, pointed—object and hurl it squarely at Hunter's irritating head.

Blithely stroll into danger, indeed.

Kate stopped her mount, Whistler, when she reached the edge of Pallton House's grounds. It wasn't all that far to the bluffs, she thought with a wistful sigh. Pity she couldn't go. She imagined it would be safe enough. Smuggler's Beach itself was another quarter mile away from where she and Mirabelle had stood and looked out over the English Channel. And she knew for a certainty that there would be no smugglers about until night.

With another sigh, she turned Whistler about, intending to have him walk a bit longer, until she was sure his muscles were warmed, and then race him back to the house. She nudged him forward with her knees.

He balked.

She tried again and added a verbal command. "Walk."

He moved, but only in a series of prancing side steps.

"Good heavens, horse, whatever is the matter with you?"

She backed him up three paces to remind him who held the reins, and then turned him in a circle to do the same. "Now then, are you quite done misbehaving?"

He shook his head and snorted, which she might have found amusing, if he hadn't been acting so strangely. His ears were twitching back and forth, and he was swishing his tail as if annoyed. She scanned the ground around them, wondering if uncertain footing or a small animal might have frightened him.

Finding nothing amiss, she gripped the reins firmly and urged him forward with her heels.

He lunged ahead, then spun completely around, nearly unseating her.

And then he bolted.

Kate tried everything she could think of to make Whistler stop, or at least slow down. She used her knees, shouted commands, and applied steady pressure on the reins. But he continued galloping forward, head turned to one side. Battling her own panic, she shortened her grip on the reins and pulled with all her might. Once . . . twice . . . To her absolute horror, the left rein broke off in her hand.

She stared at the useless piece of leather for one baffled, horrified heartbeat, before letting it fall. There was nothing she could do now but reach for Whistler's mane and hold on.

❊ *Nineteen* ❊

*H*unter stifled the urge to race his stallion across the countryside. He couldn't be certain where Kate was. The groom had seen her ride east, but she could have veered off to the north, or down to the beach after she'd been out of sight. He couldn't risk missing her in haste, or—

He saw her, a dark spot in the distance—too far in the distance, well past the edge of the grounds, and moving much too fast. His heart stopped in his chest, the air backed up in his lungs.

Somehow, something Miss Willory had done had caused Kate to lose control of her horse.

Battling back a sick roll of fear, he gave the stallion his head.

Kate was a fine horsewoman, he assured himself as he closed the distance between them at a breakneck pace. He'd heard Whit mention as much more than once. She hadn't lost her seat when the horse bolted, so there was no reason for her to lose it now. If she could just hang on until her mount wore himself out—

Kate's horse veered sharply, heading straight toward the bluffs.

The roll of fear became a wave of terror. He bent low in the saddle and pushed his mount for more speed. He had to reach Kate before her horse reached the bluffs.

No horse would run off a cliff intentionally, not even a panicked one. But the terrain was unfamiliar to Kate's mount, rocky and markedly uneven in places. The earth at the edge of the bluffs was loose and unstable in patches. The horse could slip, fall, and tumble off the cliff. Or come to a sliding halt at the edge and throw Kate off the cliff, or . . .

Bloody hell, he wouldn't think about it. It didn't do either of them any good for him to think about it. Ruthlessly wiping his mind clear of all visions of Kate tumbling off the bluffs into the sea, he concentrated on going faster.

How far away was he, now? Fifty yards? How far away were the bluffs? Two hundred, three hundred yards? There was time, he told himself. He could see where their paths would intersect. They had time. He would make it.

Leaning low over the stallion's neck, he brought his horse alongside Kate's less than fifty yards before the cliff. Kate was clinging to her mount's back, her fingers tangled in the mane. Hunter stretched out his hand for the left rein, only to discover it was missing. He leaned farther to grab the bridle, only to have the horse toss his head and veer out of reach.

The cliff loomed closer.

Bloody, buggering, hell.

He reached over one last time, grabbed Kate around the waist and dragged her off the horse.

"I have you," he said hoarsely, setting her in the saddle in front of him. He wrapped one arm tightly around her and slowed his mount with his free hand. "I have you. You're safe."

He wasn't certain whose benefit he was speaking for, he only knew he needed to say the words.

As his horse slowed to a walk, he watched in horror as Kate's mount rushed the last few yards to the cliff. He came to a sliding stop not three feet from the edge, his hoofs digging deep grooves into the loose earth. Kate wouldn't have been able to keep her seat. She'd have been thrown clear off the edge into the water below.

Kate seemed to realize how close she'd come to catastrophe. He could feel her trembling, hear the way her breath came in ragged gasps. "The rein . . ."

He pulled her harder against him, brushed his lips through her hair. "It's all right, Kate. You're all right."

"The rein. It came off in my hands." She stared down at them now as if she expected to find an explanation there. "I pulled, and it came straight off."

"It's all right. It's over."

The trembling grew more pronounced. "I'd have gone over. Right over the cliff."

Hunter stifled a frustrated groan. He couldn't hold her properly in the damn saddle. And he couldn't pull her off and into his arms, not the way he wanted, while they were in an open field.

He turned his mount about and led him at an easy trot back along the coast until the bluffs smoothed out into a small slope that ran into the sandy beach. He followed the beach back up until the bluffs formed once again, blocking the beach from the view of anyone riding along the fields above.

He dismounted, lifted Kate down after him and gathered her into his arms.

She was still trembling.

He kissed her cheeks, her eyelids, her mouth. His hands moved over her, brushing along her arms and back, her face and shoulders. He wanted to soothe and comfort. He wanted to make her stop shaking.

"It's all right, Kate. It's all right."

Kate couldn't keep still. She couldn't keep the tremors from wracking her body. She tried pressing herself closer to Hunter, burrowing her face against his chest, wrapping her arms around him, and gripping handfuls of his coat at his back. But nothing seemed to help. Nothing erased the memory of the cliff rushing up before her and being powerless to save herself.

"I couldn't stop him. He wouldn't stop."

He slipped an arm under her knees, carried her to a sheltered spot between two towering boulders, and sat in the sand, cradling her in his lap.

"It's over, sweetheart. It's done. I have you."

He did have her—wrapped warm and safe in his arms. She relaxed in his hold as his voice floated over her, pushing aside the memory of the wind whipping in her ears and the sound of hoofs pounding on the ground. She breathed in his familiar scent, letting it erase the smell of Whistler's sweat. Hunter had her now. She was safe.

His arms tightened around her. "Stop shaking, sweetheart."

She let out a shuddering sigh against his chest. "I have," she whispered. "That's you."

Hunter blinked at Kate's words.

That's you.

Bloody hell, he *was* shaking. He hadn't realized. He'd

been too focused on Kate's distress to notice the tremor in his arms. Merely a reaction to extreme physical exertion, he assured himself, and patently refused to acknowledge that he'd engaged in physical acts in the past that were far and away more extreme. And not once had they ended with him shaking.

Kate lifted her head and pressed her lips to his in a soft kiss. "I'm all right."

Was she comforting him now? Was he being *soothed*?

Did he care as long as she kept doing it? He decided he didn't, not when it involved feeling the heat of her mouth against his. Willing to be consoled, he wrapped a hand around the base of her neck, pulled her closer, and took the kiss deeper.

On a quiet sigh, she shifted in his lap and twined her arms around his neck. And then *she* took the kiss deeper, tasting him with her tongue, parting her lips in an invitation for him to do the same.

He accepted what she offered, slanting his mouth over hers again and again until the remnants of the panic he refused to acknowledge were washed away by desire; until they were both trembling with need instead of fear.

He should stop, a small part of his brain admonished. He shouldn't allow the encounter to progress past a kiss. They were on a beach, for pity's sake.

A larger part of his brain reminded him that it was a beach at least a mile from the house and hidden from both field and sea by rock. He wouldn't be able to take his time, he wouldn't be able to do all the things he'd fantasized, but he could have her. He could make her his.

He'd always been a proponent of majority rule.

He let his hands slip to her shoulders, careful of her healing cut, down her torso, around and up her back to work the buttons of her gown. Just a few, just enough to pull the bodice down over her shoulders, until there was only her thin chemise between him and the skin he craved. He didn't let himself take at first. Lowering her to the sand, he tormented them both by tracing kisses down her neck, along her collarbone, and finally across the neckline of her chemise where fabric met heated flesh. He dallied there, enjoying the sharp contrast in textures, almost as much as he enjoyed her sharp gasp of pleasure when he used his tongue to sample the skin just beneath the seam.

He could have stayed there, teasing her, listening to the sounds of her pleasure for endless minutes. He would have, if they'd been in a bed behind a locked door. And if an extended period of denied passion hadn't been tearing at his control.

"I want you." He pulled the chemise down slowly, following the movement with his mouth, whispering words against her breast. "Want you." He brushed his hand lightly over a small pink nipple, squeezed his eyes shut on a groan when she arched toward him. "Please."

It wasn't begging. He didn't beg. It was seduction—the sweet words any man gave any woman he was trying to bed. Even as he made the excuse, a small part of Hunter knew it to be a lie. But not even the smallest part of him cared. Not now, not while Kate's soft form was arched beneath him in desire.

Whatever words he needed to speak, whatever lies he needed to hear, he'd offer them and more. Though he'd deny it later, in that moment, he'd have offered anything, everything he had, if it meant he could have *her*.

"Kate."

"Yes."

Another tremor ran through him and he wasn't certain if it was one of relief or anticipation or even, heaven help him, nerves. She would be his now. *His*.

He ran his hands over her possessively, wishing he could strip away all the layers of clothes between them. He wanted to see her naked and spread out before him like an offering. He wanted to feel every inch of her skin pressed against every inch of his own. Next time, he assured himself. Next time, when they were married, he would undress her in slow stages and linger over every curve and plane. For now, it was enough, it was more than enough, to remove or push aside the most inhibiting articles of clothing, to feel the soft weight of her breasts, to slowly push up her skirts as he followed the long curves of her leg with his palm, to swallow her gasp when he discovered the heat at the juncture of her thighs.

He listened to her whimpers and sighs, relished the way she twisted beneath him in need as he poised himself against her entrance. Not yet, he ordered himself, not until she was moaning. Not until she moaned his name.

"Hunter."

"Andrew," he whispered. For reasons he didn't care to ponder, he needed to hear her say it.

"Andrew," she moaned against his mouth, sending a shiver racing along his skin.

He entered her slowly, giving her body a chance to grow accustomed to his, and giving himself the chance to savor every glorious moment.

She dug her fingers into his shoulders, lightly at first, then with increasing pressure as he pressed deeper. When he pushed through the barrier that marked her as an innocent, he could have sworn the nails in his shoulders drew blood.

"I'm sorry, sweetheart." He wrapped his arms tight around her. "I'm sorry. It will get better."

Her voice was hesitant, notably devoid of passion, and unless he was much mistaken, just a little patronizing. "Yes . . . all right."

She was attempting to spare his feelings, he realized, and nearly laughed. He might have laughed, if they hadn't both been experiencing two very different, but very real varieties of discomfort in that moment.

He wanted to move. He *needed* to move.

"We'll wait," he whispered, brushing his lips across hers. "As long as you like. We'll wait."

Ignoring the instinct that demanded he push inside her until he was sated, he kept his arms around her and stayed still, perfectly still, until her grip eased and he could no longer feel the hard pounding of her heart against his chest. When he was certain, absolutely certain, the worst of her pain had passed, he loosened his hold and set himself to the task of rekindling her passion.

He took her mouth in a long, drugging kiss and ran his hands over her again, rediscovering the places that had made her whimper and sigh before. He whispered words of encouragement, sweet endearments that made her smile and blush.

She sighed when he slid his palms down the sides of her breasts, whimpered when he brushed the sensitive skin at the back of her knee and moaned when his fingers found the spot where their bodies were joined.

He moved inside her then—slowly at first, gauging her reaction. When she moaned again and arched up to meet him, he quickened the pace. He watched her, transfixed, as she threw her head back, her eyes closed and her lips parted on a cry of pleasure.

Beautiful, he thought through a haze of desire. She was beautiful in her passion.

And then all thought was lost to him. There was only the building need, the long, hard strain to meet it, and the breathtaking sight and feel of Kate finding her release a moment before he took his own.

It was several long minutes before Hunter had the wherewithal to roll onto his back and tuck Kate against his side.

"Did I hurt you, sweetheart?" He'd meant to have more control. He'd meant to give her his name, a bed, and *then* his control, but it was a bit late to change the order of things now.

"No. Well, some at first," she admitted, and he could have

sworn he felt the cheek on his chest warm. "But then no. It was . . . I don't know what to call it . . . Wonderful?"

He shouldn't ask. He shouldn't. He just couldn't help himself. "Did you hear music?"

"Music?" She lifted her head to peer at him, then the water, then him again. "No. I told you, the sea stops it . . . Why are you laughing?"

"Never mind, sweetheart," he chuckled, tucking her head back down to his chest. "I'll explain another time."

Kate considered insisting he tell her now, then decided she had neither the energy, nor the interest. Her body felt deliciously weary, as if she'd spent the whole day running about in the sun and now wanted nothing more than to fall asleep in the cool shade. Her mind, on the other hand, was a riot of thoughts and feelings. She couldn't have fallen asleep if her very life depended on it.

She'd lain with a man. She frowned a little against Hunter's chest. What a terrible misrepresentation of the facts that turn of phrase was. It rather sounded as if the two of them had taken a nap.

She'd made love with Hunter, that description was far superior. And it fit her circumstances perfectly, because she was, in fact, in love with Hunter.

She could no longer classify what she felt for him as a strong attachment. Much to her dismay, she'd realized that as Whistler had raced toward the cliffs. Finally, she had truly fallen in love. Finally, she had found her prince. And she was going to die before she had a chance to do anything at all about it.

She had an urge to do something about it now—perhaps tell Hunter how she felt. But that sort of thing took a considerable amount of courage, and after a terrifying ride over the fields toward almost certain death, she was feeling a bit drained of courage.

Maybe it would be best if she let him speak of his feelings first. Surely he intended to at some point. She wasn't quite so naïve as to believe a man would only make love to a woman he was in love *with*, but when that man had also been courting that woman it seemed at least *plausible* that he should love her. And when that man had plucked that woman from a runaway mount, it seemed . . . well, not inevitable, exactly, but certainly more likely than just plausible. And when that man—

"I can practically hear you thinking," Hunter commented.

Oh, she sincerely hoped not. "I was . . . I was thinking that you caught up with me just in time." She'd thought it right after he'd pulled her from Whistler, which made it at least partially true.

His arm tightened around her shoulders. "I know. It's all right. You didn't fall."

"I didn't mean you saved me just in time, although that's true as well. I mean I saw you just in time. I thought to jump."

"Jump?" She felt him start, and lift his head to look down at her. "Off your horse?"

"It seemed a better choice than letting myself be tossed off a cliff. I wasn't sure Whistler would throw me, but it was becoming more likely with every passing second. And I thought I'd have a better chance at surviving a fall from a horse than I would a fall from the bluffs."

He put his head back down, took a deep breath and let it out slowly. "Calculated risk," he murmured and ran his hand down her hair. "Smart. You're an intelligent woman, Kate. I'm sorry for giving you the impression I thought otherwise."

Kate thought throwing herself from a racing horse fell more along the lines of desperate measure, but knew it wasn't in her best interest to argue the point. "Perhaps I overreacted to our argument a little," she began before recalling his comment about blithely strolling into danger. "No, I don't think I did. But I don't wish to argue about it any longer."

Soft laughter rumbled in his chest. "Fair enough."

"I'd rather hear any theories you might have as to why Whistler bolted as he did. And what happened to the rein. It's as if the bridle simply fell apart, but why on earth—?"

"Miss Willory."

"Beg your pardon?"

He blew out a hard breath. "We need to dress. I'll explain on the way back."

"Must we go back just yet?" she asked, even as she used one hand to pull up her chemise and gown. She wasn't quite ready to abandon their romantic interlude but neither was she comfortable continuing it half naked.

"I'm afraid so." He sat them up. "Others will be out looking for you by now."

"Whatever for?"

"Because," he reached around to fasten the buttons of her gown. "Lizzy knows Miss Willory was in the stable at the same time as you, and by now she will have told Mirabelle, Mrs. Summers, and your mother, who have no doubt sent other riders to look for you."

Kate felt her mouth fall open, but it was several seconds before she could make any sort of sound emerge. "Miss Willory had something to do with this?"

He gently shifted her off his lap so he could stand and put his own clothing to rights. "I've no doubt she sabotaged your tack—put something under the saddle, cut the rein. She's responsible for the piano bench as well, and for Mr. Potsbottom's mistaken belief that you were hoping for his attentions."

"She told Mr. Potsbottom . . . Good heavens," she breathed. "Has she come unhinged?"

"Not entirely, or she would have confessed to all." He tucked in his shirt and pulled on his coat. "As it stands, she'll only accept responsibility for the piano bench."

"But you're certain she—"

"Absolutely."

She shook her head in bewilderment. She could scarce believe it. Miss Willory had tried to hurt her. The woman had very nearly killed her. Which reminded her . . .

"Hunter?"

He finished buttoning his coat. "Hmm?"

"Do you think it's necessary we tell everyone *everything* that happened?"

He paused in the act of tying his cravat in a loose knot. "Do I think it's *necessary?*"

"Yes . . . Oh, I didn't mean . . . not everything, not . . ." Feeling terribly self-conscious, she waved her hand around to indicate the general vicinity of where they'd lain on the sand. "Not us. I meant what happened with Whistler. Must we tell my family I nearly went over a cliff? I can't see how their knowing would benefit anyone. And a longer ride *would* explain our, er, longer absence. And—"

"And you want to avoid being fussed over," he guessed and bent down to pull her to her feet.

"Oh, I'm going to be fussed over. But the magnitude of that fussing depends on how willing you are to be circumspect in your retelling of events." She pushed a few stray pins in her hair back into place, then gave up the effort. No one was going to comment on the appearance of a woman who'd been on the back of a runaway horse.

"You want me to lie," he translated.

"Yes, please."

He smiled at her hopeful tone. "As I intend to see Miss Willory pay either way, I don't see why not." He pulled her close to place a soft kiss on her brow. "Let's get you back to the house. I'll tell you what I know of Miss Willory's treachery on the way."

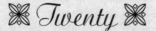

Twenty

Kate sat up in the bed she'd been not so much ushered, as bullied into upon her return to Pallton House, and glared at her brother.

"This is absurd. I was plucked from a horse, not thrown from one. I'm not injured, or ill, or even tired. There is absolutely no reason for me to be in bed."

"And yet you will remain in it until dinner," Whit ordered, and jabbed a finger at her. "And return to it one hour after dinner, or I'll have you packed and on your way to Haldon by morning."

Rather than argue, she fell back against the pillows, and upon the tried-and-true younger sister insult of sticking out her tongue.

Whit fairly growled at her. "I'm in earnest, Kate. You'll stay. And you'll drink the tea Lizzy's gone to fetch, and the broth, and—"

Mirabelle stood from where she'd been seated near the window and cut him off with a wave of her hand. "Quit badgering her, Whit. Go help your mother and Mrs. Summers see to Miss Willory."

Whit's lips pressed into a line. He looked to the door, back to Kate, then the door again. Caught, Kate thought, between protecting his sister and aiding his mother. She might have felt sorry for him, if she wasn't already annoyed with him. And feeling sorry for herself.

All evening in bed when she hadn't acquired so much as a single bruise from her misadventure. A bit of fussing she understood and expected, but Whit's reaction, in her opinion, was excessive.

Whit jabbed his finger at her one more time. "You'll stay," he snapped, and marched out the door.

"This is ridiculous," she grumbled after he left.

"But you will stay," Mirabelle guessed and took a seat on the edge of the bed. "Because he was scared half to death by what happened today, and having you safely tucked away for a few hours makes him feel better."

That was, indeed, the reason she'd stuck out her tongue rather than argue with him. "It's still ridiculous."

"It is, rather," Mirabelle laughed. "You're a good sister to indulge him, Kate."

"You'll remind him of that the next time I spill something in his study, won't you?" she jested. In truth, she'd not have given up the argument *quite* so quickly had she not felt guilty for having stayed with Hunter on the beach rather than returning to the house to let her family know she was unharmed. "I hadn't realized there was such a fuss at the house. Was it absolute panic and mayhem when Miss Willory's treachery was discovered?"

"Contained panic and limited mayhem," Mirabelle assured her. "I came across Lizzy in the hall not long after Hunter left. She informed me of what had happened. I instructed her to send word for Whit, and find Mrs. Summers. Then I sent every footman, maid, groom, and able-bodied person I could find to search for you. Then I went to look for your mother, who I found taking a stroll with Lord Brentworth in the garden. The three of us confronted Miss Willory in her room." Mirabelle snorted in disgust. "She has denied everything, for all the good it will do her. Lord Brentworth has instructed her to take herself off first thing tomorrow morning."

Kate blew out a long breath. "Do you think she's gone quite mad?"

"I think she's gone quite evil," Mirabelle replied. "Lizzy told me that Miss Willory is responsible for more than sabotaging your tack."

Kate nodded. "The piano bench."

"Yes, but that concerned me less than the mention of Mr. Potsbottom." Mirabelle gave her a hard look. "Something about him accosting you in the hall?"

"It was nothing." Kate strove to keep an indifferent tone, as if the incident with Mr. Potsbottom was a trivial matter. "He wanted a kiss, that was all. Such an unfortunate name, don't you think? Potsbottom. Mother says bottom is common in Yorkshire, but—"

"Kate."

Kate pulled a face. She should have known Mirabelle wouldn't be put off so easily. "You'll not lecture me for this, Mirabelle. You've kept secrets of your own."

Mirabelle opened her mouth as if to argue, then closed it again to press her lips into a line. "I don't care for the fact that you have a point."

"I'm sure you don't," Kate replied with a small smile—a very short-lived smile. "Oh, dear. Does Whit know what Mr. Potsbottom's did?"

"Not as of yet, but . . ." Mirabelle rolled her eyes. "Don't look at me like that, I've no intention of telling him. I only meant you should brace yourself for the possibility that he'll hear of it. Lizzy might tell him, or Mr. Hunter." Kate was surprised to see her friend begin to worry at the counterpane with her fingers. "Do you suppose it's because I banned her from Haldon—?"

"No." Kate shook her head adamantly. "No, I'm certain it's not. The, er, event with Mr. Potsbottom occurred well before that. You're not responsible for this, Mirabelle."

"Why would she go to such lengths to hurt you, then?"

"Hunter had a theory. He thought she might wish to see me removed as—How did he put it?—the most, um, 'the most eligible young lady in the house,' or something to that effect." She remembered perfectly that he'd called her "the most desirable young lady," but that was hardly complimentary to Mirabelle. "Miss Willory is in desperate need of a husband. A rich one."

"Lord Martin?" Mirabelle guessed.

"Initially, I assumed it was Lord Comrie, or possibly Mr. Potsbottom. Then I assumed it was Lord Martin. But *then* I realized it was Hunter."

"There are few, if any, who are richer." Mirabelle gave her a speculative look. "You've spent a great deal of time with him as of late."

"Well, you've spent all your time with mother and Lizzy and Mrs. Summers. I had to find someone willing to spare a few moments for me—"

"You don't truly expect me to believe that argument, do you?" Mirabelle cut in with a small laugh.

"No, but I've had it prepared for several days. Seemed an awful waste not to use it."

Mirabelle made a prompting motion with her hand. "Well, now that you have . . ."

Kate shrugged, but the casual gesture belied a sudden case of nerves. It wasn't every day a woman realized she was in love. Nor was it every day that a woman lost control of her horse, was rescued by the man she loved, gave her virginity to that man—while they were out-of-doors, no less—and then found herself sitting in bed considering the possibility of explaining her very eventful day—less the giving of her virginity, of course—to her sister-in-law.

She cleared her throat. "Yes, I have spent time with him, and . . . and I have enjoyed that time very much. I've come to know him well, I think." She laughed a little. "Do you know, before I came to know him, I thought him much too charming, and polished, and entirely too prone to looming."

"Looming?"

Kate nodded. "But now I think he's just the right sort of charming, and polished, and . . . and I've no idea how to make looming into an adjective. Loomy? Loomisome?" She waved the matter away. "He looms splendidly, at any rate, and I've . . . grown rather attached to him. Perhaps strongly attached to him. Perhaps more."

"Are you in love with him?"

She bit her lip, hesitated a moment, then gathered her courage and nodded. "I am."

"You're certain?"

"Of course I'm certain." What sort of question was that? "He's everything I had hoped to find. And nothing at all I had expected."

"I don't think any woman expects to find a loomisome man," Mirabelle commented with a smile.

Kate knew that smile. It meant she was being humored a little. "You believe I'm being fanciful."

"Oh, I *know* you're being fanciful," Mirabelle laughed. "That's not what worries me."

"Why should you be worried at all?"

"Because . . ." Mirabelle frowned thoughtfully, as if searching for the right words. "Because I don't want you to be disappointed. I don't want you to wish for more than you might receive."

"Wishing only for what one expects to receive isn't wishing at all," Kate countered. "It's . . . it's . . ."

"Expecting?" Mirabelle offered.

"Yes, exactly. And where's the fun to be had in that?"

Mirabelle sighed. "I could make a very long list of all the ways one can enjoy expectation, but I suspect it would only fall on deaf ears."

"Under other circumstances they might very well," Kate admitted. "But if you know something about Hunter that I do not, I'll listen with both ears."

"I hardly know the man at all, really," Mirabelle replied

with a shake of her head. "He just seems to me to be . . . guarded."

"He is, rather."

Mirabelle hesitated, then reached forward to take Kate's hand. "I love you, Kate, dearly."

Kate winced a little. "I'm not going to like what you say next, am I?"

"It's not so very terrible." Mirabelle squeezed her hand gently. "You're *not* guarded, Kate. You . . . you're . . ." She squeezed her hand again.

"Spit it out, Mira."

"You're vulnerable."

Kate snatched her hand away. "That's a perfectly awful thing to say."

"Please don't misunderstand," Mirabelle pled. "You're not weak, or helpless, not in the least. You're simply romantic. Sweet and fanciful and . . . open. It's part of what I love about you. Your eagerness to love. But that eagerness, I fear, leaves you exposed. Leaves your heart exposed . . . to men like Lord Martin."

As much as she disliked admitting it, Kate knew there was some truth to what Mirabelle said. She had been enamored with the idea of falling in love since she'd been a small girl. She'd dreamed of her prince for longer than she'd dreamed of hearing her symphony performed in a theater. And she had, at one time, allowed herself to be blinded to reality by her dreams. But her infatuation with Lord Martin had been just that—an infatuation. She'd fancied herself in love, but in comparing what she had felt then, to what she felt for Hunter now . . . well, there *was* no comparison.

"I never loved Lord Martin," she told Mirabelle. "Not really."

"No, but you wanted to, very much. Are you certain, absolutely certain you're not . . . eager to love Mr. Hunter as you were Lord Martin?"

"Hunter isn't Lord Martin."

"He certainly isn't," Mirabelle agreed readily. "And I must say I am glad to see your tastes improved."

"As am I," Kate admitted with a smile. "But that's not at all what I meant." She blew out a short breath and searched for the words to explain herself. "Lord Martin I wanted to love because I *did* love the idea of him. I was so certain he was a prince. But with Hunter I wanted to . . . well, not hate him, that's too strong, but strongly dislike because he didn't fit any of the requirements I thought a prince, or even a gentleman, should. And yet I've come to love him despite my unwillingness to do so. It's not the idea of him I love. It's just him, faults and all. I know that puts me in a vulnerable position as you said, but—"

She broke off midsentence when Mirabelle shook her head. "Exposing one's heart under those circumstances isn't something you can help, or should avoid. And what you describe certainly does sound like love. Particularly, the faults bit."

Kate rolled her eyes. "You're terribly romantic."

Mirabelle laughed and reached for Kate's hand once more. "I am happy for you. Although, I must admit, I had rather hoped to see you fall in love with Mr. Laury. Your mother wished for the same, though I believe the events of today may have changed her mind."

"I suspected she wished to see me with Mr. Laury. She was not particularly subtle in her matchmaking."

"Mr. Laury's disposition necessitated a direct approach."

Kate snorted. "Mr. Laury's disposition would necessitate the use of shackles and a sturdy chair, if you wished for him to remain in my presence for more than five consecutive minutes. He's quite terrified of me."

"Yes," Mirabelle sighed. "It's most odd. He's quite charming in the company of others, you know. And you're not at all terrifying."

"You've not seen the havoc I can wreak with a cream pastry."

"Everyone has seen the havoc you can wreak with food. Including your very tidy Mr. Hunter." Mirabelle grinned suddenly. "He plucked you from a runaway mount. You must have enjoyed that immensely."

In truth, plucked was something of a misnomer. It implied a certain efficiency and effortlessness that had been notably lacking from her rescue. She'd been grabbed, yanked—which had hurt her shoulder some—hauled, yanked again when her boot had caught in the stirrup, hauled once more, and then unceremoniously dropped across the saddle.

"I did, rather," she confessed with a happy sigh. "Once the terror had passed."

"Naturally."

Hunter had never laid a violent hand on a woman in his adult life. He would have liked to have said the same for his childhood, but the world he'd lived in then had been markedly different.

He recalled the fight he'd had with Miss Fannie Stansworth at the age of nine. She'd been eight at the most, a head shorter than him, and after his gloves. To his complete humiliation, she'd taken them and left him with a fat lip, a spectacular black eye, and an invaluable lesson. When it came to survival, gender was of less import than strength, cunning, and in the case of Fannie Stansworth, the willingness to do whatever it took to endure.

He'd never lost another fight to a girl after that. But he'd never picked one either. He'd used his hands only in defense.

He didn't want to use them in defense at the moment. He wanted to walk through the bedchamber door he'd been glowering at for the last five minutes, wrap his fingers around Miss Willory's neck and squeeze until her eyes rolled back in her head.

Which was why he was not going to walk through the door. He'd let the Coles see to Miss Willory's punishment for now. Later, when the image of Kate racing toward death was a little less vivid in his mind, he'd make a visit to her family in London. Miss Willory would live out her life isolated in the country, or he'd buy up and call in every debt in the Willory name.

Resolved, if not anywhere near to satisfied, he stepped back from the door, just as Whit opened it and stepped into the hall. The sound of Miss Willory's wailing assaulted his ears for a split second before Whit slammed the door closed behind him.

"I need a drink," Whit announced and turned for his room.

Hunter fell into step beside him. "How did it go?"

"She continues to deny having anything to do with what happened today. I have never, *never* been so tempted to strike a woman in my life. Kate could have been killed." He stopped and turned around toward Kate's door. "Are we quite sure she wasn't injured?"

"Not a scratch on her." Aside from the healing cut on her shoulder. And he was certainly in a position to know. "As far as I could see."

Whit stared at Kate's door a moment longer before turning around again to resume their walk. "I've informed Miss Willory that she'll go to the country, and stay there, or I'll ruin her name and see her family in debtor's prison."

"I've always known you were a man of sense. You'll speak with her family in London, I presume?"

"As soon as the mission is over."

"I'll come as well."

Whit threw a glance over his shoulder as they reached his room. "Not your responsibility, Hunter."

"I'll come."

Whit shrugged and opened his door. "Suit yourself. Drink?"

Hunter nodded, waited while Whit poured two glasses, and then took a seat in a chair by the fireplace. "I'll own myself surprised you've not taken a swing at me as yet."

"A swing?" Whit frowned at him and leaned against the mantel. "What the devil for?"

"It was my mission to keep Kate safe."

"Saved her from a runaway horse, didn't you?"

"Should've kept her off it to begin with."

"True enough," Whit agreed without heat. "But so should have I." He shook his head. "Neither of us could have possibly known Miss Willory was capable of something like this. I've known the girl my whole life. Disliked her for ninety percent of it as well, but I'd never have guessed she was dangerous. Aside from that, your mission is to keep Kate safe from smugglers, not demented young ladies looking to thin out the competition in the marriage mart."

Because it was in his best interest to be in the good graces of Kate's brother, and because he didn't want to dwell on how close Miss Willory had come to being successful in thinning out the competition, Hunter decided to change the subject. "Since you've brought up the topic of smugglers, I'll ask if you learned anything from Lord Martin today."

Whit shook his head. "Hadn't time."

"Well, as it happens, I did. The shipment arrives tonight."

"Tonight?" Whit straightened from the wall. "You're certain?"

"I am."

"And you came by this information how, exactly?"

"Coincidence," he lied. "I heard him make a comment to another guest."

"Who?"

"I wasn't in position to see. I walked along the outside of the house after we spoke this morning, and I overheard the comment through the parlor window, by the time I arrived in the actual room, Lord Martin had just maneuvered his way into a game of chess with your sister." It amazed him, sometimes, how proficient he'd become at deceit over the years.

"I assume you put an end to that."

"Immediately."

Whit nodded once in approval before taking a sip of his drink. "Well, the information is useful, but we can't act on it without a location."

"Smuggler's Beach would be my guess," Hunter remarked, a little surprised it hadn't been Whit's guess as well.

"Bit obvious, don't you think?"

"Not for the likes of Lord Martin."

Whit swirled the brandy in his glass. "The more I speak with him, the more I'm convinced he's not in charge of this operation."

"I agree. But with nothing else to go on, Smuggler's Beach remains our best hope."

"We'll not find anything."

"Are you suggesting we not try?"

"I'm suggesting we think it through," Whit corrected, just a little testily in Hunter's opinion. "It might be wiser to trail Martin rather than wait on the beach."

"Lord Martin isn't going anywhere. He's not the sort to help unload crates."

"He might fancy himself useful in a supervisory role and be present for that. He's vain enough for it."

"True. He might also be expecting a shipment at the house." In fact, given his offer to Kate to deliver an entire barrel of brandy, it was highly likely.

Whit nodded. "Right. I'll stay here and keep watch for—"

"You expect me to go to the beach on my own?" Hunter asked, raising his brows. He could request Mr. Laury's assistance, of course, but Whit wasn't aware of that.

"You'll not be capturing a whole boat of smugglers," Whit said defensively. "Just following the goods."

"Better if there's two of us." And better if the second agent was one Hunter knew from experience would keep his head in the unlikely event things went badly at the beach. He leaned back against the chair and stretched his legs out before him. "If we're discovered, you can fend off our attackers while I run for reinforcements."

A corner of Whit's mouth hooked up. "Why don't I get to run?"

"Your sense of honor wouldn't allow it."

"Neither would yours."

"It would suffer, it's true. But someone would need to survive to tell the tale to William. I'm willing to make that sacrifice for crown and country."

Whit snorted. "Patriotic bastard, aren't you?"

"I have my moments." He smiled, feeling calmer for the drink and the banter. "I'll pay off one of the staff to keep an eye on Lord Martin—fetch us from the beach if he goes anywhere. Shall we leave at say, eleven?"

"Eleven, then," Whit groused. He scowled at his drink for a moment, then drank the remainder of it in one swallow and set the empty glass on the mantel. "I need to check on Kate."

With that pronouncement, he turned and strode from the room.

Hunter stared after him. What the devil had gotten into the man? It wasn't like Whit to suggest they not follow a lead, no matter how unlikely it was they would find anything. In fact, it went against his very nature. Whit was a details sort of man. He checked and rechecked everything. So why would he suggest they not check Smuggler's Beach?

If Hunter hadn't been absolutely sure of the man's uncompromising sense of honor, he'd suspect Whit was hiding something.

He would obtain Kate's opinion on the matter after dinner, he decided. She knew her brother better than most. He'd have preferred to speak with her now, but after he'd brought her back to the house, he'd been none too subtly brushed aside by her brother, her sister-in-law, Lizzy, Mrs. Summers, and the dowager Lady Thurston. The last had made him distinctly uncomfortable when she'd grasped his face in her hands and, with her eyes bright with tears, brought his head down to place a kiss on his brow. She'd murmured something about being wrong, then something about sons and nephews that made absolutely no sense to him, and then Kate had been bustled away. He estimated the odds of getting a moment alone with her now were fairly long.

Setting aside his drink, he rose from the chair and went to inform Mr. Laury of the newest turn of events, and to see if a certain stable boy was interested in earning another sovereign.

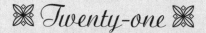

✤ *Twenty-one* ✤

𝒯o Hunter's vast amusement, Simon hadn't been nearly as interested in earning another sovereign as he had been in earning two. But after much consideration, deliberation, and considerable negotiation, he owned himself mildly intrigued by the idea of one sovereign, half.

Hunter gave him the half in advance and promised the rest after the job was completed. And the rest, he decided, would be the full two, simply because the boy had had the gumption to try for it.

"He'll be rich as Midas by the time this house party is over," he informed Kate as they sat together in a quiet corner of the parlor after dinner.

"Do you think it's wise to trust a member of the staff to

watch over Lord Martin?" Kate asked, brushing a piece of lint from the soft lilac skirts of her gown. "I thought you expected at least some of them to be involved."

"Not a twelve-year-old boy," he replied and watched her brush at another part of her skirt. She was nervous, he realized with a small smile. She was nervous because they'd not spoken since they had returned from the beach. "Lord Martin wouldn't trust a young servant with his secrets."

"Twelve is old enough to keep a secret. But, yes," she admitted after a moment's reflection, "you're right. Lord Martin would assume otherwise. Is it safe for him? He's only a child, really."

"Old enough to serve on a warship," he pointed out.

"Of which I do not approve," she replied in a hard tone. "But that is neither here nor there, at the moment. What if he's caught hiding in the closet by another staff member, or what if he's caught by the smugglers in an attempt to reach you and—"

"He knows this land like the back of his hand," Hunter cut in. "The beach is a favorite haunt for any local youth interested in engaging in a spot of mischief. In addition, he knows not to approach the beach, for any reason, if there are signs of activity. And he's not to go into the house until the staff is abed. If, by some bizarre twist of fate, someone catches him, I'll see to it he's taken care of. Satisfied?"

"As to his relative safety, yes. But, the staff is very loyal to Lord Brentworth, presumably that loyalty extends to his son. Simon might decide to protect Lord Martin, even if he's not aware of what he's protecting Lord Martin from."

"He might have been that loyal," Hunter agreed, "but then I offered him the coin."

"Not everyone's loyalty can be bought."

"I'm not buying his loyalty. I'm buying his temporary cooperation."

Kate shook her head. "You're paying him to be disloyal

and so the principle remains unchanged. You must admit that not everyone's cooperation, as you put it, can be acquired through bribery."

"I don't," he countered, "because everyone's can. It's simply a matter of price."

"That's not true." She straightened in her chair. "My loyalty can't be purchased."

"Not even if the price was the well-being of someone you loved?"

"What do you mean?"

He tapped his finger on the arm of his chair, thinking. "Suppose, for example, a band of gypsies snuck into Haldon and spirited away every member of your family—"

"The gypsies that pass through Thurston land really aren't prone to kidnapping."

"This particular band is," he assured her. "And they have commanded you to take a letter containing state secrets to France and—"

"Where in the world would they have gotten such a letter?"

"They stole it off William. What does it matter?"

She bit her lip in an obvious attempt to keep from laughing. "Well, I should like to know the sort of gypsies I'm dealing with."

"The sort who have promised to return your entire family to you in small bits and pieces should you refuse to betray your country by taking the letter to France." He leaned back in his chair. "What would you do?"

"I'd come to you for help."

He couldn't help finding that a very gratifying answer, indeed. "A wise decision. Sadly, I've been spirited away as well."

"I see. Determined lot, aren't they, to have kidnapped so many people? Might have been easier just to deliver the letter themselves."

"Too late now," he informed her with a shake of his head. "All their manpower is needed just to guard the prisoners. What would you do, Kate?"

"Well, I suppose if that *highly* unlikely scenario was to take place, I would deliver the letter as commanded," she admitted. "But I should like to point out that gypsies aren't any more prone to acts of espionage than they are to kidnapping. Also, that's not a bribe, it's a threat, or possibly blackmail. *Also*, it's quite morbid."

It was, and he didn't know why he'd pressed the issue, except it seemed important that she understand why Simon took the coin.

"Everyone has something they are willing to go to any lengths to obtain, or keep," he told her. "For many, it's coin. For some, it's rank and power. For others, such as yourself, it is the people they love."

"What of you?" she asked quietly. "What would you go to any lengths to obtain?"

You. I'd do anything for you.

He shoved that unbidden thought ruthlessly aside. "I'm very fond of apple tarts."

She blinked once, then spluttered out a surprised laugh. "Is that how the gypsies caught you? They lured you away with the promise of pastries?"

"Shameful, isn't it? You should have let them dice me into pieces."

"I'll know better next time." She gave him a speculative look. "If I promised you a pastry now, would you reconsider letting me take a lantern tonight to—?"

"No."

She slumped a little. "I thought not."

"But speaking of tonight," he said, eager to change the subject from her walking to the bluffs at night. "Whit is behaving oddly about our mission. Something the matter with him?"

Kate frowned and looked to where Whit sat talking to Mirabelle next to the fireplace. "He looks a trifle sulky, perhaps. But we did have something of a row, earlier." She looked back to him again, her cheeks growing a charming pink. "You don't think he knows about, er, about us, do you?"

"I've no doubt your brother's reaction to that bit of information, should he come across it, would be something more substantial than a sulk."

She blew out a breath of relief. "Yes, that's true. He'd beat you senseless."

"He'd try."

"I can't respond to that without being disloyal to someone." She waved her hand in a dismissive gesture. "Tell me what he's done that's odd."

"He doesn't want to go to Smuggler's Beach. He's of the opinion that we'll find nothing."

"Did he say why?"

"Thinks it's too obvious a spot."

Kate smirked. "If Lord Martin really is the man in charge of the operation, then too obvious would be a mark in favor of the location being Smuggler's Beach."

"That's what I said, essentially."

"And what did Whit say?"

"He argued a bit more, then gave up to check on you."

"That *is* strange. Well, not the part about checking on me, but the rest, certainly." She shrugged. "Perhaps he had a row with Mirabelle before he had one with me."

Hunter glanced at the pair of them. "And likely hoped to make up for that row tonight." He looked back to Kate in time to see her pull a face, even as her cheeks turned a brighter pink.

"I'll thank you not to put such images in my head. Whit is my brother."

"Whit is a healthy man with a pretty wife," he returned, for no other reason, really, than to prolong the blush.

"Beautiful wife," she corrected. "And please, do stop. Tell me what am I to do while you're away." She laughed when he gave her a hard look. "I mean about Lord Martin. If it turns out you've the wrong beach, you'll not be able to apprehend Lord Martin, and he'll expect me to meet him behind the wall at five."

"Write a note and slip it under his door," he instructed. "Tell him you fear being caught and you'll meet him at an unspecified time in the future. In London, or at Haldon. I'll let Simon know he is to expect to see you."

"But—"

"No arguments, Kate. If he does take it into his head to bring along a barrel of brandy after all, then he'll bring help. You may be certain of your safety in regards to Lord Martin, but you can't be certain of what men who haven't a title to protect them from the gallows might do, should they suspect a trap."

"Yes." She nodded reluctantly. "Yes, you're right. I'll pen the note. I . . ." She trailed off and turned her head at the sound of Lord Brentworth's laughter mixed with the dowager Lady Thurston's voice on the other side of the room. "Lord Brentworth has paid my mother a great deal of attention today."

"He's a healthy man with a pretty widow in—"

"Oh, don't," Kate half groaned and half laughed. "I beg of you, speak of something else."

"Very well. I'd like a moment with you in private."

"Now? I can't possibly. *You* can't possibly. You and Whit will need to leave soon. If Lord Martin thought to bring the brandy at five in the morning, then the shipment must be arriving only a few hours before. You'll want to be there by midnight, won't you?"

"Tomorrow, after I return," he clarified, and saw her eyes widen in surprise. And well they should. They'd shared a number of private conversations in the past. He'd never asked for any of them a day in advance. But this was different. This was to be a proposal of marriage, and it would have the hallmarks of respectability. Some of them, at any rate. He did plan on closing the door, and kissing her, and he'd chosen not to speak with her brother in advance—no point in giving the man the option of saying no, was there?—and he wasn't going to wait bloody weeks for the bans to be read. He'd obtain a special license. But other than that . . . very well, he wasn't entirely certain why he felt the need to ask in advance. It just seemed the thing to do. It seemed the sort of thing she would like.

"Will you give me the moment?" he asked quietly.

"Yes." The blush returned. "Yes, of course."

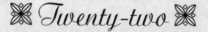

❈ *Twenty-two* ❈

*I*t took Kate four attempts to pen a note to Lord Martin. Her first try she threw into the fire because it felt stilted and unnatural upon reading. The second was discarded because it was much too dramatic, and the third because she spilled half a glass of watered beer onto the page.

The fourth and final note, she deemed acceptable, and after waiting until she was certain the other guests had gone to sleep, she very carefully crept to Lord Martin's door, only to discover that he was not among those abed. There was a light shining from his room, and the sound of voices within. To Kate's shock, one of those voices belonged to Miss Willory. Her tone was clipped and hard. Without conscious thought, Kate leaned forward to catch the words.

"It hardly signifies which room I'm in now," Miss Willory

fairly snapped. "The Coles have already begun a campaign to ruin me."

"It's true, then?" came Lord Martin's reply. "You took a knife to Lady Kate's reins and—"

"I did nothing of the sort, though my innocence makes no never mind to them. And you, of all people, would have the least cause to blame, had I made some effort to remove Lady Kate from the house."

"What do you mean by that?"

"You are much too friendly with her. If she suspected the smuggling—"

"I've always been friendly with Lady Kate."

"You've always tried. Which is why it would have been best had she left. Or better yet, not come at all. I own myself amazed you didn't confess all to her at the first opportunity."

Kate shifted her weight to lean closer to the door. So *that* was the true reason Miss Willory had attempted to be rid of her. Miss Willory had been afraid Lord Martin would give away their secret. To give credit where credit was due, Miss Willory was right. Lord Martin *had* given away their secret.

Lord Martin must have been contemplating that very thing. Kate could make out the sound of a chair squeaking, as if Lord Martin was fidgeting in a seat. "It's just a bit of smuggled brandy—"

"Oh, never mind." There was a pause in which Kate imagined Miss Willory waving her hand dramatically. "The point is, the Coles have ruined things for me. I've no other choice now, but to make a life for my family on the continent. And for that to occur, tonight must proceed without mishap. Tell me what you are to do."

"For pity's sake. We've gone over it a thousand times."

"Then we shall go over it a thousand and one. What are you to do?"

Even through the wood of the door, Kate could hear Lord

Martin's aggrieved sigh. "I am to go one half mile past Smuggler's Beach, and wave my lantern in a great sweeping arc."

"Until?"

"Until the signal is returned. I say, how long will that take, exactly? I can't be waving a lantern about for hours, you know. Why can't we send a servant—?"

"I'll not trust a servant with this," Miss Willory cut in impatiently. "What are you to do once the shipment arrives?"

Another sigh from Lord Martin. "Pay the captain, send the brandy to town, and retrieve your letter."

"No. You are to retrieve the letter, *then* pay the captain and send the brandy into town. The letter first, Martin. How many times must I tell you?"

"No need to get testy. I dare say I can manage to retrieve one letter. Though why your friend couldn't post it same as everyone else—"

"He had reason. Tell me again, what are you to do?"

"Oh, for pity's sake . . ."

Kate stepped away from the door as her mind sorted through what she'd heard. The shipment would not be arriving at Smuggler's Beach, but a half mile away. And by all appearances, Lord Martin was neither in charge of the operation, nor aware there was more going on than brandy smuggling. Miss Willory, on the other hand, quite clearly knew there was more at stake. It was *her* secret Lord Martin had referred to during their chess match.

Hunter and Whit needed to know. Simon would warn them once he saw Lord Martin leave the house, but he wouldn't be able to tell them about Miss Willory's involvement. And if Hunter and Whit apprehended Lord Martin before he delivered the letter, there would be nothing tangible tying Miss Willory to the operation.

Tucking her note away, with a mental note to deliver it after Miss Willory had returned to her own room, Kate turned from the door and headed straight for a supply closet at the end of the hall. She reached for the handle, before deciding to knock softly, instead. She didn't want to startle the boy hidden inside.

"Simon? It is Lady Kate. I've a message for Mr. Hunter."

Hunter crept up the back stairs of Pallton House twenty feet behind Lord Martin. He kept to the shadows, and rolled his feet heel-to-toe as he walked, eliminating the sound of footfalls. But it wasn't because of Lord Martin that he took such care. The man was clearly oblivious to being followed. It was because the hair on the back of his neck had stood up the moment they'd come into sight of the house. Someone else was watching. Hunter assumed that someone was Mr. Laury, but it didn't pay to take chances.

Lord Martin, blissfully unaware of having at least two sets of eyes trained upon him, practically skipped down the hallway, happy with his success.

It had been the same the whole way back from the beach. Not once had Lord Martin looked behind him to see if he were being trailed. Hunter supposed the man's behavior made sense, in a way, if he believed himself to be involved in nothing more nefarious than a bit of brandy smuggling. And if the man was a fool. Hunter figured the latter was obvious, and the former highly likely, given the detailed message Kate had sent with Simon.

Whit had appeared alternately baffled and irritated by Simon's appearance on the beach, though whether his reaction had stemmed from the news itself, or the fact that the news came from Kate, Hunter hadn't been able to determine. He'd been preoccupied for the next hour as he and Whit maneuvered their mounts back up the steep hillside, across the fields in the dark, and then found a spot from which they could watch for the smugglers without being detected. The last had required they take up a position some distance from the beach, but they had been close enough to see Lord Martin meet two other men from town with a horse-drawn cart. Then it had been only a matter of time before the boat arrived, the cargo was unloaded, and Lord Martin accepted the letter from the captain. Hunter had left Whit to follow the cart into town, while he'd followed Lord Martin back to the house.

He stepped into the shadows now as Lord Martin turned and knocked softly on Miss Willory's door. Miss Willory appeared almost instantly. After a quick glance down both ends of the hall, she grabbed Lord Martin's arm, pulled him inside, and promptly shut the door again.

Hunter moved toward his own room, but stopped when a door behind him opened softly. He spun around and reached for the pistol at his side.

Kate's blonde head peaked out from the door. "Hunter. Is it done? Where's Whit?"

"Kate." He blew out a quick breath and put the pistol away. "Get back in your room."

"I am in my room," she whispered. "Is Whit—?"

"He's well. I—" Bloody hell, there was no point in standing in the hallway. He gently urged Kate inside, and followed her, leaving the door cracked open an inch so he could keep watch. "How did you know I was here?"

She pulled her wrap tightly around her night rail. "I've been keeping watch. Out the window first. I saw Lord Martin. When I heard footsteps, I watched under the door. I recognized Lord Martin's boots, then I thought I saw yours. Then I heard a door open and close down the hall. I assumed Lord Martin met with Miss Willory and—"

"Never mind." He couldn't help but smile at the picture of Kate down on all fours to peer under the door. "You delivered your note to Lord Martin, I presume?"

She nodded. "Miss Willory took to her own room shortly after I sent Simon to you. He reached you, then? You received the message?"

"The shipment arrived a half mile from Smuggler's Beach, just as you said. Well done, Kate. Very well done."

Even in the semidarkness of a single lit candle, and the very first light of dawn peeking through the window, he could make out the bloom of pleasure on her cheeks. "I merely overheard a conversation."

"You gained sensitive information and passed it on in a safe and expedient matter. Sometimes, that is the whole of an agent's mission." He caught and held her gaze. "You've done well."

"Oh, well, thank you." She cleared her throat delicately. "Everything went as expected at the beach, then?"

"As far as the smugglers are concerned, the run couldn't have gone more smoothly. Whit's following the goods into town." He glanced into the hall. "He wasn't happy about it."

"He wanted to return to the house?"

"No, I don't think so. He just appeared angry in a general sense, and that after he was done appearing genuinely shocked at finding the smugglers. He's still behaving oddly."

She took a step closer to him, visibly agitated. "Will he be all right, going into town alone? What if he's discovered and captured? What if—"

"He won't be. He'll follow from a good distance. Even if the smugglers come to realize he's there, which they won't, he'll be able to make an escape. Once . . ." He trailed off and held a hand up for silence as the door to Miss Willory's room opened and Lord Martin stepped into the hall. They waited in silence until Lord Martin made the short journey to his own room and disappeared inside.

"Will you confront Miss Willory now?" Kate finally whispered when Lord Martin's door closed with more force than Hunter considered advisable for a man attempting to be sneaky.

He shook his head. "No. She'll be followed when she leaves. Miss Willory is likely no more than a courier. We want the individual she's to meet."

"A courier," Kate repeated. "However did she become involved in such a scheme?"

"She was approached for the mission, no doubt. Her family's financial straits; her reputation for being a woman of considerable ambition; her connections to a gullible peer with the means to finance a smuggling run." He rubbed at the back of his neck, where the hair was once more standing on end. The residual effects of having been watched by both Miss Willory and Kate, he told himself. "She would've been an irresistible target."

Kate shifted in an effort to see around him. "What do you suppose the letter contains?"

"We'll find out soon enough."

He motioned for Kate to back away from the door as the feeling of being watched grew. He drew out his pistol a moment before a soft male voice sounded from the other side of the door. "Actually, I believe that leg of the mission to be my responsibility."

In a heartbeat, Hunter had the door opened just wide enough to train his weapon on the man stepping from the shadows.

Kate's voice came out with a slight crack. "Mr. Laury?"

Mr. Laury tilted his head to look around Hunter's form. "Are you going to invite me in, Lady Kate? Or shall I wait in the hall until we are all discovered?"

Hunter lowered his weapon and stepped back to let the man inside.

Mr. Laury tossed him a questioning look before taking up the position at the door. "If I'd known you meant to bring Lady Kate into the investigation," he whispered. "I'd not have asked you to keep my involvement to yourself."

Hunter shrugged. "Had I been certain you'd keep Kate's involvement to yourself, I might have brought you in."

"Fair enough," Mr. Laury replied agreeably. "My only orders were to trail the paperwork, at any rate."

"You've some talent for trailing," Hunter admitted.

Mr. Laury's lips curved up. "I doubt I'd have made it around the door before you noticed."

"You wouldn't have."

Kate took a step toward them. "I do wish someone would afford me the courtesy of an explanation."

"Mr. Laury was attempting to avoid you," Hunter informed her, stowing away his pistol once more.

"He's been successful," Kate replied.

"I'd no other choice." Mr. Laury looked away from the door to give Kate a brief smile. "My knowledge of all things musical is limited. You'd have discovered that if we spent any amount of time together."

"But . . . you . . . I've heard you sing."

"I can carry a tune, and play a piece or two on the pianoforte, nothing more. I wouldn't begin to know how to compose an original piece."

Kate shook her head. "Why on *earth* would you pretend such a thing?"

"Because musical aptitude was a requirement for an invitation to Baroness Cederström's salon. And an invitation to the salon was a requirement for spying on a possible traitor . . ."

Mr. Laury trailed off, glanced out the crack in the door and held up a hand for quiet. The three of them stood in silence for a moment before Mr. Laury turned to them once more and grinned. "She's off, which means I am as well. Lady Kate, Mr. Hunter, it's been a pleasure."

As quickly and quietly as Mr. Laury had appeared, he was gone.

Kate blinked at the empty doorway. "I . . . Good heavens. Mr. Laury, an agent. I can scarce believe . . ." Her eyes moved to him. "You knew."

"I did." Hunter shut the door softly. "I didn't want you to seek him out. You weren't to be involved, remember?"

Kate frowned at him. "You could have simply ordered me not to speak with him."

"Awareness can be communicated with more than words. Mr. Laury would have known."

Kate pressed her lips together for a moment in obvious annoyance. "There is no way for me to counter that without positing the argument that I am a skilled actress."

Hunter swallowed down a chuckle and stepped forward to bend his head and catch her eye. "I didn't want to risk anyone learning of your involvement. I didn't want to risk you being sent back to Haldon. I wanted you here, with me. Would you like me to apologize for being selfish?"

She ran her tongue across her teeth. "Are you attempting to charm yourself out of trouble?"

"Possibly." He gave her a hopeful smile. "Is it working?"

"Possibly," she conceded with a twitch of her lips. "I'll have to think on the matter." She gestured at the closed door. "What happens, now, to the letter, and Miss Willory?"

"Mr. Laury will trail Miss Willory. The letter will be confiscated, its intended recipient apprehended. Miss Willory will likely be exiled."

"And her family?"

"They may join her, if they like."

Kate was quiet a moment before speaking. "She did this to save them."

"You feel badly for her?"

She looked down and fiddled with the tie of her wrap. "You told me there are some things people will do anything to keep. Miss Willory wants to keep her family solvent. It may not be a noble cause, but she's never known another life. I imagine she feels she had no other choice."

"She did." There were times a person found himself completely out of choices, he knew. But this was not one of those times. "She had other options. More than most."

"Yes, I know." She blew out a short breath. "The smuggling . . . that is why she did those things. Broke the piano bench, encouraged Mr. Potsbottom, and sabotaged my tack. She was afraid Lord Martin would tell me of the smuggling."

Hunter ground his teeth. "I find my limited sympathy has flagged."

She smiled a little at that. "What of Lord Martin?"

"I suspect his punishment will be minor, given that he appears to be innocent of treason in his intentions. But it's up to William."

She nodded and went back to thoughtfully toying with her wrap. It was a long and flowing concoction of ivory, covering her from neck to toe. He wanted to reach out to pull the tie loose and slide the material from her shoulders. Then he wanted to loosen the thick braid of pale hair that fell down her back and use handfuls of it to pull her in for a kiss. But more than that, he wanted to have the conversation he'd asked her for in the parlor.

The idea of it brought on a sudden and unexpected case of nerves. Excitement, he corrected, he was *excited*. It was anticipation that had him stalling. He was within moments of seeing his plan come to fruition. He was within minutes of acquiring the hand of Lady Kate Cole.

Only she'd ceased, at some point, to be just another, or even the ultimate, acquisition for him. He couldn't put his finger on when it had happened, or how it had happened. He only knew that it had. There was no denying the terror he'd felt when he'd seen her horse charge toward the bluffs, nor the staggering relief that had washed over him when he'd pulled her safely into his arms.

He was attached to Kate, there could be no mistake. Which was not to be confused with in love with her. She was important to him, and it followed that her well-being was of concern to him, but he was not in love. He would never be in love.

But perhaps it was best he felt more for her than he allowed himself to feel for others. She was to be his wife, after all. A man ought to feel a little bit . . . well, *more* for his wife. He intended to feel more for any children they might have. Not too much—children had the unfortunate characteristic of being small and fragile—but certainly more than he did, say, his cook. That was only natural.

Moreover, Kate was of a romantic bent. She'd want something other than mild interest from her spouse. She'd be unhappy without it. She was too sensible and too much a member of the *ton* to refuse an offer of marriage now that he'd taken her innocence, but she'd not be happy in their union without some level of affection. And it had been his plan from the very start to make her happy. What good was acquiring a rare jewel and then showcasing to the world that one wasn't capable of properly caring for it?

Only he wasn't acquiring her, he reminded himself, because she wasn't an acquisition.

He resisted the urge to drag a hand through his hair. The whole business of trying to figure through what Kate was, and was not, to him made him uncomfortable. Which is why he shoved it aside.

He liked her very much. They would marry. He would make her happy. That was quite enough figuring through.

He cleared his throat. "I'd like the private audience I requested from you last night, Kate."

Kate looked up, her blue eyes rounding. "What? Now?"

"Yes. Why not?"

"Because," she replied, as if the answer were patently obvious. "I'm in my night rail."

He gestured at her. "You've been in your night rail for the past half hour or more."

"And you've had a private audience, mostly. That's not the point." She shook her head. "I'll meet you in the sitting room in half an hour."

"But—"

"It's nearly time for Lizzy to rise. If she comes in while you're here and I'm not properly clothed, it will be a disaster."

"Why don't you simply lock—?"

"The sitting room in half an hour." She moved past him to open the door. After glancing down both ends of the hall, she reached to snag his arm and propel him across the threshold. Before he could utter another word of protest, the door was shut with a soft click.

Kate dressed in ten minutes, cajoled her hair into something approaching respectable in under five, and, in an attempt to retain a bit of pride, decided to stall the remaining fifteen minutes. She brushed at the white muslin of her skirts, straightened a small stack of music on her nightstand, and occupied her mind by wondering if her suspicions were correct and Hunter was about to offer marriage. Quickly deciding that was most certainly the case, she turned her imagination toward what sort of proposal she might receive.

Something traditional, she mused. He *had* made a point of formally asking for a private audience. Even if he'd then suggested she hold that audience in her night rail, it still indicated some desire for a conventional proposal. Likely he would give a small speech as well. It wouldn't be overly flowery—the man wasn't given to theatrics—but she imagined the charmer in him would see to it that it was eloquent. There was a distinct possibility there would be a hint of practicality to it as well. He was a businessman, after all. Nothing wrong with being practical about the matter, she told herself. Nothing at all. But it was matters of the heart that had her pacing the floor, twisting her fingers in the skirts she'd just smoothed, and grinning like a lunatic.

She'd found her prince. They had fallen in love. He was going to propose. It was a dream come true.

Pulling the watch he'd given her from her pocket, she

noted that she had managed to stall for all of four minutes. That was really the most that should be expected of a woman in her position.

Kate walked through the house at a respectable pace, conscious of the muted sound of footsteps and sleepy voices coming from the servants' quarters. The staff would think it odd to find a guest about so early, but they would think it stranger yet to find that guest dashing through the halls. She reached the sitting room without meeting a soul, and after one last brush of her skirts, let herself in quietly. Hunter was standing in front of the windows, his back to the door. He turned when she entered, and to her great delight, crossed the room to take her mouth in a long, warm kiss.

It was, she decided, a perfectly lovely way to begin a proposal.

He released her mouth and taking her hand, led her to a settee by the window. "Will you sit?"

She bit her tongue to keep from laughing. Was the man nervous? He had to be, to suddenly become so formal. And she must be as well, she realized as she took her seat. She'd not uttered a syllable since she'd entered the room, and for the life of her, she couldn't think of one to utter now.

She waited while Hunter sat next to her, brushed his hands down his thighs, cleared his throat, twice, took one of her hands in his, and then finally got around to the business of speaking. "Lady Kate Cole, would you do me the great honor of becoming my wife?"

She blinked at him. Well, that certainly was . . . brief. Abrupt, even. She rather thought there might be some sort of lead in to the affair. Maybe nerves had made him hasty. Maybe he simply needed a spot of encouragement.

She gave him what she hoped was an exceptionally encouraging smile. "I am delighted that you should offer, Hunter. And there is a *very* strong possibility that I should like to marry you, but . . ."

Oh, dear. How to go about asking for what she wanted, without sounding as if she was fishing for compliments?

"But what?" Hunter prompted.

"But I . . . I would like to hear your reasons for offering first."

"All right," he agreed with a single nod. "To begin, I took your innocence not twenty-four hours ago."

She pulled her hand away. "That's your only reason?"

"Not my only reason, no," he was quick to reply. Unfortunately, he was just as quick to add, "But it is *a* reason, a sound one."

"It could be the very best reason in the world, but it's hardly what a woman wishes to hear in a marriage proposal."

"I suppose it's not." He recaptured her hand. "Kate, darling, I have wanted you for my wife for some time. How could I not? You're the most beautiful, compassionate, and talented woman I have ever met."

It seemed fishing would only net her compliments after all. Apparently, a direct approach would be necessary. "I am asking how you feel about me."

This time it was he who pulled away. "How I feel?"

"Yes," she said carefully, rather disconcerted by his reaction. "About me."

"I see." He rose from the settee suddenly, and tugged a little on his cravat. Both very bad signs. "I am very fond of you."

"Fond?" One was fond of pastries, and sunshine, and freshly washed linens on the bed. "Just . . . fond?"

"Very fond," he corrected.

"Like apple tarts," she whispered in disbelief.

"Beg your pardon?"

She squeezed her eyes shut and shook her head to clear her thoughts. When she looked at him again, she was certain her feelings were evident on her face. "You feel nothing more than fondness?"

He licked his lips, another act of nerves she might have wondered at if she hadn't been preoccupied wondering at his lack of passion.

"Should I?" he asked.

"I . . ." She swore she could see the edges of her vision grow red. "*Should you?*"

"What I mean is, is it necessary for us to feel more in order to wed? We've—"

"Of course it's necessary."

"Very well," he conceded on a sigh she could have done without hearing. "I have other feelings for you. I respect you. I desire you more than I have any other woman. I . . . I have a great deal of . . . of . . ." He cleared his throat, directed his gaze over her shoulder, and finished on a mumble. ". . . affection for you."

"And?" she prompted when he said nothing more.

"And what?" he asked impatiently. "Would you have me list everything I feel for you without offering me something in return?"

She was tempted to point out that *she* wasn't the one who had offered a marriage proposal, but only because her feelings were raw. In all fairness, she couldn't judge him for not declaring himself if she wasn't willing to do the same.

"No, of course not," she said. "You're absolutely right."

He nodded in a supremely satisfied sort of way, which was something else she could have done without. She let it pass and concentrated on the daunting challenge of admitting her love for him.

"I . . . I too have a great deal of respect for you." Oh, dear, this was more difficult than she'd anticipated. "And I too feel a physical . . . that is . . ."

"You desire me," he supplied a bit dryly.

"Yes, thank you. And I . . . I . . ." She cleared her throat. "I . . ."

His mouth curved up in something akin to a smirk. It was

all the motivation she needed. She straightened her shoulders, caught his gaze, and held it without blinking until his smirk disappeared.

And then, quite clearly, she said, "I am in love with you."

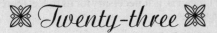

❋ *Twenty-three* ❋

I am in love with you.

Hunter went very, very still. He couldn't have heard her correctly. He couldn't have possibly. "I beg your pardon?"

Kate tipped her chin up. "I am in love with you."

Very well, he had heard her correctly.

He hadn't expected to hear those words from her. He'd worked to earn her loyalty, her trust, and her affection. Maybe, just maybe, some small, irrational part of him had hoped for her love as well, but it would have made him the worst sort of hypocrite to expect it.

He wished he could move. He wished he could think of something better to say than, "I hadn't expected that."

Because, really, there had to be an infinite number of more eloquent things to say in that moment.

Kate certainly seemed to think so. She gaped at him. "*That's* all you have to say? I tell you—"

"No, no. I beg your pardon." Regaining the use of his legs, he stepped forward to take her hand yet again and draw her to her feet. "Forgive me. I'm . . . overwhelmed."

He couldn't ever remember feeling so overwhelmed.

"Oh, well." She smiled a little, a blush forming on her cheeks. "That's all right, then."

He wasn't certain it was all right. "It's a priceless gift," he told her. It was also a tremendous responsibility. "I'm grateful for it." And afraid of it. "I'll treasure it." While it lasted.

"I'm glad it pleases you," she murmured.

And then she stood there, waiting—*pointedly* waiting. Clearly, she expected to hear the words returned.

Bloody hell. What the devil was he supposed to do now?

His first instinct was to lie. So were his second and third. But his fourth and final instinct banded with reason and together they declared telling her the truth his best chance at success. Provided, of course, he managed to relate that truth in a way that suited his purposes.

Kate might, in the excitement of the moment, believe anything he cared to tell her. That would certainly work to his advantage in the short term. He could have them married by special license within the week.

But in the long run, it would be disastrous. Kate was an intelligent woman. Eventually, she would discover the lie. And then what? If she knew the marriage to have begun on a pretense, would she leave him? Despise him? Take lovers? Use her family's wealth and influence to obtain a divorce? The idea of any of those outcomes turned his stomach into sick knots.

Better all around if she understood from the very start what he could offer her, and what he could not. And then it was simply a matter of convincing her that what he offered was of far greater value than what he could not. He could do that. He'd conquered greater challenges than convincing a woman of the *ton* that love was not a prerequisite for a successful marriage.

"There is something you need to understand, Kate. Something . . ." He shook his head. He couldn't just blurt the words out. He'd never make her understand that way. He needed to start at the beginning. "Where did you first meet Lizzy?"

She made a helpless motion with her hands. "What on earth has that to do with anything?"

"Humor me, Kate, please."

"All right," she said slowly, still shaking her head in obvious bafflement. "I met her in Benton as a child."

"And?"

"And what? We were children. She was an orphan. My mother offered her a home—"

"The details, Kate. Tell me the details of the day you met her."

She blew out an irritated breath. "Very well. It was a long time ago, but . . ." She scrunched her face a little in thought. "But I seem to recall it was winter. My mother was shopping for . . . I've no idea, she's always about shopping for something. I remember that I was bored, and when I saw a little girl my own age sitting on a bench in the square, I snuck away and went to sit next to her. She told me she was waiting for someone . . . someone with an unlikely sounding name. I can't seem to recall—"

"Puck."

"Yes, that's . . ." Her eyes grew round. "How did you know that?"

"Because . . ." He swallowed hard. "Because that's what I told her to call me."

"I . . . You . . . You're . . . ?" Her mouth continued to work without sound for a moment before she managed, "You knew each other? As children?"

"We both have the misfortune of having spent a portion of our youth at St. Michael's workhouse in London."

"A workhouse . . . but I thought . . ." She stepped back slowly to retake her seat. "I could have sworn Whit mentioned your father was a merchant, or—"

"He was a linen draper. He inherited a modest shop from his father, along with a comfortable house we shared with my widowed aunt and her son." He rolled his shoulders. He didn't like telling his family's story. He didn't like remembering. "Modest and comfortable weren't enough for my parents. They insisted on the best of everything. My mother even saw to it I received an education fit for a peer. She had visions of me becoming a man of law, I think. I might have at that, if my father had been as skilled a businessman as he pretended to be. We lost the shop to debt when I was eight. By the time I was nine, we'd lost everything else."

"And went to the workhouse?"

"After a time, yes." After the last of his mother's jewelry had been pawned and the money it garnered spent. "They separate men and women upon admission, but children of a certain age are allowed to stay with their mothers. We told the mistress I was nearly two years younger so I could do the same." He smiled wryly. "We were fortunate she wasn't a particularly observant woman."

"And Lizzy?" Kate asked, her voice rather stunned. "She was with her mother as well?"

"Her grandmother. The woman was nearly blind, completely deaf, and regularly forgot who Lizzy was. Lizzy couldn't have been more than four years of age at the time. For some reason, she took to me. She was always following me about." He laughed suddenly. "She annoyed the devil out of me. She was so persistent. In her presence, her questions, her cheerfulness. I couldn't make heads or tails of her, and I couldn't make her go away."

"She grows on you," Kate murmured.

"She does. She did. She hardly gave me a choice." Day after day she'd appear at his side, relentless in her chatter, in her campaign to make him smile. She was always successful. "My mother and I looked out for her. We taught her to read from an old copy of *A Midsummer Night's Dream*." The workhouse had claimed a small room as its school, but little to no education was actually provided.

"Puck," Kate said, nodding.

"She had a lisp then," he told her. "She had trouble with the 'r' in Andrew. We used nicknames instead. Puck and Titania."

"She did have a slight lisp when I first met her," Kate murmured. "I'd forgotten."

"She had a weaker constitution then as well," he said darkly and wished he and Kate were having this conversation later in the day so he could justify going to the sideboard and pouring a drink. "Poor food. Bad air. Lack of adequate clothing and heating. It was difficult for her. There was an outbreak of scarlet fever. She and her grandmother were two of the first to fall ill. I did what I could for her, for both of them."

That was when he'd begun sneaking into the kitchen at night to steal extra food. He took to picking the locks on supply closets as well, obtaining extra blankets he put on Lizzy at night and hid away in the morning. He'd even crept into the rooms of staff while they slept and taken money, a pocket watch, even a wedding band. There'd been a great to do when the staff discovered the thievery. Every healthy resident over the age of eight had been punished. He'd felt bad for it, but not badly enough to stop stealing.

"Lizzy recovered," Kate said quietly.

"She did, but her grandmother did not. Nor did half the inhabitants of the workhouse." He swallowed past a dry lump in his throat. "Including my parents and cousin."

Her hand went to chest. "I'm sorry. I'm so sorry. Your aunt?"

"She survived."

"I'm very glad you had someone," she said softly.

A part of him wanted to nod and leave it at that. But a greater part of him wanted her to know everything, and all of him wanted her to understand. "I didn't have her for long. After the sickness passed, she discharged herself from the workhouse."

"Discharged? You mean, she *left* you there?"

She'd walked through the front gate while he'd begged her to take him and Lizzy with her. Bloody well *begged*. He cleared his throat. "Yes. She was grieving for her child—"

"That isn't an excuse to abandon another."

"No. It isn't." But he'd always preferred to think of her as a tragic figure—a woman who'd lost her mind after the death of her husband and only child. Better something be horribly wrong with her, than something be lacking in him. He cleared his throat yet again. "At any rate, she disappeared. I waited until Lizzy grew well again and then I took her away. I thought she'd not make it through the winter."

"You brought her to Benton."

"We were merely passing through." The money from the stolen goods had only purchased passage as far as Benton. "I wanted us farther from London before we stopped for any length of time. Getting out and away from London had become . . . important to me." It had become an obsession. He'd wanted Lizzy away from the poverty, the filth, the disease. From everything that could take her from him. "I went in search of food and told her to wait in the alley behind one of the shops. I should have known she wouldn't sit still that long. I returned to find her sitting on a bench speaking with you and your mother."

"I saw you, didn't I? I did. I *did*," Kate repeated. "You were staring at me from the other side of the square."

"I couldn't stop staring at you," he admitted. "It had been a long time since I'd seen a girl with hair like yours." And he couldn't ever remember seeing someone give away the shoes on her feet, not willingly.

"I realize it's not the most pertinent bit of information at the moment, but I can't help but ask, weren't there any children at the workhouse with blonde hair?"

"There weren't any children at the workhouse with *clean* hair," he clarified. "Blonde doesn't look blonde when it's filthy."

"Oh, I see. I'm sorry."

He shook his head. "What do you remember after that?"

"After your staring? I looked away for a moment, trying to get mother's attention. And when I turned back again, you were gone."

"Moved some, but not gone. I was still watching. I saw your mother hold out her hand. And I saw Lizzy take it. And leave." He'd told her to wait, told her not to leave, and she'd walked away.

"You said nothing?"

"Lady Thurston's reputation has always preceded her," he explained. "I knew Lizzy was better off."

Kate licked her lips, studying him. "You must have been very angry."

"Not at Lizzy or your mother. At life. At the unfairness . . . She was the last person on earth I . . . the last person I cared for." He'd loved her. And it had broken his heart, cleanly split it in half, to watch her walk away from him into a life he was certain he could never give her. That heartache had translated into an impotent, helpless fury. And that fury had driven him not to simply prosper over the years, but to acquire wealth and power beyond the dreams of most men. Never, *never* again would he find himself in a position where he was impotent, or helpless, or heartbroken.

Kate would understand that. He opened his mouth to ask if she did, indeed, understand, but Kate spoke first.

"I remember Lizzy speaking of you. Mother had people search for anyone who might be looking for her, but . . . but we assumed you were a creation of Lizzy's imagination. After a time, she believed it too. I . . ." A line suddenly formed across her brow. "Why are you telling me this now? I'm glad to know your connection to Lizzy of course, but why now?"

He stepped forward to crouch down in front of her. "Because I want you to understand. I won't do it again, Kate. I can't. I'm not capable of it."

"Not capable of what?"

"Of what you've offered me, but—"

"What I've . . . You mean love?" Her face paled. "You're saying you're not capable of love?"

"There are so many other things—"

"Would you be capable of it if I were someone else?" she asked in a thready voice. "Someone—?"

"No." He reached for the hand she had twisted into her skirts. "No, there's only you."

"Only . . ." She swallowed hard. "Only I'm not enough."

"You are. You're more than enough. You're everything I've always wanted."

She stared down to where their hands were joined. Slowly, she pulled hers away. "You courted me, made love to me, and offered for me knowing all along you would never love me?"

She asked it quietly, but it wasn't a question, it was an accusation. He searched for the words to defend himself and found he hadn't any. He tried evasion instead. "Kate, sweetheart—"

"Why?" She shook her head. "Why did you court me at all?"

"I've told you why. I'm fond of you. I desire you. I can offer—"

"You could feel those things for any woman," she cut in, the first hints of anger tinting her voice.

"I want *you*."

"And I you. But apparently, neither of us wants in the manner the other needs."

"I . . ." He stood up and dragged a hand through his hair. "What the devil does that mean?"

"It means I need your heart along with . . . everything else. And you want everything else, but need to keep your heart."

He didn't find the workings of her mind quite so fascinating now. He found them frustrating. And terrifying beyond measure. Was he losing her? He couldn't possibly be losing her. He'd explained, hadn't he? They should be at the point of understanding now. They *would* be at the point of understanding if she would just be reasonable.

"Kate, be reasonable. People regularly marry without . . . without . . ."

"You can't even bring yourself to say the word," she grumbled.

"Without considering matters of the heart," he bit out. It was exceedingly difficult to make her understand when she wouldn't let him finish his own sentences.

"Yes, most often because they haven't any other choice." She shook her head slowly. "I am sister to the Earl of Thurston. I've more wealth and status than I shall ever need, and a family that would never insist I sacrifice my happiness in a bid to acquire more."

"You think there is nothing I can offer you that you don't already possess?"

"There is nothing you are *willing* to offer that I don't already possess."

"What of children?"

"Children would be wonderful," she admitted. "And Whit and I are both testimony to the fact they can be happily raised in a home with only one loving parent. But the possibility of that is not sufficient reason to enter into an ill-advised union."

"It bloody well isn't ill-advised." He threw his hand up in an impatient gesture. "And you may very well already be with child."

She rose slowly from her seat, as if she ached. "Should that circumstance arise, I may have to reconsider matters, but unless it does, I'll marry for love, or not at all."

"You love me. That is more than most in the *ton* can claim. Can't it be enough for now, and—?"

"If it were enough to earn your love in return, it would be."

"Kate, you have to understand—"

She didn't, apparently. She'd turned and walked from the room before he could finish his sentence.

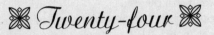

� Twenty-four ✦

$\mathcal{K}$ate wondered a little that she was able to walk down the hall, past staff and guests as if nothing was amiss. She wondered that she was able to walk at all. The hurt was enormous. It sat heavy in her chest where her heart ought to be and beat out a steady rhythm of pain in time to the rushing of blood in her ears. It bloomed out from there—sharp tendrils that wound through her belly and out to her arms and legs down to her very toes. Her head hurt. Her eyes burned. Even her jaw ached from clenching.

Hunter didn't love her. He'd all but promised he never would.

The burn at the back of her eyes increased as she dragged herself up the back stairs.

Was it irony that she should have spent so much time dreaming of a prince who loved her without bounds, only to have fallen in love herself with one who would not love her in return? That he *could* not, she refused to believe. At least in the sense that he was incapable of love entirely. Everyone was capable of love. It was Hunter's choice to keep his heart locked safe behind a wall of mistrust.

She couldn't blame him for having constructed the wall, and a portion of the pain she felt now was not only for her, but for the hurt boy he'd been. But he was no longer a helpless boy. He was a grown man of wealth and power. He made his own choices. And he chose to keep the wall.

Though he'd assured her otherwise, Kate couldn't help wondering whether he would have chosen to take the wall down if she'd been a different sort of woman. Someone less stubborn, or less distracted, or less clumsy. Someone he thought was worth the risk.

The first tear fell as she pushed through her bedroom door. A half dozen more fell before she closed the door behind her.

Hunter didn't love her. He never would. She'd mistaken the wrong man for her prince, again.

She made it to the bed, crawled atop the counterpane, found a pillow to bury her face against, and began to weep in earnest.

"Kate?" Lizzy's soft voice filtered through the sound of her own crying. "Lady Kate?"

"I'm sorry, Lizzy." She managed to turn her head from the pillow and choke the words out between the sobs. "But please go away."

"It's Mr. Hunter, isn't it?"

She couldn't answer. She couldn't do anything but turn her face back into the pillow, and cry harder.

Hunter walked along the beach, oblivious to the seagulls swooping overhead, the golden light of morning dancing across the waves, and the salty breeze that blew off the water. He was oblivious to everything but the thoughts and emotions simmering in his mind. Uncomfortable with the latter, he focused his attention on the first.

It was for the best that he fought back the urge to follow Kate after she left the sitting room. The woman was being stubborn and unreasonable. A few hours to herself would be a more effective remedy for that than a few hours spent listening to him demand she *cease* being stubborn and unreasonable. Furthermore, giving Kate a bit of time to think provided him with time to develop a new strategy, or at the very least, figure out what had gone wrong with the first.

He'd been so sure telling her the truth would work to his benefit. It should have. It *would* have, if she'd given him a chance to convince her he'd make a fine husband. They'd have a good marriage, no less happy for not being a love match. What the devil was wrong with a match made out of fondness and respect?

I'll marry for love or not at all.

He grimaced at those words.

Obviously, he had misjudged what it was about her novels that captured Kate's interest. She wasn't merely a dreamer. It wasn't just a life of adventure she wished for. It was love. The woman was a hopeless romantic, with a very heavy emphasis on hopeless. She fancied herself in love with *him*, after all.

You're a good man.

That's who she was in love with—the good man. The charming gentleman who made her laugh, brought her thoughtful presents, and offered her adventure. She hadn't the first inkling that he'd done those things for himself, hadn't the slightest idea that the charming gentleman was nothing more than one of many personas he'd created over the years.

She hadn't the foggiest notion that the man she loved didn't exist.

If she even suspected half the things he'd done in his life, she'd have nothing to do with him now. He wasn't a good man. He wasn't a prince from one of her books. He—

Something small and sharp caught him on the side of his head. He whirled around and found Lizzy standing not ten feet away, her eyes red and her face set in mutinous lines. She wore a full apron covered with pockets and held a decent-sized seashell in her hand.

She'd hit him with a shell?

"Lizzy? Why the blazes are you tossing shells at me?"

"You've hurt her. You made her cry."

Kate was crying. And Lizzy had been as well. Oh, damn. "Sweetheart—"

"You'll not call me that!" She hurled the next shell and hit him on the shoulder, as soon as it left her hand another appeared in its place.

"All right. I'll not call you that." Hunter held up his hands in surrender and eyed her warily. "You've a great many pockets on that apron. How do you keep the contents straight?"

"I fill them all with the same thing."

He'd been afraid of that. "I see. Lizzy, try to understand—"

He ducked before a particularly sharp half shell could take out an eye, then ducked again.

"*Pax!*" He dodged the next projectile, braced as she raised her arm to hurl another. "Titania, *pax!*"

She froze in place, her eyes wide. Slowly, ever so slowly, she lowered her arm. "What did you say?"

He ran his tongue across dry lips. Why should he be nervous? He'd intended to tell Lizzy at some point. He'd known he'd have to once he told Kate. He just hadn't intended to tell her quite so soon, and he hadn't thought to tell her like this.

"You called me . . ." Lizzy opened her mouth, closed it again. "You called me Titania, didn't you?"

He nodded, and waited for her to remember. Heart in his throat, he waited to see if she *would* remember.

"Titania. I've not been called that since . . ." She stared at him, her eyes narrowing. "Since I was a very little girl."

"You were five. We were in London."

The shell she'd been holding fell to the ground with a soft thud. "Puck?"

The distance from the shore to Pallton House was no more than a hundred yards, but to Hunter it seemed a hundred miles. He was, in a word, *exhausted*. He'd been up for more than twenty-four hours. He'd completed a mission. He'd offered for, and been denied, the hand of the woman he wanted to marry. He'd informed a grown woman that, as a child, she'd been the nearest thing he'd ever had to a sister, and then discussed that exceptionally uncomfortable topic for well over an hour, which left him no further along in his strategy for winning Kate's hand than he had been an hour prior.

By the way his mind and body dragged, Hunter imagined he'd be no further along an hour hence. He needed sleep—a brief nap to clear his head.

He had time enough, he told himself as he climbed the steps of the terrace. Kate wasn't going anywhere. The house party wasn't over yet. There was a fortnight left for him to put a new strategy into play.

He could make her come round in a fortnight.

She wasn't going to come round.

Hunter stood next to Kate on the front steps of Pallton House and watched as trunks were loaded onto the Thurston carriage. He'd woken to the sound of it—the hustle and bustle up and down the hall. He'd followed the noise and movement and found Kate standing in the midday sunlight, watching her mother, Lizzy, and Lord Brentworth give directions to the footmen loading the carriage that would take them back to Haldon Hall.

He couldn't quite wrap his head around it, simply could not grasp that Kate was leaving. He turned his eyes from the drive and stared at her profile. Neither had spoken when he'd come outside. He'd been unable to find the right words. He'd been unable to do most anything beyond stare and wonder at the sudden ache in his chest.

The ache grew, spurring him to say *something*. "Don't do this, Kate."

"It's for the best," she replied softly, keeping her gaze straight ahead.

"Running away is never for the best."

"I'm not running away. I'm going home. To Haldon." She fiddled with something on the front hem of her gray spencer. He couldn't see what, because she wouldn't turn to face him. "You'll be welcome there, should you decide that is what you want."

He hadn't a response. He wasn't sure what, if anything, the offer meant. So he changed the subject, and his tactic.

"The other guests will talk. They'll speculate Miss Willory scared you off and—"

"Let them."

Kate's mother called up as Lord Brentworth took her hand to assist her into the carriage after Lizzy. "When you are ready, dear, the carriage is prepared."

Kate nodded in acknowledgment. She barely turned her head to speak to him. "Good-bye, Hunter."

She stepped forward and suddenly the ache gave way and a panic unlike any he'd ever known raced through his veins. Chasing close behind was fury. His arm shot out to grab her elbow. "I'll not come for you," he growled. "I'll not bloody beg."

She looked at his hand a moment, and then for the first time, looked at him.

"Would it change anything," she whispered, "if I did?"

It would change everything.

I'll beg.

I love you.

Say the words. Even if they're lies, say them.

He dropped his arm.

She nodded, turned, and walked away.

❋ Twenty-five ❋

*H*unter had a new strategy. He was going to win Kate back with flowers, presents, charm, and an adventure or two. He was going to convince her by using every means at his disposal that she couldn't live without him. It was, he could admit, a rather uninspired strategy, but it *was* a strategy.

He reminded himself of this as he sat in his room at Pallton House, staring into a glass of brandy he hadn't a clear memory of pouring. At a guess—a highly inebriated guess—he had reminded himself of his strategy every half hour for the last eighteen hours, which also happened to be the frequency at which he envisioned getting on his horse, riding to Haldon, and begging Kate not to leave him. It was humiliating how strong the temptation was to chase after her. But he wasn't going to give in, he told himself and took a long swallow of his drink. He wasn't going to make a terrific ass of himself—women weren't charmed by asses, terrific or otherwise—just because he couldn't stop thinking of her. Or because he missed her smile, and her laugh, and the damn dimple at the end of her nose.

He wasn't going to make an ass of himself just because he hurt.

He rubbed the heel of his hand against his chest. Shouldn't *not* loving the woman hurt less? Hadn't that been the point of not falling in love—to *not* hurt?

He glowered at his drink. Hadn't not hurting also been the point of getting foxed?

"Waste of perfectly good brandy," he grumbled and set the glass aside.

He glanced up at a knock on his door, and the sound of Whit's voice coming from the other side. "You decent, Hunter?"

"Haven't you heard?" he asked, letting his head fall back against the chair. "I'm better than decent. I'm bloody good."

Whit opened the door. "What?"

"Nothing." He waved a hand impatiently. "Come in, then."

Whit frowned at him a moment before crossing the room to toss a letter in Hunter's lap. "Mission's over. William wants you in London."

"Can't ride. Drunk."

Whit stepped closer and bent forward to sniff. "You do smell flammable. Hell, man, it's eight in the morning."

Hunter glanced at his window. He hadn't noticed the sun had come up. "What of it?" he groused. "I'll go to London when I'm sober. Anything else?"

"Yes, as a matter of fact." Whit took a seat across from him. "I wish to discuss Kate."

"Why? Mission's over, as you said."

"This doesn't pertain to the mission," Whit replied. "Do you know the excuse she gave for leaving the house party early?"

"No."

"She said she was homesick. Said she couldn't compose properly in an unfamiliar room." Whit snorted and leaned back in his chair. "Chit's not been homesick a day in her life."

"Is there a particular reason you're telling me this?"

"There is." Whit tapped his finger on the edge of the chair. "Your mission required you to spend a good deal of time with my sister while she was here. I saw the looks that passed between you at meals and over games of chess in the parlor. I know my sister. I know her heart." He stopped tapping. "I know you broke it."

A demand of satisfaction from Kate's brother, Hunter

thought with resigned disgust; it was a fitting end to the courtship. "Took you long enough to seek me out."

"I wanted to think the matter through, and give you time to do the same."

"Time changes nothing."

Whit surprised him by shrugging. "I'm not quite as eager to call you out as I was eighteen hours ago."

"Generous of you."

"Not really. Mirabelle promised to take our son and emigrate to the Americas should I try it."

"Ah."

"She did give me leave to bloody your nose a bit, though."

"Have done with it then," Hunter invited with a wave of his hand. He didn't bother getting up. No point, really, if he was just going to fall back down again.

Whit sat up in his chair, and his voice grew cold. "Is there a *particular* reason I should?"

Hunter was just sober enough to know when a diplomatic reply was in everyone's best interest. "Broke her heart, didn't I?"

Whit, apparently satisfied by that answer, snorted and leaned back once more. "By the looks of it, she broke yours as well."

"Don't have one to break."

"If I believed that, even for a moment, I'd not have let you within a hundred yards of my sister."

"You don't know me as well as you think."

"I do." A small smile pulled at Whit's mouth. "You've what—five, six months left of your obligation to the War Department?"

Hunter bolted upright, waited for his vision to catch up, then demanded, "You know? You know and would allow me to have anything to do with your family?"

Whit's smile grew. He motioned toward the decanter of brandy. "May I?"

"What? No. Yes. I don't care." What the devil was the man talking about?

Whit helped himself to a small drink and returned to his chair to sit back and let out a long contented sigh. "I've been waiting a good while to have my revenge on William."

"Revenge?"

"You'll be wanting your own soon enough."

Hunter was vaguely aware of grinding his teeth. "What do you know?"

Whit took a sip of his drink. "I know you financed, among other things, a very successful smuggling operation for a time." He took another sip. "I know you were apprehended with some of your goods, and that among those goods was correspondence between a French patriot and an English spy." He took yet another slow sip. "I know those letters were planted."

"They bloody well were," Hunter snapped. At least, they had been in the sense that one of his men had acquired them without his permission or knowledge.

Whit's smile grew into a positively wolfish grin. "They were planted by William."

A long period of silence followed that announcement. Whit continued to sip his drink. Hunter stared at him, his sluggish brain struggling to catch up to his hearing.

"You lie," he finally managed.

Still grinning, Whit shrugged and finished his drink. "Ask William yourself. He intended to tell you in a couple months' time."

Hunter went back to staring as Whit set his glass aside and rose from his chair to take his leave. He paused at the door and turned back. "Regardless of your reasons for working for the War Department, you've been an extraordinary agent, Hunter. The best . . . aside from Alex and myself, of course. And you've been a good friend."

"Because I helped make you rich."

"That didn't hurt. Neither did stepping in front of that bullet for me."

Hunter resisted the urge to shift in his seat. "Just a scratch."

"Sober up. Get to London." Whit's grin returned. "Give William my regards."

The ride from Pallton House to London took six hours by horseback. Hunter's head throbbed as every hoof beat against the road. He'd averaged it out to be roughly three hundred sixty beats per minute, sixty minutes an hour, for six hours. That was roughly one hundred thirty thousand throbs. And he was going to bloody William's nose for each and every one of them.

It mattered little to him that William hadn't been the reason he'd reached for the brandy, nor that it hadn't been William he'd thought of while he'd spent half the day trying to undo the damage that brandy had done, nor that it hadn't been William he'd thought of during the vast majority of the long ride. It was William who was going to pay.

And now that he was perfectly sober, he decided to make Whit pay as well. The man had known of William's treachery and not said a word until now. What sort of good friend kept secrets such as that? It was possible, of course, that Whit had only recently learned of the deception, but that minor detail wasn't going to save him.

Fuming, throbbing, and eager to make William pay for both, Hunter climbed the front steps to William's town house, lifted a fist to pound on the front door, then paused.

There were questions he wanted answered and if those answers turned out to correspond with what Whit had told him, he wanted satisfaction. The latter was easily obtained with his fists, but the first would be troublesome to acquire from an unconscious man. Even a man with a broken nose could be difficult to understand.

He'd give William a chance to explain himself, he decided as he pounded on the front door. Perhaps he'd have a little fun with the man first—let him squirm a bit. *Then* he'd bloody his nose.

A maid showed him in and ushered him down the hall to the study where William sat working behind a desk piled with paperwork.

"Mr. Hunter to see you, sir," the maid announced before taking her leave.

"Hunter, my boy." William barely spared him a glance. "You're late. And you look like hell."

"I was drunk."

That got the man's full attention. "Were you?"

"Very," he assured him and took a seat in front of the desk.

"Any particular reason?"

"None whatsoever." He stretched his legs out before him. "Just fancied the idea."

"I see, and did this idea occur to you before or after your mission was officially over?"

"Before," he lied. "*Well* before,"

"I see," William repeated and narrowed his eyes. "Habit of yours?"

"I wouldn't call it a habit, not really. I'm more of a dedicated hobbyist." He raised his brows. "Problem?"

William set his pen down, hard. "Have you forgotten your obligation to me? To the War Department?"

"No. But I have decided to no longer meet it."

"You'd risk the hangman?"

"No," he said clearly. "*Apparently*, I wouldn't."

William opened his mouth, closed it, and sat back in his chair with a disgusted grunt. "*Damn* Whit. I should never have told him."

"Damn you!" Hunter snapped, straightening in his chair. "You *lied* to me."

William heaved the sigh of one very much put open. "Yes. Yes, I did. Extensively, in fact."

"You planted evidence that marked me as a traitor."

"Strictly speaking, it wasn't planted. Never left my pocket. I just pulled it out—" He broke off at Hunter's narrow-eyed glare. "Very well, I planted it."

"I thought I'd been an unwitting traitor." That had eaten at him, the notion someone had gotten the better of him, that someone had used him. "I thought I'd hang." That hadn't sat well with him either. Nor did the realization that someone *had* used him sit well now.

He jabbed his finger at William. "I should call you out."

"You'd certainly hang for shooting me."

He jabbed his finger again. "I should beat you senseless."

"Might want to hold off on that until I explain why. Or don't you want to know?"

Hunter snarled but dropped his finger. "Why, then?"

"Because I wanted you as an agent and, at the time, it was the only way to gain your cooperation." William gave Hunter a pointed look. "Would you have come to work for the War Department simply because I had asked?"

"No."

William nodded. "I needed you. You are one of very few who can move about in every level of society as if it was his own, because at some point, every one of them was your own. You've been, among a multitude of other things, a pauper, a thief, a merchant, and by the time you were brought to my attention, a guest at some of England's most elite tables."

"Is that why you didn't confiscate my wealth?" Hunter demanded. "Because you knew I'd need it to find any level of acceptance in the *ton?*"

"Well, that, and because I do have *some* sense of fair play. It was never my intention to punish you, merely make use of you."

"Do you expect me to express gratitude for that?"

"For that, no. For giving you the opportunity to prove yourself, yes."

"Sanctimonious ass," Hunter snarled. "Prove myself to whom? You? The Prince Regent?"

"To yourself," William informed him. "Admittedly, it wasn't for your own well-being that I planted the letters, but it worked out to your benefit all the same. Your obligation to me—"

"There was no bloody obligation."

"Your perceived obligation, then," William corrected. "It gave you time away from your less savory pursuits. It gave you a chance to become the man you believe you've only pretended to be."

Hunter gave himself a moment to try to decipher that last bit. "What the devil does that mean?"

"It means you're a good agent, Hunter. One of the most reliable I've ever had."

"I haven't had a choice, have I?"

"Certainly you have," William countered dismissively. "You could have left. Nothing stopped you from simply disappearing years ago."

"And have your men hunt me down like a fox run to ground?"

William waved that argument away. "You know how to stay hidden, how to evade."

"From the likes of McAlistair?" The man had been an assassin. A highly successful assassin.

William seemed to think about that, scratching at his nose before his face split in a sudden grin. "I'd have paid good money to see a contest such as that. It would have been epic."

It would have resulted in the death of one or both of them. "You're positively macabre, aren't you?"

William shrugged. "It's the nature of the business. Speaking of which . . . I'm retiring from it."

"I . . ." Hunter bent his head to pinch the bridge of his

nose. Just like that, the man wanted to change the subject. "I'm delighted for you. Or I express my deepest condolences, whichever you prefer. May we return to the matter at hand?"

"It is the matter at hand. I'm naming you as my successor."

His head snapped up. "What? Me? What the devil for?"

"Because you're a good man, a trustworthy agent. Didn't I just mention that?"

"I . . ." He held a finger up. "A minute."

He needed a damn minute to wrap his throbbing head around the bizarre conversation. William had planted evidence, misled and used him, and was now offering him a position of exceptional prestige and power. There were, he decided, only so many surprises a man could absorb in a short amount of time. William, no doubt, was aware of this.

"Make no mistake," Hunter said in a cool tone. "We're not finished with the matter of the planted letters. But to address your attempt at changing the subject—Whit, Alex, and McAlistair are fine agents as well." They were also better men, but he wasn't about to begin a discussion on that. "Ask one of them."

William shook his head. "This isn't a job for a peer. It requires one be a mite . . . flexible, shall we say, in one's morals."

"McAlistair's flexible enough."

"He lacks diplomacy."

The years McAlistair hadn't been an assassin, he'd been a hermit. "He does that."

"You'll take the position, then."

"No. I . . . The offer is . . ." He dragged a hand down his face. He had no idea what the offer was except astonishing, and unacceptable. "No. I can't do it. I'll not risk . . ." He wanted to say he'd not risk leaving Kate by staying with the War Department. But he wasn't hers to leave, was he? "I'll not risk it."

"Not so much of a risk, to be honest. The vast majority of it is paperwork." William nudged a stack on his desk, and curled his lip. "Bloody lot of paperwork. But my Mrs. Summers has insisted she'll not have another husband employed by the War Department. I have promised to retire."

"You're willing to make this sort of sacrifice for her?"

"It's not a sacrifice, to be honest. I've been planning my retirement for some time. But yes, *were* it a sacrifice, I would make it, happily, to be with the woman I love." He tilted his head. "I imagine you know something about how it feels to be in love."

"I don't," he snapped instinctively.

William snorted derisively. "You bloody well do. And saying otherwise won't change the fact. I can see it in your eyes. They're bloodshot."

"I was drunk."

"Bah. You've fallen in love with our Lady Kate." William winced sympathetically. "Hurts a bit, doesn't it? I hadn't expected that, myself."

"Sanctimonious ass *and* an idiot."

William appeared to ignore him in favor of twisting his lips in thought. "It's worked then."

Forget bloodying noses. He was going to strangle the man. "*What* worked?"

"Right." William nodded and heaved his put-upon sigh once again. "I cannot adequately express how tired I am of telling this, but . . ." He heaved yet another sigh. "Almost twenty years ago, the late Duke of Rockeforte tricked me into a deathbed promise. A promise that I have spent a number of years attempting to fulfill."

Again, Hunter wasn't certain he wanted to know. "The nature of this promise?"

"That I help the children of his heart find love." He laughed suddenly. "Your expression is no doubt very near to the one I gave Lord Rockeforte."

"That is the single most preposterous deathbed promise I've ever heard."

"So I thought at the time, and for many years after. Even Lord Bucknam's request to have his sixteen hounds looked after seemed reasonable in comparison. But now . . . well, it's still damned unreasonable," he admitted. "But Rockeforte wanted happiness for the children he loved, and there's nothing preposterous about that. Kate, as I am sure you have guessed, was one of these children. And you are her match. You may thank me for that at your leisure."

"I could beat you now and get the details later," Hunter growled. "What did you do?"

"Nothing too extreme, I assure you. I merely exaggerated the possibility of Kate becoming embroiled in the smuggling operation and assigned you to watch over her. Lord Martin was no threat to her. Boy thought he was bringing in a bit of brandy and a love letter over, that's all. No idea Miss Willory was using him to smuggle a message containing the whereabouts of a French saboteur. We've caught them, by the way, Miss Willory and her contact. I'll let Martin's father see to his son."

Hunter spoke around a clenched jaw. "Miss Willory nearly killed Kate by sabotaging her tack in a bid to remove Kate from Lord Martin."

"Whit mentioned that in his letter." William dragged a hand down his face. "No wonder, really, that Whit sought his revenge now. In my defense, I hadn't expected Miss Willory to be involved."

"Whit knew of this . . . of everything?"

William winced. "Yes, and no. He knew of the matchmaking business. I was less forthcoming with him in regards to the mission. He believed it entirely fabricated."

That certainly explained Whit's reluctance to spend the night on Smuggler's Beach, his surprise at finding actual smugglers, why he'd allowed Kate to attend the house party to begin with, and why Mr. Laury was given orders to keep his mission secret. Bloody hell.

"Who else knew?"

"My Mrs. Summers, Lady Thurston, and the Dowager Lady Thurston, though the last two were less . . . enthusiastic, shall we say, in my choice of match for Kate."

"Sensible women."

"Cautious women. They don't know you as Whit and I do."

He wasn't going to have a discussion on that topic either. He could barely comprehend the one he was having now. "You do realize your entire ridiculous ruse was utterly pointless? I'd been planning to acquire Kate's hand for some time."

"Some time," William repeated with a roll of his eyes. "Hell, man, you do overthink things. Can't fathom why you bother, as you always plow straight through the obstacles in your path as if you don't see them. By the look of you, I'd venture to say that strategy mucked things up a bit this time, didn't it?"

"I—"

"Well, I said you were a good man. Never said you weren't an arrogant, shortsighted fool."

"I can't very well be both."

"Certainly, you can. I'm a sanctimonious ass, aren't I? I lied to Whit. Lied to you—planted false evidence so I could use your unique position in society for my own ends, and I feel quite justified in having done so. And yet I am a good man."

He was, in fact. It stunned Hunter to realize it. William Fletcher was a right bastard—particularly just then, to his mind—and a good man. He was a lying, manipulating, schemer . . . Who'd spent years fulfilling a promise to a friend, and his whole life in service to his country. Hunter found himself at a loss for words.

William, bastard that he was, had no difficulty taking the

ensuing silence for complete agreement. "Delighted you con-
cur. It's never a good idea to mistake minor imperfections for
gross deficiencies of character." He reached for his pen with
one hand and pointed to the door with the other. "Now, go
smooth over whatever mess you've made with Kate. I want
my obligation to the late duke to be at an end."

Still reeling, Hunter tossed his hands up in a combination
of disbelief and defeat. "Certain there aren't any other con-
fessions you care to make before I take my leave?"

William looked at the ceiling for a moment as if considering. "No. No, nothing comes to mind."

"You're absolutely sure?"

"Yes, I believe I am quite done."

"Splendid."

Hunter arrived home feeling bewildered, rather discontent,
and *exceedingly* annoyed with himself for having let William
distract him from the aim of administering a bloody nose.
Leaving his horse to the care of a groom in the mews, he
walked to a side door, scowled at it a moment, then walked
round to the front of the house to stand on the sidewalk in
the last light of a long summer's day and take a good look at
his home.

Taking up a significant portion of the block, the house
was far and away the largest building in the neighborhood.
Which was the very reason he'd bought it. In fact, it was the
only reason he'd bought it. He'd wanted the grandest, the
most impressive, the most imposing. He'd certainly gotten
the last. The house appeared impenetrable, wholly inde-
structible. Napoleon's army wouldn't be able to beat down
the massive front doors.

"I don't like it," he announced to absolutely no one. "Don't
like a damn thing about it."

He didn't like the dark color, didn't care for the top-heavy
look of the attic, didn't understand why there were so many

chimneys sticking out of the roof. Surely he didn't have that many fireplaces. Why would anyone need that many fireplaces? The house looked like it had the bloody pox.

"Beggin' your pardon, sir, but is everything all right?"

"What?" He blinked, lowered his gaze from the roofline and found a maid waiting at the open front door, a concerned expression on her young face. "Yes. Yes, everything's fine, Anne."

Except that everything felt very wrong, he thought darkly, and climbed the steps to follow Anne inside. He absently handed her his gloves and hat, absently declined refreshments from a waiting footman, and then absently returned the greetings of the staff that arrived in the front hall to welcome him home. He had an inordinate number of staff, he realized after a time. Perhaps it was they who used all the fireplaces.

Eventually, when the last had come and gone, he stood there in the gigantic front hall of his colossal, pox-ridden home, and wondered what he was supposed to do with himself.

For the first time in his adult life, he felt utterly devoid of purpose. Which was absolutely ridiculous, he assured himself. He had his fortune to cultivate, investments to tend, businesses to watch over, and Kate to win back with charm, thoughtful presents, and . . . Bloody hell, he must have been *stupendously* drunk to have believed that strategy would work. It was the same strategy he'd tried at Pallton House. And what had it gained him? Nothing more than a rejection of his offer of marriage, a magnificent headache, and a nagging ache in his chest.

He rubbed at the ache now. It had been there while he'd sobered up, while he'd ridden to London and while he'd spoken to William. But now, with nothing to distract him, it was beginning to spread into the tight ball of pain it had been before he'd drank a vast amount of coffee and gone to London.

Perhaps the key to easing it was simply to distract himself with . . . with what? His fortune? His investments and businesses? How was that to work when he couldn't scrounge up even an ounce of enthusiasm for the idea?

He couldn't scrounge up an ounce of enthusiasm for anything at the moment. Anything beyond the idea of Kate, who, no doubt, wasn't the least bit enthused by the idea of him.

He could hardly blame her. A little time and the vast amounts of coffee had bought him a small amount of clarity, and with it, an ocean of remorse.

I'm very fond of you.

Like apple tarts.

What the devil had he been thinking? He should have remembered the jest he'd made the night before about apple tarts. He should have remembered a great many things. He should have remembered the novels she read were about love, not just adventure. He should have remembered that her friends and family all had love matches of their own. He should have remembered the way her eyes lit up when she'd watched Evie dance with her husband at Lady Thurston's ball.

But he'd been too focused on *acquiring* her. He'd gone after her hand and all it represented in the eyes of society in the same way he'd gone after his fortune, with blind determination.

He'd not once, not *once* since she'd left Pallton House given a thought to what her hand represented. He no longer cared. She could be a fisherman's daughter, a seamstress, a scullery maid and he wouldn't want her less. He wouldn't miss her less. He wouldn't be less remorseful for having broken her heart. And in breaking, lost it.

The pain bloomed.

Bloody hell, it hurt. Just as it had when he'd lost his parents and cousin. Just as it had when his aunt had turned her back on him. And just as it had when Lizzy had walked away.

Just as it had every other time he'd lost someone he loved.

He squeezed his eyes shut on a groan. "Oh, *bugger* it."

He loved her. Despite swearing he never would, despite taking every precaution known to man to *ensure* he never would, he'd fallen deeply, hopelessly, and irrevocably in love.

And now he was paying for it, just as he had in the past.

No, that wasn't right. That wasn't right at all. It wasn't anything like what had happened before. Kate wasn't dead, for pity's sake. She'd not walked away to a place or a life unknown. She'd not left, abandoned, or forgotten him. She wouldn't. It wasn't in her nature. Isn't that part of what had drawn him to her in the first place—her absolute loyalty to those she loved?

She'd just . . . very understandably backed away, a little. And very courageously invited him to follow, he realized, remembering her invitation to risk a visit to Haldon.

This time, it had not been he who'd been willing to beg. It had been he who had turned away.

And this time, he thought with a growing sense of hope and urgency, he wasn't a powerless little boy who didn't know how to make things right again.

"Beggin' your pardon again, sir, but—"

"No." Without turning his head, he jabbed a finger in the direction of Anne's voice. "There will be no more begging."

"Er . . . Yes, sir. It's only that you've been standing there—"

"Never mind that. I need my coat and gloves. Where . . . ?" He looked around him, uncaring that the grin growing on his face likely made him look a veritable loon. "How the devil do you find anything in this monstrosity?" He turned and jabbed his finger at Anne again. "We're getting a smaller house."

"I . . . Yes, sir." She backed away slowly. "Very good, sir. I'll just fetch your things, then, shall I?"

"My things, yes," he said distractedly and then called after her as she turned and fled. "And have someone ready my horse!"

He was going to make things right.

❈ *Twenty-six* ❈

*T*he symphony was done.

Kate sat back in her chair and stared at the piles of paper littering her writing desk.

She'd finally completed it, finally discovered why she'd not been able to complete it before. Anger, grief, and heartache, *that's* what the missing piece of her symphony had needed. She hadn't been able to hear them before, because she hadn't been able to feel them. Well, not feeling them had ceased to be an impediment. She'd felt all of them and more during the return trip from Pallton House. She'd felt as if she would drown in them.

Desperate to do something, anything really, with those feelings *besides* drown in them, she'd gone to her room the moment she'd arrived at Haldon, pulled out her supplies, and begun to compose. She'd worked until her eyes burned and her fingers cramped, until the red light of dawn filtered through her window and grew until the gold light of early day. And then she'd eaten, slept for a few hours, and begun composing once again.

What was it now, she wondered blearily, seven o'clock in the evening the day after she'd left Pallton House? It seemed odd that she had only been awake for a few hours.

"Have you a moment, Lady Kate?"

Kate glanced up to see Lizzy standing in the open door between their rooms. She looked anxious, Kate realized. She was biting her lip, and there were circles under her eyes. Worry and guilt were added to the heartache. Had something happened while she'd secluded herself away to lick her wounds?

"What's the matter, Lizzy? What's happened?"

"Nothing's happened. Nothing's the matter, not really. I don't wish to interrupt." Lizzy hesitated, then walked in and eyed the papers strewn across the desk. "Your symphony, isn't it?"

"You're not interrupting," Kate assured her. "It's done."

"Is it?" Lizzy's face brightened. "Is it really? You've finished the whole of it?"

"I have."

"That's wonderful," Lizzy breathed. "An entire symphony. I can't imagine. It's . . . well, it's wonderful, isn't it? You must be very excited."

Kate nodded, and wished she could, in fact, feel some level of excitement. In truth, she'd rather the symphony have gone unfinished than experience the pain that had inspired its completion. "I'm glad it's finished," she said evasively. "What is it you wished to speak to me about?"

"Oh, right." Lizzy looked down and began fiddling with the edge of her apron. "A letter arrived from Lord Thurston to your mother an hour ago. Mr. Hunter has returned to London."

"I see," Kate said carefully. She knew Lizzy had spoken with Hunter about their shared past, but aside from that, neither had broached the subject of the real reason they'd left Pallton House.

The guilt she was experiencing grew. There had to be much more for Lizzy and Hunter to discuss than they could have in the short time they'd been given. And though Kate had encouraged Lizzy to stay behind with Mrs. Summers, Mirabelle, and Whit so she could further her friendship with Hunter, Lizzy had adamantly refused. Kate had no doubt that refusal stemmed from her loyalty to her friend and mistress.

"Would you like to go to London, Lizzy?"

"I wouldn't." She pulled a face. "Why should I want to go to London? You know I don't care for it there."

"Wouldn't you like to speak with Mr. Hunter again?"

"I'll speak with him next time he comes to Haldon Hall and . . ." Lizzy trailed off and winced. "I'm sorry, I know you wouldn't care to see him."

"It's not that I wouldn't care to see him, it's only . . ." Only that she wanted to see him so terribly that she hurt with it. She shook her head. "Never mind. If it's not Mr. Hunter you're troubled over, what is it?"

"It is Mr. Hunter, in a way." Lizzy bit her lip again. "It's what we spoke of. Well, part of what we spoke of. We didn't speak of it exclusively, or even a very great deal. He mentioned it almost in passing, although he was quite clear—"

"What is it, Lizzy?"

"He offered to take care of me."

"Oh?"

Lizzy nodded. "A house of my own in Benton and a yearly allowance."

"I wondered if he would." She and Evie had planned to offer the same in a few years' time. "Will you accept?"

"I don't know. What he offered is . . . it's ridiculous, is what it is," Lizzy huffed. "He told me I could have Bethel Manor. Said he bought it a year ago with me in mind and—"

"Bethel Manor? Good heavens." The house and grounds were enormous. She and Evie couldn't afford anything quite that grand. They'd chosen a small cottage not far from the town square, and they'd had to borrow the money from Whit. "And a yearly allowance?"

"Five hundred pounds, plus salaries for staff."

"Five hundred pounds and Bethel Manor?" Kate felt a smile form. "You're richer than I am."

Lizzy's eyebrows winged up. "Am I really?"

"I don't have five hundred pounds a year and my own manor house, do I?"

"I don't have it as yet either." Brow furrowed, Lizzy walked to the bed to take a seat on the end of the mattress. "I don't know what to do. I've always been a lady's maid. I don't know how to be anything else."

"You've never been just a lady's maid," Kate replied, shifting in her seat to face the bed. "You're a friend. You always will be."

"It puts me in an awkward position, to be neither servant nor lady."

"Then be something else entirely," Kate suggested. "You could open a shop. A bookseller's shop. Oh, that would be lovely."

"Benton all ready has a bookseller's."

"Yes, but Mr. Kirkland caters to the gentlemen. And a town can never have too many booksellers." She smiled a little at Lizzy's pained expression. "Something else, then. A milliner's, a bakery, a blacksmith's if you like. Whatever it is that tickles your fancy."

"It's not to be a blacksmith," Lizzy said dryly. "Or live in a house as grand as Bethel Manor."

"Well, whatever it is, whatever you decide to do, you know you'll have the support of every Cole at Haldon."

A light blush bloomed on Lizzy's cheeks. "Thank you."

Afraid Lizzy was still hesitant to take Hunter's offer of assistance because of her, she added, "I should tell you though, that I'll be giving mine most grudgingly if you refuse what

Hunter would give you. I don't fancy supporting you in your decision to be a twit."

"I suppose I'd have to be, to deny myself a windfall," Lizzy replied on a laugh. "Thank you. I want to put my mind to the matter a bit longer, but I feel better for having spoken with you."

"You're welcome."

Lizzy bobbed her head, then looked about the room for a moment. "I'll feel better for having said this too—'Tisn't good for you to spend so much time in here."

"Yes, I know." She nudged the papers on her desk. Now that the symphony was done, she wasn't at all sure what to do with herself. Rising from her seat, she shoved the papers into the center of her desk and lifted the front lid to enclose her work inside. "I believe I'm done with composing for a while. Perhaps I'll go for a stroll."

She hesitated a moment, and then, before she could talk herself out of it, went to her vanity to retrieve the pocket watch Hunter had given her. A walk in the garden, she decided, might be just the thing to distract her from the heartache she no longer had a way to vent now that she'd finished the symphony.

After twenty minutes of meandering along the gravel paths without giving a single thought to the flowers, trees, and bushes around her, she was forced to admit that a walk in the garden was an entirely ineffectual means of distraction.

The pain was relentless. She feared it always would be. Though she knew time could heal a great many wounds, in that moment it seemed impossible that she should ever feel truly happy again. She needed Hunter too much. Loved him so deeply it made even the most poignant romances she'd read in her novels now seem hopelessly shallow. And she would, without doubt, always love him in the same way.

Not too many years ago, had she proclaimed to Evie and

Mirabelle that such a love could exist, they would have teased her good-naturedly and informed her that she was being fanciful. And not too long ago, she would have laughed and admitted—if reluctantly—that they were right.

But she wasn't being fanciful now. She wasn't insisting she loved Hunter with every fiber of her being because she *wished* to love Hunter with every fiber of her being. At the moment, she'd have given nearly anything to feel less for him. How could she not, when he hadn't a fiber of love to spare for her?

Battling back tears, she stopped to sit on a stone bench, and reach into her pocket to pull out the watch. She traced the gold inlay with her thumb and felt the watch ticking, steady and sure, beneath her finger. For the life of her, she couldn't explain why she'd taken it out of her vanity. She wasn't using it to keep a consistent tempo of any music. She'd simply wanted it with her. She wanted to feel the steadiness.

That's what Hunter wanted too, she thought dully— steadiness, certainty, constancy. It was what he had gone without as a boy, and it was what he needed now.

She'd offered him a love that constant. She'd offered to *beg*, for pity's sake. She closed her eyes as a wave of humiliation washed over her. Oh, what had she been thinking?

That I love him.

That I'd do anything for him.

That I wanted him never to doubt either.

Surely he couldn't have doubted after that. Except . . . she *had* left. She'd walked away as he'd stood there, watching her from the steps. She'd gone even after he asked her—albeit in a very roundabout sort of way—not to go. She'd left him, just as his aunt had, and Lizzy.

It was different, of course. He didn't love her as he'd loved his aunt and Lizzy. But it was the same, in that she was supposed to be someone who loved him, and she'd left.

"Oh, dear."

But what else could she have done—remained at Pallton

House, pretending to enjoy the house party as if nothing was wrong? As if he'd not broken her heart? Besides, she'd only gone to Haldon, not Australia. He must have understood she was only going away a little and only because he'd hurt her.

She rolled her eyes at the ridiculous qualifications. A little? What difference did a little make? What difference did it make that her reason for going away was valid? She had still claimed to love him in one minute and left in the next. How was he to understand and trust that the love she offered was constant from behavior such as that?

She should have waited a little longer, should have taken the time to make certain he understood that she would always love him.

Perhaps she should explain herself in a letter. No, that would never do. She wasn't certain she could convey what she felt in a letter, and like as not, receiving a letter from her would only reiterate the fact that she was some distance away.

Perhaps she could speak with him when her mother took her to London for the Little Season. But that was months away. She couldn't possibly wait that long. Perhaps she should go to London sooner. Perhaps she should go tonight.

She bit her lip, calculating the risks and benefits of such an endeavor. London was only a short distance away. She could easily make the trip, speak with him, and be back at Haldon by morning. She'd wait until after midnight, and she'd take at least two footmen she could trust to keep her secret. Whit and Mirabelle hadn't yet left Pallton House, and her mother and Lizzy would be fast asleep by then. With any luck, she could get to London, speak with Hunter, and return to Haldon without any member of her family being the wiser.

There was the possibility that it would change nothing. Probably, it would result in a lecture about being impetuous. Without doubt, she wouldn't deserve one. She wasn't being impetuous,' she decided and rose from her bench, she was taking a calculated risk.

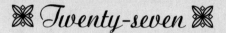

❋ *Twenty-seven* ❋

*H*unter eyed the wall beneath Kate's window and blew out a short breath.

One would think, given the woman's romantic nature, that she would have a trellis or the like about for her prince to clamber up—a balcony for him to climb onto at the very least. Or perhaps trellises and balconies were only for white knights and doomed lovers. Probably, princes were meant to use the front door. Very probably, princes were not meant to use the front door in the middle of the night. Which meant he would be climbing the wall.

No matter, he had more practice sneaking in and out of windows than most. In addition, the exterior walls of Haldon were made of uneven stone. It would be an easy thing for him to find handholds and footholds . . . relatively easy. He'd always been better at opening locked doors than crawling through windows.

He eyed the wall a little longer, blew out another short breath, and found a handhold. The climb, he soon discovered, was not quite as easy as it looked. The stone was chipped and jagged in places, and worn smooth in others, so that he alternated between feeling as if he were trying to scale a rose-bush, and attempting to climb a waterfall.

By the time he was two-thirds of the way up, he was a little out of breath and a little put out with himself for not having thought to search out a ladder in the stable. Granted, scaling a ladder wouldn't be quite the romantic gesture that scaling a wall was, but Kate would probably have appreciated it more than finding him broken and bloody beneath her window. Then again, if she was *very* angry with him . . .

He pushed that thought aside and concentrated on navigating the remainder of the wall. When, at last, he reached the window, he breathed a sigh of relief to find it was not only unlocked, but wide open. He moved the drapes aside, slipped silently over the sill, straightened, and then, shocked by what he found, stood where he was, unable to move a muscle.

During the ride from London, he'd fantasized, countless times, about how his little escapade might play out. He imagined finding Kate sound asleep in her bed, the covers up to her chin and her pale blonde hair spread across the pillow. He'd envisioned stealing softly to her bed and kissing her awake. He'd imagined her lids fluttering open and the fog of sleep slowly clearing from her blue eyes.

But nowhere in his daydream had Kate been standing in the middle of her room dressed in cape, gloves, and bonnet, and staring at him as if he had two heads and a tail.

Likewise, his daydream had not contained any variation of the question, "Where the devil are you going?" But that was what came out of his mouth, because it was the middle of the damn night. Where the devil *was* she going?

Her hand flew to her heart. "Hunter? What are you doing here? Has something happened? Miss Willory—?"

"No, no. We caught her and her contact. It's done. I . . ." She looked so beautiful. So perfectly beautiful standing in the stream of moonlight from the window. "I . . . Oh, hell."

He crossed the room in three strides to pull her into his arms.

"I missed you," he whispered raggedly a second before he bent his head and kissed her, everywhere—her mouth, her cheeks, her brow, her nose. He even pulled off her bonnet to brush his lips across her hair. If it was within reach, he pressed his mouth to it. He couldn't help himself. A well of panic he'd not realized he'd been keeping at bay since he'd left his house washed over him now. He was so close to having what he truly wanted. She was right there, right there in his arms. But if he made a mistake, if he did something else wrong, if he couldn't make her believe, if she left him . . .

"It's all right, Hunter."

He was trembling. He could feel his arms shaking, as they had after he'd pulled her from Whistler on the bluffs. But he couldn't fool himself into thinking it was from physical exertion. Not this time. Not while his legs felt as if they might give out beneath him and his breath shuddered in and out as if he'd run the whole distance from London.

Kate's hands ran slowly up his back, down again. "It's all right."

It wasn't. It wouldn't be if, if he'd been wrong and he really was helpless. It wouldn't be if he couldn't make things right.

"I want to make things right."

She pulled back a little to study his face. "Then I'm sure you will," she said softly.

Not just absolute loyalty to those she loved, he realized as the panic began to dim, but absolute faith. He wasn't at all convinced he could live up to it, was quite certain he'd not done a thing to earn it, but he'd be damned if he couldn't find the courage to try and keep it now.

Feeling a bit calmer—though by no means confident—he took her hand and led her to the pair of chairs in front of the fireplace. He sat her in one, took a seat in another. And then promptly stood back up again to begin pacing the room.

"Hunter?"

"A moment."

Too late he realized he should have spent less time on his ride to Haldon daydreaming about waking Kate with a kiss, and more time planning what to say once she woke. Because knowing he had to try to earn the love and faith she offered, and knowing *how* to try were two very different animals. He wanted to simply tell her that he loved her and leave it at that. But he *needed* to tell her everything else. He needed her to know the man he'd been.

The idea of it terrified him. Bad enough that he should have fallen in love, but to hand her his heart, and then all the reasons she should drop it and walk away went against every instinct he'd honed since he'd been a boy. And though earning a lifetime with the woman he loved, and not self-preservation, had been his purpose in coming to Haldon, he couldn't keep from stalling a bit before coming round to that purpose.

He stopped in his pacing to light a few candles and then nod his chin toward the bonnet he'd tossed aside. "Where were you going?"

"Er . . ." She shifted a little in her seat, a bright blush forming on her cheeks. "To London. To see you. I was being . . . I was taking a calculated risk. I wanted . . . to tell you that I love you. Even though I left Pallton House. I wanted you to know that I will *always* love you."

He let out a long breath and felt the last of his panic ease. *"Excellent."*

"Yes, well. I'm delighted you think so." The blush died away rather quickly. "You said you wished to make things right?" she prompted.

"Right. Right. I . . ." The trouble with constantly reinventing oneself, he realized with disgust, was that a man had no practice answering for who he'd been. "I'm a good man," he tried and nodded as if to drive the point home to both of them. "I may not be a great man, but I am a good one."

She, in turn, shook her head in bafflement. "Yes, I know. Why—?"

"There are things, portions of my past you aren't aware of. A time when I was . . . less good."

"It doesn't change who you are now."

"No, it doesn't." It felt incredible to be able to say that, and believe it. It didn't feel nearly as pleasant to say, "It could change how you feel about me. How—"

"No," she cut in, her voice resolute. "It won't. Nothing could."

"I was a liar, a cheat, and a thief." He spit the words out quickly, afraid he would lose the courage.

"I see," she said slowly. "What did you do?"

"I lied, I cheated, and I stole," he replied in a tone that was both dry and cautious. "Mostly, I stole. I was using the phrase in a literal sense."

"Oh." She frowned thoughtfully. "What did you steal?"

"Food, coin, whatever I could. Whatever I needed." Once or twice, it had simply been what he wanted, but it wasn't necessary to admit *every* sin in one night. "Life was difficult for a time, for a long time, after I left Benton. I did what was needed . . . what I felt was needed to survive. And to thrive. I picked pockets, slipped into homes, took—"

"You went into people's *homes*?"

"Yes."

"Good heavens," she breathed. "How often?"

He sincerely hoped she wasn't looking for an exact number. He'd not cared enough at the time to keep count. "As often as I needed until I was old enough to acquire what I needed in other ways."

"What other ways?" she asked in a tone that said she wasn't entirely sure she wanted to know.

"I did apply myself to legal work," he assured her. "I also cheated at cards and used my ill-gotten winnings to finance a variety of enterprises. Some that were reputable, and some that were less reputable, but vastly more profitable, like smuggling."

"You were a smuggler."

"I was until William caught me."

"Is *that* why you went to work for the War Department? Why you might have hanged?" She opened her mouth, closed it. "What on earth were you smuggling?"

"Wool out and brandy in, as the majority of smugglers do. Until a few hours ago, I was under the impression I had unwittingly smuggled correspondence between spies. As it happens, that was a . . . misunderstanding."

"That is a *significant* misunderstanding."

"It was. But it's been . . . cleared up." Almost. There was still the small matter of retribution.

"Well . . . all right." She shook her head, clearly bewildered. "Is there anything else you'd like to tell me?"

He almost wished there were, just so he could keep talking. The longer he talked, the longer he delayed the moment of judgment. Then again, the longer he kept talking, the less likely that judgment would fall to his favor.

He shook his head.

She was quiet for several moments—several excruciating long moments to his mind—as if digesting everything he'd said. "Do you feel better for having told me all of this?" she finally asked.

"I don't know." How was he supposed to have an answer for that before she'd told him how *she* felt about it?

"Did you tell me thinking you might feel better?"

He dragged a hand through his hair. "I don't know."

"Well, why did you tell me?"

"I . . . I thought you should know. I needed you to know. And I suppose I needed to make a gesture."

"Like the gesture of climbing through my window?"

"I was afraid words would not suffice."

"It depends on the words," she replied softly.

He crossed the room to pull her to her feet and cup her face in his hands. He took a deep, fortifying breath, and then took the biggest risk of his life. "I love you. I'm in love with you. I adore you. I could provide a speech, if you need it. Something poetic like you've read in your books—"

"No. No, that isn't necessary," she said unsteadily. She closed her eyes and let out a long, shaky sigh, then another, much shakier sigh.

When the first tear slid down her cheek, he pulled her into her arms with a groan. "Sweetheart, don't. I'm sorry. I'm so sorry."

The tears that had briefly clouded her eyes when she'd broken Lord Brentworth's vase had hurt him to see, but the heartache she quietly cried out now was his doing, and his alone. He couldn't stand the thought of it. He held her, rocking her back and forth, whispering hoarse words of apology in her ear, and despite his earlier assertion that there would be no begging, he found himself doing just that. "Stop now, sweetheart. *Please*, stop."

She nodded against his chest, but another minute passed before the soft shuddering of her breath eased into a more natural rhythm.

Sniffling, she pulled back to look up at him. "You're certain? You'll chance it?"

He studied her face. Her eyes were puffy, her nose red, and her cheeks blotchy. She was the most exquisite thing he'd ever seen. "For you, *with* you, I'd chance anything."

"Oh." She closed her eyes again. "Oh, that *is* excellent."

"I'm delighted you think so too." He kissed her forehead and gently wiped away the tears with his fingers. "Does this mean you'll forgive me?"

She sniffled again and opened her eyes once more. "For hurting us both, yes. For the man you were? If you need it, I certainly will. But I've never known that man, so . . ." She trailed off, sniffled once more and eyed him a little curiously. "You weren't, by any chance, a pirate at some point in your colorful past?"

"A pirate?" he repeated, caught between bewilderment at the non sequitur, a relief so great it threatened to overwhelm him, and a joy so sharp he wondered he was able to feel anything else at all.

She'd forgiven him. She'd offered to forgive him for everything.

"The image does suit you rather well," she explained.

"No." He retrieved a handkerchief from his pocket and handed it to her. "Pirating is one sin I cannot claim."

"Pity." She wiped the remaining dampness from her cheeks and smiled. "I imagine it would be quite exciting to be married to a pirate, even a former one."

"How do you feel about being married to the current head of the War Department, instead?"

Slowly, she lowered the handkerchief. "Well, er, William Fletcher is a very nice man, but—"

"I meant me, sweetheart," he explained on a small laugh. "William is retiring. He wants to name me as his successor."

A smile bloomed on her face. "A nice and very wise man."

"You may change your mind about that once I tell you his role in our . . ." He recalled William's disgust for the number of times he had been forced to relate the story of his deathbed promise to the late Duke of Rockeforte. "No . . . no, I do believe I shall let him tell you the details of our mission together. I'm done with talking for the moment."

And with that proclamation, he bent his head to Kate's. As their lips met, he thought that this, *this* was the kiss he should have given her from the start. There was no purpose beyond feeling, no thought given to who had the upper hand. It wasn't a test or a lesson or a frantic bid to ease a pain or battle back fear. It was simply love—given, received, and destined to last forever.

Epilogue

Kate struggled, *almost* successfully, not to squirm in her seat. It was terribly difficult to remain still and wait patiently as a small crowd filed in to take their seats in the theater. But it wasn't the many curious eyes glancing in her direction that made her anxious, nor that some of those glances also held a distinct air of disapproval along with the curiosity. It was excitement that made her reach out and take Hunter's hand in an effort to steady herself.

Brushing his thumb across her wrist, he turned to her, his dark eyes filled with concern, with pride, and with love. "Nervous, darling?"

"Excited."

"And happy?"

"Yes." She grinned and looked out over the audience from their box. "Oh, yes."

Because curious, disapproving or both, the people had come. They'd come to hear the premiere of Lady Kate Hunter's first symphony.

She couldn't quite believe it. Even now, after months to prepare herself, she couldn't quite fathom that she was only minutes away from hearing her greatest musical endeavor performed in front of an audience.

Mr. Lucero, owner of the theater had been surprised, and notably hesitant after learning the symphony brought to him for consideration had been composed by a woman, but in the end he'd announced that the "unfortunate gender of the composer" would not deter him from bringing a masterpiece to light.

The "unfortunate gender" bit she could have done without, but "a masterpiece" quite made up for it. Having her dream come true *more* than made up for it.

Having *another* dream come true, she corrected.

As the chandeliers were raised, Kate looked about her, her heart swelling with happiness. There were Sophie and Alex, and Mirabelle and Whit, Evie and McAlistair, Mrs. Summers with her Mr. Fletcher. Lizzy was in attendance, and still blushing at the eyes Hunter's footman had been making at her earlier. Even her mother had a new suitor, the inestimable Lord Brentworth.

And here was she, Lady Katherine Hunter, with the prince of her dreams.

INTERACT WITH DORCHESTER ONLINE!

Want to learn more about your favorite books and authors?
Want to talk with other readers that like to read the same books as you?
Want to see up-to-the-minute Dorchester news?

VISIT DORCHESTER AT:
DorchesterPub.com
Twitter.com/DorchesterPub
Facebook.com (Search Pages)

DISCUSS DORCHESTER'S NOVELS AT:
Dorchester Forums at DorchesterPub.com
GoodReads.com
LibraryThing.com
Myspace.com/books
Shelfari.com
WeRead.com

✂ ☐ **YES!**

Sign me up for the Historical Romance Book Club and send my FREE BOOKS! If I choose to stay in the club, I will pay only $8.50* each month, a savings of $6.48!

NAME: _____

ADDRESS: _____

TELEPHONE: _____

EMAIL: _____

☐ I want to pay by credit card.

☐ **VISA**   ☐ **MasterCard.**   ☐ **DISCOVER**

ACCOUNT #: _____

EXPIRATION DATE: _____

SIGNATURE: _____

Mail this page along with $2.00 shipping and handling to:
Historical Romance Book Club
PO Box 6640
Wayne, PA 19087
Or fax (must include credit card information) to:
610-995-9274
You can also sign up online at **www.dorchesterpub.com**.
*Plus $2.00 for shipping. Offer open to residents of the U.S. and Canada only.
Canadian residents please call 1-800-481-9191 for pricing information.
If under 18, a parent or guardian must sign. Terms, prices and conditions subject to
change. Subscription subject to acceptance. Dorchester Publishing reserves the right
to reject any order or cancel any subscription.